DEEP BURN

A STATION SEVENTEEN NOVEL

KIMBERLY KINCAID

Burn
deep! ♡

[signature]

KIMBERLY KINCAID

DEEP BURN

This book is dedicated to Rachel Hamilton,

who is the biggest cheerleader a

girl could ever ask for. Capelli is

all yours, doll!

ACKNOWLEDGMENTS

Writing a book is always a team effort, particularly so with DEEP BURN. This book wouldn't be in y'all's hot little hands if it weren't for the following people.

Nicole Bailey with Proof Before You Publish, whose patience is unending (I really mean this!), and Jaycee DeLorenzo with Sweet n' Spicy Designs, who knows just where to place a photograph to get maximum ab exposure, thank you for being my dream team. Geoff Symon, who is just brilliant and never bats an eye when I send him messages like, "Exactly how much blood is in the human body, anyway?"—thank you for guiding me toward the proper forensics. Any mistakes or liberties are solely mine (and I took a few!), but all the knowledge is Geoff's.

Robin Covington and Avery Flynn, there isn't enough gratitude for the plot sessions in the minivan, the phone calls that kept my hero and heroine (and villain!) in line, and all the support you give me on a daily basis. Huge thanks to Skye Jordan, who pushed me through the early stages of this book. I'm also grateful for the guidance and kindness of Laura Kaye and Cristin Harber, whose praise for the Station Seventeen series humbles me and makes me giggle.

To my family—Reader Girl, Smarty Pants, and Tiny Dancer, who really earned an ice cream party for this one. And an extra-special shout out to Mr. K, who helped me write a computer expert hero with a whole lot of gadgety toys and online cloak and dagger. If I'd been left to my own devices, Capelli would've barely been able to figure out DropBox. Thanks, honey!

Lastly, to my readers, who always have room for more firefighters (and cops and paramedics and chefs and Army Rangers and and and) Thank you for making my job possible.

INTRODUCTION

A note to the reader about time warps

If you've been with Station Seventeen from the beginning, you may note a timing issue in this book. If you haven't, that's okay. The stories all stand alone, and this passage won't spoil anything for you!

This book picks up a few months after the last one, SKIN DEEP, left off, and it follows chronologically. But many of you know, I wrote a novella, DEEP CHECK, that is labeled "1.5" in the order of things.

Funny thing about that. DEEP CHECK was part of an anthology that was released between this book in your hands and SKIN DEEP (thus, the 1.5) But since DEEP CHECK had to happen according to the end of the hockey season, as our hero there is a hockey star, I had to write it out of chronological order with the Station Seventeen timeline.

DEEP BURN takes place in January-February, where DEEP CHECK is actually June of the same "year." So while you got DEEP CHECK first, the events in the book don't actually happen until after the events of DEEP BURN take place.

All of that is to say that's why you won't see Finn Donnelly in this book. Because he hasn't come back to Remington yet! But I couldn't pass up a chance to bring you his and January's story in the anthology, which had a specific release date and timeline, so...I time warped a bit in order to do that.

Thanks for letting me bend the rules!

CHAPTER 1

Shae McCullough wanted exactly three things: a long, hot bath, a heaping plate of chicken Parmesan, and her bed occupied by a very sexy man looking for an equally sexy time. But since she was a mere five hours into her twenty-four hour shift as Station Seventeen's only female firefighter, she'd have to settle for a three-minute buzz through the house shower, a slab of meatloaf that could probably stunt-double as a brick, and a bunk full of co-workers who she'd never see as anything other than the brothers she'd never had.

Thank God she got to run into burning buildings for a living. That made all the other shit worth the price of admission.

"You done in there, Princess? Walker and Slater came out like ten minutes ago," she called, balancing her towel and her bag of toiletries in one hand as she placed a sharp knock on the shower room door with the other. After five years of hauling hoses and fighting fires, Shae was used to rotating in for showers at Seventeen.

Just like she was used to a double dose of side-eye from her engine lieutenant, Ian Gamble, when she got brash enough to do things like call him Princess. Which—admittedly—was pretty often, but come on. Was it really her fault she got just as sweaty during their training as everyone else, or that the lieutenant in question took longer showers than a fifteen-year-old girl? She needed a scrub-down like nobody's business, and she wasn't going to get one by meekly waiting.

"McCullough." Gamble opened the shower room door, a frown etched over the already hard line of his jaw, and while the expression probably would've tempted most people to tuck tail and run, Shae just returned it with a bright smile.

"Hey, boss. You thinking about finishing up anytime soon, or were you going for some sort of record with your loofah?"

One dark brown brow arched all the way up. "You know, I'd give you more drills for being a pain in my ass, but the problem is, you'd probably fucking enjoy them."

"I do love me a good obstacle course. Or—oooh!" Shae paused, her pulse doing a hop-skip in her veins. "If you want to send me out with squad next time they practice rope rescue from the tower, I won't complain. Or even—"

"Yeah, yeah. I get it, you little adrenaline junkie," Gamble said, and although Shae knew he was fighting like mad to *look* mad, a hint of a smile tugged at the corners of his mouth. "Anyway, I'm done in here now. Obviously." He dropped his black-coffee stare to his ridiculously muscular body, which was covered in a sheen of shower water, a half-dozen inky black tattoos, and—thankfully—a towel.

In truth, Shae's gratitude had nothing to do with embarrassment or impropriety. If Gamble had decided to trot out bare-assed to ration up shit for cutting his shower short, she'd have responded with the same smile/sarcasm combo as if he'd been wearing a full set of turnout gear. Not that he wasn't a good-looking guy, because hey, the truth was kind of hard to miss when it was standing in front of you in nothing but a scrap of cotton and a scowl. But Shae's normally hyperactive libido didn't so much as twinge for Gamble, or anyone else whose name got yelled out at A-shift's roll call. Work relationships, even ones that stayed strictly between the sheets (or in the back seat of a car…or up against a wall…or…) were one of the very few things firmly in her "never" column. She had to trust the guys at Seventeen with her life, and they had to trust her with theirs. Fucking that up with a bunch of more-than-friends feelings?

So not on her agenda. After all, hot guys could be found damn near anywhere. But guys she could really trust when the world went pear-shaped?

Not so much.

Shae grinned, straightening to her full five foot eight as she reached up to clap Gamble's shower-damp shoulder. "Awesome, because after those ladder drills you just put us through, I need a threesome with my soap and shampoo."

She'd no sooner nudged past him, though, than the high-pitched blare of the all-call sounded off from the overhead speakers, and the karma of being a smartass came back to bite her square on the seat of her sweaty, seen-better-days uniform pants.

"*Engine Seventeen, Squad Six, Ambulance Twenty-Two, Battalion Seventeen, structure fire, four hundred block of Crestridge Drive, requesting immediate response.*"

"So much for that threesome," Gamble said, making a quick grab for his uniform pants as Shae dropped her toiletry bag on the counter like a bad habit and turned to haul her cookies toward Engine Seventeen.

"Ah, it's all good," she called over her shoulder, even though she really *did* need the lather/rinse/repeat. "I'd rather get down and dirty with my helmet and Halligan bar anyway. See you in the rig."

The words barely made it past the shower room door before Shae heard the thing thump closed. Moving briskly and tempering her breath against the inevitable press of her pulse in her ears, she locked her focus on the fastest path to the engine bay. Her five years of tenure as a firefighter had earned her the operator's spot on Engine Seventeen, and God, if there was anything that came close to the rush of running into a burning building, it was driving the big-ass vehicle that would get them all there in the first place.

"Hey, hey, McCullough," came the twangy Southern drawl of Seventeen's rescue squad lieutenant, Gabe Hawkins, less than a second after he entered the hallway from the common room with more than half the house on his boot heels. "You ready to drive that engine like you stole it?"

Shae channeled her adrenaline into a laugh, because it was either that or redline on the stuff, and she was none too interested in letting the natural response of her brain veto all the hard-fought training she'd put to her body. "That all depends."

"On...?" Hawk asked, blond brows raised.

"Your goals," Shae said. "If initiative is what you're after, then my answer is yes with hell yes on top. But if you're asking as a rescue squad lieutenant, then my answer is no, sir. I wouldn't even dream of doing such a reckless thing with a department-owned vehicle."

"You would too, you little kiss-ass," joked Kellan Walker, her fellow engine-mate, who also just so happened to be a former Army Ranger and the current live-in boyfriend of one of the toughest female detectives in Remington.

Not that his badass résumé kept Shae from stepping up to the plate to answer him with a ball-busting grin. "Haters never prosper, Walker."

"I'm pretty sure that's cheaters," Kellan flipped back,

giving her shoulder a friendly nudge with his own as they hoofed it to the double doors at the end of the hall.

"Oh, please." Shae nudged him in return. "If we're going to dwell on semantics, I prefer to think of myself as an opportunist instead of an apple polisher."

Hawk's pop of laughter echoed off the cinderblock walls of Station Seventeen's triple-wide engine bay as he headed for the squad vehicle on the far side of the room. "Opportunist it is. If squad needs extra hands on search and rescue for this call, you're in, McCullough."

Freaking *yes*. "Thank you!" Shae called out, hustling over the buffed concrete floor toward Engine Seventeen. Her excitement at the chance to run headlong into potentially grave danger—along with the banter that seemed laid back on the surface—probably seemed odd or even callous to most outsiders, she knew. But much to the chagrin of her parents and the bewilderment of her two older sisters, Shae just wasn't a day-jobber. God, the mere *thought* of all that staid routine gave her the fucking sweats.

From blood to backbone, all she wanted was adventure. If she had to shred a little convention to find it?

All the better. She'd never been much for propriety anyway.

Clattering to a stop beside the bright red and white engine, Shae methodically slowed her breathing even though her movements kicked into double-time. As Engine Company's operator, she didn't have the luxury of being able to gear up on the way to the scene like Gamble and Walker and their rookie, Luke Slater, which meant she had about six nanoseconds to Houdini her way into the turnouts she'd left prepped and ready to go next to the front of the vehicle.

"Hello, baby," Shae murmured, toeing out of her running shoes and skinning into her bunker pants with one swift slide. "Come to momma."

Another seamless move had her suspenders in place over the shoulders of her navy blue RFD T-shirt, then the comforting weight of her coat on top of that—*breathe in*—and another still put her behind the wheel of the engine—*breathe out*. Shae's heart thudded against her sternum in a solid bid to get her brain to give in to the triple-dog-dare coming from her central nervous system. But giving in to her physiology would only get her the world's fastest tap-out, so she tightened her belly along with her seatbelt and kicked the engine into a low, diesel-fueled growl.

Gamble stealthed his way into the officer's seat next to her, which was downright goddamn freaky considering he was roughly the size of a professional wrestler and a lumberjack combined, and Shae grabbed her headset from its resting spot over her right shoulder. By the time she'd maneuvered the thing into place, Gamble had put eyes on both Walker and Slater in the step behind them and given up a clipped, "fall out" over his own headset, and hell if he had to tell her twice.

"Okay, let's see what we're dealing with here," he said, turning his attention toward the dashboard monitor that gave them updates from emergency services as Shae steered the engine from the fire house garage into the deceptively sunny January afternoon. "Dispatch has report of a house fire at four ninety-two Crestridge Drive." With a few keystrokes, he clacked the rig's GPS to life. "Looks like the nearest major cross street is—"

"Glendale," Shae supplied, her brain mapping out the city blocks of their call area that she'd long since memorized.

"That's in North Point." Walker's voice was slow and full of caution as it filtered over the shared channel. "I know the neighborhood from the Julian DuPree case."

Shae's stomach squeezed. Kellan had been a somewhat inadvertent part of the police investigation that had taken down one of Remington's nastiest criminals a few months ago, and he had the literal scars to prove it.

"It's a rough part of the city," Slater agreed quietly into his mic, and Shae nodded to turn the assessment into a trifecta. Run-down houses with poor construction and even poorer upkeep, all crowded together like a mouth full of crooked teeth? It was a five-star recipe for Very Bad Things, especially when fire joined the party.

"Well, wherever it is, it's burning pretty good," Gamble said. "This report from dispatch has flames showing on Alpha, Bravo, and—shit. Charlie sides of the residence."

Unable to help it, Shae gasped, the sound of her shock mixing in with the soft static on the line. "Already?"

It wasn't as if burning houses didn't attract attention, and dispatch never sat on their thumbs when someone called 9-1-1 to report a fire. How the hell could a house—even a small one—burn *that* fast? Unless…

Gamble leaned in for a closer look at the update flashing over the monitor and bit out a top-shelf curse. "And to put the frosting on this little cupcake, the 9-1-1 caller is reporting the house to be a known meth lab."

"Oh, hell," Shae murmured. They knew better than to take call-ins as gospel—after all, civilians could run the gamut from mistaken to malicious. But the solvent-based chemicals used to cook crystal meth were highly flammable, not to mention highly toxic. A fire could definitely start and spread more quickly than usual with those sorts of extra-curriculars going on.

"Alright. Gear up," Gamble said gruffly, the same thoughts doubtlessly going through his head. "Squad will take point if there's a hazmat situation, but it looks like this one's gonna be all hands on deck, so have your masks ready to go. And McCullough?" He spared her the briefest glance from across the front of the engine, but God, she felt every inch of his seriousness as he added, "Don't dawdle getting us there."

"Copy that, Lieutenant." Locking down her focus even further, Shae stared through the engine's windshield and dropped her foot a little harder over the accelerator. Maneuvering through traffic oddly soothed her nerves—*right turn on Hamilton Avenue, breathe in. Cut over to Queen Anne Street to save a few seconds, breathe out*—and by the time she pulled up to the dilapidated two-story house at the end of Crestridge Drive, her mind was as lasered in as her body.

Which was great, because the scene in front of her was a pure shit show.

"Radios on," Gamble called out amidst the heavy thump of bootsteps on the pavement as they all clambered out of the engine damn near simultaneously. Shae flipped the switch on the two-way at her shoulder without looking, taking in her surroundings instead. Her gut filled with dread as her gaze swept methodically from left to right, and the sensation didn't get any better when she reversed it for a lightning-fast double-check, just as she'd been trained to.

Bright orange flames licked upward from all four windows on the first floor, carving a path for the steady plumes of smoke that followed. There were no signs of entrapment—nobody stumbling through the front yard with panicky reports of a family member still inside; or worse yet, leaning out the second-story windows hollering for help. Still, Shae had been on far too many calls to feel relief until search and rescue came up clean. Although the yard was surrounded by a sturdy perimeter of padlocked chain link fencing all the way around, the house's front door appeared otherwise unimpeded. But between the swiftly moving fire and the harsh tang in the air that Shae immediately recognized as some sort of chemicals burning, an easy breach would be all the silver lining this call was going to cough up.

The two-way radio on her shoulder crackled to life. "Okay, everyone," came Captain Bridges's calm, controlled voice. "Hawk, you and Dempsey are on search and rescue, but make it fast. Faurier, you and Gates get a vent on this roof. Gamble, tap a hydrant and get those water lines ready to go. Send anyone you can spare with Hawkins for that sweep. If there are people trapped in this house, we need them out now. Go."

A litany of "copy that"s filtered over the line, followed quickly by Gamble's voice in real time as he pegged Shae, Slater, and Walker with a piercing stare.

"Walker, you're with me. I want those lines prepped five minutes ago. Slater, today is your lucky fucking day. You're with McCullough, backing up squad on S&R."

Whoa. Score one for the rookie. Shae's brows would've shot toward the brim of the helmet she'd just buckled into place if she'd had so much as a second to spare. But Gamble and Walker were already moving toward the back of the engine to ready the hoses, and shocked or not, she wasn't about to lag behind.

"Alright Slater," Shae said, looking the rookie in the baby blues at the same time she grabbed her Halligan bar from the storage compartment to her left. *Breathe in. Breathe out.* "Time to put the last three months' of training to work. You're on my hip. Not in my dance space, not ten paces behind me, but on my hip until you're told otherwise. You copy?"

"Copy." To his credit, Slater's nod was firm as he fell in at her six, his own Halligan already in hand. They reached the gate to the front-yard fence just as Ryan Dempsey, the newest member of their rescue squad but the best at breaching everything from back doors to bank vaults, took care of the padlock with a quick snick of his bolt cutters.

"Now that *that's* out of the way," Hawkins said, the serious set of his jaw a complete one-eighty from his earlier cockiness as he led them over the narrow concrete walkway and up to the house. "Dempsey, let's make hay on getting this front door knocked in. I've got a feeling we ain't gonna have time on our side for this sweep. McCullough, Slater, you're on floor one. Dempsey and I will take floor two."

Shae nodded, both her lungs and her muscles squeezing beneath the familiar weight of her SCBA tank and the rest of her gear as the four of them clattered to a stop in front of the timeworn threshold of the house. "Copy that, Lieutenant."

Heat and potent, chemical-laced smoke poured from the house, grabbing Shae by the throat before Dempsey could so much as get his Halligan bar between the door hinges.

"Masks on," Hawk barked, but Shae had been halfway there. Reaching the rest of the way up, she yanked her mask over her face, the oxygen from her SCBA kicking in with a low hiss. Thankfully, Slater's instincts were as good as his training, and he mimicked her movements to follow Hawk's command after only a brief hitch.

Hawkins jerked his chin at the three of them. "Let's rock and roll, y'all."

With a hard jerk of his Halligan and a perfectly placed kick, Dempsey sent the front door flying on its hinges, and a few seconds later, they were all over the fiery threshold.

"Okay, Slater," Shae said, scanning the space around them as soon as Hawk and Dempsey cut a path into the house and headed for the stairs. *Damn* this place was burning fast. "This fire already has a lot of teeth. We're going to have to split up if we want to cover the whole floor in good time."

Dividing forces wasn't unusual for S&R, although considering the hairy factor of this call along with Slater's rookie status, it wasn't ideal. But he'd done plenty of S&R on Gamble's hip at smaller fires, and he was coming into his own. Plus, they really didn't have a choice.

Which he seemed to realize all too well, because he answered with a tight, definitive nod. "Copy that."

"You take the Delta side and I'll go Bravo. Be quick but don't rush." Flames climbed the walls around them in irregular patterns, heat and uncut adrenaline forcing an instant sheen of sweat over Shae's brows, and oh hell, as much as she loved the rush of her job, they needed to do this sweep and get gone. "Don't be shy about using your radio if you need it. I've got your back. Go."

She turned toward the left-hand side of the house, her boots already in motion on the floorboards. The place was fully involved, the fire spreading at a rate that bordered on ridiculous for a run-of-the-mill house blaze. Keeping her eyes wide open for both people and potential hazards, Shae moved into what she guessed to be a living room, surveying the sparsely appointed space.

"Fire department! Call out!" she bellowed past her mask. The windows were covered by dark, heavy curtains, which made visibility jack with a side of shit even though they'd already been half-eaten by the quickly moving flames. An odd sensation plucked at Shae's spine, growing both stronger and stranger as she took in the erratic pathways of fire and the sheer intensity with which they burned. The couch in the middle of the room was in even worse condition than the curtains, and a fresh bloom of sweat trickled between her shoulder blades as she crouched down low and picked up the pace into the next room.

"Fire department, is anyone—"

Shae's words crashed to a halt at the sight of a figure lying slumped on the floor. Things went from bad to cluster fuck when she registered the table along the far wall holding what looked like a full-scale science experiment, complete with two—dammit, three portable gas burners, and her heart launched against the wall of her

11

chest, smacking every last one of her ribs for good measure.

"Sir! Sir, can you hear me?" she called out, dropping to her knees beside the lifeless figure. She palmed his shoulder, assessing him for obvious injures with a lightning-fast glance. But then flames rolled out over the ceiling above her, sending the curtains from the window in a heavy, flame-fueled thump, and dammit, there was no more time to waste.

"McCullough to command," Shae reported into her radio, shifting the unconscious man onto his stomach to get him in position for a fireman's carry.

Captain Bridges came back with a steady, "McCullough, this is command. Report."

"I've got an unresponsive civilian down on floor one, Bravo side. Affirmative on the meth lab, too. This fire is going to flash over, Cap, and soon."

"Command to McCullough, copy that. Are you clear for the primary exit?"

Shae shot a gaze toward the living room, now clouded by a nearly impenetrable haze of dark gray smoke. Not gonna be a cakewalk with fiery debris raining down harder by the second and the pretty much nonexistent visibility, but… "Affirmative, Command."

"Good," Bridges said. "Hawkins, Dempsey, Slater, I want you out of there *now*. McCullough, paramedics are standing by at the primary exit. Fall out."

"Copy that."

Coiling her muscles so hard they burned, Shae hooked her hands beneath the man's linebacker-esque shoulders, stabbing her boots into the floorboards. Her training merged with her survival instinct and the adrenaline already cooking in her veins, and she hauled the guy up and over her shoulders despite what had to be a fifty-pound weight difference. Shae forced her lungs to expand—*breathe in*—and her heartbeat to slow as she retraced her steps—*six, seven, eight, nine*— through the room and toward the front door. Shock popped in her veins at how rapidly the path through the living room had deteriorated, but with the window frame and half the wall around it now totally engulfed in smoke and flames, the front door was still her best viable exit.

Breathe out. With a deep-down burst of energy, Shae powered her way to the door. The thing stood wide on its hinges from Dempsey's earlier breach, and finally, *finally* she got close enough to see fragments of blue sky and clear daylight beyond the threshold. For a second, Shae's senses short-circuited, her vision and balance and brain all scrambling to adjust to the searing brightness of the sun as she cleared the front door. But then Parker Drake and Quinn Copeland rushed up the concrete walkway, and the hard clack of the gurney wheels yanked her focus all the way into place.

"He was down when I found him," Shae said after lowering the guy to the gurney and tugging her mask from her face to suck in a lungful of natural air. Parker's gloved hands became a blue nitrile blur as he started a rapid trauma assessment, concern knotting his nearly black brows.

"Between the smoke and the fumes, that's not too shocking. Ah, dammit. No pulse. Starting compressions."

Shae shifted back to give him room to work, and God, what a cluster fuck of a call. "Is everyone else clear?" she asked Quinn, swiveling her gaze over the chaos of the scraggly yard. But before the worry in the woman's dark blue stare could form an answer, Slater's voice tore over the radio.

"McCullough! *Shae.* Help!"

Her breath slammed to a stop at the same time her pulse rattled at her throat. "Slater, what's your status? Are you hurt?"

"Negative. I'm not injured or trapped," came the immediate reply over the line. "But I…I can't fall out…you need to see this."

Shae turned toward the actively burning house behind her, and something snapped, hard and definite in her gut. "Dempsey and Hawk are clear, right?" she asked, reaching for the mask propped high over her forehead.

"Yes, but…" Parker frowned in confusion, transferring his stare to hers as Quinn slid monitor leads into place over their patient's chest. "McCullough, Cap ordered everybody to fall out. You can't—"

She was geared up and halfway back to the threshold before Parker could even finish.

"McCullough to Command. I'm going back in for Slater." The call-in would earn her an epic ass-chewing, Shae knew. But if she wanted to have Slater's back like she'd promised, she needed someone else to have hers.

"McCullough, this is Command," Bridges bit out, and yyyyep. He was pissed. "Stand down *immediately* while I assess the scene. Do you copy?"

"Sorry, sir. Too late," she clipped into her radio as she shouldered her way back through the door and into the hazy space of the foyer. "Slater, what's your location?"

"Here! I'm here." Thankfully, the rookie stood a handful of paces inside the doorway, upright and unhurt. But Shae's sharp blast of relief at the sight of him screeched to an end at the fear in his voice as he added, "Come quick."

He led her through the smoke-filled space to the right of the foyer, which was a near-identical layout to the side of the house she'd already cleared. Two long tables stood end to end in the middle of the first room, both filled to the gills with enough chemicals to make Shae's throat go tight beneath her hood.

"Slater," she started, but still, he pressed farther past the smoke and spreading flames, coming to a sloppy stop just inside the second room.

"I saw him just after Cap gave the order to fall out. I rolled him to check for spinal injuries, just like we're supposed to before we move anyone, but—"

Shae's stomach twisted, a shiver running the length of her spine despite the hell-hot conditions surrounding her on every side. The man on the ground was slumped over and lifeless, much as her victim had been. The giant pool of blood spreading out beneath him from the gaping, ear-to-ear slash wound on his neck?

That was definitely different.

Breathe in. Breathe out. Breathe...breathe right. Fucking. Now.

"Okay, Slater." Shae forced the words from her throat, marshalling every ounce of calm that she owned past her gag reflex and the reckless slamming of her heart. "We need to get this guy out of here."

Still, Slater didn't budge. "He's dead, isn't he?"

"We need to get him out of here," she repeated, hoping like hell he wouldn't notice her definite dodge of the question. "Are you good to take point?"

As wide as the rookie's eyes were behind his mask, Shae couldn't risk letting him lag behind her, and they had to fall out, *fast*. Shae maneuvered the victim closer for extraction, her boots slipping in the pool of blood beneath her feet, and Slater stood frozen to the floorboards, his stare unmoving.

Dammit. *Dammit.* "Slater, look at me. *Look!*" The scalpel-sharp edge in her demand grabbed his attention—thank fuck —and he lifted his stare from the blood now soaking through her turnout gear to meet her gaze. "I've got you, and you've got point. We're getting this guy out of here, nice and easy, but I need you to lead the way. Do you copy?"

"Okay, yeah. Yeah." Slater's nod was still a little wobbly, but Shae would have to take it.

"Good." She took one last look at the man on the floor, her gut pitching as she reached for her radio. "Command, this is McCullough. We're going to need another ambo. And, Cap?"

She hooked her arms beneath the victim's, the unnatural loll of his head on what little was left of his neck sending a fresh twist of dread from her helmet to her heels.

"Call the cops and tell them to get out here as quickly as they can. This place is a murder scene."

CHAPTER 2

If idle hands were the devil's workshop, then James Capelli was about to become a master carpenter for the Prince of Darkness. But the intelligence unit at the Thirty-Third hadn't seen anything more serious than a string of low-level smash and grabs since before Christmas, and as the guy who ran all of their surveillance and tech, if they weren't busy, he wasn't busy.

Which wouldn't be so bad, except that whole devil's workshop thing? Freakishly accurate in Capelli's case.

"Okay. Time to stay busy," he murmured, sliding his glasses higher over the bridge of his nose and killing the pang in his rib cage before it had a chance to fully form. Leaning back in his sleek black desk chair, Capelli sent a calculated stare over his work space. Eight years of running IT and surveillance for the Remington Police Department had given him plenty of time to cultivate the perfect technical environment, and he'd done it bit by bit (literally, because geek humor was a beautiful thing.)

Although he'd personally designed not only the network

Sergeant Sam Sinclair and the four detectives in the intelligence unit used on a daily basis, but the state-of-the-art digital display board they used to collect and cross-reference data on any given investigation too, Capelli's deep-down pride and joy was his own work space. An array made up of six twenty-seven-inch touch screens that could provide individual images or enlarge one across the entire display. Seamless connections to any database a cop could think of—as well as a handful no one other than Capelli could think of but hey, might be useful one day. Enough bandwidth to effectively run a small island nation, and hell if shit like this wasn't exactly why he shouldn't have free time on his hands.

His mind was always on, always alert and processing and moving at warp speed. And if he didn't use his walnut for good, his past history would rear up in an instant to become an all-too-present reality.

One that would land him in jail. Or worse.

"Listen up, people. We have a case."

The sandpaper edges of Sinclair's voice hooked Capelli's attention, along with everyone else's from around the large, shared work space of the intelligence office.

"Okay." Detective Isabella Moreno looked up from the stack of paperwork on her desk as if she'd just been handed a Presidential pardon, her brown eyes glinting in true *let's do this* fashion. "What're we looking at?"

Sinclair didn't skip a beat. "Captain Bridges over at Seventeen just called in a pretty nasty fire at a residence housing a meth lab in North Point."

"Was there a problem with the call?" Alarm streaked over Moreno's face, but Sinclair canceled it out with a quick, tight shake of his crew cut.

"All first responders are accounted for and uninjured."

"Oh. Good," she said, although the simplicity of her

answer was a poor match for the relief flooding through her stare. Logically, Capelli didn't find Moreno's reaction out of the ordinary; after all, she and her boyfriend, firefighter Kellan Walker, had filled their grave-danger quota for at least a year with the DuPree case—or okay, maybe for a decade. Possibly forever.

Emotionally, though? The response was as foreign to him as if Isabella had started spouting ancient Sanskrit backwards. Investing that much emotion in another person, whose behavior and actions you couldn't predict or know inside and out one hundred percent of the time, without fail? Christ, it was an engraved invitation for disaster.

Once bitten, twice no fucking thank you.

"Alright," said Moreno's partner, Liam Hollister, the confusion in his tone depositing Capelli back to the reality of the intelligence office and the potential case in front of them. "So a meth lab in North Point got a little crispy around the edges. I'm not trying to thumb my nose at a case or anything, but isn't vice going to try to swipe this one since there are drugs involved?"

"Probably," Sinclair said, tipping his gray-blond crew cut at Hollister in concession. "But seeing as how there were also two bodies at the scene, that's a pissing contest they're not going to win."

"Hey now." Detective Shawn Maxwell propped his elbows over the paper-littered surface of his desk, his black eyebrows sky-high. "Bodies do give us dibs."

"That they do," Sinclair agreed. "So let's run this. According to the ID in his wallet, the first victim is Lawrence Richardson, also known as the L-Man and a member of the Scarlet Reapers. Died of what looks to be smoke inhalation on the way to Remington Memorial, but docs are still working on an official cause of death. Lawrence has been arrested for a handful of petty misdemeanors and two prior counts of felony drug possession, one six months ago, one a year before that. Both kicked down to misdemeanors, but he did thirty days in lockup for number two."

Sinclair gestured to the digital board at the front of the office without pausing. Not that he needed to. After eight years, he knew Capelli almost as well as Capelli knew him back, which by deductive reasoning meant he also knew Capelli would have the details on display by the time he was done turning around. Which, of course, he did, along with Richardson's mug shot and a full list of his previous charges, because—*hello*—that was protocol. Why fuck with a streamlined process for data gathering when said process worked?

"Second victim is Malik Denton, also a known member of the Scarlet Reapers," Sinclair continued, and at this, Detective Addison Hale piped up from the desk closest to Capelli's.

"So this *is* drug related," she said, the ends of her blond hair brushing over the shoulders of her long sleeved T-shirt. "I mean, the Reapers are the third largest gang in Remington, and they're not exactly known for selling Girl Scout cookies. Plus, the L-Man died of smoke inhalation. Hardly shifty considering the fire likely started while these two jokers were cooking up a bunch of meth."

Capelli knew the look on Sinclair's face, and huh, that was weird. It wasn't agreement. "Not so fast. Denton's throat was cut nearly all the way to his spinal cord."

Shock sizzled a fast path through Capelli's veins, his fingers freezing over his keyboard. "Whoa. That's pretty out of the ordinary for the Reapers." Not to mention pretty personal for a gang murder. Unless the killer wanted to send a serious message or settle a serious vendetta, anyway. "Any evidence that the L-Man did the slice and dice or does it look like they're both vics?"

"Preliminary crime scene reports are still coming in," Sinclair said.

"So even if this wasn't some sort of revenge thing against either Denton or the Reapers"—Moreno paused, her frown clearly marking the hypothesis as the long shot it was —"we've got at least one homicide with what's got to be zero viable evidence between the blaze and the water used to put it out, and our only chance at getting any sort of lead is the hope that this wasn't an internal gang hit, *and* that the other members of the Scarlet Reapers will cooperate. With us. In an investigation that's bound to implicate them in multiple felony drug crimes for the meth lab alone."

"Mmm hmm." Sinclair nodded. "That about sums things up."

Well. At least Capelli wouldn't have to worry about the idle hands thing for a while.

"I'll start running background on Denton and the L-Man —dump their phones, comb their social media. Oh, and I'll sniff around for online chatter about any rival gangs who might have a beef with the Scarlet Reapers, too."

He shifted back toward the keyboard in front of him, his brain already halfway through the process, but Sinclair kept the surprises coming by shaking his head.

"Do it on the way to North Point," he said, pinning Capelli with an ice-blue stare that brooked less than zero argument. "We don't have more pressing case work here, and you've got sharp eyes. With that photographic think-trap between your ears, you'll be able to grab the details of this one better if you're directly on-scene. Given how much potential this case has to be a righteous pain in the ass, the more we've got to go on from the start, the better."

For a second, Capelli's ingrained instinct to stay one step removed from all things directly criminal warred with Sinclair's admittedly sound logic. But while he didn't normally hit a fresh scene with the rest of the team, this certainly wouldn't be his maiden voyage in the field. Plus, the look-see would keep his brain busy, which he not only wanted, but needed, so he squashed his unease with a quick lift and lower of his chin.

"You got it, Sergeant."

"The fire is out, but Captain Bridges has to run a pretty tight protocol because of all the chemicals inside, so it might be a while before we can get anyone from the crime lab past the front door," Sinclair continued. "Hollister, I want you and Moreno out there to canvas the neighborhood in the meantime. Maxwell, you and Hale go talk to the two firefighters who made the find on the bodies and see what they can tell you. Capelli, you stick with them and start piecing together the basics until we can get inside the house. Let's go."

All four detectives kicked into the simultaneous motions of double-checking the Glocks in their side holsters and the badges at their hips. Not technically being a cop, Capelli had neither, so he slid his black canvas jacket from the back of his desk chair, grabbed the organic Granny Smith apple sitting on top of his desk, and catalogued his thoughts in order of priority—*grab phone records, cross-reference timelines and whereabouts of the victims with social media posts, pull bank records, credit card statements, any open investigations on the Reapers by vice and the gang task force unit*—until Maxwell and Hale finished their lock and load.

"I'll drive," Maxwell said, reaching for the keys on the pegboard in the front of the intelligence office, but Hale slipped in to lift them with a giant grin on her face and half a second to spare.

"Not today, big man! You can, however, duke it out with Capelli for shotgun. I'll even referee."

"Actually," Capelli said, calculating Maxwell's reach and edging a full step outside of it, just for an ironclad margin of error in case the guy had gotten quicker since Capelli had last pissed him off. "I've got to take shotgun regardless so I can access the police database from the dashboard unit and start running case background on our way to the scene."

While Capelli had fully expected the hard glint in Maxwell's stare, it still tagged him right in the survival instinct. "You'd better find something good," the detective said, tugging a black knit hat over his shaved head as they made their way down the hallway and toward the stairs leading to the main hub of the Thirty-Third precinct. "And don't think you're driving back, Hale. My patience only goes so far."

"Oh, bullshit," Hale said, so gleefully that Capelli had to wonder whether she had a death wish lurking somewhere beneath her blond ponytail and bright smile. "Once you get past that dark-stare, big-badass, moody-broody-tough-guy thing you like to broadcast like the six o'clock news, you're really just a big teddy bear."

Given how astronomically high the odds were that Maxwell was, in fact, reaching the outer limits of his already scant patience, Capelli swallowed his laugh and one-eightied the subject. "So, we're headed to four ninety-two Crestridge Drive." He bit into his apple and scrolled through the rest of the text alerts Sinclair had routed to his cell phone, scanning for the highlights. "The docs over at Remington Mem have confirmed smoke inhalation as the probable cause of death on the L-Man, but we'll have to wait for the autopsy to know for sure."

"Any word on whether or not he could be our ax man?" Maxwell asked, cutting right to the chase as they descended the last of the steps at the back of the precinct's busy front lobby.

"Let's see." Capelli scrolled through the rest of the alerts, and whoa, plot twist. "Actually, all signs point to no. The hospital report says there were no signs of blood anywhere on the L-Man's hands or clothes."

Maxwell's chin lifted a fraction of an inch, but it was the only sign of his surprise. "So either the L-Man had a full-on wardrobe change before he died…"

"Or he didn't kill Denton," Hale finished.

Capelli weighed the facts from the report, running the probabilities in his mind. "Although it's not *impossible* that he killed Denton, given this? It's pretty unlikely. The most probable scenario is that the L-Man was trapped in the house during the fire and his death was an accident."

"Or he was locked in and murdered too," Maxwell offered, and Hale chimed in with,

"At a fire that might have been an accident or might have been set on purpose to hurt both of them. *Or* cover up the murder…murders?"

Jesus. Calling this case a righteous pain in the ass might've been a gift.

Needing some concrete facts, Capelli tapped the image files that the doctors at Remington Memorial had sent over of both bodies. "Denton's neck wound *is* pretty significant," he mused.

Hale looked over his shoulder, immediately wincing even though she didn't break stride over the threshold of the precinct. "Ugh. That's grisly as hell." She shuddered, but the unease on her face told Capelli it had little to do with the January weather they'd just walked into.

"It's not your average slash job," Capelli agreed, zooming in on the screen for a closer look at the wound so he could catalogue the particulars. "Sinclair wasn't exaggerating about his throat being cut nearly all the way to the spinal cord. Whoever did this was either really pissed or using a machete."

"You think the murderer used a machete?" Maxwell's

breath puffed around his face in the afternoon cold, his brows lifting to the edges of his cap in question, and Capelli lifted his hands in apology.

"Sorry, figure of speech. I mean, I guess the killer *might've* used a machete," he conceded, because there really was a lot of gross tissue damage. "But I was referring more to the size and depth of the wound being comparative to a larger weapon. Truth is, unless it's still sticking out of someone, not even the ME can definitively know if a stab wound was made by a scalpel or a broadsword."

Maxwell huffed out a soft, half-humorless laugh. "You, my friend, have a very wide and very morbid base of knowledge."

The irony of the words stuck into Capelli like a hundred razor-sharp pins, and time for a redirect, stat. "Yeah, but I'm fucking awesome at *Jeopardy!*"

Hale raised a brow, but couldn't cover up the twitch of her lips that accompanied the gesture. "So what you're saying is we're not going to get far on a murder weapon unless there's one gift-wrapped and waiting for us at the scene."

She popped the locks on their department-issued unmarked Dodge Charger, her boots thumping softly over the pavement in front of the precinct, and Capelli shook his head as he fell into step beside her.

"No. Probably not."

"Weapon aside, though, throat slashing isn't exactly the method of choice for a gang murder. We might get lucky if another one pops in the database."

Capelli thought for a second, rolling through mental file after mental file until... "Nope. At least not on any gang-related case intelligence has worked in the last eight years."

At Hale's look of shock, Maxwell simply shook his head. "What, did you forget we were riding with Encyclopedia Brown over here?"

Even though Capelli had a particular sore spot for nick-names, he had to crack at least a small smile at the mention of the one that had been administered by his teammates half a decade ago—even if his memory *was* technically more eidetic than photographic.

"Hey," he said, sliding into the Charger's passenger seat. "If the brain pan fits..."

"Use it," both detectives chimed at the same time.

After giving Hale one last mighty stink eye, Maxwell origamied his way into the back seat of the car. "Which two firefighters made the find?"

Excellent question. Capelli thumbed down to the last text Sinclair had sent him. "Let's see. Looks like Luke Slater and"—his chest squeezed in a weird, involuntary pang —"Shae McCullough."

There was no rational reason why his pulse should accel-erate at the thought of Shae McCullough. As part of the intelligence unit, Capelli crossed paths with the firefighters and paramedics at Seventeen here and there on cases, and both the cops at the Thirty-Third and the first responders on A-shift all killed more than a little of their spare time at the Crooked Angel bar and grill together, too. Subjectively, Capelli couldn't deny that Shae *did* skirt the boundaries of gorgeous with that long, lean frame and that wavy, honey-brown ponytail worthy of its own damned shampoo commercial. But he'd spent enough time around her to know she defied logic every time she turned around, hopping spontaneously from one thing to the next with no regard for a process or a plan. Not being able to predict Shae's patterns in order to figure her out drove him crazy enough to turn his otherwise steady composure into a dim fucking afterthought every time he clapped eyes on her, and *that* could mean only one thing.

No matter how tempted he was to wrap that ponytail

around his hand and find out what she looked like bent over his bedsheets, he needed to keep his distance from Shae McCullough.

Clearing his throat even though the conversation had lulled, Capelli took another bite of his apple and tapped into the RPD's database on the computer wired to the Charger's dashboard. The tasks in front of him calmed the chaos that had rattled through his brain like a five o'clock freighter at the thought of Shae, and he methodically kicked off background checks and online searches for any information he could find on their two victims as he finished eating. To his surprise—and dismay—his ten minutes of digging turned up precious little in terms of anything useful. Even after they'd been waved past the uniformed officer standing sentry three houses down from the cluster of emergency vehicles blocking the end of the street, Capelli still had virtually no more to go on than when they'd left the Thirty-Third.

If the scene in front of them was anything to go by, he wasn't going to get much else in person, either.

"Damn." Following Capelli out of the car, Maxwell sent a frown over the scorched and torched mess that had been a small, more-than-slightly rundown house just like all the others on Crestridge Drive just a few hours earlier. "That smell will wake you up in the morning."

"The chemicals used to cook meth definitely have a distinct smell when they burn," Capelli agreed, and hell, even inhaling through his mouth did nothing to help calibrate his senses to the sharp, bitter-burnt scent riding the air around them. "Hydrochloric acid, sodium hydroxide, touline, acetone…it's all pretty toxic stuff."

"You storing away a how-to guide over there?" Hale asked as she slammed the Charger's driver's side door, and even though her tone painted the words as the joke they were, the suggestion that he was well-acquainted with the process still sent a jab of unease to Capelli's gut.

"Recipes differ, of course." He lifted one shoulder halfway before letting it casually drop. "The rest is just chemistry." A subject he'd aced in middle school with his eyes closed and one hand tied behind his back. Not that it was how he'd gained the knowledge he'd just offered up. "Anyway, the chemicals definitely have the potential to be pretty dangerous. I'm not surprised they ignited a fire, or that Bridges wants to be careful about the cleanup."

Maxwell nodded, his gaze moving toward the red and white fire engine parked in front of the still-smoldering house. "Speaking of which…"

Capelli moved his eyes from the scene of the crime just a fraction too late to see Shae before she saw him first, and not only was her bright green stare brimming with all of its usual intensity, but her face was smudged with soot and traces of dark red streaks and spatters that could only be one thing.

His heart took a slap shot at his sternum without his brain's consent, and *fuck*, so much for having any composure around her.

Again.

"Thanks for getting out here so quickly," Captain Bridges said, approaching the three of them with Shae and a clearly shaken Luke Slater on either side. "This scene gave us a whole lot more than we bargained for."

"So we heard," Hale said, sympathy flickering over her face by way of a small smile.

Bridges nodded. "I'm sorry you can't get into the house quite yet, but there are enough volatile chemicals and toxic fumes in there to fill half a warehouse. Lieutenant Hawkins and squad have their hands full with hazmat protocols."

"Understood." Hale's eyes moved over the scene quickly, but with care. "We'd like to get as much information as we can in the meantime to see if we can start piecing together what happened."

"My two paramedics are still at Remington Memorial, finishing up the paperwork on the smoke inhalation victim," Bridges said. "Paramedics from Station Six transported the other victim for an official call on time of death."

"We got the update on the bodies from dispatch on the way over," Maxwell said, softening things by adding, "Hell of a call, like you said."

"Yes. Well, of course you're welcome to talk to firefighters McCullough and Slater here about the find. I'll be sure to alert Sinclair when the house is safe for your crime scene techs to go through. Just let me know if there's anything else we can do."

"We definitely will. Thank you." Hale shifted her gaze from Captain Bridges to Slater, and Christ, even though the rookie wasn't a small guy by any stretch, he looked like he'd blow over in one half-decent gust of wind, his normally light brown skin both pale and sweat-sheened. "Hey, Slater, why don't you and I head over to the engine to talk?" she asked. "I'd love to get out of this cold."

He blinked at Hale once, then twice, before nodding. "O-okay. Sure."

Shae waited until they'd moved out of earshot with Captain Bridges not far behind before she split a stare between him and Maxwell. "You guys always do the divide and conquer thing with stuff like this?"

It was a weird question, which made Capelli pause in an effort to figure out why she'd asked it. But Maxwell either didn't notice or didn't care that she'd swerved into unexpected territory.

"It's SOP," he agreed. "Your reports of the scene are the only thing we have to go on for potential leads right now.

The details will stand up better in court if they can be corroborated in individual interviews."

"Yeah, well, do me a favor and go easy on him, would you?" She tipped her chin toward the spot where Slater and Hale had climbed up into the back of the engine, and Capelli's curiosity sparked, good and hard.

"Why?" The question was out before he could capture it, and Shae's brows took a sky-high route over her forehead.

"Beeeeecause less than an hour ago, he stumbled across a murder victim who'd lost more than half his blood volume from a wound that turned out to be four tendons shy of decapitation?"

Heat crept up the back of Capelli's neck at the obviousness in her tone, and the fact that he'd missed the visceral aspect she so clearly hadn't. "All I meant was that he didn't do anything wrong. Hale's taking his statement, not interrogating him," he said, but Shae's brows—and her frown—didn't budge.

"And all *I* meant was that while Slater's tough, he's still a rookie. This was his first loss in the field. He's taking it about as well as you'd expect."

Maxwell nodded, stepping toward her on the pavement. "Copy that. We're all on the same team, McCullough. We're not here to upset either of you. We just need to do everything by the book."

"I know," she said, her courage sliding into concession fast enough to make Capelli a little dizzy from the whiplash. "I just…it was pretty bad in there. I think we left 'upset' in the rearview forty-five minutes ago."

Shae wrapped her arms around her rib cage, a visible shiver working a path over her frame. Not surprising, really, since she was standing in thirty-nine degree weather in nothing more than a sweat-damp RFD T-shirt and her bunker pants.

"Where's your coat?" Capelli asked, taking note of the half-dozen other firefighters milling around the street in front of them, all of them bundled to their chins in full gear.

A wry smile tilted the corners of her mouth upward just slightly, although the gesture lacked any traces of true humor. "Did you miss the part about the victim's blood volume, then?"

Oh *hell*. Capelli's throat tightened. "I don't miss details," he told her, shrugging out of his jacket reflexively. "I was just considering the established facts, and since you didn't specifically mention you'd been the one to pull Denton from the fire..."

Surprise skated over Shae's face as her eyes dropped to the jacket he held out in offer. "Oh. No thanks. Calls like this tend to knock a girl's body temp out of whack. I know it sounds crazy, but the cold actually feels nice."

Capelli was tempted—not a little—to tell her that with as much body heat as she'd probably spent on the call, welcoming a chill didn't sound crazy so much as bat shit insane. Physiology didn't *work* that way, for Chrissake. But in the entire time he'd known her, Shae had never done the same thing twice, let alone done anything in a logical fashion, so he settled on, "I take it you *were* the one who pulled Denton from the fire, then."

Although he hadn't crafted the words as a question, Shae answered them anyway. "Yes. Slater made the find, but I made the extraction."

Capelli's brain buzzed with a whole new set of inquiries. Maxwell must've been on the same wavelength, because he said, "Why don't you start from the beginning and tell us everything that happened."

"Okay." She launched into a play-by-play that covered most of what they already knew, from the presence of the reported meth lab in the house to getting an unconscious L-

Man out to paramedics, and finally to Slater's discovery of Denton on the other side of the house.

"Hang on." Capelli replayed her words in his brain, but wait, they couldn't be accurate. "You disobeyed a direct order to go back into the house for Slater once he found Denton's body, even though you knew how bad the fire was?"

If the sudden stubbornness in Shae's jaw was anything to go by, her report was *entirely* accurate. "My captain has already promised to read me the riot act, thanks."

"It just seems like a pretty reckless decision to put your personal safety on the line in those specific conditions. Not to mention breaking rank, which is never a good idea."

Shae's chin snapped up, her hands moving to her hips as she took a step back on the faded asphalt to pin him with a stare. "You really see things in black and white, don't you?"

"I see facts," Capelli countered, inhaling slowly to offset the uncharacteristic thrum in his chest. Christ, this woman pushed every last one of his buttons. "You knew the fire was going to flash over. Your captain gave you a direct order to fall out. You went back into the house anyway."

Obvious surprise lifted Maxwell's brows. "I think what Capelli meant to say is—"

"Exactly what he did say," Shae finished, although her stare never wavered from Capelli's. "Yes, I knew shit was going sideways in the house, and yes, I disregarded a direct order to re-enter the scene anyway. But there's another fact you're forgetting, and it's the most important one of all."

Either she was mistaken or speaking figuratively, because he never forgot a fact. Hell, he never forgot anything, not even when he desperately wanted to, but now wasn't exactly the time for examining semantics. "And what's that?"

"When Slater and I crossed that threshold, I told him I had his six, which means when he needs me, I'm there. Period. I don't just see facts, Capelli," she said, her green eyes glittering with enough conviction to make his heart pump faster in his chest. "I see everything."

And just when he thought she couldn't throw anything more unpredictable in his direction, Shae swiveled on her boot heels and walked away.

CHAPTER 3

Conrad Vaughn despised the sound of his name. Not that many people called him by it, or for that matter, even knew what it was. His last boss—sanctimonious bastard —had insisted on addressing everyone formally, and since the guy had also been a mouth-foaming sociopath, Vaughn hadn't really felt the need to push the issue. Of course, now Julian DuPree was a *dead* mouth-foaming sociopath, which really just validated the shit out of Vaughn's current plan.

He needed a career path that didn't involve having a spectacular fuckwit for a boss. The problem was, nearly every person he'd ever met fell squarely into that category. The rest? Well, they were even dumber.

Kicking his worn-out black Converse sneakers over the cracked concrete beneath them, he let his always-racing mind take the thought and spin. In truth, Vaughn had always had a hate thing for working for the highest bidder. While the revenue stream of setting up security and counter-surveillance for Remington's underbelly didn't necessarily suck, it wasn't enough to set him up in a tiki bar on Kauai, either—and the job security wasn't exactly cement when chances were high that your employer could end up *in* cement. Not that Vaughn really minded the criminal activity, because playing for Team Dark Side sure beat the hell out of all that work-hard, honest-living bullshit most sheeple did.

But each of his bosses had shared the same flaw; namely that they were all dumb enough to lead with their emotions rather than their gray matter. Which meant that at a certain point, shit always went tango uniform. DuPree was case in point. That motherfucker had been so far away from his happy place that he'd nearly gotten Vaughn caught in a raid by RPD's finest. He'd been able to escape, of course, but only because the intelligence unit's Head Geek In Charge had once been his partner in crime—literally and figuratively. As decent a hacker as James Capelli was, he was also as predictable as high tide. But even after eight years of total radio silence between them, Vaughn had still been smart enough to know the guy's every move before the first neuron even fired to turn it into an action.

No honor among thieves, really. Rapists or murderers either. But between hackers least of all.

Still, James might be calculable to a fault, but he also didn't have his head lodged quite as far in his colon as the rest of the RPD. After the whole DuPree debacle, Vaughn had needed to spend three goddamn months bouncing all over the grid in order to be absolutely sure he'd escaped his old buddy's detection, all while staying *off* the grid in various flophouses and cesspools. The sabbatical had provided him with a much-needed reality check, as well as the time to come up with the perfect plan to fix his problem.

After all, he was far more intelligent, more calculated and intuitive, than anyone he'd ever met, let alone worked for. Why earn their money like a chump when he was smart enough to just take it instead?

Good old-fashioned extortion might not be glamorous,

but it was making for a hell of a payday. And on the rare occasion his former employers hadn't bucked up and wired him the money he deserved for outsmarting them, he was all too happy to follow through on his threats to make them pay in other ways.

Liiiiiike setting all their shit on fire and laughing while it burned.

A grin slid over Vaughn's face, his chest filling with satisfaction at the thought. Sinking lower in his hoodie, he took a sip of the sixty-four-ounce slushy in his hand and lowered himself over his favorite park bench. Okay, so 'park' might be a bit of a stretch for this section of Atlantic Boulevard, especially considering how many blow jobs and dime bags had likely been traded here in the last twelve hours, but really, he wasn't about to alert the grammar police. It was the perfect spot for him to take care of business—solid visuals on all four arms of the compass for fifteen feet, three separate exit points in case he needed to ghost, no cops dumb enough to wander this far down the wooded path and no criminals likely to linger if they saw that the space was already *ocupado*.

Which was stellar, since killing people in public was *such* a pain in the ass to cover up.

And, hey, speaking of murder…

Vaughn set his drink aside and took the burner phone he'd bought for this very occasion out of his back pocket, keying in a number from memory. The call wasn't necessary, per se, but since he hadn't been able to extract a payday from Raymond Allen, a.k.a. Little Ray and the leader of the Scarlet Reapers, a little pay*back* was the next best thing.

The phone on the other end rang only once, and outstanding—Ray was keyed up enough to give him the upper hand right out of the gate.

"Who the fuck is this?" the guy demanded, and okay,

rightfully so. It's not like gang leaders gave out their private cell numbers like Halloween candy.

Which was exactly why Vaughn had called it. "Now, now. Is that any way to greet an old friend?"

And three, two, one...Yahtzee. "You little piece of scrawny, no-good shit! I'm going to rip your goddamn head off and piss down your neck," Ray snarled, and Vaughn gave up a soft tsk.

"Such nasty profanity. I'm hurt, Little Ray. Truly."

"Not yet, but you're gonna be, Shadow." Even covered in venom, the name Vaughn had earned made him smile as Ray hissed it into the phone. "After what you did today, you're a dead man."

"Actually, I'm alive and kicking," Vaughn told him, slapping a bored-as-hell expression over his face as he scanned the park around him in a covert three-sixty. All clear, exactly as he'd predicted. Duh. "Heard you had a pretty bad afternoon, though."

The silence humming over the line was so loaded, Vaughn could've used it to make a kill shot from fifty feet away, and finally, Ray bit out an answer. "A bad afternoon? You blew up my business. Killed Malik *and* the L-Man. Cut Malik's throat from ear to ear."

Yeah, that had been irritating. Vaughn had always hated wet work. The stink of blood and piss and pure, primal fear didn't wash off for fucking days. He'd tried to just tranq the guy into next week like he had the L-Man. At least that way Vaughn would've been able to let the smoke do the job and keep the shoes he'd put on this morning. But the sufentanil he'd jammed into Malik's neck hadn't knocked the dude out fast enough to just leave him there to die from smoke inhalation, and no way was Vaughn dumb enough to chance letting him survive. He'd been forced to go with his backup plan, i.e. actually using the scalpel he'd pressed to Malik's jugular when he'd stealthed up on him from behind. But at least the hack job he'd done afterward would be some added fun for the cops to try and (not) figure out.

"To be fair, I told you I would," Vaughn said, his pulse moving faster in his veins even though his words remained perfectly metered. "Or did you think I was bluffing when I said you could either pay me two hundred thousand dollars or I'd torch you to the ground?" He paused just long enough to let the salt sink into the wound before he topped it off with rubbing alcohol. "Oh, you did. That's so unfortunate for you. Ah, well. I guess now you know."

"You think I'm just gonna stand by for this?" Ray spat into the phone. "Nah, man. I'm gonna find your skinny ass, and when I do, you're gonna wish your momma had never spread her whore legs for your old man in the first place."

The insult struck unexpectedly, swift and deep, and anger beckoned from the place in Vaughn's belly where he kept it well-buried. But emotion was for pussies, and the anger would only make him weak and impulsive, so he stuffed it back with a smile. "To be honest, I'd rather you'd just paid me like I told you to. But it looks like neither one of us is going to get what he wants, so we might as well call this a draw."

Ray let out a lungful of disgust. "After what you just did, you want me to let you *walk*?"

Shifting his weight over the cold, rickety slats of the park bench, Vaughn sighed. Emotions made people so fucking stupid, honestly. "I'm sure you won't, but the reality is, you should. Look at the facts. I ran the Scarlet Reapers' security for six months. That makes me pretty much the high lord of your dirty laundry. Add in the harsh reality that me and my skinny ass managed to singlehandedly kill two of your most loyal associates *and* turn your biggest operating center into a giant pile of ash, and it's not really a logic leap to know you shouldn't keep messing with me."

"You ain't the high lord of a goddamn thing. How do you know I didn't change all that security shit up after you left?" Ray asked, and oh, look. Vaughn's favorite bluff.

"Because while you may be a bottom-feeding Neanderthal, you're surprisingly not a terrible businessman. You hired me because I'm the best. And even on the off chance you did change the security system you paid me to implement after I left"—of course he knew the guy hadn't, because he'd left loopholes in the Scarlet Reapers' system like any halfway decent hacker would and should—"you don't really think I didn't keep my own records, do you?"

The string of nasty swear words that followed led Ray exactly where Vaughn wanted him. "You little fuck! I'm going to take you apart, one limb at a time."

"No you're not," Vaughn said with a laugh he actually felt. "I'm the Shadow, remember? I could be right behind you and you wouldn't know it until I tapped you on the shoulder."

He waited out the obligatory five seconds it would take the guy to check his surroundings out of paranoia before continuing. "This is your endgame, Little Ray. You can't exactly file an insurance claim against your losses, so you're out all that product, your biggest and most productive meth lab, and the personnel." Vaughn ticked each one off on his fingers even though the bare trees around him were his only company. Oh, the numbers were so fucking beautiful, though, constant and predictable and precise. "You can't go to the cops for the murders without them looking at everything about you, right down to what you ate for breakfast. And while you *can* spend all your time and energy trying to get revenge, it'll only be a waste of both."

Vaughn pushed to his feet, and this time, his heartbeat did accelerate, his mouth curling into a smile. "I'm a shadow. You're not going to catch me, man. No one ever does."

Popping the lid on his slushy, he didn't even bother

pressing the button to end the call before dropping the burner phone first into the cup, then into the nearest trash can on his way out of the park.

⌒

AFTER FORTY MINUTES in the shower and half a bottle of vanilla-scented body wash, Shae gave up trying to get the stench of that afternoon's call off of her. It was figurative, of course—although between the second victim's blood and the giant cocktail of toxic fumes in the air at the scene, she hadn't exactly smelled like posies when they'd finally returned to Seventeen. She and her engine-mates had filed back into the fire house without conversation or fanfare, although she'd definitely caught the severity of the frown and side-eye combo Gamble had pinned her with as he'd handed over a replacement coat from the equipment room.

Blowing out a breath, Shae cranked the lever for the shower farther toward "hot" even though her skin already stung from the heat of the spray. She was well-acquainted with the symptoms of adrenaline letdown, along with the best methods to compartmentalize the grislier aspects of her job so as not to go nuts on toast. Sadly for her personnel file, Shae was also rather cozy with her emotions writing her an engraved invitation to the hot seat. Between Gamble and Captain Bridges, the censure she surely had in her immediate future was going to smart like a sonofabitch.

Not that she wouldn't pull on her big girl panties and take it. After all, no matter how much of a no-brainer her actions had been, she *had* disregarded a direct order when she'd gone back into that house for Slater, which meant she'd earned every syllable of the ass-chewing waiting for her outside the shower door.

But hot seat or not, she wasn't going to change the way

she did her job. Yes, she'd been tenacious (and okay, maybe a *teensy* bit insubordinate), but she hadn't put anyone but herself in possible danger, and she hadn't signed on at the academy because she'd wanted a thumb-twiddling nine to five. She'd learned the life-is-short lesson the hard way, and God, if her number could be up at any moment, she was going to make *all* her moments count, risks be damned.

It just seems like a pretty reckless decision...

Capelli's words echoed in her ears, hiking her chin to attention beneath the shower spray. Reaching out, Shae stopped the water with a swift turn of her wrist, her heart beating faster even as she took a deep breath to counter it. She might jump in with both boots first most of the time (okay, fine. All the time), but she was still a damn good firefighter. She wasn't going to make any apologies for that.

No matter how much she felt like Capelli had examined the facts and only the facts, then completely dismissed her *and* the reason for her actions with that one little melted chocolate stare.

"Now you really are losing your marbles," Shae muttered, snapping her towel from the hook outside the shower stall. Sure, Capelli was more methodical and observant than most —and seeing as how her closest friends were a bunch of first responders of varying specialty, that wasn't exactly small potatoes. She wouldn't expect the guy in charge of tech and surveillance for Remington's most elite police unit to be a dumbass, though, and anyway, his eyes weren't all *that* melty.

Okay, right. She officially needed a giant fucking Hershey bar and a pair of orgasms, stat.

Finishing up her dry off/get dressed routine, Shae shouldered her duffel and headed out of the shower room. The house was fairly quiet, although after a really pear-shaped call, that wasn't unusual. Her boots called out a series of soft thumps on the linoleum as she made her way to the locker room to stow her bag, then another as she redirected herself to the laundry room with this morning's sweaty and smoky uniform in tow.

She clattered to a stop on the threshold at the sight of Slater with his hands braced on either side of the washing machine and his head hung low over his chest.

"Hey," she said quietly, and although he lifted his chin, he didn't turn to look at her.

"Oh, hey. I was just, ah, you know. Doing some laundry."

Although a pile of navy blue cotton sat directly in front of Slater on top of the washer, the machine itself was silent, the plastic container of detergent next to his hand sealed up tight. Something shifted behind Shae's breastbone, and she stepped up next to him to put her clothes on top of the dryer.

"Popular choice. You want to combine forces? We can probably fit all of this into one load."

"Yeah, sure." Slater nodded. But instead of stepping back on the linoleum to move his clothes and open the washing machine door, he stuck to his spot and said, "I really fucked up today."

Usually she was the one surprising people, so it took her a second to recalibrate. "You didn't fuck up, Slater."

He arched a black brow toward his nearly shaved hairline in a clear expression of doubt. "I froze, McCullough. I heard the captain's order on the radio. I knew what I was supposed to do when I found that victim, and I couldn't make myself do it. There was so much blood, and the guy's neck was just"—the color drained from Slater's normally light brown complexion—"I've never seen anything like that. I knew I was supposed to call in directly to Bridges for orders, but I didn't. Instead, I panicked."

Shae knew she could give him a bunch of there-there platitudes like any regular person would. Hell, the call had been hairy enough to warrant a bucketload of them. But since she was about as far away from regular as a girl could get, she gave in to the wry smile tempting the edges of her mouth instead. "I hate to break it to you. That just means you're human."

"Yeah, but I can't afford to let my emotions railroad me on a call."

"No, you can't," she agreed, because as much as she didn't want to kick the guy when he was down, she wanted to bull-shit him even less. "But you also can't forget you have them, because you do. And if you ever *aren't* scared on call, that's when you need to hang it up."

Slater's chin snapped to attention. "You were scared today?"

Shae laughed, and judging by the rookie's expression, she'd reclaimed the upper hand in the surprising-people department. "I saw exactly what you saw, Slater, so in a word? Hell yes. I have emotions all the time—especially on calls. The only difference between me and you is that I've learned how to manage mine during a fire. You think I never need backup?" she asked. "Or that Walker or Gamble don't?"

"Well...no. I guess not," Slater admitted slowly.

"That's exactly why we do everything in pairs." She soft-ened her voice, but not her resolve. "Because ninety percent of our job is unpredictable, just like today. Any given call could go about a thousand different ways. This one was rough. One of the worst I've seen in a long time. But you'll figure out how to manage your emotions on calls. Good fire-fighters always do."

The sound of a feminine throat clearing captured their attention from behind them, and Shae's stomach tilted a little bit closer to her knees at the sight of their fire house admin-istrator, January Sinclair, standing in the open doorway.

"Sorry to interrupt," said the petite blonde, tucking the stack of file folders in her grasp against the hip of her dark gray pencil skirt. "Captain Bridges would like to see you in his office, Shae."

Even though she'd been expecting the request, her pulse still pushed a little faster in her veins. Slater opened his mouth—presumably to make a protest of some sort—but this wasn't exactly Shae's first rodeo, so she gave up a tiny head-shake to let him know she'd be fine. Turning to follow January down the long stretch of hallway that connected the two wings of the fire house, she straightened her shoulders and smoothed a hand over her fresh uniform before stepping over the threshold of Captain Bridges's office. He sat stiffly behind his desk, his normally calm demeanor painted over with a serious layer of I'm-not-happy, and Gamble looked equally twisted out of shape from his spot in one of the two chairs across from the captain.

"McCullough. Shut the door," Bridges clipped out with a tight nod. Unease filled Shae's stomach—nothing good ever came from the old shut-the-door request that wasn't a request—but she did as she was told before moving to stand beside the empty chair next to Gamble.

Bridges didn't tell her to sit before folding his hands over his desk, and okay, wow, he really *was* mad. "This is familiar territory for you, so I'm not going to go through any pleas-antries. Disobeying a direct order from a superior officer is not only unacceptable, but it's completely irresponsible. Your actions were dangerous and made without regard for your engine-mates."

Shae's cheeks flamed with indignation. He couldn't be serious. "I went back into that house *specifically* for one of my engine-mates," she protested.

"And what if someone else had to go in after *you* because you'd recklessly run into a situation you couldn't handle?"

The thought made her pause, but only for a millisecond. "But I did handle it. Slater and I were just fine."

Funny, that little fact didn't make a dent in Bridges's anger. "You're far from fine. You dove headfirst into a snap decision that wasn't yours to make instead of standing down while I assessed the situation and handled it accordingly. You acted foolishly, without one iota of thought or respect for the chain of command," he said, and the words arrowed all the way through Shae's chest, rocking her heartbeat and her waning calm.

She managed to inhale, although she had no fucking clue how. "With all due respect, sir, I'm not stupid."

"You may not be, but your actions were." A frosty silence filled the space of his office for a minute, then another, before Bridges added, "Do you think Slater doesn't learn from you?"

If he'd asked her to stand on his desk and sing show tunes, it might've shocked her less. "No, sir." Her conversation with Slater two seconds before she'd arrived in this room was case in point that the rookie was paying attention, and well.

Gamble triple-knotted the you're-in-deep-shit factor of the conversation by leaning forward in his chair to chime in. "I could've kept Slater with me on lines, or I could've waited for a different call to send him on S&R with Walker. But I didn't. I picked you, McCullough. I trusted you to take him in there and show him how to be a good firefighter."

The implication that she wasn't slid over her like an ice bath. "How does having his back at all costs not teach him exactly that?" she asked, but Bridges knocked her question down, hard and fast.

"Because you disobeyed a direct order, Shae. I'm not saying you shouldn't have Slater's back. I'm saying you should let me have yours and trust that I'll do my job, which is to make the best choices to keep *all* of you safe." He paused, his voice growing quieter but no less intense. "This is a dangerous profession, McCullough. I'm sure I don't need to remind you that we lost a firefighter in this house nearly four years ago."

The words stunned her so thoroughly that for a second, she couldn't speak. Of course she remembered Asher Gibson. He'd been their candidate before Kellan had arrived from the academy and Dempsey had moved over to squad, one of her engine-mates and a part of the Seventeen family just like everyone else. The day he'd died in that house fire had leveled them all. Including Shae.

"Yes, sir," she managed, her mouth dust-dry, but Bridges didn't scale back on his censure.

"There's no room for freelancing in this fire house. You might've gotten Slater out of that house today, but what you taught him was that it's okay to fly by the seat of your bunker pants and break the rules. Now I have to worry about you *and* him going commando every time the all-call goes off."

Shae's breath jog-jammed, squeezing her lungs as Bridges's words sank deep under her skin. "You don't have to worry about me, Cap. I'm a good firefighter."

"I'm afraid that's not what I saw today," he said, sitting back in his desk chair to spear her with a stare. "I've got no choice but to write you up and take you off active duty for two weeks, effective immediately."

No. No fucking way. She'd go crazy in the first two minutes. "You want me to sit on my hands for two *weeks*?"

At least here, Bridges gave up a pause, albeit a microscopic one. "Not entirely. You're on restricted duty for the rest of today's shift, helping January here in the office until she goes home for the night. Then first thing Monday, you'll report to the arson investigation unit and let them put you to work there for two weeks."

"Arson investigation," Shae repeated. On one hand, it was better than two weeks' worth of being benched completely.

On the other… "You're sending me to the place where paper-work goes to die?"

Now Bridges didn't hesitate. "They do solid work over there, and clearly, you need to slow down and be reminded what proper protocol looks like. Two weeks of procedure and paperwork will do you some good."

She opened her mouth, the impulse to argue sparking on her tongue. But the hard set of the captain's jaw told her he wasn't going to budge, and Gamble's dark, serious stare only reinforced her shitty odds.

No matter what she said, she was going to be wrong. Too hot-blooded. Reckless. Impetuous.

So as much as she hated it with the intensity of a thousand burning suns, Shae had no choice but to scrape up what little was left of her pride and say, "Great. I'll go find January and get started."

CHAPTER 4

Capelli sat back in his desk chair, staring at the precise piles of data he'd compiled in total disbelief. Statistically speaking, the odds that this much information wouldn't yield so much as a glimmer of a lead had to be astronomically high. Yet this case seemed bound and determined to defy any sort of normalcy, so really, he shouldn't be surprised.

Christ, they had nothing. And if there was one thing Capelli hated above all others, it was a puzzle he couldn't analyze and figure out.

Especially when said puzzle came with two dead bodies attached to it.

"Okay," he murmured, looking at the copy of the main case board screen he'd pulled up on his monitor. The intelligence office was quiet and semi-dark, with Isabella having left to swing by the sufentanil for dinner and Hollister, Maxwell, and Hale calling it quits to celebrate their Friday night at the Crooked Angel not long after that. Sinclair was still in his office, which wasn't really a fair barometer, because Capelli had a hard suspicion that the guy actually lived in his office rather than the apartment he rented a few blocks away. But the quiet would give Capelli a chance to get some work done, and the work would keep him busy.

Weekends were the hardest, with all their idle time.

He forced his eyes to focus on the screen and his pulse to remain status quo. Scanning the monitor on the desk in front of him, he tapped the touch screen to maximize the crime scene reports, re-reading each one even though he'd memorized them by default the first time through. He was better with numbers and images than words, though, and sometimes the repetition offered up a new angle.

At this point, anything would be better than the nothing he had, so he planted his elbows on his desk and read.

The excessive amounts of water needed to put out the fire had pretty much rendered any evidence that might have been left behind useless, for both the murder and the meth lab. Not that their crime scene techs hadn't gone through and collected what little they could anyway, but Capelli knew far better than to think that between the soaking and the fire that had required it, any fingerprints or viable DNA samples —or, okay, any clues at all—had survived. Getting anywhere with the Scarlet Reapers had been a bust, too. Their leader, an absolute mountain of a dude who ironically went by Little Ray, had been unequivocally unhelpful when Maxwell and Hale had reached out for a little knock and talk after they'd left the scene of the fire.

They might get lucky with physical evidence on the bodies, but for now, if Capelli wanted to get anywhere, he'd have to rely on background checks (nothing), chatter from confidential informants (*nada*), and the information gathered from the interviews done at the scene (nil.)

Well, shit. Good thing he loved a challenge.

Closing his eyes, Capelli pictured the scene reports in his mind, marshaling the words into order so he could look at the details in his mind's eye, like a photograph. Slater's account had been pretty basic—yes, he'd assessed the fire and seen the chemicals, no, he hadn't seen the victim until Bridges had made the call to fall out. After that, the only detail he'd been able to recall with any accuracy was the blood that had been everywhere, along with the fact that Shae had run back into the house to grab the victim and lead Slater to safety.

Now Capelli's pulse did jump, rendering him stupid for the second time today. While the reaction wasn't entirely unnatural considering Shae's lack of regard for anything resembling a rule or the all-emotions, all-the-time way she'd abruptly ended their conversation before walking away from him at the scene, it *was* still dangerous.

Actually, check that. His uncharacteristic reaction wasn't really the problem.

The impulsive thoughts about the even more impulsive firefighter who had caused it, not once, but twice today? Now those were downright fucking dangerous.

I don't just see facts, Capelli, came that infuriatingly sexy, borderline overconfident voice from the spot where his memory had stored it with care.

I see everything.

"You're here awfully late."

Sinclair's words delivered him back to the intelligence office with a hard jolt. But since Capelli had been programmed ages ago never to show surprise, he opened his eyes slowly, keeping his face blank and his body angled toward the computer monitor for just a beat longer before turning to give his boss a run-of-the-mill smile.

"You taught me well. Not that I gave you much choice."

"Hm." The corners of Sinclair's mouth twitched in the smallest suggestion of amusement, an expression he kept in place as he said, "Well, I'm not giving you much choice now, either. It's late, and it's Friday to boot. This case isn't likely to get much warmer until we get those reports from the ME's office and CSU, and even then, leads are going to take both work and luck. Go home, Capelli. Decompress. I don't want to see you again until Monday morning."

Without letting his own smile slip, Capelli weighed all the logical reasons he could craft into an argument for staying. But Sinclair knew him better than pretty much anyone, just like Capelli knew from countless past attempts that there was a zero percent chance the guy would ease up on his demand, no matter how good of an argument he made. Which meant Capelli's only viable option was to ghost.

Greeeeat.

He pushed back in his desk chair, his movements perfectly measured even though his heartbeat worked over-time in an effort to unsteady them. "You're the boss."

"That's what they tell me," Sinclair said. Turning on his heels, he moved back toward his office, tacking on a quiet but serious "good night" before disappearing through the door. Capelli resignedly went through the motions of powering down his machines, making certain to leave all traces of the case behind him on his desk for Sinclair's bene-fit. He didn't really need the files anyway—thank you, eidetic memory—and even if he did, he could use his laptop at home to pull them from the RPD database faster than most people could order a pair of pizzas. What he did need, though, was to keep his over-active brain from wandering. Making all sorts of suggestions he'd be tempted to consider. Sliding back into the past.

Don't go there. Not even in your head.

Check that. Especially not in your head.

Grabbing his jacket from the back of his desk chair, Capelli shouldered his way into the thing and headed through the glass double doors leading out of the intelligence office. His past wasn't a secret (public records were funny that way), nor was his history with Sinclair. While no one in the unit ever started a conversation with "hey, remember that time Sinclair arrested Capelli on multiple felonies and instead of throwing his ass in jail where it belonged, he gave him a job instead?" they never really dodged it either. Mostly because it was the truth.

Disclosure was a presentation of facts. And facts were everything.

That Capelli's had turned him into a white knight and a black king at the same time just made his personal chessboard extra-fucking-special.

He walked the same path as always out of the intelligence office—down the second-floor hallway to the open stairwell, sixteen steps to the main floor of the precinct, ten paces to the front door. As if there were some switch in his subconscious connecting work and the rest of the outside world, his stomach began to rumble the minute his boots had crossed the threshold of the Thirty-Third. Capelli did a mental scan of the contents of his fridge, and yeah, unless he wanted to eat mayonnaise or some leftover vegetable Lo Mein of dubious quality, he was going to have to grab some groceries on the way to his apartment.

Shifting a little deeper into his jacket, he let his mind turn even as he surveyed the street and the sidewalks around him. Today's case, and the frustrations that went with it, had him wound pretty tight. He needed to keep his brain occupied, but keeping the rest of him busy might not be the worst thing in the universe, either. Truthfully, it had been a while since he'd blown off any steam between the sheets, and if he was jacked up enough for Sinclair to kick his ass out of the building, maybe he should take the hint.

Maybe, just maybe, if he got laid, he'd finally stop thinking about Shae McCullough's smart mouth, and all the hot, impetuous-as-hell things she could probably do with it.

"For Chrissake," Capelli muttered, slipping the words far enough under his breath that he was certain no one on the sidewalk had overheard him. He needed to get his thoughts of Shae—and her sexy, overbold mouth—in line and out of his head, once and for all. Ordering his grocery list in his head, he made a beeline for the Stop 'n Shop six blocks away. The place was essentially empty of other shoppers courtesy of his Friday night timing. But since that just meant a more time-efficient circuit up and down the usual aisles for the usual items, Capelli was all for the solitude.

At least, he *was*...until he rounded the corner of aisle twelve and caught sight of the woman in front of him in the frozen food section.

Her back was completely to him as she leaned down to drop a few ready-made dinners into her cart, but with a view like the one her low-slung jeans and form-fitting shirt were treating him to, Capelli was all too cool with that. The woman's brown-gold hair spilled down her back in long, thick waves, her dark green top cropped just short enough to have revealed the sweet, muscular curve of her lower back when she'd bent forward. Heat rushed under his skin to head directly south, and damn, it looked like a more primal part of him than his stomach wanted attention.

Hard attention. Fast attention.

Right-fucking-now attention.

Before he could cage the wild, sudden impulse pumping through his bloodstream, he covered the space between himself and the woman in a handful of strides. Her shoulders tightened just slightly, a sure signal that she'd heard him and he wouldn't startle her or—worse yet—come off like a total creeper. Striking up conversations with strangers in the Stop 'n Shop wasn't exactly his MO, even if they were sexy enough to make him drop his normally cautious demeanor. He might like control—crave it, even—but come on. He wasn't a monk. Especially not with a woman like this in front of him.

"If you're trying to choose between the Salisbury steak and the chicken piccata, I'd go with the steak. Although personally, I'm more of a spaghetti and meatballs kind of guy."

The woman shifted, just enough for Capelli to catch the vanilla and brown sugar scent of her body lotion.

But the attraction making his heart beat faster and his dick half-hard turned into a bolt of pure shock when she turned on her three-inch boot heels, and he found himself nailed into place by Shae McCullough's brassy, sassy smile.

~

SHAE WASN'T sure what surprised her more—unexpectedly running into Capelli at the Stop n' Shop at nine o'clock on a Friday night, or the fact that her girly bits were currently an involuntary hot zone at the sight of the slow, sexy smile that had been riding his mouth when she'd turned around.

"Spaghetti and meatballs, huh?" Shae inhaled to counter the thrum of her pulse, grateful that they were surrounded by wall to wall freezers on both sides of the aisle. "I'll be honest, I didn't have you pegged as a frozen dinner kind of guy."

In fact, all the leafy greens and bottled water and items in his cart boasting words like *multi grain* and *organic* suggested he wouldn't touch a frozen dinner with a forty-foot pole. Which could only mean one thing.

James Capelli was flirting with her.

"*Shit*. I mean"—he cleared his throat, tugging a hand through his dark blond hair and taking a step back on the overly buffed linoleum—"I apologize. I didn't mean to be so forward."

"Really?" Surprise of a more traditional sort rippled through her chest. "Because I've gotta tell you, you kind of nailed it."

She'd been trained to be more aware of her surroundings than most people, so she'd heard Capelli's footsteps the second he'd turned the corner of the otherwise dead-empty aisle, just as she'd caught the darkly flirty intention in his smile when she'd turned around. He might not have ever aimed a look like that in her direction before, but Shae wasn't thick. She knew attraction when she saw it.

Just like she knew when she felt it back.

"Yes, really," he said, driving her surprise into confusion. "I didn't recognize you."

Shae gestured to her jeans and long-sleeved top with a laugh. "I'm hardly in disguise. Look, I'm not even wearing a coat. Again."

The revelation seemed to unnerve him another notch. "Your back was turned, and you just...you normally wear your hair in a ponytail, is all."

He gestured to her hair at the same time she reached up to skim a hand through it. "Ah," she said, her confusion waning slightly. "Must've forgotten to pull it back tonight, I guess."

At that, his brows tucked from behind his dark-rimmed glasses. "You don't have a routine?"

"You do?" Shae asked. She was about as familiar with routine as she was with astrophysics. Which, come to think of it, might be right up Capelli's alley.

"Well, yes. I..." He broke off with a wave of one hand. "It's not important. Anyway, how come you're grocery shopping? Aren't you supposed to be on shift at Seventeen until tomorrow morning?"

Just like that, her gut did a flawless impersonation of a rusty corkscrew. "Yeah, that's a long story that should probably be told over one too many gin and tonics," she said, tacking a smile over her face even though it was a poor fucking fit. A few seconds ticked by, punctuated by the strains of some pop song on the overhead speakers and Capelli's chocolate-colored stare, and jeez, how had Shae not noticed the sexy-factor of those glasses before now?

She shifted her weight from one boot to the other, trying to displace the warmth prickling between her thighs. "So how's your murder investigation going?"

It was a bit of a lame attempt to swerve the subject from her admittedly shitty day and her even shittier benching, she knew. But his shoulders loosened just a fraction beneath his black canvas jacket as he opened his mouth to answer, so score one for subterfuge.

"Slow, but we're still working on it. We don't have a whole lot of evidence to go on though."

"With how quickly that fire moved through the house, I can't say I'm shocked," Shae said, a thought percolating in the back of her mind. "Hey, did you hear anything from arson yet on the cause of the fire?"

He shook his head. "No, but the fire marshal has to do a scene inspection first. The only reports we have so far are the ones we took from you and Slater at the scene. Why?"

"The fire was really intense, and the flame patterns seemed kind of...I don't know. Wonky."

"Wonky," Capelli repeated, dark blond brows lifted as if she'd just started speaking in tongues.

She mirrored the expression right back at him. "Yeah, you know. Weird. I was wondering if they thought the fire had been set intentionally."

"Oh." He paused for a second, clearly thinking. "Well, it definitely wouldn't be the first time some dirt bag tried to use arson to cover up a murder, but we haven't seen a proven case like that in Remington in the last five years. There were a ton of chemicals at the scene today, all of them volatile and highly flammable. That seems like the most likely cause of the fire, and it probably had a lot to do with how quickly the blaze spread."

Shae opened her mouth, set and ready to argue. Yeah, she'd responded to a good half-dozen fires that had been obvious meth-cooking accidents, but still. *Proven* arson was pretty uncommon, period—mostly because it required a lot of undisputable evidence, and fires didn't usually leave a ton of that behind. But burn patterns told stories just like DNA and blood spatter and anything else at a crime scene, and Shae knew what she'd seen. Even if all she had to go on was a weird gut feeling.

Which would probably fly with Capelli about as well as a box full of bricks, and on second thought… "You're probably right. I'm sure the fire marshal and the arson unit will look at everything carefully and let you know if the fire was deliberate. The scene this morning was pretty crazy. Guess my mind is just caught up in the adrenaline of the whole thing."

"Speaking of which"—he looked at her, his expression unreadable yet not unkind—"I should apologize for earlier."

"Okay," she said, elongating the word until it nearly grew into a question. "I'm not sure I follow."

Capelli slid a hand over the front of his long sleeved T-shirt, his gaze dropping to the floor for just a breath before he lifted his eyes back to hers. "For our conversation earlier this morning," he clarified. "I don't normally conduct interviews for the intelligence unit, and I guess I'm not used to a lot of face-to-face, especially at crime scenes. I didn't mean to offend you with anything I said, though."

"You didn't mean to call me impulsive?" Shae's disbelief edged out her surprise, but only by thiiiis much. She might not know him all that well, but she wasn't blind, and she certainly wasn't an idiot. She'd seen advanced algebra equations less calculated than this man. If he'd called her impulsive, it was because he meant to.

"Well, no. I mean, yes." Capelli paused. Took a breath. Let it out slowly. "You did behave impulsively on the call. But Slater was pretty rattled. You two are engine-mates. Logically, it makes sense that you were just looking out for him when we showed up to question the two of you about the scene."

A pang unfolded in her chest, swift and deep and completely unexpected. "I was," she said, giving the odd sensation a second to dissipate before adding, "I appreciate the apology, but you don't have to worry about offending me. At least, not over something like that."

"You weren't mad?" he asked, his doubt obvious.

"Oh no, I was plenty pissed," Shae said. She wasn't about to scale back on the God's honest, no matter who she was talking to. "I just tend to burn bright, then burn out in the anger department. I don't really see much point in holding grudges. Life's really too short."

Capelli nodded, the fluorescent lights overhead glinting off his glasses. "I guess that's good to know for the next time I piss you off."

Shae very nearly laughed, until his expression told her he wasn't kidding. God, he was so serious.

Suddenly, impetuously, she wondered what it would take to undo him.

"We should probably stop meeting like this, you know," she said, her legs taking a step toward him before her brain recognized the command to move.

Her blood flared hotter when he didn't take a step back to counter it. "Us running into each other is purely coincidental," he replied. "I didn't even know you shopped here."

"Relax, Capelli." This time, she did laugh. "It was a joke." At his continued lack of a smile, she added, "Because we've run into each other unexpectedly twice in one day."

"Oh. Right, of course," he said, still going no joy on a smile.

Rather than backing down, though, Shae tried again to get him to loosen up. "And actually, I don't shop here, but I was out for a walk and I got hungry, so…"

She gestured to the small grocery cart behind her, filled with a stack of frozen dinners, a six-pack of ginger ale, and the king-sized Hershey bar she'd been craving all damned day.

"So here you are," Capelli said. "Unexpectedly."

Shae's pulse quickened, a deep pull of attraction spearing through her belly at the way his eyes had flared over the last word. Between helping each other at scenes from time to time and all hanging out at the Crooked Angel after hours, the cops in intelligence and the firefighters and paramedics at Seventeen knew each other both professionally and socially. A hookup or two had been known to go down between the group of friends—hell, Isabella and Kellan had even moved in together. Shae might have a pretty hard and fast rule against extra-curricular relationships with her fellow firefighters, but as she stood there on the linoleum looking at the hey-now angle of Capelli's shoulders beneath that jacket and the serious/seriously sexy look on his handsome, clean-shaven face, she had to wonder why the hell she'd never slept with him.

Then again, with the way his stare had just lingered on her mouth for a second longer than was cordial, she could probably remedy that gaffe right. Now.

"So what do you say we trade this six-pack of ginger ale for a six-pack of beer and go heat up a couple of these meal-sicles together?" She let her smile hang between them for just a beat, then tacked on, "I'll even give the spaghetti and meat-balls a shot."

"I'm not sure that would be such a good idea."

Surprised, Shae paused. "You never know. It might be fun."

Now it was Capelli's turn to pause. "I'm sure it would be a lot of fun, actually."

"What's the matter, Capelli? Aren't you a fun kind of guy?"

The tight spot between her legs filled with nine kinds of heat at the idea of just how much *fun* might be lurking under all that controlled composure of his. Again, his eyes lowered to rake slowly over her smirk, and oh God, how could she feel him so much when he wasn't even touching her?

Shae closed the rest of the distance between them save a scant inch, completely uncaring that they were smack in the middle of the frozen food section. "I mean, we're not exactly strangers. It seems kind of silly for us to spend Friday night alone when we could be having a little fun, don't you think?"

"I think..."

Capelli trailed off. Lifting one hand, he brushed the pad of his thumb over her bottom lip. The hot, unfettered sensations from the contact stunned Shae into place, turning her breath into a soft gasp and her nipples into aching peaks. He reversed the path of his thumb, the teasing, barely there touch making her sex clench. She parted her lips under his attention, pressing forward with every intention of letting him kiss her senseless right there in the grocery store, when the *clack clack clack* of shopping cart wheels filtered in from the next aisle over.

Just like that, Capelli's head whipped up. Yanking his hand from her lips as if she'd scorched him, he stepped back swiftly to regain a full bubble of personal space.

"I'm sorry," he said, his expression neutral and his brown

eyes as cool as the freezer case behind him. "I really can't. Have a nice night, McCullough."

He turned on his heels to walk a precise line toward the end of the aisle and out of Shae's line of vision, leaving her more turned on and pride-stung than ever as she stood there trying to figure out what the hell had just happened.

CHAPTER 5

After three hours of working in the arson investigation unit, Shae considered putting her eyes out with a spoon. It wasn't that the people were so bad; on the contrary, Natalie Delacourt, who'd showed her the ropes this morning, and Frank Wisniewski, who had worked in arson since the dawn of time, were actually rather nice.

The glacial work pace and the never-ending policies and procedures, though? Yeah. Cue the utensil drawer.

Blowing out a breath, Shae sat back in her desk chair and surveyed the mini-Mount Everest covering her small, makeshift work space in the corner of Natalie's office. Yes, being kicked down to arson had put a dent in her normally bulletproof armor, but her two-week penance on the paper trail might not smart so much if she hadn't been so summarily dismissed by Captain Bridges on Friday. Add in Capelli's weird duck and run in the grocery store after what she'd been certain had been a sure thing, and her already precarious ego was about as brittle as it could get without breaking.

"Want some confetti to go with that pity party?" Shae

muttered under her breath, swiping a file folder from the top of the pile by her elbow. Okay, so her pride had taken a pretty nasty one-two, but come on. She wasn't exactly a stranger to being told she was too impulsive, too capricious, too brash. She'd been tough enough to field those beliefs from everyone around her for the last eight years.

After all, watching your best friend die right in front of you when she'd been laughing ten seconds earlier tended to do a number on a girl's fortitude. Not to mention her perspective.

But backbone was the one thing Shae managed with any level of consistency. If she could handle a four-alarm fire, she could certainly handle a little dressing-down from her captain and a sexual Heisman from James freaking Capelli. Even if she *had* spent the majority of her weekend swinging between hot and bothered over the latter.

Stupid melty brown eyes.

Placing her elbows over her desk, she popped open the file folder between her fingers and read the report inside even though both her patience and her brain were halfway to tapioca by page two. Italian restaurant versus faulty wiring, a twenty-five-year-old building along the notoriously low-rent North Point pier, a grease trap that sounded like it hadn't been cleaned since the turn of the century…yeah, the restaurant never came out on top in a case like that. Shae flipped to the next page, her report already halfway written out in her head per Frank's instructions, when a glossy eight-by-ten photograph of the scene slipped from the back of the folder and drifted to the floor.

Holy fire damage, Batman. Shae reached down low to pick up the photo and give it a more careful look. She might be far more used to seeing a scene during a blaze than after the fact, but the extent of the damage to the restaurant was damned close to unreal. Curiosity spinning, she moved the written reports from the fire marshal and the responding firefighters aside, dropping the folder over her teeny-tiny desk to examine the rest of the photos more closely.

There were only six, but God, they spoke volumes. The place was a total loss, the walls bearing all the telltale signs of an electrical fire, with scorch marks running the length of the wiring that had been underneath the drywall and burn patterns that had rendered the outlets and switches nearly unidentifiable. Nearly all of the building-killing damage was centered in the back of the restaurant, which wasn't exactly a giant shocker considering the description of the grease trap above the fryer. Not that much seemed to be left of the thing, or most of the kitchen and adjacent office and half the dining room, either. But something about the scorch patterns and the sheer extent of the damage seemed both odd and familiar, swirling and poking and tugging at Shae's brain until finally, all the dots connected in a hard, magnetic snap.

"Hey, Natalie?" Shae asked, looking up at the redhead with her heart halfway to her throat. "Do we have the reports from the house fire that Seventeen responded to on Friday?"

Natalie blinked at her from across the cramped office space. "Not yet. The fire marshal wanted to give the RPD's crime lab plenty of time to go over the scene. He isn't even scheduled to go out there for his inspection until tomorrow morning. Why?"

"Because there are a lot of similarities between that fire and the one that went down at this restaurant by the pier two weeks ago, and something about the restaurant fire looks weird to me."

"Okay," Natalie said, the crease between her auburn brows marking her doubt. "Define 'weird'."

Shae lifted the photograph from her desk, flipping it outward in display. "See the burn patterns here, along the walls? And all this crazy damage in the kitchen?"

Natalie leaned forward in her desk chair, her brown eyes narrowing as she took a minute to examine the picture. "There's more damage than your average restaurant fire, but that doesn't automatically make it arson. In fact, those scorch marks are textbook for faulty electrical."

"Exactly." Despite what should be a slam dunk, Shae's heart beat faster against the crisp white top of her uniform. "But if the crappy wiring sparked a fire"—she turned the picture to trace the burn marks by the fryer with one finger—"and that's what ignited the grease trap, which made the place burn so hot, so fast"—she whipped the second picture in place of the first to hammer home the extensive damage to the kitchen—"then why does the office, which is clear across the room from the grease trap *and* the point of origin of the fire, look like it sustained the most damage?"

"Fire doesn't really discriminate," Natalie said with a matter-of-fact shrug. "I'm sure you don't need me to tell you that. Put enough stuff in a small space like an office, and flames won't have any trouble ripping through it, just like they did through the rest of the restaurant."

Shae lowered the photos to her desk, her thoughts going Mach 2. "True. But the fire would've had to travel across what? Eight, ten feet of ceramic floor tiles in order to reach the office?" Not impossible, but also not likely without foul play or fairy dust, especially since the dining room looked just as torched.

A feeling that Natalie didn't seem to share, if her expression was anything to go by. "The fire might have spread over the walls and ceiling. Without a full set of pictures, it's tough to say exactly how the fire moved from one room to the other. The point of origin is pretty clear from that shot of the switches and outlets, though. This was definitely an electrical fire."

That may be, but... "You're assuming the fire started in only one place," Shae said, prompting Natalie to laugh.

"Multiple points of origin can't happen by accident. It's impossible."

Adrenaline perked in Shae's veins, her pulse pressing faster against her eardrums. "Right. So what if this fire wasn't an accident?"

Natalie's shoulders met the back of her desk chair with a thump. "You're telling me you think this restaurant fire was set on purpose, and there's some kind of tie-in with the fire you responded to on Friday."

"I'm telling you I think it's possible," she corrected, mostly because Natalie was looking at her like she'd lost her faculties. But Shae's gut was screaming of things not right, and she'd been at the scene of that house fire firsthand. She knew what she'd seen, just like she knew in her gut that she wasn't wrong about this. "Listen, I get that it's kind of low on physical evidence. But I'm telling you, between the intensity and the extent of the damage, there's something off about these two fires. Don't you think it warrants at least a *little* digging?"

After a second that felt like an hour, Natalie said, "We could ask Frank."

Yessss. Excitement bloomed behind Shae's breastbone. Straightening the photos as best she could in less than a breath, she scooped up the file folder and followed Natalie across the hallway. Frank's office was a carbon copy of Natalie's, minus the pretty pot of African violets on her windowsill and times about thirty on the number of file folders towering from the box marked "incoming" on his desk.

"Everything okay, Delacourt?" he asked, although since he hadn't moved his eyes from his computer screen or so much as paused in whatever he was typing, Shae had to admit, she had no idea how he even knew they were standing in the doorframe.

"I'm not sure. Shae found something in the report for that restaurant fire from a couple weeks ago—Fiorelli's, down by the pier? We wanted to get your take on it if you've got a second."

Frank's mostly gray brows tugged downward to match his frown, and while he still didn't stop typing, he did at least slow down. "Shoot."

Realizing she had a very thin window for what little of his attention she was going to get, Shae didn't mince words. "I think this fire—and one that happened on Friday in North Point—is arson."

"Arson." Frank exhaled slowly, pushing back from his keyboard to cross his arms over his barrel chest. "And what makes you think these fires were set deliberately?"

She launched into the same explanation she'd given Natalie, describing the weird behavior of the fire at the meth lab-slash-murder scene in comparison to the even weirder damage patterns in the photos of the restaurant fire. The retelling only cemented Shae's resolve, and by the time she'd gone through all the details, she was more convinced than ever that something nefarious was going on right under their noses.

"Some of this does make sense in theory," Natalie started, but Frank dismissed the idea with a wave of one beefy hand.

"And in reality, all of it can be refuted by more reasonable explanations. No offense, McCullough." His genuinely apologetic expression didn't make Shae want to scream any less. "I know you're used to a lot of action. But the reality is, we're not exactly like an episode of *CSI* over here. Arson is a lot more out of the ordinary than most people think. The chances that you stumbled onto not one, but two of them in your first few hours here...let's just say I'm impressed with your imagination."

A shocked huff crossed Shae's lips. He couldn't be *serious*. "So you think I'm just making this up?"

"In the thirty years I've worked in arson investigation, do you know how many firefighters I've had assigned here short-term?" Frank asked, the odd re-direct shocking her enough that she shook her head by default.

"No."

"Probably a hundred, maybe even two. And do you know how many of them were sure they'd found a case of arson on their first day here?"

Shae's face flushed, but still, she pressed her boots into the thinly carpeted office floor to stand her ground. "I'm not imagining things."

"Neither is the fire marshal," Frank said, pointing to the file folder in her hands. "He did a site inspection of that restaurant. If he says the fire was accidental and caused by faulty wiring and the evidence we have backs that up, then that's what happened."

"But it might not be that cut and dried. If you'd just look at the burn patterns again—"

Frank cut her off with a shake of his balding head. "Listen, McCullough. I appreciate that you're giving these files a hard look, but we're up to our eye teeth in them. Leaping to conclusions on little more than impulse isn't going to get you far on this job, and you'll need a hell of a lot more than a couple 'what if's all spit-balled together for me to green-light an investigation that goes against what the fire marshal has already said. So do me a favor, would you please? Stick to reality so we can get some work done around here. You're dismissed."

"I'm really sorry," Natalie whispered once Shae finally got the command to her legs to about-face and move back into the hallway. "Arson's just notoriously hard to prove, and we tend to go by the whole 'simplest explanation is the best explanation' mindset around here."

"Thanks for trying," Shae managed, trying like hell to calm the frustration cycloning through her rib cage. She had two weeks to go here in arson. Common sense dictated that she should fill out the report and move on; after all, Frank wasn't necessarily wrong. A reasonable argument could be made that these fires had both been accidents, and that they were both completely unrelated to boot.

Oh, screw reasonable. There had been two *bodies* at that house fire, and just because the odds weren't in her favor, that didn't make her wrong. Shae might not be able to prove it with a thousand irrefutable facts, but these fires didn't feel unrelated, and they sure as hell didn't feel like accidents. If Frank wouldn't listen to her, she'd just have to find someone who would.

Which was exactly why, instead of filling out her report like Frank had clearly told her to, Shae waited until Natalie's back was turned, then slipped the entire case folder into her laptop bag.

∿

CAPELLI WAS a complete and total idiot. More specifically, he was an idiot with a raging hard-on that had refused to leave him in peace ever since he'd heedlessly touched Shae McCullough's mouth three days ago.

And didn't that just make the fact that he'd been sitting in the intelligence office for the last four hours reeeeeally fucking awkward.

Capelli turned toward his laptop monitor, mashing back on the thought. Yes, Shae had flirted with him, and even though it had defied every ounce of logic he owned, for a hot, reckless minute, he'd flirted right back. But a woman that wild and impulsive was like top shelf tequila. The first shot might be a rush, but the rest of the bottle got real dangerous, real fast. Capelli had to keep his head on straight and his control locked down, for this case and for his sanity.

Because if he got a taste of Shae McCullough, he knew goddamn good and well he wouldn't stop until he'd taken her back to his place to drink down every wicked inch of her.

Starting with that curve in her lower back.

Slapping his hands over the keyboard in front of him, Capelli forced himself to open the active investigation file for the Denton murder—not that any of the information had changed since he'd last looked at it an hour ago. They still hadn't seen official reports from either the ME or the crime scene techs, and although he had gotten the preliminary photos of the scene from the latter, the images had left him just as empty-handed as ever.

Still, perfect murders were a statistical impossibility. There had to be *something* that would get Capelli from point A to point B, some scrap of detail that would lead his brain to a set of facts he could parse out and put together in a logical fashion. All he needed was to find it, to uncover the right set of details to get him on the path to solving the puzzle and doing good…

Sinclair stuck his head out of his office, clearing his throat and pegging Hollister with a look from across the room. "Caught a robbery/assault at a pawn shop over on Norton Avenue. Maxwell and Hale are still stuck in court on that domestic homicide from last summer. You and Moreno up for a little adventure?"

"Always," Hollister said, grabbing his jacket while Isabella did the same.

"Good. I'll have dispatch tell the unis at the scene that you're on your way." Sinclair's ice-blue gaze moved over the quiet desks and otherwise empty office space to land on Capelli. "Looks like you're holding down the fort."

"Copy that." He had plenty on his plate with this homicide investigation, thin as it was. He murmured a pair of "see ya later"s to Hollister and Moreno, but before he could settle in and get to work, the sound of an all too familiar voice hit him directly in the solar plexus.

"Hi, Isabella." Shae stood just inside the glass doors of the intelligence office, and oh sure, *now* she had her hair pulled back in her trademark ponytail.

Moreno pulled up short, her brown eyes wide with surprise. "Oh! Hey, McCullough. Is everything okay?" She dropped her voice, but not enough that Capelli missed her adding on, "Kellan told me Bridges took you off active duty for a couple of weeks."

Capelli's pulse tapped faster with shock and something a little deeper that he couldn't quite identify. She'd been benched? Christ, that explained why she'd been in the grocery store instead of on shift Friday night.

Along with why her smile had gone tighter than a tourniquet when he'd mentioned it.

"Yeah, I'm fine," Shae said. "At least, I am as far as that's concerned." The way her lips pressed into a thin, white line as soon as she'd finished speaking didn't agree, but Capelli wasn't about to point that out. He was halfway to eavesdropping as it was, and Shae McCullough's state of mind was none of his damned business. "But I was wondering if I could talk to you about that fire down in North Point."

"Ah." Isabella swung a harried glance toward the door, where Hollister stood waiting. "I'm actually headed out on a robbery call. Did you remember something about the scene that you wanted to add to your report?"

Shae shook her head, but funny, the negative did damn little to erase the determination creasing her gold-brown

71

brows. "No, I...it's kind of complicated. I think it's important, though."

"Okay," Isabella said, clearly torn. "Capelli's up to speed
on the case. Why don't you talk to him about it, then I'll
catch up when I get back?"

Shae's shoulder blades snapped together beneath her
quilted navy blue RFD jacket, her perfectly heart-shaped lips
parting at the suggestion, although Isabella didn't seem to
have caught the reaction. Of course, Capelli had not only
seen it in spades, but his stupid, treasonous, no-thoughts-
left-behind brain would probably replay the subtle movement of Shae's mouth over and over again in vivid detail for
hours after she left.

Fuck. He really was an idiot.

"Sure, yeah," Shae said slowly. Her tone painted the
words with all the enthusiasm of someone agreeing to a
double-decker root canal, and truthfully, Capelli was with
her. He needed to be putting together plausible scenarios
based on the facts of this case. Being distracted by Shae's
bold, bright green stare and insane curves? Not going to
help, thanks.

But balking would only pique Isabella's attention—and
not in a good way—so he aimed a perfectly polite look at
Shae instead.

"Come on in and have a seat," he said, pushing up from
his desk to grab the extra chair from beside Maxwell's work
space. Capelli placed the chair close enough to his for them
to talk, yet far enough to keep her at arms' length, literally,
and she gave their surroundings a nice long look-see before
settling stiffly across from him.

"Quite the setup you've got here," she said, gesturing to
the array mounted over his shoulder and the crime scene
board to her left, which was currently switched off. But the
sooner they got down to business, the faster he'd be able to

systematically go through what little he had on this murder to piece together the most likely viable hypothesis.

So he replied, "Thanks. You had something on the fire?"

Again, her shoulders hitched, but only for a second before her eyes sparked with fierce resolve. "I think your murderer is also an arsonist, and I don't think the fire he set on Friday was his first one."

Capelli's pulse stuttered at the multiple whammies in her statement, his brain scrambling to order the parts of her accusation by importance.

First thing's first. "Do you have any proof of that?"

Shae paused. "That's where this gets a little complicated."

"That's a no," he said, and dammit, he needed leads he could use, not a bunch of wild what-ifs that couldn't even be substantiated.

Shae, however? Not backing down so easily. "It's not *necessarily* a no. If you'd just hear me out, I have a theory—"

"A theory." Jesus, this was getting crazier by the minute.

"Yes." One hand slid to the hip of her navy blue uniform pants, locking in tight. "A theory. You know, a coherent group of general propositions that can be used as principles of explanation and prediction?"

Capelli's jaw would have unhinged in shock if the rest of him hadn't just been so unequivocally turned on. "I know what a theory is."

"Well, good, because I have one, and even though I can't back it up with concrete facts per se, I still think it's important."

For a hot second, he considered pushing back. Shae was smart—anyone with a double-digit IQ could see that—but she wasn't exactly prone to logical thoughts. Besides, he wasn't a fucking rookie, flying by the seat of his damned pants and praying for a happy landing. He had a method for figuring out cases. One that considered all the facts and the probabilities that went with them in order to get to the most likely scenario. One that he'd crafted over time and proven again and again. One that worked.

Except.

Capelli was painfully short on facts (or, shit, *anything*) and this case was growing cold, fast. Weighing the current situation in his head, he arrived at the option most likely to give him the outcome he was after.

Took a deep breath. Exhaled with a dirty, internal curse. And said, "Okay then. Why don't you start from the beginning?"

CHAPTER 6

Shae looked at Capelli as if he was one taco short of a truck, which he had to admit, felt plausible given the circumstances. But part of forming the most likely scenario was ruling out all the things that *hadn't* happened at that crime scene, and if Shae could help put one more of those in his "no" column, far be it for him to stand in her way.

"Oh. Okay then," she said, shifting slightly in her chair. "Well, I'm working over at arson investigation for the next two weeks, helping them review cases and file reports." She paused to wince, and with good reason. The regs alone were probably giving her an epic case of the shakes. "I stumbled across this restaurant fire from a couple of weeks ago, and something about the damage and the burn patterns are wonky."

Capelli's brows lifted. It was the same word she'd used on Friday to describe the damage at the meth lab fire. Still... "No offense," he said. "But you're going to have to be more specific than 'wonky.'"

Shae's brows lifted right back. "Fine. According to the report, the restaurant fire was caused by faulty electrical.

And before you interrupt to tell me that almost certainly *wasn't* the cause of the fire at your murder scene, I know."

"Okay," he said, his brain scrambling for a re-direct, because pointing out the inconsistency had been exactly what he'd intended to do. "Did the fire marshal think there was anything odd about the cause of the restaurant fire when he did his site inspection?"

"No." But rather than admitting strike two like any rational person would, she sat up taller in her chair, poised to argue even harder. "He noted that the scorch patterns were consistent with an electrical fire, and actually, he's not wrong. But there's something off about the rest of the damage. Look."

Shae reached into the brown leather laptop bag she'd placed by her feet and pulled out a file folder bearing the crest of the Remington Fire Department, and holy hell, she had more brass than a college marching band.

"Please tell me that is not an active case file."

"Technically?" she asked, prompting Capelli's gut to pang even harder. Like there was any other *way*.

"McCullough, you can't just waltz out of the arson investigation office with stuff like this." She was committing at least three different policy violations, and those were just the ones he could think of off the top of his (admittedly overactive) head.

"I get that I'm sort of bending the rules," Shae said, her green eyes flashing beneath the harsh fluorescent lighting overhead. "But none of this information has been scanned into the RFD database yet. I didn't have any other way to show you the file other than to bring it here, and you need to see it. This restaurant fire might not have started in the same way as the one from Friday, but they have a lot in common. They both look accidental—"

"Odds are high that's because they actually are," Capelli

said past his frown, but she continued even more emphatically, as if he hadn't just offered up a perfectly logical response.

"Both scenes sustained a huge amount of fire damage in a small amount of time—"

But again, he shook his head and took the rational road. "Also not outside the realm of plausibility. Volatile chemicals have the potential to create a lot of heat and damage, especially given the right combinations and enough things in their path to burn. Same with faulty wiring."

"Fine." Shae pushed the word through her teeth. "Then how do you explain that in addition to the other similarities, both fires have more than one potential point of origin?"

Capelli opened his mouth to put a spike in this argument, once and for all. Scanned, then re-scanned every detail of the fire at the murder scene in his head just to be sure his facts were straight.

And stopped.

"The restaurant fire has more than one potential point of origin?" he asked, his breath kicking from his lungs as his thoughts suddenly shuffled into an entirely different order. True, the most probable cause of the meth lab fire was a combination of toxic chemicals and a mismeasurement of the heat used to cook them. Even so, Capelli couldn't definitively pinpoint one specific starting point for the blaze, nor could he come up with irrefutable evidence that the mismeasurement—and thus the fire—had been accidental.

Which meant there was a chance, however unlikely, that Shae was right.

"I think so," she said, and the scenarios in his head jerked to a graceless halt.

"That's not what I asked you." For Chrissake, he'd met people who *thought* the earth was flat as a fucking two-by-four. He needed facts, not conjecture.

A muscle in the otherwise delicate line of her jaw twitched. "Oh for the love of...*yes*. Although the primary cause looks like faulty electrical, the restaurant fire could have more than one point of origin."

Whipping the file folder open, she flipped to an eight-by-ten photograph of what had once been a commercial-grade fryer, leaning forward in her chair as she continued, "The fire marshal reported that the fire started with the faulty wiring in this wall right here, then traveled to ignite the grease trap above the fryer, and bam. There's your blaze."

Capelli took in the photo, the details finding a probably-permanent home in his brain. "Highly likely."

"But"—Shae swapped the photograph of the fryer for two of some fire damage so bad, he could only lodge a best-guess at what had once been in them—"the restaurant's office is clear across the kitchen, and it sustained at least as much damage as the rest of the scene, arguably more. So did more than half of the dining room. The place is on the pier, near at least a dozen other businesses, so it's not like it burned unnoticed for an extended period of time..."

She let the rest hang, and he filled in the blanks all too easily. "So you think the fire had to have started in all three places at once in order for it to have caused so much damage in that amount of time."

"Yes. Not only that, but I think the same thing happened at the scene of that meth lab fire," Shae said. "I don't know if I'd have made the connection so easily if I hadn't been there to see the fire in action, but that house wasn't just burning, Capelli. It was a freaking inferno, and I'm telling you, normal fire might burn that hard under the right circumstances, but it doesn't spread that fast naturally. I think the burn patterns and the amount of damage at both scenes suggest multiple points of origin are at least a possibility. Which means the fires must have been set on purpose."

Sitting back in his desk chair, Capelli clicked through a few possible sequences of events in his head, but damn, each one had more pitfalls and potential snagging points than the last. Not to mention a metric ton of gray area.

"If these two incidents are related—and I'm not saying I think they are—you're talking about a highly intelligent, highly calculated perpetrator," he said slowly. "And there were obviously no victims at the restaurant fire, so there isn't even a clear motive for someone to torch the place." At least with the meth lab fire, the whole 'covering up a murder' thing worked in their favor on that count.

"Not yet," Shae argued, knotting her arms over her chest. "But I've been knocking down fires for five years, and I know what I know. Something about these two scenes don't wash, and despite what the fire marshal says, I think it warrants a deeper look."

He paused. What Shae was proposing was unlikely at best; after all, the theory of Occam's razor existed for a reason. Common sense dictated that the simplest explanation was usually the right one, and hers was damn close to crazy.

Crazy, but not impossible, came a whisper from the back of his brain. She might not have looked at either scene conventionally, or even rationally, but he couldn't refute her theory that these fires were arson beyond all doubt. At least not without going to both scenes to gather more intel.

More intel he might need in order to catch an arsonist and a killer.

Fuck.

His silence seemed to unnerve her, though, and before Capelli could figure out a way to verbalize his thought process or any of the places it had led him, Shae let out a frustrated huff.

"Look," she bit out, stabbing him with a stare that put

every last ounce of her frustration on full display. "I get that you need something concrete—"

"I do," he agreed, but she barreled on, her voice growing stronger by the syllable.

"—and that what I'm saying is maybe a little unlikely, and I'm jumping to conclusions because I'm too impulsive and reckless and I should just stick to the facts and forget everything else—"

"McCullough," he tried to interrupt, but Jesus, she was on a tear.

"—and maybe I *am* impulsive to go with my gut, and I knew you of all people wouldn't believe me, because of course you want it all in black and white and you *never* think outside the box, but—"

"McCullough—"

Shae shook her head, jabbing a finger into the air as she continued, unchecked. "I mean it, Capelli. Impulsive or not, this is serious. Something's not right with these fires. Two people died! And frankly, I'm really freaking tired of being dismissed right now, so if you could just—"

"*Shae.*"

She blinked once before her dark gold lashes fanned up in surprise. "What?"

"I believe you."

"You do?" Shae's lips parted even though her eyes didn't budge. Her fingers flexed against his palm, and only then did Capelli realize he'd pressed forward to grab her uplifted hand and wrap his fingers around hers in a firm, hot grip.

Shit. He let go and briskly slid back to reclaim the space between them, although a tiny, dark place inside of him gave up a harsh protest. "I do," he said, smoothing his voice into perfect calm despite his rioting pulse. He had to find his center and keep focused.

"It's true that you don't have anything by way of hard

evidence"—he held up a hand to stanch her clearly brewing argument before she started in again—"but I do think there's a chance, however slim, that the inconsistencies you've noted could theoretically point to arson."

"Okay." Shae sat up straighter in her chair. "So what do we do in order to find out for sure?"

"We follow protocol." Turning toward his desk, Capelli palmed his cell phone, and a handful of keystrokes later, Sinclair came out of his office.

"McCullough." His gray-blond brows lifted so slightly at the sight of Shae that no one but Capelli would have likely even noticed. "Nice surprise. You're not on shift today?"

Her shoulders did the up and at 'em against the back of her chair, and *that* was something even a blind man would have noticed. "No. Actually, I'm spending a couple of weeks over in arson investigation, and I came across something I thought you'd want to know."

She replayed the details, step by step. Sinclair went for a full-on frown when she pulled out the hijacked file, but Capelli had to hand it to the guy. He was smart enough to let Shae run her story from stem to stern before he said so much as a word.

"So it's your feeling that both the fire marshal and a thirty-year veteran from arson investigation are wrong on this, and that somehow, these two fires were set on purpose by the same person who killed Malik Denton."

Any reasonable person on the planet would have paused at the doubtful edge in Sinclair's tone. So of course, Shae didn't. "Yes. That's exactly what I think."

Sinclair swiveled his gaze toward Capelli. "And you agree?"

"I can't rule it out as a possibility," Capelli corrected, and Sinclair read between the lines in less than a breath.

"But you can't rule it in, either."

"Not without more information." Gesturing to the laptop on his desk, he formed a mental list of the variables that would provide the best shot at a lead, as well as the ones that would help eliminate dead ends. "First, we'd have to go over both fire scenes pretty carefully, ideally with the help of someone who has experience with interpreting fire behaviors and burn patterns."

That was going to be easier said than done, since second-guessing the fire marshal's report was certainly bound to piss off just about every single person in the arson investigation office. But if these fires had been set by the person who'd killed Malik Denton, there could be something at one of the scenes that would give them the break they so desperately needed in solving this murder case.

"Okay." Sinclair nodded in agreement. "What else?"

Capelli pushed his glasses higher over the bridge of his nose and thought. "We're also going to need a close look at the fire marshal's report from Friday's scene so we can compare it with the one from two weeks ago for similarities."

"There isn't a report on the meth lab fire yet," Shae chimed in, capturing both Sinclair's and Capelli's full attention. "Natalie over at arson told me the fire marshal wanted to be sure the crime lab was done collecting evidence first. He's not supposed to go out to the scene until tomorrow."

"Spectacular," Capelli muttered. Between that and the ME's report, he'd probably be waiting for the better part of three days, even with a rush request.

Sinclair seemed oddly untroubled at Shae's revelation, though. "All right. If more information is what we need to either link these fires to our murder or prove they're a dead end, then let's go get it. I want the two of you on this together."

Capelli's spine snapped to full attention. "Wait, what? You want me *and* McCullough on this?" He wasn't even technically a cop, for Chrissake. And neither was she. Plus, he had methods for analyzing data. Tested methods. Legitimate, time-proven methods.

Methods that Shae McCullough was bound to either blatantly disregard or totally fuck with. Possibly not in that order.

"For preliminary investigative purposes?" Sinclair asked, leaning against the edge of Maxwell's desk to fasten him with a stare. "In a word, yeah. All my detectives are out on calls, and I've got a murder case that's growing frostier by the minute. I'm not inclined to wait for a report from the fire marshal when I can send you to check the murder scene for details right now, and as far as analysis goes, you've got the best eyes on the team."

Well, shit. Of course his boss had to go and have a logical point. "Yes, but..."

Nope. Sinclair wasn't having it. "We're perfectly within our jurisdiction to go through the scene before the fire marshal does, and anyway, I don't want you to do his job. I want you to do yours," he continued. "You'll go out there to look for information on the murder, and properly interpreting the fire may now be part of that."

"It might," Capelli said, and his agreement was just the fuel Sinclair needed to keep going.

"Good. Like you said, you need someone who's well versed with burn patterns to help you shake this out, and Shae has firsthand knowledge of how the meth lab fire went down. That makes her an excellent resource."

"I'd be happy to go back to the scene for a walk-through if you think it would help," Shae said, the spark in her green eyes putting Capelli another notch closer to being overruled.

Sinclair nodded, just a quick lift and lower of his chin. "Good. I'll reach out to Captain Bridges as a courtesy to make sure he's okay with you assisting us on this case. I'm sure he's got good reasons for sending you to arson investigation for two weeks."

"Oh, he does," she agreed with a frown, and dammit, even that didn't seem to budge Sinclair's resolve.

"And I'm not about to go over his head on that. Find or no find, working recon on this case today won't get you off the hook there. You're still going to have to do whatever time he's assigned to you at arson."

Shae—being Shae—didn't even skip a beat. *Fuck.* "You guys have two bodies to account for, and arsonists put firefighters' lives at serious risk. I'm okay with making up the lost time on desk duty if it gets you closer to catching this guy."

"First things first," Sinclair said, snatching the words right from Capelli's mouth. "Let's find out if there *is* an arson to go with our murder, and then we'll go from there. I'll get the gears moving with Bridges, but I want the two of you out at that scene as soon as he gives up an all-clear. And, McCullough?"

She met Sinclair's stare with one of equal resolve.

"You might've made a good find with your amateur detective work, but around here, we take protocol seriously. When you're on my watch, you'll do the same. No exceptions. Do you copy?"

"Yes, Sergeant," she said, waiting until Sinclair had gone back into his office and shut the door before turning to Capelli and sealing his fate with an infuriatingly sexy smile.

"Well. It looks like for better or for worse, you're stuck with me."

CHAPTER 7

Shae's heart tapped an excited rhythm against her breastbone as she followed Capelli down the hallway outside of the intelligence office twenty minutes later. Bridges had given her the green light to survey the scene of Friday's fire with Capelli, although he'd texted her the instant he'd gotten off the phone with Sinclair to remind her in no uncertain terms that she'd better keep her nose spic and span while she did. In her defense, she hadn't gone looking to break the rules when she'd popped open that file on the restaurant fire—in fact, she'd been trying to suck it up and do the exact opposite so she could grit her way through Bridges's punishment and get her ass back to the action of Station Seventeen, where it belonged. But working with the intelligence unit to catch some lowlife who had committed both murder and arson?

That was *so* much better than sitting in some stuffy office filing even stuffier paperwork. So she'd impulsively fractured a few little rules by borrowing the file. Was it really that big a deal if it ended up getting intelligence the lead they needed?

She could help. If her experience as a firefighter could

help Sinclair's team figure out who was setting these fires and why, she could potentially save lives.

And hell if that wasn't the biggest reason of all to jump right in.

"Okay!" Shae said, smacking her hands together and rubbing them with borderline glee. "What do we do first?"

Capelli frowned slightly before descending the stairs leading to the Thirty-Third's first floor and bustling main hub. "We make a plan, obviously."

"So we're not going to go out there and see what strikes us as odd, then investigate from there?" A step-by-step plan seemed a little rigid, and by "a little", she really meant "a shit-load". Then again, this was her super-serious, super-sexy partner in crime they were talking about. Shae probably shouldn't be shocked that he wanted to go by the book. Hell, with all that smoldering determination lurking in his stare, he'd probably *written* the book.

She cleared her throat and kicked aside the hard tingle running from her spine to her more delicate parts at the errant reminder of Capelli's sexiness. She was here for the case now, and anyway, he'd made it wickedly clear the other night that he'd only been interested when he'd thought she was someone else.

Capelli looked at her over one broad shoulder as they cleared the bottom of the stairs and began navigating their way through the bustling lobby of the Thirty-Third. "We'll be far more efficient with a specific strategy in place, especially since there's no report from the fire marshal for us to use as a baseline yet. The crime lab already went through the scene to collect whatever evidence they could for the murder."

"So now we just have to go through and figure out the fire, then see where it fits with your dead body."

"It's not as easy as it sounds," he said, pushing open the main door to the precinct. Rather than going through, though, he shifted back so she could go first, and ooookay, so much for that tingle between her legs taking a hike.

"Thank you." Shae slipped past him, their boots falling into step together a few seconds later as they descended the stairs leading to the tidy sidewalk in front of the stone and brick building. "And for the record, I don't think this is going to be easy. But I definitely think it's going to be fun."

Capelli exhaled, his breath puffing around his face before scattering in the chilly afternoon air. "I'm pretty sure that word doesn't mean what you think it means."

But Shae just grinned. "Oh, it does. I just have a very wide net when it comes to adventure."

"You don't have to remind me," he said. Ah, she'd kind of earned that one, what with the whole showing up unexpectedly/illicitly borrowed arson file thing.

"I know I might not go about things in a very orderly way, which probably drives you bat shit insane," Shae said, slowing to a stop next to the dark blue unmarked car where Capelli had just done the same. "But I'm not making light of this. I really do want to help. We're both on the same side here."

She braced herself for a response that held more of the same high-logic, low-tolerance-for-anything-not-in-black-and-white attitude he'd dished out ever since he'd questioned her at the scene of the meth lab fire.

So her jaw damn near dropped to the pavement when he said, "You know what, you're right."

"I'm sorry, what?"

Capelli pulled a key fob from the pocket of his black canvas jacket and pressed a button, the locks on the unmarked car popping open with a heavy click-*click*. "I said, you're right. As impulsive as I think your methods are, you wouldn't have come here if you didn't want to help. Intelligence has two dead bodies and exactly zero leads, and at this point, you and I working together does give us the best statistical chance of making any headway on the case."

"Aw," Shae said, unable to keep her tart laughter in check. "You sweet talker. I bet you say that to all the girls."

"Actually, I don't." He paused, dropping his hand halfway to the passenger door handle and turning to step toward her instead. "But I'll do whatever it takes to solve this murder."

A sudden flash of hot intensity moved through his stare, cutting through the methodical calm she was so accustomed to, and for a second, her breath froze to a stop in her lungs. "Oh," she finally managed, although the word sounded oddly soft as it escaped. "Okay then. Partners?"

Shae stuck out her hand, the exhilaration in her chest resurfacing quickly at the slight hint of a smile on Capelli's face as he wrapped his fingers around hers for a firm shake. "Partners with rules," he qualified.

"Excellent!" She didn't even bother dialing back her grin. Not that she ever bothered to dial back anything else either, but... "This is going to be so much fun. Come on—I'll be Starsky, you be Hutch."

Huh. Looked like that tiny smile of his had a very short shelf life. "That's not really how any of this works," he said, leaning in to open the passenger side door so she could slide into the car.

"Okay, fine," she said after he'd slammed her door and moved around to let himself into the driver's side. "I'll be Hutch. So how do you want to work the plan?"

Capelli traded his darkly framed glasses for a pair of Ray-Ban aviators, but not before giving her a look that seemed to question her sanity. "The way I always do. We'll examine the scene, consider all the variables, then weigh possible scenarios based on our findings."

Shae's brows went up. "You make it sound so serious."

"That's because it is," Capelli said, matter-of-fact.

"I know." She thought of the body she'd recovered at the meth lab fire, instantly sobering. "I guess I just meant that your plan is really technical. Don't you ever go with your gut?"

He navigated traffic, which was thankfully light. "I can't quantify my gut, so no."

"So you never trust something on pure faith?" she asked, surprise knocking through her veins at the concept.

"No."

"Never ever?"

"No."

Whether it was the utter conviction of his tone or the sudden tension radiating from his body, she couldn't be sure. But something about Capelli's reply kept her from pushing back.

"Okay then. If you think we should go with the facts, I'm game to start there."

They settled into silence for a few minutes, and oddly, it wasn't stiff or uncomfortable. Shae watched the buildings go by in flashes of brick and sunlight and glass, but wait. Something about the path Capelli was on wasn't right.

"Aren't we heading to North Point?" she asked, pointing out the window to the turn he totally should have taken but had bypassed without pause.

"Mmm hmm. But first we're swinging by the arson investigation office so you can return that file."

God, he was so rules-oriented that she was almost tempted to laugh. "But what if we need it?"

"We won't need it."

Capelli didn't elaborate, but come on. Facts were his jam. He couldn't really mean that. "We *might* need it," Shae argued, but he shook his head, resolute.

"You took it without permission, McCullough, and rules are rules. The file needs to go back." He paused for a second, then continued as if he'd anticipated her argument. "We need to look at the fire at this murder scene independently of the one at the restaurant anyway. Comparing them right off the bat might tempt us to stretch, and the last thing we need is to jump to conclusions that aren't there. Analyze first, then hypothesize."

Shae opened her mouth. Then closed it with an internal curse. Dammit, his process *did* sort of make sense. Even if it was uber rigid.

"Okay, okay. I'll put the file back before we go."

A few more minutes had them at the arson investigation office, and a few more after that had the file safe and sound on her temporary desk in Natalie's office. Captain Bridges must have let Frank and Natalie know she wouldn't be back for the rest of the day, because neither one of them batted so much as a lash at her parting "see you tomorrow", even though it was barely one o'clock.

Shae settled back into the passenger seat of the unmarked police car, and as tempted as she was to argue that maybe they should loosen their plan of action to *include* some action (God, she was so. So. Tempted), she didn't. Capelli made his way through downtown, crossing over to the dingier and less reputable streets of North Point, and Shae gestured out the windshield at the intersection they were quickly approaching.

"I know your GPS probably says to keep going on Hamilton, but if you turn here on Queen Anne and use the side street as a cut-through, you'll save a little time."

"If that was faster, the GPS would say so," he pointed out, but Shae just shrugged.

"Sure. And if the GPS knew that the light at Hamilton and Glendale takes conservatively a month to turn green, and that the intersection is the third most dangerous in all of Remington, it would tell you to take Queen Anne."

Capelli slowed for the four-way stop sign at Hamilton and Queen Anne, using the opportunity to look more carefully at the digital map on the dashboard screen before engaging the turn signal and taking her advice. They looped back through to Hamilton and Glendale, where—ha!—a huge line of cars sat waiting for the light on the other side.

His brows traveled toward his neatly combed hairline, and he surprised her with a deferent nod. "Thanks."

"You tried it just to prove me wrong, didn't you?" She capped the question with enough of a smile to remove any heat it might've carried. After all, she tested boundaries on a daily basis. Far be it for her to get pissy over someone else returning the favor.

"I tried it to test the theory," Capelli said, lifting one hand from the steering wheel in concession a second later as he added, "But in fairness, no. I didn't think going that way would be faster."

"See? Sometimes I use my powers for good," she teased. "And sometimes, the most logical way isn't the best path between two points."

The downward twitch of his lips was a direct translation of *let's not get crazy*, but he didn't voice it. "Do you know South Hill that well, too?" he ventured instead, and oh, what the hell. She indulged him.

"Pretty much. The south side of Remington is easier to navigate though. Well, except for the construction cluster fuck going on over where the mayor is building his new McMansion," Shae added. The thing was actually more monstrosity than mansion, but then again, Mayor Bradley Aldrich III was all about flash and dazzle. The stupid thing had turrets. Plural. Who even *did* that in this day and age, seriously?

"You must go on a lot of calls in this area to be so familiar with the traffic patterns," Capelli said. The observation brought her back to the here-and-now of the moment, and she nodded, giving the area around them a good scan through her window.

"We do. Seventeen is right between North Point and South Hill, but we tend to come down here more often. Usually the calls are pretty small time—medical assists and small fires. Stuff like that. I've responded to enough car wrecks at that intersection to tell you the stats on that one are definitely legit, though."

"So some of the calls you go on aren't quite so small time, then."

Capelli's voice lifted in curiosity—just slightly, but it was enough—and Shae met it with a nod.

"Well, yeah. Obviously, this one we're going to check out was pretty bad. And there was that fire three months ago that ended up being related to the DuPree case." Her brain skimmed the place where she'd compartmentalized the double homicide that sociopath had committed, then tried to cover up with a nasty fire, and her heart began to pound. *Breathe in. Breathe out. Breathe in...*

"I remember it," Capelli said. He stayed quiet for a few passing blocks, but the hard set of his jawline told Shae his thoughts were far from idle. He didn't say anything, though, and by the time they'd crossed over to Crestridge Drive and came to a stop in front of the scene of Friday's meth lab fire, her heart began pounding for a whole new set of reasons.

"Wow," Shae said, taking in the window-scorched and worse-for-wear house in front of them. "This place is definitely a loss."

"That may have been the point," Capelli reminded her. "We won't really know until we go in and take a closer look."

She thought about the challenge in front of them, adrenaline and excitement swirling low in her belly. "And here I thought you'd never ask."

Getting out of the car, Shae scanned their surroundings in more detail as they walked a path over the crumbling sidewalk. The tang of stale smoke still hung low in the air, sliding through her senses with her first full breath. The bright blue sky was an odd backdrop for the dingy, fire-eaten house, which—whoa—bore dark, angry scorch marks around all but one of the windows and fresh sheets of plywood nailed over three of the ground-level spaces where the glass had stood.

"Further proof that the Halligan bar is eight and a half pounds of 'fuck shit up,'" she murmured under her breath.

"I'm sorry?" Capelli's brows breached the top rim of his sunglasses, and Shae gestured to the boarded-up windows.

"It's standard operating procedure for us to break the windows and use the hoses from the exterior when a fire's running too hot to fight from the inside. I'd kind of forgotten how bad the damage looks a few days later, though."

She eyeballed the house again as they continued their approach on the walkway. Yellow tape stamped with the warning *No Trespassing by Order of the Remington Police Department* had been threaded across a six-foot swath of the part of the chain link fence where the gate was centered, and she didn't hesitate to slide a palm beneath it to swing the waist-high door on its hinges.

"Come on, let's get a closer look."

"We'll have to be careful," Capelli said with a pointed glance and a truckload of implication.

But Shae didn't even break stride on the front walkway. "Not to put too fine a point on it, but I ran into this place when it was burning down. I'm pretty sure I can handle a walk-through now that the fire's out."

"I didn't say you couldn't handle it," he replied, and funny, his tone backed the words right up. "I said we'll have to be careful. If we go too fast, we might miss something important."

Shae's feet tempted her to hitch in surprise, but dammit, he did have a point. "Okay," she said, forcing her steps to slow despite the squall of protest from her adrenal gland. They made their way up the rest of the front walk, then past the posted notices from both the police department and the fire marshal taped across the front door. Her breath tightened, speeding up at the sight of the extensive scorch marks covering the walls and ceilings of the foyer and the heavy layer of waterlogged soot coating the floorboards in streaks and ashy puddles.

Damn. Forget going slow. Finding something they could use in this mess?

That was going to take forever.

Capelli, however, didn't seem daunted in the least. "Right." He slipped off his sunglasses, quickly replacing them with his regular pair. "So the house is two levels with no basement. Our best bet would be to start upstairs and work our way down here. Provided it's safe to do that," he added, his gaze lingering in doubt on the admittedly rickety staircase in front of them.

Eh, Shae had seen worse by a mile and a half. "Should be fine," she said, testing the first few steps to be sure. "I wouldn't trust what's left of that railing though."

Dodging the look of disdain flickering over his ridiculously handsome face—God, messing with him was kind of fun—she led the way to the top of the staircase. "So why start upstairs when the bodies were found on the first floor?"

The question seemed to distract him from his irritation well enough. "Because the bodies were found on the first floor."

"Ah," she said after a beat of confusion. "You want to rule things out before you start ruling things in."

"Exactly."

Shae looked down the narrow upstairs hallway in both

directions, measuring the condition of the walls and floors with a careful glance. Two doors on either side, both spaced almost evenly apart, one of which might yield the needle they were looking for and the rest of which would just be a whooole lot of haystack.

Game. On.

Pushing up the sleeves of her navy blue RFD jacket, she led the way down the hall leading toward the Delta side of the house. "Hawkins and Dempsey did search and rescue up here. They didn't report anything unusual, but the place was burning pretty hard by the time we rolled up."

Capelli nodded, following her into the room at the far end of the hallway, which turned out to be a small bedroom. "So I see."

"These scorch marks are pretty consistent with a fire traveling up from the main floor." Shae pointed to the grimy baseboards, tracing the damage up the walls with a sweep of her finger. "All the burn patterns in here are actually pretty textbook."

She noted a couple of other details, none of which made her alarm bells start clanging. Luckily, the fire hadn't destroyed everything in the room. *Un*luckily, the place had been so sparsely appointed from the start, with just a bare, soot-smudged mattress in the middle of the room and a battered nightstand bearing a lamp, a couple of empty Red Bull cans, and some ruined drug paraphernalia, that it was pretty much a useless victory.

They made quick work of scanning the rest of the rooms upstairs, all of which yielded the same amount of *nada* in terms of both evidence of arson and clues that might tie in to the murder. By the time she and Capelli made the return trip back down to the main level, Shae's chest bubbled with frustration.

"Well, if ruling things out was your goal, then you just hit a grand slam," she grumbled, her boots shushing over the ash-covered floorboards at the bottom of the steps in the foyer.

Capelli lifted one shoulder halfway before letting it drop. "I wasn't expecting a whole lot upstairs. And anyway, we did learn something important about the fire while we were up there."

Doubt tugged the edges of her mouth into a frown. "What's that?"

"It isn't where it started. Which means…"

Shae's heart kicked against the crisp white cotton of her uniform shirt. "It had to have started down here."

"And that's why I definitively rule out the least likely possibilities first. It's almost always easiest to do."

"God, you really *are* Starsky," she murmured, turning over the methodical process in her head.

But Capelli dismissed the notion before the words had even fully disappeared into the smoke-stale space between them. "I'm on the RPD's payroll, but I'm not a cop. This is all just part of my job. Speaking of which…" He gestured to the Bravo side of the first floor, and Shae blinked herself back to the task in front of them.

"Right. I did the search on this side of the house." She walked into the first room, her thoughts shifting through everything she could remember about the call. The space was veiled in shadows thanks to the boarded-up windows over her shoulder, but of course, Capelli was prepared.

He clicked the button on the Maglite he'd produced from his jacket pocket. "The damage is definitely more extensive down here," he said, swinging the beam slowly over the room to illuminate it fully. Angry black scorch marks marred the walls in more places than not, and what the furniture had looked like in its glory days? Yeah, that was anybody's guess.

"Yep," Shae agreed, taking one last look at the charred

remains of the couch now sitting crookedly in the middle of the room. "This was already burning heavily when I did my sweep, too."

"And you found Richardson in here?" Capelli's footsteps echoed in muted thumps as he moved into the next room, which held a lot more natural light thanks to the one-way trip the curtains had taken to the floor courtesy of the flames.

Shae nodded, her memory churning along with her gut. "Right by the table."

"I'm assuming that's what this was." He gestured to the ash-covered kindling littering the far wall. The chemicals Shae had seen when she'd last been there had all been removed as part of hazmat protocols. Not that she was surprised—with how flammable they were, leaving them anywhere close to the scene would've been a surefire recipe for a flare-up, even once the fire was technically out. But from the warped and buckled floorboards to the fire-ravaged drywall both beside them and above their heads, the sheer damage to this whole section of the room might as well have been a fifty-foot neon sign.

The fire had started here.

Shae's heart began to pound, her gut locked with certainty. "Yes. This part of the room was burning the hardest. See where the fire ignited this wall here, then traveled up to the ceiling and continued over to the wall over there?"

"So this is almost certainly the point of origin," Capelli said, his voice so quiet that he seemed to be talking more to himself than to her.

But she answered him anyway. "It is. If someone mixed the chemicals improperly and left them over one or more of these portable burners long enough"—she pointed to the barely recognizable black metal stands that had been washed to the corner of the room, ruined heating coils and frayed electrical cords set beneath each one—"it would have definitely ignited a fire that would leave burn patterns exactly like these."

Capelli's eyes moved over the room with such deep concentration, Shae would swear he was memorizing every detail. Finally, he looked at her and gave up a slow nod. "I guess there's really just one question left to answer then."

Her brain filled in the blank at the same time he said, "Is there another point of origin that would make this fire arson?"

With care that bordered on excruciating, Capelli retraced his steps to the front of the house. Although she had no idea how, Shae resisted the urge to elbow her way around him, forcing herself to slow the thrum in her chest and the anticipation in her veins as best she could by double-checking their surroundings for anything she might have missed. The process yanked her back to the last time she'd been here, her memories combining with the adrenaline already doing its very best to commandeer her senses. Finally, they made their way through the foyer and into the other side of the first floor, her breath catching tight in her lungs at the sight of the scorch patterns—some scattered, some in clusters, all dark and destructive—covering nearly every surface. Shae's chest squeezed harder at the wide, gruesome stain on the floorboards where Denton's body had been, and a sheen of cold sweat bloomed between her shoulder blades, causing her uniform shirt to hug her skin.

She'd forgotten, not accidentally, how much blood there had been. The sticky press of her gloves against her palms as she'd adjusted her grip on Denton's body to keep her hands from slipping. The coppery smell, like a bag full of dirty pennies, that had punched her in the throat the second she'd taken her mask off.

The bones of Denton's spine, four of which she'd been

able to count with ease through his gaping, gory wound when she'd finally laid him on the gurney outside the house.

Shae tore her eyes from the floor just in time to see Capelli looking not at the scene, but at her instead, and she shook her head before he could verbalize the *are you okay* clearly brewing on his lips.

Breathe in. Breathe out. Do your job.

Help solve the case.

"Slater found Denton's body over here. Obviously." She swallowed and turned to study the rest of the room, the task calming her brain even as it kept her pulse at a steady clatter. "He was shielded from a lot of the fire by that armchair, but it also made him a little harder to see at first."

"CSU went over that part of the room pretty carefully," he said. His voice carried a slightly softer tone than usual, and despite how desperately she wanted to help with the case, God, she was grateful as hell not to have to relive the memory of dragging Denton out of there.

Marshaling her thoughts back to the fire itself, Shae squinted, trying to firm up the picture in her mind. "Most of my focus was on Slater when I came back in here, but I definitely remember that this table had the same kinds of chemicals all over it as the one in the other room."

She reached out to skim her fingers over the warped surface of the tabletop, which had only sustained less damage than its counterpart on the other side of the house because it was a heavy plastic and metal folding table rather than made of wood. "There," she breathed, pointing to a huge, upward bloom of fire damage on the interior wall. "Yeah, look. There must have been another one of those portable gas burners plugged into this outlet."

Shae scanned the wreckage in the room, her heart beating faster in anticipation, and come on, come, on—ah! A mangled unit with four connected burners lay upside down on the floorboards a few feet away.

Her brain spun. "If someone left enough chemicals over the burners in both rooms, then threw some more around as accelerant, that would explain how the fire spread so quickly."

"Spreading out the chemicals does make sense," Capelli said, his stare moving meticulously over the table and the burn patterns behind it. "Less risk that the fire would accidentally cause an explosion that could hurt the person setting it that way."

"Exactly," Shae said, undisguised excitement kicking through her chest. "So do you think maybe this was some kind of argument gone wrong? Lawrence kills Denton, then sets fire to the house to try and cover up the murder, only he gets over-zealous with the chemicals and eats too much smoke before he can get out?"

Capelli frowned. "I think you're jumping ahead of the facts."

"How's that?" She slid a hand to the hip of her uniform pants. "With how closely these burn patterns match the ones on the other side of the house, there's no way there weren't two points of origin for this fire. It's definitely arson."

Although Capelli didn't argue with her, he also didn't agree, and for the love of fucking pockets, what more could the man *want* by way of evidence?

"That doesn't mean the L-Man set it, or that he killed Denton. He didn't have any blood on his hands or clothes. Still, there is more damage on this side of the house." Again, his brows bent in concentration, his shoulders locking into a broad line as he continued to examine the room. He seemed more lost in thought than scrutiny, but damn, he sure didn't pull up on his intensity in the switch.

"There are two points of origin, but they couldn't have

been set simultaneously by one arsonist. It's likely that whoever did this started the fire over here first, which gave it more time to burn. That still makes Lawrence the most likely suspect," she insisted. "Either that or you've got the world's luckiest criminal on your hands."

Sure, the chemicals used to cook meth were toxic, but the chances that a third party could kill Denton, set the fire, *and* ensure that Lawrence would be overcome by the fumes and smoke before he escaped the house? Capelli of all people had to know how steep the odds were on that one.

A soft chime interrupted whatever he meant to say in response. He slid his cell phone from the back pocket of his jeans, giving her a fast glance of apology as he pressed it to his ear, and after a few minutes' worth of "mmm hmm"s and "I see"s, he lowered the phone with an exhale.

"Actually, it looks like our guy has more brains than luck after all. The ME just finished the autopsies, and it looks like both Richardson and Denton were pumped full of sufentanil just before they died."

"Sufentanil?" Shae blinked. "What is that, specifically?"

"It's a synthetic opioid that's used as a painkiller or an anesthetic in small doses," Capelli said.

She pushed past the confusion in her brain, thinking and processing, and oh God. "What about in larger doses?"

"In larger doses, it would render a person fully unconscious—even if the building they were in was burning down around them. Which means not only were Lawrence and Denton *both* murdered and this fire was set by a third party…"

Dread centered itself behind Shae's breastbone, digging in deep. "But whoever did it is still out there, and we have no idea who he is or how to find him."

CHAPTER 8

Vaughn tugged the key to his apartment building from the pocket of his hoodie and fought the deep-seated urge to puke. From the neatly swept sidewalk to the oversized planters boasting fancy yet tasteful winter greenery, everything about this place made his teeth hurt. At least in the shitholes and the slums of North Point, what you saw was exactly what you got. But here in the upstanding part of the south side, Vaughn was stuck with a bunch of fake cheer and rah-rah work ethic crap.

Fuck, this extortion plan couldn't work fast enough to get his ass out of Remington and permanently planted on a beach, Mai Tai in hand and millions in his offshore bank account.

Vaughn slumped just far enough into his hoodie to look standard instead of suspicious. Making certain the glance he swiveled over the area surrounding the entryway was as casual as it was indifferent, he slid the key into the lock on the building's front door and tugged the thing on its hinges. Five days had passed since his Playing With Matches adventure in North Point, and while Little Ray had given up some semi-decent attempts to find him (presumably in an effort to shoot him in the face, blah blah blah), Vaughn was far too smart not to stay four steps ahead of the idiot.

Even if he'd had to find a vacant apartment in the goddamn sweet spot of South Hill in order to do it.

"Oh, hello, Brian. Just coming home from work, dear?"

He looked up at the tiny, birdlike old lady belonging to the voice, hating his aw-shucks smile with every ounce of his being as he slipped it over his face. "Oh, hi, Mrs. Abercrombie. I sure am. Those third graders know how to wear a teacher right out."

Normally, Vaughn cut a wide-as-shit berth around anyone and everyone around him, because truly, so many of them were just so fucking stupid. But elementary school teacher Brian O'Connell, a.k.a. the fictional renter of the poor schmuck whose apartment Vaughn was squatting in while the guy was serving overseas, had been an all-too-easy persona to pull over on the old bat. Since he might be stuck here for at least a little while, it was better to have the building busybody think he was such a *nice* boy than to be suspicious of him.

Mrs. Abercrombie pressed her inch-thick glasses higher on her nose, her hands fluttering over the front of her horribly floral housecoat. "I'll bet you keep those kids busy right back! It's so lovely to have such hardworking young people living in the building."

Briefly, Vaughn wondered if old Mrs. A had an online retirement fund he could drain before he got out of this hellhole. "Not as lovely as it is to be here. You have a nice evening."

He crossed the threshold of his stolen apartment T-minus three seconds from sugar shock, and oh yeah, this was more like it. Turning to flip the two-inch deadbolt he'd installed less than a minute after he'd stolen the place, then propping the solid steel door jammer beneath the doorknob and bracing it against the floorboards, Vaughn exhaled in relief. The security in the building itself was good but not great, which was exactly what he needed. Too little and he'd pull a fucking hamstring taking countermeasures, but too much, and he'd have to blow his wad to make sure he stayed under the radar. This place still used regular keys instead of higher tech key cards that could be tracked for usage, and the closed-circuit cameras at all the main entry/exit points were monitored by a private security company that Vaughn had hacked one-handed and half-asleep.

Which was exactly how he knew Mrs. Abercrombie went to Bingo twice a week at the church up the street, the medical intern down the hall was either not home or in a sleep coma, and the blonde with the fake tits in 6A? He didn't even want to get *started* on some of the freaky shit that chick was up to in her free time. But he had eyes on everyone, which was the most important step in staying undetected.

If he saw every piece on the board, he could control the strategy to outmaneuver and outsmart every last one of the players.

Vaughn grabbed a bottle of Mountain Dew and a bag of Doritos from the once-tidy kitchen before parking himself at the work station he'd set up in the living room. Powering up his laptop, he threw a handful of chips into his cakehole as he scrolled through the list of alerts he'd set up for various databases, his dusty orange fingers freezing over the keyboard as one in particular caught his attention.

Remington Fire Department, Office of Arson Investigation.

"What the fuck?" His heart thumped out a steady stream of *you've got to be shitting me*. Vaughn had flagged the RFD's database just to keep tabs on the two fires he'd been forced to set so far. He'd rigged the causes of both to look accidental enough on the surface, and really, it wasn't like most people tended to give a shit about a meth lab run by gang members and a shitty Italian restaurant that had really been the front for the local Mob. Setting fires to make his nastier payback-related crimes harder to investigate was ironically a little nugget he'd borrowed from his good, dead buddy, Julian DuPree. Only since Vaughn had been far more meticulous along with far less emotional about the whole thing, he'd been certain both cases would be open and shut, at least as far as the fires themselves were concerned.

Yet the fire at Little Ray's meth lab and the torch job he'd done at Fiorelli's when that Mafioso prick had refused to pay up were currently marked as "active, pending further investigation", and huh.

Guess it was time for more countermeasures.

Vaughn scrolled through the reports, his mind spinning like a Tilt-a-Whirl at a sideshow carnival. While he wasn't worried he'd get caught—*that* would take an act of God and Congress put together—he did need to figure out what steps the RFD was taking so he could outwit any advances they might get lucky enough to make.

Eh, looked like they had precious little to work with. Knowing how difficult it would be to prove arson with all the gray-area maybes he'd left at both scenes, Vaughn would bet his left nut that the idiot fire marshal would still be knocking around theories a month from now. Actually linking those fires to him on top of it? File that under "never gonna happen".

"Let's see who else is doing background on these babies," he murmured. With any luck, it would be that fucktard, Wisniewski. Ol' Frank couldn't even find his ass with both hands and a three-way mirror.

Clicking through the rest of the report, Vaughn landed on the sign-off page, and sure enough, Wisniewski's name flashed up at him from the bottom of his laptop screen. But it was the one next to it that made him pause, and he narrowed his stare over the screen with a curse.

Shae McCullough, Engine Company, Station Seventeen.

He sent a rude noise through his teeth. Those firefighters at Seventeen were *such* a righteous pain in the ass. Kellan Walker had been a big part of the sting that had taken down DuPree, and now this chick McCullough was shoving her nose into an arson investigation.

The question was *why.*

Three keystrokes and just as many seconds had her personnel file splashed over Vaughn's laptop screen, and holy shit on a swizzle stick, 'pain in the ass' didn't even begin to cover this woman. She'd been written up a half-dozen times in her five-year tenure with the department, which was ironically also the number of letters of commendation she had to her name. Her latest misstep—insubordination, natch—had landed her ass-first in arson for what looked to be another week and a half. She'd obviously put all of her cases under a fucking microscope, and now Vaughn had to deal with her to ensure that the ones with his name on them stayed cold long enough for him to grab his payday and get gone.

He re-read McCullough's file and sorted through a handful of possibilities. While popping her would probably be fun, it also carried a high likelihood of being both messy and suspicious. She was only pushing paper in arson for seven more days, after which the case would presumably get dumped in Wisniewski's big, fat, lazy-as-hell lap. So really, all Vaughn had to do was distract her a bit, maybe rattle her a little bit more, and bam! He'd be on his way to becoming a permanently unsolved mystery, yet again.

Leaning all the way back in his desk chair, he uncapped his Mountain Dew, the bottle letting out a soft hiss that echoed his mood as he flipped the lid to the crumb-laden surface of his kitchen table-slash-desk. Yeah, this firefighter bimbo would be easy enough to scare off in the short-term, but if the RFD was going to eagle-eye the fires he was setting as payback in this extortion scam, then logic dictated that he needed to set less fires in order to stay under the radar.

Because the very last thing Vaughn needed was to have the cops up his ass again. Keeping that from happening had been his whole reason for wanting get-out-of-Dodge money in the first place.

He needed to get gone, because he sure as hell wouldn't live through getting caught.

His survival instinct sparked, and he clack-clacked his way to the police department database, slipping into the file on the meth lab murders. He'd known the autopsies on Malik and the L-Man would come up hinky—there was no masking sufentanil, and while he could alter chemistry to create the perfect environment for a meth lab fire, he couldn't change it completely, especially not in a pair of bodies that were deader than fucking chivalry. But the cops still looked like they had no leads and their heads in their asses, so at least that was some good news.

Still. With the RFD looking into both fires now, there were a couple potential moves on the intelligence unit's chessboard that hadn't been there yesterday. It was unlikely as shit that any of them would turn into anything that would lead the cops in Vaughn's direction; then again, he'd felt the same way about those assholes when they'd been on DuPree's tail.

His old pal James might have gone all straight and narrow like the pussy he'd always been, but he wasn't a dumbass by any stretch of the imagination. And didn't *that* just put the guy on a very short list.

Tossing back another swig of Mountain Dew, Vaughn cracked a grin as he wondered if the cops James worked with had a clue what the guy's former life looked like. That he used to hack banks and business payroll databases to con people out of their hard-earned money. That he'd memorized and analyzed countless security details specifically to get around them during B&Es. That he'd been raised to recklessly lie, cheat, and steal like the common criminal he was.

Of course, James thought he'd reformed, and wasn't that a kick in the pants. Damaged goods or no, the guilt of what he'd done—to his own mother, of all people—was probably messing with the guy's head something fierce. But guilt was for the weak, and if there was one thing you couldn't escape, it was who you were at your very center.

Underneath that holier-than-thou façade, James Capelli was a delinquent. Calculating and cold and good for nothing but crime.

After all, Vaughn hadn't nicknamed that fucker the Wraith for nothing.

Vaughn's heart picked up the pace, pressing louder against his ears in the quiet of his stolen apartment. Reformed or not, James *was* still smarter than nearly anyone Vaughn had ever met. Not smart enough to catch him, of course—*duh*. But if there was a chance the intelligence unit might catch wind of this extortion scheme, it would make the rest of his plans infinitely harder to throw into motion.

Which meant that after he was done throwing Shae McCullough's concentration a couple of curve balls, his best strategy was to stop chipping away at his end game and crank the stakes up nice and high.

CAPELLI WALKED into the Crooked Angel bar and grill and checked every point of entry he could see even though he'd been in the place no less than a thousand times and had memorized the layout after his first visit. Not that the Crooked Angel had changed much over the last eight years, other than a subtle swap or two of some tables and booths, some updating of the sports memorabilia decorating the darkly paneled walls, and the addition of white lights strung overhead, presumably to soften the place up a little. But the habit of putting eyes on every viable entry point to calculate all the possible escape routes in case something went sideways was about as ingrained as inhale/exhale, and Capelli wasn't a tech and surveillance specialist just for grins and giggles.

Make that a tech and surveillance specialist with a wide-open arson case, a double murder, and still no viable leads in sight, and thank God he was in a bar, because right now he *really* needed a drink.

"Hey, Capelli!" Isabella looked up from her seat at the intelligence unit's regular table in the front of the softly lit dining room, her expression betraying her surprise. "I didn't think you were coming out tonight."

"I wasn't," Capelli said, nodding a quick greeting at Hollister, Hale, and Maxwell as he shrugged out of his jacket and slung it over the back of an empty chair. "But Sinclair kicked me out of the office."

Isabella gave up a knowing laugh. "Yeah, he has a tendency to do that. Come on, I'm going to the bar anyway. I'll buy you a drink."

She led the way through the Thursday-night crowd at the Crooked Angel, walking past a handful of occupied four-top tables and the neon-covered jukebox before turning to look at him over one shoulder. "Listen, I need you to do me a favor."

"Sure. Name it." Although Capelli hadn't been expecting the request, his answer was automatic.

Unfortunately, so was Isabella's ability to read people like the Sunday *Wall Street Journal*. "Stop beating yourself up over this case."

Capelli's steps were perfectly steady even though his pulse didn't share the luxury. "I'm not beating myself up over this case," he said, not too fast or too slow or too loud.

But one dark brow lifted to call his finely crafted bluff. "I'm going to pretend you didn't just try to pull that over on me."

The palm she'd placed on her hip told him in no uncertain terms that arguing with her would get him nowhere, so he lifted a hand in an unspoken concession and stepped in to an empty spot at the bar.

"I'm working hard," he amended, sticking to the truths he could easily tell. "But come on, Moreno. We've got a killer who likes to set things on fire, two bodies, and no leads. I know the L-Man and Denton weren't exactly Boy Scouts, but…"

"Someone murdered them, and it looks like that same person has set more than one dangerous fire. It's a thorny case with barely any evidence and you want justice so no one else gets hurt. Trust me, I get it." Isabella's stare moved, seemingly out of pure instinct, to the back of the Crooked Angel, where the firefighters from Station Seventeen were all hanging around the pool table in the alcove by the bathrooms. Capelli's breath quickened without his permission at the sight of Shae standing between Kellan and Quinn Copeland, and Christ, couldn't his physiology do him a solid just this fucking once?

She threw her head back and laughed long and loud at something Quinn had said, and looked like the answer to that question was a great, big, resounding *no*.

"Anyway." If Isabella had noticed a change in Capelli's demeanor or the direction in which his stare had wandered, her expression didn't give her away. "All I'm saying is you spent the better part of the day poring over those reports from the fire marshal, and the better part of the week investigating and examining the other case details. I know it's important. Just don't forget to breathe a little while you're at it, okay?"

A twinge of guilt settled between Capelli's ribs before spreading out to form a dull ache. But it wasn't as if he could actually tell her he put his nose to the grindstone more out of mental necessity than decency, that if he didn't work, he'd play. So instead, he took the only option he had to end the conversation.

He lied.

"Okay," Capelli said. "I won't forget to breathe."

Swallowing back the bitterness the words had left behind, he turned to catch the attention of the tall, dark-haired woman serving up martinis to two women a few bar stools down, and a few seconds later, she came over to greet them with a darkly lipsticked smile.

"Hey, you two. How's the bad-guy business?"

Isabella returned Kennedy Matthews's smile with one of equal size and wattage. "Booming. Lucky for us, we're booming back. How are things here?"

"The liquor is flowing, the bar stools are full." Kennedy gestured to the busy dining room around them, lifting a delicately pierced eyebrow. "As far as I'm concerned, everything's right as rain."

If Capelli thought about it, there were really no surprises in the fact that tough-as-spikes Kennedy ran a successful business. He doubted she'd take so much as a syllable of shit from a two hundred fifty-pound linebacker.

Kennedy turned toward the beer cooler built in beneath the top of the glossy wood of the bar. "You two want your usual?"

"Please," Capelli said. He slid his wallet from his jeans to cover the round even though Isabella was sure to give him a ration of shit for it, and sure enough, as soon as he beat her to the punch, she gave him a pretty sour look. It turned into an ear to ear grin as soon as Kellan approached, though, and Capelli made a mental note to thank the guy later for the inadvertent save.

"Hey, there you are. Everything okay?" Kellan asked as he arrived beside them with Shae and Gamble not too far behind, and Capelli took a long and much-needed draw from the beer in his hand.

"Yep." Isabella pressed up to her toes to brush a thankfully swift kiss over Kellan's cheek. "Everything's perfect. Capelli and I were just tying up some loose ends."

"All work and no play?" Gamble asked. But before Capelli could offset the question with a no-big-deal reply, Shae surprised him with a tart laugh.

"Right, Gamble. Because that's not all sorts of pot and kettle and bullshit coming from you."

It took balls the size of Canada to stand up to a guy Gamble's size—the dude was six-five if he was an inch, and between the tattoos, the muscles, and his six-year stint in the Marines, most of which was spent in Spec Ops if rumor served, Capelli was fairly certain he was the baddest badass in the bar (which was saying something, because hello, Maxwell was still over by the front door with Hollister and Hale.) Of course, that didn't seem to bother Shae, which was just further proof that her audacity was, in fact, limitless.

Even more surprising was the fact that Gamble merely shrugged one shoulder in response. "You might have a point, McCullough. But it takes one to know one."

"Now that, I won't argue." She paused to turn her attention to Capelli. "So did you get any more leads on the case?" she asked, and seriously, he would never figure out how she kept managing to unnerve him with little more than a curious stare.

"No."

"No?" The pause that followed was loaded with surprise. "But I went through everything arson had on both fires and emailed everything over to you before I left tonight, just like you asked."

That last part earned him a deeper frown. Despite her numerous protests, Capelli had dropped Shae back off at the arson investigation office after they'd left the scene in North Point yesterday. Yes, she'd been eager to help, and yes again, her input as they'd gone through the house had been shrewd and spot-on. But they'd done the job Sinclair had asked. As soon as the fire marshal had seen all the facts, he'd opened an investigation into the meth lab fire, and had agreed—albeit grudgingly—to re-examine the scene of the restaurant fire in light of what he and Shae had found. She had her work in front of her, and Capelli had his. Well, he *would*, once he finally caught a break in this frigging case.

The pieces were there. They had to be. All he needed to do was focus, to figure out which facts were important and how they fit together before this killer made a repeat performance.

And without Shae McCullough shaking his concentration or control.

"Sorry," he said, realizing only belatedly that his one-word answer had pretty much killed the conversation. "We're still running through the facts on our end to come up with some possible scenarios. The victims having sufentanil in their systems isn't helping any of this make sense, though."

Kellan's chin snapped to attention. "Wait...did you say sufentanil? As in, the narcotic?"

"Uh, yeah." Confusion warred with the adrenaline

starting to tap dance through Capelli's veins, and he lowered his beer to the bar. "How do you know what sufentanil is?"

"Because I've been up close and personal with it. That's what DuPree's thugs drugged me with last fall on the night you guys took him down."

Although his voice remained quiet and steady, Kellan ran a hand over the back of his neck as he spoke, and Isabella's shoulders tightened around her spine.

"I never knew that," she said.

Kellan flashed her a glance that contained some sort of emotional shorthand Capelli couldn't decipher before answering with a nothing-doing nod that seemed to put Isabella more at ease. "I had an extensive tox screen run after everything went down so any drugs in my system wouldn't send up a red flag on my controlled substance screenings for the RFD. It came back positive for sufentanil, but I never thought to mention the drug specifically. Still, it's not exactly garden variety, so..."

"That's kind of a weird coincidence, isn't it?" Shae asked, the excitement and curiosity in her stare doubling up and tagging Capelli right in the solar plexus.

"Not necessarily," he said, his brain spinning fast enough to put his mouth at a serious disadvantage. "I mean, yes, Kellan's right in that sufentanil isn't very common. But it's hardly a calling card, either. And anyway"—disappointment squeezed his gut as he lined up his thoughts, recalculated according to the facts of the DuPree case, lined them up again—"DuPree is dead, which makes the likelihood of him being tied to this crime statistically zero."

Isabella planted her boots into the floorboards and straightened her spine to its fullest height. "Which is a good thing for several reasons, not the least of which is that we're all off the clock. We'll be back on the case first thing in the morning," she said, the glint in her eyes broadcasting her determination. "But for tonight, I'd love nothing more than to ditch any and all thoughts of Julian DuPree."

"I'll drink to that," Gamble said, lifting the dark brown bottle in his hand and clinking it against Isabella's before taking a long draw that dropped the topic once and for all. Conversation drifted to the hockey game on the TV over the bar and Capelli paid attention well enough to follow along. But something niggled at the back of his brain, dancing just out of reach every time he got close enough to latch on to it, and the more he tried to focus, the bigger his frustration grew.

His brain wouldn't allow him the luxury of compartmentalizing the way the rest of his unit-mates did, much less let him actually shelf his thoughts in order to relax. He was always calculating. Processing. Seeing numbers and schemes and ways around the rules, and if he didn't channel that into something good like working this case, he'd land on his default.

Fuck. He needed to get out of here and work on this case. The sooner, the better.

Capelli eased out of the conversation strategically, adding less, taking a step back from the larger group that had formed at the bar, then another. The hockey gods did him a solid by dishing up a high-action game—the New Orleans Cajun Rage was having a hell of a Cinderella season, and Capelli sank his brain power into analyzing the stats real-time in order to predict the winning margin. Isabella and Kellan talked happily with his sister Kylie and her boyfriend Devon, who worked for a local private security company in the city. Gamble stood over by the jukebox with a curvy redhead, the two of them exchanging the sort of body language that suggested neither one of them was in danger of being sainted anytime soon.

Capelli hung back another degree. Shae had wandered to

the other end of the bar a few minutes ago, and another surreptitious glance around the hustle and chatter of the Crooked Angel's dining room told him she was either in the ladies' room or she'd left for the night. Just as well, despite the treasonous tug in his rib cage saying otherwise. They might've worked surprisingly well together yesterday, but tonight she'd gone right back to pushing both her luck and his buttons.

He needed to focus, and it sure as fuck wasn't going to happen with Shae McCullough in his dance space.

Nodding a wordless *see ya later* at Isabella and Kellan and the rest of the firefighters from Seventeen, then going through the motions again for Hollister, Hale, and Maxwell at the front of the bar, Capelli buried his hands low in the pockets of his jacket, swinging a covert glance over his shoulder as he started walking toward his apartment.

And ran directly into Shae on the sidewalk.

CHAPTER 9

"Whoa!" Capelli's hands shot out to wrap around Shae's shoulders, and for the love of all things sacred and holy, would this woman ever stop doing things he couldn't predict? "What are you doing out here?"

She gripped his jacket at the elbows, the flowery scent of her hair filling his nose and doing nothing to calm his out-of-control pulse. "I'm waiting for you," she breathed, her voice just one step above a whisper.

Great. Now his pulse *and* his dick were out of control.

Capelli cleared his throat, ignoring the protest rising up from the primal part of his gut as he lifted his palms from the soft cotton of her sweater and took a step back on the concrete. "Why?"

"Because." Shae blinked, but only once before her expression turned to steel and her voice shifted to match it. "I know you're going to work on this case, and I want to go with you."

"No." The word pushed past his lips before he realized it would tell her she'd been on the beam about his intentions to go home and dig back into the case, and God dammit, this woman turned his equilibrium into pudding.

Shae's exhale was all frustration. "Why not?" she asked, but then seemed to think better of waiting for him to answer. "Look, we were a good team, going through the scene of that fire. I'm your contact at arson. Sinclair *told* us to work together."

"That was just for yesterday," Capelli argued.

Of course, she stepped right on up to the plate. "Maybe, but it worked." Sliding her hands to her hips, she said, "Come on, Capelli. You're just as stuck with the murder investigation as I am with the arson. You're going to work on the case anyway, and I'm game. We could help each other out."

Her eyes flashed with the sort of undiluted intensity that made him want to simultaneously run screaming and pin her to the nearest flat surface to fuck her senseless, and hell if that wasn't the crown jewel of reasons to stay away from her. Not only could he not predict anything Shae would say or do, but he couldn't predict anything *he'd* say or do or even feel when he was around her.

"No," Capelli said again. He turned to move around her once and for all, but her hand shot out to wrap around his bicep.

"Please," she said, and truly, he couldn't tell what stunned him more—the word itself or the need with which she'd spoken it. Some emotion he couldn't be sure he'd seen, much less identify with any certainty, darted over Shae's face in the glow of the ambient light being cast down from the bar behind them. "I want to help. Not just tag along for a day or send you reports from arson, but really *help*. So could you please do me this one fucking favor just for tonight and let me?"

"Okay."

The word sailed out of his mouth before his brain could lock it down, and speaking of not being able to predict what he'd say in her presence. Jesus Christ, was he insane?

"Really? You want to work together? Tonight?" Shae asked, and if her wide-eyed stare was anything to go by, the two of them were a matched set in the surprise department. But as much as the idea made Capelli's defense mechanism want to self-destruct, from a logical standpoint, teaming up with her again wasn't the worst plan ever. For whatever reason, his normally ironclad system wasn't working. His brain was working too much.

He needed to figure out what he was missing in this case, and as cracked as it was, reason dictated that working with Shae might at least help more than it hurt.

She didn't wait for him to realize out loud that he'd agreed, much less give him a chance to recant. "Yes! You won't regret this. So do you want to go back to the precinct?"

Shit. Clearly, he hadn't thought this through. "It's after hours," he said slowly. "I was actually going to work from home."

Shae didn't skip so much as a beat or a breath. Naturally. "That works too. I can just follow you there if you want."

She pulled a set of car keys from the pocket of her jeans, but Capelli shook his head. "I live eight blocks from here, so I walked."

"Oh." Her brows lifted. "Alright, then. Why don't I give you a ride? I'm parked a block over, on Delancey."

"Okay." They started to walk, the chilly night air settling in around them, and he eyed her thin gray sweater with a twinge of concern. "I realize you're not a big fan of outerwear, but aren't you freezing?"

Shae looked down at her body as if it had just now occurred to her that a coat in January might actually be a decent idea. "I guess I didn't really think about it when I left my apartment."

"You didn't notice the whole thirty-five degrees thing and

go back to grab a jacket?" he asked, unable to keep a wry tone from lacing over the words.

She lifted her obviously coat-free arms and laughed. "No offense, but for a guy who works in the intelligence unit, you kind of suck at the whole detective thing. Anyway, like I said the other day, the cold doesn't really bother me. I guess my internal thermostat is just a little left of center."

"Kind of like the rest of you?"

She hitched in surprise, just for a fraction of a beat, and dammit, could he have put his foot in his mouth any more thoroughly?

"I'm sorry," he said. "I didn't mean—"

But she cut off the rest of his apology with a deep, unexpected laugh. "I don't make any apologies for who I am, Capelli. So please, don't make apologies for noticing."

The no-bullshit way she claimed her personality was as palpable as a touch, slicing through him with an odd brand of jealousy he didn't see coming. They walked the rest of the block in silence, their footsteps creating a steady rhythm on the pavement. Shae hit a button on her key fob, and the lights on a mud-splattered Jeep Liberty flashed through the night-time shadows.

"Sorry it's in need of a bath," she said, although the grin on her face was far from apologetic. "I did a little off-roading over the weekend and haven't had time to hit the car wash yet."

"A little off-roading," Capelli repeated, and who knew her grin could grow even bigger.

"Okay, so I might have spent six hours on the trails out at Spearhead Valley. But it's too cold to go rafting, and my mountain bike has a flat. Off-roading was the next best thing."

Capelli took in the state of her Jeep, unsure whether to be a little bit stunned or a whole lot impressed. "It sure looks that way. Hey"—he lasered in on her windshield, where a bright white slip of paper stood out in stark contrast against the dusty glass—"looks like someone left you a note."

"Ah, it's probably just some ad. I swear, that new pizza place over on Fourth Street is wallpapering the city with them." Shae pressed up to her toes to pluck the single sheet from beneath the windshield wiper, but her movements froze less than a second later.

A shiver touched Capelli's spine beneath his jacket, lingering at the base of his neck. "Shae? What's the matter?"

"Nothing," she said, shaking her head with a self-deprecating sound that fell just shy of a laugh.

Nope. Not tonight. "Try again."

Releasing a sigh, she handed over the note, and a bubble of adrenaline rose quickly in his chest at the sight of the bold block letters printed across the page.

I SEE YOU.

"Jesus," Capelli bit out. Taking an instinctive step toward Shae, he swiveled a methodical stare over their surroundings, vaguely aware that she was doing the same. Nothing looked unusual—all four streetlights on the block were fully functional and shining away. Nobody lurked on either street corner or in any of the cars parked quietly on the street, but still, his heart thumped in steady warning. "We need to call intelligence."

"What? No." Her fingers wrapped around his wrist before he could get more than halfway to his pocket for his cell phone. "Don't be ridiculous. It's probably kids playing some stupid prank. Fifty bucks says there's one on every car out here."

A lightning-fast re-check of the other vehicles on either side of them proved her wrong.

"Can you think of anyone who might want to scare you? Anyone you might have pissed off?" Capelli asked.

Despite the situation, Shae's lips folded over a smile, and she lifted a brow at him in the streetlight spilling down from overhead. "I irritate a lot of people—including you, might I add. But no, Mr. Paranoia. I don't know anybody who would even think of trying to scare me on purpose. I'm telling you, this is just some random idiot getting his chuckles on."

"Chuckles or not, protocol dictates a call-in on something like this," he said, taking another look at the admittedly generic, possibly pseudo-threat in his hand.

"And how many times do call-ins on notes like this turn out to be actual, real-deal threats?"

Capelli hesitated, unable to do anything but. "Not too often," he admitted, although he kept the single-digit figure of the percentage to himself.

Not that the non-disclosure mattered, because not only had Shae proven her point with the question, but the expression on her face said she knew it. "Look, I might love a good adventure, but I don't have a death wish, Capelli. If I thought for a second that this was a legitimate personal threat, I'd call intelligence myself. Besides, I'm about to spend the next few hours with you, right?"

"That's the plan," he agreed slowly.

"Okay. So if anything out of the ordinary happens, we can both call in the cavalry, and if it doesn't, we'll know this was nothing. But truly, I don't want to waste intelligence's time over something stupid when we could be making real headway by working on this case."

Logic *and* determination. Talk about hitting a guy where it hurt. "Fine," he said after a second that felt more like ten. "But we're going by my definition of out of the ordinary, and I'm walking you to your car later, just in case."

"Sounds fair."

After one last look around them that yielded nothing other

than a whole *lot* of nothing, Capelli reluctantly slid into the passenger seat of her Jeep. He placed the menacing note in his lap, careful not to touch it any more than he already had, just in case. Five minutes' worth of easy directions had them in front of his apartment building, where there was thankfully a vacant spot in reach of the security cameras by the front entrance.

"It might be a little tight," he said, eyeballing the space and considering the dimensions of her Jeep.

But Shae just laughed, the throaty sound making him wish the space between them was both bigger and nonexistent all at the same time. "Nope. I've got this."

Twenty seconds and one extremely skillful parking job later, Capelli stood totally corrected. "Guess I forgot about the whole driving the fire engine thing," he said, allowing a smile of his own to poke at the corners of his mouth.

"And that's just one of my many talents," she quipped back, and okay, yeah. Time to go. Now. Before the dark, wicked back rooms of his brain could conjure up exactly what she might be good at in vivid, cock-hardening detail.

"Right." Clearing his throat twice for good measure, Capelli got out of the Jeep and led the way toward the glass double doors of his building. *Nine steps through the lobby. Six steps past the mailboxes. Do not look at her flawless ass in those jeans. Focus.* "So, um, do you live nearby?"

Blessedly, Shae didn't seem fazed at all by the subject change. "About ten minutes from here. But I move to a new apartment every couple of years."

"You haven't liked any of the places you've lived?" he asked in surprise, but she shook her head to cancel it out.

"The apartments are just fine. It's staying in one place I'm not a fan of."

"So you move all over Remington?"

"Mmm hmm." She looked at him with wide-open honesty

for just a second before following him into the elevator. "I like having options. How about you?"

The quiet sounds of the elevator moving upward became the backdrop for his pulse pressing against his eardrums. "I've lived here for eight years."

More specifically, eight years had passed since Sinclair had walked him down the exact hallway he was now walking down with Shae and pressed the key into Capelli's palm. He hadn't been able to afford the place—shit, everything he'd owned that hadn't been seized by the RPD had fit into the duffel bag that had been on his shoulder. But Sinclair had worked out some sort of legal judo with the landlord that neither man would talk about, let alone let him repay, and Capelli had been an upright tenant ever since.

"Are you sure?" Shae asked, her smile cutting through his thoughts with an odd sense of calm as they crossed the threshold and moved through the small, tidy space of his apartment. "Because no offense, but this place is neat enough to give me hives. Don't you have any clutter? Dirty dishes? Anything even remotely resembling imperfection?"

Startled, Capelli froze halfway out of his jacket. "I'm far from perfect."

"I didn't mean it in a bad way," she said, her shoulders lifting in a shrug delicate enough to belie their obvious strength as she moved to sit down on the couch a handful of feet away. "You're just really organized."

It was a perfect segue, not to mention an even better dodge and deflect, and he took it even though part of him didn't want to. "Speaking of which"—he finished shrugging out of his jacket, hanging it up neatly before grabbing his laptop from the nearby side table where he'd left it this morning—"we should get started on the case."

"I'm going to take a flyer and assume you've got a method." Shae's openly excited smile took a chip out of the tension that wound its way through his shoulders every time he thought of this case, and he nodded, sitting down beside her.

"Analyze, then hypothesize. The facts will get us where we need to be."

"So all we need to do is figure out the right way to see them," she said, causing Capelli's brows to pop at how quickly she'd caught on to his process.

"Yeah."

She leaned in, her smile growing even bigger, and *fuck*, she was unreasonably pretty when her face lit up like that. "I'm ready whenever you are, Starsky. Go ahead and start from the beginning."

CHAPTER 10

Because he had no choice other than give in to the small yet primal part of him that wanted to push this case aside and taste every inch of Shae's smart, sassy mouth, Capelli tamped down on anything not coming directly from his brain and methodically went through everything they had already established at the scene of the fire. She surprised him by listening carefully, peppering in a few technical details that the fire marshal had added to his official report before he'd handed it over to her for the investigation, then gesturing to his laptop.

"Okay, so what else do we know?" she asked, and Capelli released an exhale in a slow leak.

"It's what we don't know that's dead-ending us." He tapped his laptop to life, pulling up the photos of the crime scene along with the detailed report from CSU to keep his thoughts in order. "We have no suspect, no murder weapon, no witnesses, and no possible motive."

"And no obvious link between these two fires, other than the fact that they both appear to be arson," Shae added, although funny, none of it seemed to throw her.

"No. CSU wasn't able to pull any physical evidence from the bodies or the scene that could be definitively linked to the murders," Capelli said, scrolling through the images that the ME had sent over. "The sufentanil in both victims' systems was a big find, obviously, but not really unique enough to get us anywhere useful. It's almost as if these crimes were committed by a ghost."

Shae was quiet for ten seconds, then twenty before he realized her eyes were solidly fixed on the detailed photograph of Denton's injury splashed over his laptop screen.

"The gore doesn't bother you?" she asked, and he remembered—too late—the way she'd paled at the sight of the bloodstains on the floor yesterday.

Something twisted beneath the center of his long-sleeved Henley. "I have to look at it as evidence," he said with care. "The anatomy and the nature of the wounds are clues just like everything else. They're pieces to the puzzle, so I have to look at them from every possible angle if I want to solve the case."

Shae stared at him for a minute, those green eyes burning pinpoint after pinpoint into his skin until he couldn't stand but to ask, "What?"

"You've either got a hell of a work ethic or a bulletproof defense mechanism. I'm just trying to figure out which."

The thought of her having noticed enough of him to be able to peg either made him strangely uncomfortable and even more strangely turned on. "You were really calm with Slater," he pointed out, and at her raised brows in response, he added, "He told Hale you worked the scene like a pro, even though Denton was in bad shape. But it clearly bothers you."

"Oh, it scares the crap out of me," Shae said without pausing for so much as a beat or a breath. "I still have to do my job, though. Anyway, I'm kind of a firm believer that fear is just an opportunity to knock a little courage into a person."

"I never thought of it that way." Capelli sat back, weighing the concept of fear versus courage in his mind.

But she continued, unfazed. "I can't afford to think of it any other way. I learned a long time ago that being afraid isn't such a bad thing. It lets me know I'm not too far gone, you know?"

The reality of her words arrowed through him, sticking his breath in his lungs. He needed a redirect, and he needed it right now. "There *is* something odd about the wound, actually," he said, focusing on the facts to ground himself.

"Oh?" Shae asked, turning her attention back to the image on the screen.

"Yes." Capelli scrolled past the photograph, landing on the ME's report. "Denton's cause of death was obviously blood loss. But he bled out from a very precise cut to the carotid. All of this larger damage was done post mortem."

"How can you tell?" she asked, and as gruesome as it was, he was grateful for the technical question. At least he could speak to the facts with ease.

"Tissue damage looks different when wounds are inflicted after death. The science isn't like a stopwatch, though, so it's impossible to know with certainty exactly how much time passed between the wound that killed him and the rest of the damage. But the ME definitely put his time of death before the majority of the throat slashing."

Shae sat back against the couch cushions, obviously caught up in thought. "So the person who did this hacked into Denton to cover his tracks."

"Either that or the murder was extremely personal."

"Like some sort of message?" she asked, and he nodded.

"Could be." The intelligence unit certainly saw their fair share of revenge crimes, and some of them were exactly this nasty. "But nobody seems to have a vendetta against the gang that Denton and the L-Man were a part of, so right now, it doesn't make any sense. Then there's the sufentanil in their systems...none of it adds up."

That odd prickle he'd felt on the back of his neck at the Crooked Angel came back in full force, but the more he tried to focus on the feeling and pin it down for examination —*damn it*—the harder it was to grasp.

"It does seem really weird that both victims were knocked out by the same drug as Kellan."

"'Weird' is one way to put it," Capelli agreed. Frustrating. Infuriating. Completely fucking unexplainable. "But it still could be a coincidence."

Shae's laugh sounded oddly like a dare. "You don't believe that, though. Do you."

He took a breath to collect his patience. Or maybe it was his sanity. "I can't prove that it's not." He'd tried—all freaking day in fact—to find just one scrap of truth that would get him somewhere on this case.

"Proof." She made a noise that sounded suspiciously close to a snort. "Come on. Can't you go with your gut, just this once?"

"That's not how figuring out a case works." Pulse tapping faster, Capelli pushed up from the couch, walking to the open space of his kitchen in order to give his frustration a logical outlet.

Shae followed him the handful of steps, her chin hiked in a way that meant nothing good was in his immediate future. "That's exactly the problem, though. *None* of this works."

"We can't just chuck the rules, Shae." Was she nuts?

"I'm not suggesting we start making shit up to suit our purposes here," she said, nodding in a wordless *please and thank you* at the bottle of water he just as wordlessly offered her from the fridge. "But you said it yourself. It's what we don't know that's dead-ending us. So what can it hurt to take a flyer and go with your gut here?"

"My gut won't get us anywhere," Capelli insisted, frustration swirling hotter in his chest. "You're suggesting we try to tie an active murder investigation to a man who's been dead for months."

"Do you have any better ideas?" Shae said, and sweet baby Jesus, she *was* nuts.

"Intelligence did an extensive investigation on DuPree. He never did business on the pier, and there's no connection between him and the Scarlett Reapers. All of his clients were high end." Other than the sufentanil, there wasn't even a hint of a suggestion that the cases could be related. "Yes, it's a bit of an odd coincidence that Kellan was drugged with the same narcotic as Denton and the L-Man, but there's no point pursuing it—DuPree is dead, and his entire operation went down with him. Right now we have a killer on the loose. We don't have any time to chase highly unlikely what-ifs. We need to focus on the facts."

Not that a tiny little thing like logic was going to stand in Shae's path. "When I came to you with these arsons, they were both what-ifs too. I was going purely on *my* gut," she said, her eyes glinting greenish-gold, and the sudden pop of adrenaline in Capelli's veins warred with his diehard need for caution and order.

"You acted on your gut when you went back into that house after Slater, too, and look where that got you."

The words tightened the tension in the air, but Shae met it head-on. "Why are you so afraid to just act on something you can't measure?"

Something dark and dangerous swelled in his chest. He stepped toward her, reducing the space between them to mere inches, and there went more of his control. "I'm not afraid."

And yet, his heart pounded hard enough to negate the claim. Her stare flashed with intensity, raw and hot and so fucking beautiful that it destroyed his ability to think.

"Yes, you are," came Shae's fierce reply. "God, Capelli, why can't you just trust what you feel instead of what you can prove?"

"Because," he growled.

And then he grabbed her by the shoulders and slammed his mouth over hers.

~

A THOUSAND THOUGHTS and feelings crashed into Shae from all directions. She wanted to yell at Capelli, to shake him and call out his completely rigid ways and scatter his tightly wound composure all over the floor like marbles. But one feeling surged ahead of all the others, and it was the only one she could focus on with any sort of clarity.

More.

Her lips parted in an effort to convey the message without resorting to messy extras like words. Capelli caught on quickly, answering the movement of her mouth with a hard, deep press of his own. He was so shockingly brash, the steadfast control that normally ruled everything about him nowhere in sight, that all Shae wanted was to keep unravelling him until they were naked and sweaty and screaming, right here in his kitchen.

Her sex clenched, a heady sigh climbing the back of her throat at the thought. The sound—or maybe it was the feel of it vibrating between them—made him even bolder, and he tightened his hands on her shoulders, claiming her mouth with his tongue.

Yes, yes, fucking yes. Shae was dimly aware of the clatter of the plastic water bottle in her hand tumbling to the floor as she dropped it to knot her arms around his shoulders. Capelli's muscles flexed beneath her touch, the friction of cotton over the hard angles where his neck met his back making her nipples harden against the thin lace of her bra. Sliding her tongue out to meet his, she opened to his kiss even more, offering up the control he seemed to so desperately need.

And oh, he took it. Gripping her shoulders, Capelli swung her around, walking her back just a few swift steps until her body met the flat surface of the refrigerator behind her with a firm thump.

"*Ah.*" She moaned into his mouth. His lips twisted into a wicked smile that she felt rather than saw, and the gesture grew even darker when she arched up to fit her frame against his from chest to hips. Heat speared between her legs at the contact, the unmistakable press of his cock at the seam of her body making her clit throb in a demand for more.

"You drive me crazy, you know that?" He broke from her lips to trail a line of rough kisses over her jaw that were no less intense than the way he'd taken command of her mouth. "You make me want to lose my fucking mind."

"Mutual," Shae said, forcing the word past the greedy need building low in her hips. She turned her head to one side against the cool, stainless steel surface of the refrigerator to give him better access to her neck, and he took it with a low curse. Flattening one palm over her shoulder and lowering the other to her hip, Capelli held her close, working the sensitive skin of her earlobe with his lips and tongue. He explored without pause, tasting every inch of her jaw and neck as if he was memorizing her with his mouth, and her breath squeezed in her lungs as her sex went slick with want.

Want that became entirely more primal when he closed his teeth over the spot where her neck joined her shoulder and applied just enough pressure to make her cry out in pleasure.

"Ah. There it is," he murmured in satisfaction, and God, the gravelly, need-soaked sound of his voice alone was enough to make her want to fly apart. "Christ, you are so hot right now. I can't wait to find every single place that makes you scream."

Shae's heart thundered even as her frustration welled. As sexy as it was to think of Capelli taking the scenic route over her erogenous zones, the need in her belly had pushed far past an insistent demand. They could take their time on round two, or maybe three.

But right now, she wanted him.

Hard. Fast. And buried between her legs.

Reaching down, she freed the button on her jeans, her zipper releasing a soft hiss as it followed suit. "I can show you a good place to start."

Capelli's body went bowstring tight against hers, but thankfully, he didn't argue. Shae slid her jeans lower over her hips, exposing her teal satin panties, and his stare grew nearly black in the diffused light filtering in from the adjacent living room. Not waiting for her to get her jeans past mid-thigh, he anchored one hand at her waist, cupping the other against her pussy in a hard press that left no guesswork to his intentions.

"Christ, Shae." He grated the words at her ear. "You're so wet."

The easy slide of his fingers over the fabric between her legs was proof, the movement making her clit pulse with hot, provocative want.

"Capelli." His name collapsed past her lips, part moan and part whisper. Shae tilted her hips to maximize the contact, and *ah*, he didn't waste any time following her lead. Shifting slightly to one side, Capelli angled his stare downward, his eyes locked on his fingers as he tugged her panties aside to reveal her bare, need-slicked sex. A sound rumbled from his throat, both dirty and reverent, and she pushed forward to meet his fingers at the same time he pressed inside her.

"Oh *God.*" For a second, she couldn't do anything, couldn't think or speak or breathe. Then he started to move, and forget not being able to do anything.

Shae wanted everything.

Capelli filled her in slow, firm strokes, one finger thrusting deep while his thumb slid up to find her clit. There was nothing sweet or tender about the way he touched her, but that just made her want him all the more. Shae chased each forward movement with her hips, daring him faster and deeper until she was certain the desire pulsing through her blood would either break her in half or swallow her whole.

"I can feel how close you are," he said, a second finger joining the first. "How bad you want it."

The added pressure stretched her, daring her closer. "Please," she moaned. "Please make me come."

Something dark and wholly forbidden hardened his face, his stare glittering in the shadows. Hooking one finger around the other, Capelli pressed both into her pussy, finding some spot deep inside of her that sent sparks through her vision. Shae reached forward blindly, the blunt edges of her fingernails digging into his forearm and holding him close as he fucked her with his fingers.

She couldn't think of a word to call out that would do this any sort of justice. She'd never felt so turned on, so desperate for release, and sensation built between her legs, both pure and primal. Capelli's breath sawed out in quick, hot bursts against her neck, his hand pumping harder and harder, and with one last thrust, she shattered with a keening cry.

The climax gripped Shae in waves that stunned her with their intensity. He worked her through each shudder, pulling back only after her body had gone lax against his.

But oh, how she'd only just gotten started with him.

A sassy smile tugged at the corners of her mouth, and she reached out for the hem of his Henley. "I'm game to stay in the kitchen if that's your kink, but you're going to have to lose some of these clothes if you want to catch up."

But an unreadable expression had replaced the urgent passion that had been on his face only seconds before.

"Shae."

Capelli caught her hand to stay her movement. His tone slid past the lusty haze in her mind, making her heart squeeze with something other than arousal, and wait... "What's the matter?"

The slow, deep breath that lifted the front of his shirt served as an all-too stark reminder that he was fully dressed and fully in control. "This...I was...I mean, you're..."

Too impulsive.

"Don't say it," she managed, although the look in his chocolate-colored eyes told her that her brain had filled in the blank with gut-punching accuracy. Cheeks burning, Shae quickly righted her clothes, then locked her shoulders around her spine. "I'm going to take a wild guess and assume you'd rather work on this case alone for the rest of the night, too."

After a few seconds that lasted an eternity, Capelli said, "I think that would be the smartest plan," and God, could she be any more thoroughly dismissed?

"Right. I'll be on my way, then."

"Wait."

Her stupid, treasonous pulse tripped as he took a step toward her. Then he paused as if he'd thought far better of the proximity, his chin lifting as he fixed her with a serious, all-business stare. "The note. I need to walk you to your car."

Shae's protest burned brightly in her mouth. But she'd agreed to let him walk her safely out, and of course he'd get all uptight and argue if she pushed.

The fastest way out of here was to let him have his way, despite the fact that the chance for danger was frigging nil, so she did what any smart girl with shredded pride would do.

She took it.

"Fine. I'm ready if you are," she said, and then she walked toward the door without looking back.

CHAPTER 11

F*uck me, fuck me, fuck me.*

It was—despite his very best efforts to the contrary —the only thought Capelli had been able to squeeze from his clearly addled brain for almost an hour. One bold challenge, one flash of Shae's wild green eyes, and his control had been destroyed. Every calm, rational thought he'd ever considered having had not only pulled a disappearing act, but had left him so completely, it was as if he'd never known composure in the first place.

And he'd loved every dark, reckless second of it.

"Stop." Although Capelli hadn't spoken loudly or with force, the word still echoed through his apartment. Yes, he'd been reckless, dangerously so, but he had to move past his momentary lapse of judgment. He needed his brainpower for other, safer things, and Shae was far from safe. She was impulsive, unpredictable. Hell, if anyone told her not to do something, she'd not only do it twice, but she'd probably take pictures on top of it all. He couldn't—*could not*—dwell on the way Shae had felt under his hands and mouth. How she'd managed to sound both provocative and just the slightest bit sweet when he'd relentlessly made her come.

How much she'd made him *want*.

Inhaling deeply, he packed away his thoughts of her, once and for all. He'd walked Shae downstairs, triple-checking their surroundings and her Jeep from front to back before watching her get in and drive off without incident. She was safe. He was sane again. What he needed—now more than ever—was to keep his mind busy on this case.

Capelli fired up his laptop, placing the thing carefully over his kitchen table as he pulled up a chair. But before he could get comfortable, let alone wrap his brain back around the facts in front of him, his cell phone buzzed softly with an incoming call.

Huh. His brows lifted in surprise at the sight of the name and number on the caller ID, but the sentiment only lasted for a heartbeat. Isabella might have mellowed out some since she and Kellan had gotten serious, but she was still a detective in the most elite unit in the freaking city. Capelli should've known she wouldn't be able to fully practice what she'd preached in the Don't Forget to Breathe department.

"Hey, Moreno." He considered making some wry comment about her work ethic being the size of a small nation, but the spring-loaded pause on the other end of the line put a swift end to any niceties. "What? What's going on?"

"It's Shae," Moreno said, Capelli's heart ricocheting in his chest when she added, "how quickly can you get to her apartment on Hanover?"

∾

SOMEWHERE IN THE dim back hallways of his mind, Capelli knew he should be methodically taking notice of the things around him. If there were video cameras in the parking area beside the neatly bricked five-story building. Potential security weaknesses at the front and side doors. Whether or not the management company had installed a key card entry system that could be tracked down to when every last resident had gone to walk her Pomeranian or grab the mail. But none of that was front and center in Capelli's brain as he barged past the glass and steel doors of Shae's apartment building with his heart wedged in his windpipe.

He knew the rules. For fuck's sake, he *swore* by them. How could he have been so careless?

He didn't even consider bothering with the bullshit of the elevator. Taking the stairs two at a time, Capelli cut a fast path up to the third floor, flashing his RPD ID badge at the uniformed officer standing just outside the wide-open door of an apartment halfway down the hall that had to be Shae's.

She sat on a couch in the main living space with Hale on one side and Isabella on the other, a blanket over her shoulders and a serious frown on her face, and all the breath punched from his lungs in relief.

"What the hell happened?"

"I'm fine."

Their words crashed together, both of them having spoken at once. Taking a deep inhale, Capelli dug for his composure, biting back the string of questions exploding through his mind so Shae could continue.

"I told Isabella she didn't need to call you. Everything is totally fine."

"If that were true, she wouldn't be here, and neither would Hale or the officer at the door," he pointed out. "So do you want to tell me what's going on?"

Shae's shoulders didn't budge beneath the red fleece of the blanket around them, but she let go of a soft sigh and conceded. "I got home a little while ago and decided to take a shower."

Belatedly, Capelli noticed the way her damp hair was pinned to the crown of her head in a loose knot and the thick, bright pink socks peeking out from beneath the edges of the blanket. A stab of guilt spread out in his chest at the reason she'd likely felt compelled to shower, but he'd have to work through that later.

"Okay," he said, and Shae continued.

"Nothing looked out of sorts. The door was locked just like always when I came in, and I turned the deadbolt again before I went into the bathroom. But then when I got out of the shower and came back out here to grab something to eat…" She paused, her face turning a shade paler as she flicked a glance at the nearby coffee table. "That was sitting there."

Capelli took a step toward the table, his blood turning to ice in his veins at the same moment his adrenaline dumped his heart into his gut.

The single piece of paper read: *I SEE YOU HERE TOO*

"Oh hell," he said, winging his gaze around her casually cluttered but seemingly otherwise undisturbed living room. "And you're sure it wasn't here when you walked in the door?" God, the thought of some miscreant near her, in her apartment while she *showered*, for fuck's sake, turned his hands into fists at his sides.

"Pretty sure. I mean, not a hundred percent, but…"

Shae broke off, her mouth pressing into a thin, white line, but Isabella shook her head. "It's okay. The fact that you don't remember it being here at first is still helpful, and this is obviously a serious issue regardless. You were right to call me."

"We should have called after we found the first note on your car," Capelli said, looking at Shae. But before she could get the protest flashing in her eyes to her mouth for a reply, Isabella held up one hand.

"Why don't you come talk to me about that over here while Hale finishes talking to Shae?" she asked. Capelli's brain recognized the standard operating procedure. He knew it was important—hell, logic reminded him that the divide and conquer protocol was sometimes the most crucial part in catching the tiny details that could break a case wide open.

And yet for the first time in eight years, he found himself wanting to take a flamethrower to the rules.

He made himself nod in agreement even though it took effort, following Isabella toward the door. The half dozen or so steps and the time needed to take them allowed Capelli to regain at least a portion of his composure, and he scrubbed a hand over his face before turning to look at her.

"Please tell me you've got a crime scene unit on the way out here," he said, and Isabella nodded in the affirmative.

"I called Sinclair as soon as I saw the note. He's got CSU on the way right now. Hollister and Maxwell are downstairs talking to the building manager, trying to see if there's any security footage we can grab to pin down a potential suspect. We'll canvas the entire floor as soon as they're done."

The well-detailed plan calmed him a step further. "You have the note that was left on her car too, right?"

Moreno nodded again. Seeming to sense his need to start carefully examining and processing the facts in order of occurrence, she said, "Yes. We'll send both out for a full analysis. In the meantime, do you want to tell me what happened there?"

Capelli gave her a rundown of what had transpired outside the Crooked Angel, from where Shae's Jeep had been parked to her adamant claims that the first note had been some sort of prank and nothing more. "There was nothing out of the ordinary other than the note. Nobody hanging around, nothing suspicious at all," he said, swearing under his breath. "Still, I know better. I should have called it in even though Shae didn't want to."

Isabella tilted her head, closing the small black notebook where she'd been jotting down the details of his account. "In Shae's defense, we've seen hundreds of pranks that never amount to anything other than stupidity and boredom. In yours…" Her stare slid to the spot on the couch where Shae sat, still wrapped in her blanket and talking quietly to Hale. "This is obviously not a joke."

"These notes have to be related to this arson case," Capelli said. "Using them as a scare tactic is the most likely explanation."

"The timing seems a little too neat to be a coincidence," Isabella agreed, measuring him with a calculating glance. "But you've been working on the case together, and nobody's left any notes for you. Plus, the notes don't say anything about her backing off the investigation. We'll have to work all the angles."

Capelli opened his mouth to argue, but closed it just shy of allowing the words to form. If they were going to get anywhere, they needed facts. Evidence. Irrefutable proof. And as badly as he wanted all three, no good would come from rushing through trying to find them.

"Copy that."

Following Isabella back over to the center of the living room, Capelli chanced a look at Shae. "Are you okay?" She seemed awfully pale. "Maybe we should get Parker or Quinn over here, just—"

"Absolutely not," Shae said, her tone six times stronger than her countenance. "Nothing even *happened*, for Pete's sake!"

Hale—blessedly—chose that moment to cut in. "I'm not so sure about that, Shae. I know you're physically fine," she added, holding up one hand to quell any further arguments. "But I think we're pretty far past 'nothing.'"

"I hate to say it, but I agree," Isabella said. "Whoever left these notes isn't an amateur. Technically, there hasn't been a clear or specific threat."

Capelli's chin snapped to attention along with his pulse. No. No fucking *way*. "You're not going to treat this as a threat?"

She dismissed his question with a look that questioned his sanity. "Of course we're treating it as a threat. We don't mess around when it comes to our own. Plus, it's entirely plausible that whoever did this is also responsible for multiple felonies, including a double murder. All I meant was, we have to be careful how we go about pursuing things."

"So what do we do from here?" Shae asked. Hale exchanged some barely-there eye contact with Moreno, a gesture Capelli would have certainly missed if he owned any brain other than the one currently residing in his skull.

"We'll keep eyes on the building and your apartment for the rest of the night, just in case whoever did this decides to make an encore," Hale said, and Shae swung a startled stare from the detective to the spot where Capelli stood.

"Wait...you don't seriously think this guy would come *back* for me tonight, do you?"

"Logically?" He bought himself a scrap of calm by calculating the odds and coming up with, "It's not likely."

Moving to sit down next to Shae on the couch, Isabella put on a no-bullshit smile. "Monitoring the scene is just part of protocol, but Capelli is right. Given the circumstances, chances are very slim that whoever left these notes would come back tonight. Realistically, CSU is going to be here for at least a few hours, and anyway, I have to recommend that you not stay here for a few days regardless."

Shae's shoulders thumped against the back of the couch cushions. "Is that really necessary?"

"You had a break-in and two threats to your personal safety," Isabella said. "We have to take it seriously. Do you have anyone you can stay with?"

Shae paused, and the oddly vulnerable expression on her face ripped the words right past Capelli's lips before he could temper them with any sort of normal-person reason.

"She does. Until we get a grip on this, she can stay with me."

CHAPTER 12

O f all the circumstances by which Shae could imagine
spending the night at Capelli's place, staying out of
some creepshow's path didn't even make the top one
hundred. Yet here she stood, in her holey old Charlotte
Rogues hockey T-shirt and a pair of RFD sweats, staring at
his living room for the second time tonight, and yeah. She
officially hated this.

"Sorry you couldn't really take much with you," came
Capelli's voice from beside her, after the hard click and rattle
that signaled the front door to his apartment being locked up
à la Fort Knox.

Shae's moxie lifted her shoulders in a default move the
rest of her could barely back up. *Breathe in. Breathe out.*
"That's okay. I was already ready for bed, and I understand
why Addison and Isabella didn't want me rummaging
around just yet."

A closer perusal of her apartment had showed a handful
of seemingly random things either missing or wildly out of
place, to the point that the crime scene techs who had
arrived just after Shae had (reluctantly) agreed to stay with

Capelli had told her not to touch anything until they'd combed over every last bit of it.

For the next twenty-four hours.

"Right," Capelli said, as cautiously as if he'd just read her mind, and with how stupidly perceptive he was, she really wouldn't put the ability past him. "Well, I've got an extra toothbrush in the bathroom, and you're welcome to borrow whatever else you need in the morning. There are clean towels in the closet."

"Guess you're a regular Boy Scout, huh?"

Funny, the comment seemed to hit a nerve, drawing his shoulders into a rigid line around his neck. "Not really. I just like to be prepared."

"You didn't have to offer to put me up, you know." Shae gestured to the tidy living room around them. Her pride might have taken a back seat to the whole crazy-stalker-note thing, but there was no sense not addressing the truth now that they were standing here alone. Again. "I don't want this to be awkward for you."

The slight lift of Capelli's dark blond brows was the only betrayal of his surprise. "I might feel a lot of things about what happened between us earlier, Shae, but awkward isn't one of them."

That made two of them on the surprise. "It's not?"

"No."

"What is?" she asked, genuine curiosity pulsing to life in her veins.

"It's complicated," he answered, and Shae bit back the urge to give up a great, big amen. "At any rate, I really don't mind you staying here tonight. As long as you're okay with it, too."

"It's better than crashing on Gamble's futon." She didn't even want to get started on how it would save her from her parents' guest bedroom. As tough as she was, that might be enough to break her right now. "Don't get me wrong, I love the guy like a brother, and we're tight. But when it comes to stuff like this, he's kind of like a big, badass mother hen."

"He seemed pretty concerned about you," Capelli said. "Kellan and Quinn and January, too."

Of course half of Seventeen had blown up her phone ten seconds after she'd called Isabella, who had still been at the Crooked Angel at the time. Occupational hazard of mixing work and play. "Yeah. It took a little convincing, especially with Gamble." You could take the guy out of the Marines, and all that jazz. "But I let them all know I'm fine."

"Are you?"

The question pinned her into place with its simplicity, but she wouldn't—couldn't—tip her hand. "Of course."

Capelli looked at her, his brown eyes brimming with doubt. "It's perfectly normal to be shaken up by something like what happened tonight. The guy was in your apartment, Shae."

"I'm aware of that." Her stupid, stupid heart thwacked against her sternum.

"Isabella meant it when she said intelligence is taking the threats seriously. The whole unit is on the case."

Under normal circumstances, Shae's tolerance for dangerous situations was sky-high. Tonight, however? Not so freaking much. "Would it be okay if we didn't talk about the notes or this murder investigation until tomorrow? I'm just kind of...fried."

"Oh." Capelli blinked, but only once before giving up a slow nod. "Sure. What do you want to do instead?"

She laughed, although the sound came out way more sad and soft than she'd intended. God, what was *wrong* with her? "Truth? I want to drown this day in a giant vat of wine."

Capelli's pause told her he was trying to rate her level of

seriousness on a scale of one to ten. Finally, he surprised her with, "I have ice cream."

"You know what? That works."

Shae followed him into the kitchen, watching as he pulled a plain white bowl from the most orderly cupboard known to mankind. "I should've known you'd be an ice-cream-in-a-bowl kind of guy."

"Um, how else would you eat it?" he asked. Placing the bowl on the impeccably clean white granite counter, he opened a drawer for a spoon, then another for an ice cream scoop, and she couldn't help it. She laughed a real laugh.

"Right out of the container. It tastes better that way."

"You do realize it's physically impossible to make something taste better just by virtue of the container it's in?"

The wry expression that had snuck over his face was a clear indication that he was teasing her in his own weird, Capelli sort of way, and she teased him right back.

"Spoken like someone who's never eaten ice cream right out of the container," Shae said, unable to keep from noticing how the lean muscles of his forearm flexed as he scooped out three of the neatest portions of strawberry ice cream she'd ever laid eyes on.

He rinsed the stainless steel scoop, placing it carefully in the dishwasher before handing over the bowl and spoon. "I'm serious."

"I see that."

Whether it was the residual adrenaline in her system or the uncharacteristic, almost sweet way Capelli was looking at her, Shae couldn't be sure. But all at once, her emotions welled up, spilling past her lips before she realized they would. "I know you think I'm reckless. Too impulsive and brash. Probably even a little dangerous."

"Shae," he started, but she cut him off with a shake of her head.

"We both know it's true, and anyway, I meant it when I told you I don't make apologies for who I am." Taking a breath, she cradled the bowl of ice cream to her chest, letting the coolness seep through the cotton of her T-shirt to ground her. "I know I drive you crazy. Hell, I drive lots of people crazy. But I'm not just some dumb adrenaline junkie. I have reasons for living fast and not holding back, and they're not small."

Capelli's brows, nearly gold in the warm, soft kitchen light, lifted over the dark rims of his glasses. "You do?"

"What, you thought I was just born this way?"

The wry tone she'd wrapped around the words scattered the tension that had started simmering in the air between them, and he let a smile break over his mouth. "Yeah, actually."

He took a few steps across the floorboards, ending up at the small, two-person table on the far side of the kitchen. But rather than simply sitting and waiting for her to do the same, Capelli pulled out one of the chairs in a silent offer, and Shae felt the stress of the last couple of hours slip another notch.

Smiling her thanks, she sat and took a bite of her ice cream, and okay—it might not be enough wine to do the backstroke in, but Capelli had impeccable taste in frozen desserts.

"I hate to break it to you," Shae said. "But you're wrong there. I haven't always been impulsive. Well, not like I am now, anyway," she amended, because while she might've had a come to Jesus meeting with her lifestyle after Abby had died, it hadn't been a total personality transplant. "In fact, I was once a perfectly normal teenager doing perfectly normal things in a perfectly normal suburban city. Not one risky move in sight."

"No way." Capelli's expression suggested equal parts gentle teasing and genuine surprise, and Shae let another mouthful of ice cream linger on her taste buds before sending it down the hatch to answer.

"Cross my heart. Honor roll, student council, homecoming committee, college scholarship. The whole enchilada."

Capelli's brows creased, making the little V behind the bridge of his glasses that always formed when he was processing something. "What happened?"

She paused. But even though she didn't blab about it to everyone who happened by, the accident wasn't some sort of secret she kept locked away either, and truth be told, her fearless best friend would've had a fit at anyone getting all moony over her death.

So Shae said, "The summer after my senior year happened. I was all set to go to UNC on a full ride. Both of my sisters had gone there, and nearly everyone in my graduating class was heading off to college somewhere. It just felt like what I was supposed to be doing, too."

Although Capelli didn't say anything, his quiet stare from across the table told her he was not just listening, but listening intently, and funny how that just made more of the story pour right out of her.

"A bunch of my friends and I decided to celebrate graduation in the Smoky Mountains. We'd gone on trips like that a few times during the year, staying at my best friend Abby's parents' cabin near the Wayehutta Trail in Bryson City. My boyfriend at the time had an ATV, and so did Abby's and a few of their buddies. It felt like the most normal thing in the universe for all of us to pack up and head out for a week of fun before we all started our summer jobs."

Shae stopped, her chest squeezing only slightly at the memory of how blissfully unaware she'd truly been that life could change so drastically, so fast.

"It sounds pretty normal," Capelli said, and she smiled

around the bite of ice cream she'd taken to try and freeze out the pang behind her breastbone. Talk about normal. Knowing him, he'd probably been halfway through some triple-major degree at some Ivy League school at the time.

"It was painfully normal," she agreed. "The first couple of days were exactly what you'd expect. A bunch of off-roading and hiking during the day, a bunch more drinking and getting a little rowdy at night. The third day, we were all geared up for more of the same, but Abby's boyfriend had a nasty hangover, so she and I took his ATV out while he stayed behind to sleep in."

Shae had played the what-if game about that moment, that one tiny decision that had rippled out and touched everything that had come after it, a hundred thousand times in the last eight years. What if Tyson hadn't been hung over and had gone riding that day. What if Abby had been the one hung over and she'd stayed behind instead. What if they'd taken a different trail. What if Shae had been the one driving. What if, what if, what if…

"Anyway." She shook her head, pushing the what-if game aside. "Even though I knew how to operate an ATV, I was too chicken to drive Tyson's on the really bumpy back trails, so Abby did it."

"*You* were chicken?" Capelli asked, surprise widening his dark brown stare for just a breath before his expression grew apologetic. "I'm sorry. It's just difficult to get my head around that."

Rather than being offended, Shae bit back a laugh. Of course the first thing he'd try to do would be analyze what she was telling him.

"Abby was way more fierce than me back then. She didn't even think twice about driving." A knot formed in her gut, but she kept telling the story anyway. "A couple of the guys we were with decided they wanted to go really far up the trail that day to get to this lake none of us had ever been to before. We mapped out the trail, so Abby and I knew the terrain was going to be a little rougher than we were used to navigating, but God, we didn't hesitate."

In that second, something small yet definite shifted in Capelli's demeanor, just a slight tightening of his body against the black ladder-back chair where he sat, and yet it marked his realization as clearly as if he'd shouted. "You were in an accident."

She nodded. "We were pretty far away from the main trails, on a route none of us were familiar with, and there had been a few nasty storms earlier in the week."

Gripping the spoon between her fingers even though her stomach churned far too hard for her to consider taking another bite of ice cream, Shae inhaled. *Breathe in. Breathe out.* This part never got any easier on the rare occasions she let the story out of the box where she usually kept it tucked away.

Still, she couldn't shy away from giving it a voice. "About a half-mile from the lake, Abby and I went around a pretty sharp bend in the trail. She didn't see the fallen tree blocking our path until it was too late."

"Jesus, Shae." Capelli reached one hand across the expanse of black wood between them. Just shy of contact, he hesitated, as if the movement had been automatic and his brain had registered it on a delay. But his fingers were close enough for Shae to feel their warmth, his hand enviably steady, and she angled her knuckles against his, letting the barely there brush of their skin anchor her.

"We hit the downed tree head-on," she continued, focusing on the feel of his hand, on the one tiny spot where they touched. "Abby and I were both thrown from the ATV."

The muscle along the hard edge of Capelli's jawline twitched. "Were you badly injured?"

152

Oh, the irony of it all. "No." Aside from some nasty scrapes and bruises that she hadn't even felt in the moments right after she'd sustained them, she'd been completely unharmed. "But honestly, no one knows how. I was thrown fifteen feet from the ATV, which ended up flipping into a shallow ravine on the other side of the trail from where I landed."

"Oh." The tension that eased from his shoulders lasted for less than a second before he connected all the dots. "What about Abby?"

"Abby was…not so lucky."

Shae dropped her stare, concentrating on Capelli's fingers. He had wide, strong hands, callused in some places, yet smooth in others, and suddenly, urgently, she wanted to wrap her fingers around his and not let go.

"When we hit the tree, Abby was thrown in the other direction," she said quietly instead. "She ended up in the ravine about twenty feet below the trail, pinned beneath the ATV."

Capelli went perfectly still across from her. But unlike anyone Shae had ever confided in, he didn't interrupt, didn't offer up any of the "oh my God"s or "how awful"s she'd long since grown used to, opting instead to simply give her the space she needed to tell the rest of the story.

So Shae took it.

"It took me a few minutes to figure out what had happened, that we'd even been in an accident. But our other friends had been behind us, and as soon as they made it around the bend, they figured things out pretty fast." Thankfully, they'd all been going slower than she and Abby had, so they'd all been able to stop in time to remain safe. "Two of them went for help—cell coverage is pretty much nonexistent out on the trails—and the other two were shell-shocked enough not to be of much help."

"That's a normal physical response to really bad accidents," Capelli said, his voice softening as he added, "you must have been in shock, too."

"I was," Shae admitted, although she hadn't known it until far after the fact. "I ran down into the ravine, but one look told me I wasn't going to be able to do anything." Not that she hadn't tried. God, she still remembered crazily trying to pull the five-hundred pound ATV off of Abby with all her might. "I didn't have any idea how to help, other than to stay with Abby and tell her everything was going to be fine. I knew it was a bald-faced lie. Even though I couldn't see most of her body, I could still tell she was bleeding a lot."

Abby had been so thoroughly pinned beneath the ATV that Shae hadn't even been able to hold her hand. She'd found out later, quite by accident, that trying would have been in vain. One of Abby's arms had been crushed so badly, her hand had very nearly been severed.

Shae swallowed, completing a few rounds of inhale/exhale before finishing with, "Anyway, I lay there on the ground with her, telling her to just hang in there and that help was on the way, but she died before the paramedics even got to the scene."

"I'm really sorry, Shae."

The straightforward sentiment oddly soothed her, and she managed a tiny smile. "Thank you. Abby's death was really hard on me, obviously, but at the same time, it really opened my eyes. I decided not to go to college that fall. Instead, I drove all over the country. No plan, no routes mapped. I just packed a bag full of clothes, got on the road, and went wherever I felt like going."

"That does sound like you," Capelli said.

"It *is* me. At first my parents thought I just needed time, and maybe part of it was my way of coping and finding as much closure as I could. But after the first few weeks on the road, I knew I couldn't ever go back to living my life the way I had been. Life is too short not to live it out loud and without apologies."

Capelli tilted his head, looking at her through the soft overhead light of his kitchen. "So you never came back and went to college?"

"Nope. Much to my parents' dismay." They'd given her a little leeway, considering, but… "After the first year, their understanding turned to concern, then outright disappointment that I wasn't 'settling down'." Shae paused to sling air quotes around the words. "But I didn't want to settle down. I wanted to see things, *do* things. If any second could be my last second, I was going to make every single one of them count."

"I suppose logically, your motivation makes sense," Capelli said slowly, and God, everything really was black and white in his universe.

"Yeah, well the go-where-the-wind-takes-you lifestyle really only works if you're a trust fund baby or you like sleeping on park benches, and honestly, after a couple of years, I got tired of waiting tables and doing odd jobs to pay for the next stop on the road trip. I might be capricious as hell, but I'm not a slacker. Sitting on my ass isn't my idea of a good time. So I came back here and enrolled at the fire academy."

Capelli let that sink in for a second. "For the adrenaline aspect?"

"Funny enough, no, although that's what my parents and sisters all thought. Don't get me wrong," Shae said, because the truth was still the truth. "I do love the thrill of running into a burning building. But I don't just think it's cool for my own personal gain."

At Capelli's look of obvious surprise, she continued, even though her heart pounded at the words. "When Abby died, I felt so helpless. I know there probably wasn't anything I'd have been able to do for her even if I'd been trained," she added. "Her injuries were extensive, and I get that. But being a firefighter lets me help people when they're at their worst, when they really need it the most. And if I can help save just one person…"

She broke off to steady the waver that desperately wanted to climb into her voice. "Doing everything I possibly can to help is what I want to do with my life. Even if that means taking risks."

They sat there for a minute—or hell, maybe it was ten—Shae with her melting ice cream and her heart in her throat and Capelli just quietly studying her. Finally, he simply closed the fraction of space between their hands, sliding his fingers firmly over hers without saying a word, and as crazy as it was, Shae wouldn't have traded the gesture for all the adrenaline on the planet.

CHAPTER 13

Capelli folded the blanket under which he'd slept, double-checking to make sure the corners of the dark green fleece lined up before he placed the thing over its usual spot on the back of his couch. He'd given his bed to Shae even though she'd given *him* some shit for it, but it wouldn't have mattered if he'd been in the swankiest, most extravagantly lush suite in the Remington Plaza Hotel.

Between his going-nowhere case, the threats made to Shae, and the revelation she'd made afterward in his kitchen that had knocked him figuratively yet thoroughly right on his ass, he hadn't slept a goddamn wink.

Letting out an exhale, he eyed the hallway leading to his bedroom, where Shae was still getting dressed. CSU had cleared enough of her apartment overnight to allow Quinn to run by to grab some clothes and drop them off on her way to her shift at Seventeen, which the paramedic had done a few minutes ago. Shae had seemed like her usual self with both him and Quinn this morning, which was to say she'd swung through about four different emotions before she'd finished her first cup of coffee. None of them, however, had even been in the same stratosphere with the way she'd looked last night as she'd sat at his kitchen table and told the story of her best friend's death.

Of all the words Capelli was certain would never describe her, vulnerable was easily in the top five. Yet the second that story had crossed Shae's lips, she'd gone and shocked the hell out of him yet again.

She wasn't just impulsive for the thrill of it, or worse yet, because she didn't take a damn thing seriously. She had reasons for taking risks—no, check that. She had logical, well-*founded* reasons, ones Capelli had been able not only to rationalize, but really understand. Beneath all that brash exterior he needed to avoid like it was at the center of a five-alarm fire, Shae was a purely, deeply good person. All she wanted was to help people on their very worst days, while once upon a time, he'd engineered the most underhanded scams in Remington, conning hundreds of unsuspecting people out of their pensions and paychecks all so his drug-addicted mother and her boyfriend du jour could party like rock stars for a living.

And didn't that just make him a degenerate of the highest order, because *fuck*, despite how good Shae was and how very good he wasn't, Capelli wanted her anyway.

"Whoa." Shae's voice jolted him back from his trip down memory lane. "Are you okay? You look like someone just walked over your grave."

"I'm fine," came his default, and great. Add "liar" to his résumé. "And I don't have a grave. I'm standing right here. Obviously."

She laughed, and the part of him he'd been trying so hard to keep on lockdown prowled faster in his chest. "Lord. Are you ever *not* stone cold serious? I meant figuratively. Because you look upset," she added with an obvious—yet not unkind

—lift of her honey-colored brows, and damn it, this woman wrecked everything about him.

"Right. Sorry. I must need more coffee." Or a lobotomy. Christ, he needed to get it together. "Anyway, it's still a little early, but I'm sure Sinclair's already at the Thirty-Third. We can head over for an update on the break-in at your apartment before you go to arson today."

"Sounds good. To be honest, I'd really like to get back to normal and nail the asshole responsible for these crimes." Halfway to the door, Shae paused. "Thanks. You know, for putting me up last night. And for…listening."

"You're welcome." Capelli's gut squeezed, but his words were perfectly level. They *had* to be.

For both his sake and Shae's.

They made their way downstairs and out the front door of the building, into the slightly gray, definitely chilly morning. He watched Shae's back as much as his own as their feet hit the pavement, scanning all the potential places someone might lurk or even just hang back and pretend to casually observe. She returned the favor, her green eyes moving over their surroundings in a methodical sweep, but thankfully, the quiet side street and everything on it—including her Jeep and his Volkswagen Golf GTI—were all systems go.

"I'll meet you at the precinct," Shae said, sliding into the driver's seat and giving him a wave before pulling away from the curb. Capelli lingered for another minute, pretending to read a message on his phone. The street remained completely as expected, a handful of people in various states of hustle and go on the sidewalk, light traffic that would soon grow heavy as rush hour got going in earnest. Nobody pulled out after Shae, and no one loitered around, watching him in the same covert manner he watched the street.

Which meant that either things *were* entirely normal, or whoever had eyes on Shae was just that good.

After all, it wasn't paranoia when someone was really watching you.

Shaking off the thought, Capelli got into his Volkswagen and drove the handful of miles between his apartment building and the Thirty-Third. Shae's Jeep wasn't in the parking lot next to the precinct, though, and he ran through a quick set of possibilities for why she wouldn't have arrived ahead of him since she'd had a five-minute head start.

Nothing good came out of his mental list. At. All.

But just when Capelli was about to consider true concern, a text popped up on his cell phone.

Hey, Starsky. I stopped to run a quick errand. I'll be there in ten. Stop making that serious face.

She followed it with a bunch of smiley faces and other assorted emojis to match, and the whole thing was so freaking Shae that he had to huff out at least a soft laugh before texting back with a quick "copy that". Yes, she'd been threatened, very likely by whomever had committed the crimes they were trying to solve. But she had the entire intelligence unit freshly programmed into her cell phone, and she was smart. Tough.

Sexy. *Definitely* sexy, with those pretty blue-green panties and all that hot, smooth skin...

"Walk," he bit out under his breath, forcing his boots into motion fast enough for them to crunch the gravel beneath. Counting his steps and marshaling his breath to a slow, even rhythm, Capelli walked through the parking lot—twenty-nine paces—up the eight stairs to the main entryway leading into the Thirty-Third, and after a quick scan of his RPD badge and an exchange of "hey-how-are-ya"s with the desk sergeant on duty, he was on his way up to the intelligence office. To his surprise, Hollister and Hale were already at their desks, and (not to his surprise) Sinclair was in his office, his door closed and his phone pressed firmly to his ear.

"Hey," Hale said, lifting her gaze from her laptop with a smile far too cheerful for the pre-eight A.M. hour. "You're here early."

"I wanted to get started on the surveillance videos from Shae's apartment. See if we can't catch a break off one of them that might lead us to our murderer." Or at least off of square one, where he seemed to have taken up permanent residence.

"Great minds," Hale replied, scooping up a coffee mug claiming *Glitter is the New Black* in sparkly pink script and taking a long sip before continuing. "Hollister and I have been at it for almost an hour. Sadly, there's not much to write home about. Building management only has cameras at the front door and in the elevators."

Shit. "So if the intruder posed as a maintenance worker in order to gain access through a side door, then took the stairs once he was inside, these feeds won't show so much as his shadow."

"Our guy is smart. It's highly possible he managed to avoid the front door," Hollister admitted, looking up from his laptop.

"Alternate point of entry is what I would do to gain access without being noticed," Capelli said. "Those key cards that residents and building employees use to get in and out can easily be duped, and even more easily stolen. Either way, the only trail left behind is of the person who had the thing swiped, not necessarily the person who actually swiped it."

Hale nodded and reached for the phone on the corner of her desk. "I'll put in a call to the building manager and see if any of his employees are missing a key card, or if any residents have reported theirs stolen. It's a long shot, but—"

"Oooo, did someone say long shot? Because I'm always up for a challenge."

Shae's voice sounded off from the door of the intelligence

office, which she'd bumped open with her hip because her arms were full of two long, flat boxes. But before Capelli could move so much as a muscle to help her, Hollister bolted out of his chair.

"Are those what I think they are?" he asked, his face in full-on glee mode.

Shae handed over the boxes with a grin. "Yep! I brought breakfast."

"This isn't just any old breakfast," Hollister said, and if Capelli didn't know any better, he'd swear the detective had just drooled on his T-shirt *and* his shoulder holster. "These are doughnuts from the Holey Roller, home of the Killer Cruller."

"Jesus, Hollister. You are such a mercenary when it comes to food," Hale said, sending her gaze skyward.

Hollister took the boxes from Shae. "Clearly, you've never experienced the joy that is that cruller. Anyway, I'm a single guy. Of *course* I'm mercenary when it comes to food."

"Capelli's a single guy, and you don't see him throwing elbows to get at these," Hale pointed out.

"That's because Capelli is a health Nazi. Also, possibly insane." Hollister waggled his reddish-brown brows, and Capelli tried on a wry expression to cover the unease building in his chest.

"I'm standing right here, you know. With perfectly functional hearing and everything."

Before Hollister could pop off with a smartass answer to match Capelli's smartass comment, Isabella hustled through the door. "Oooh, doughnuts from the Holey Roller," she said, not even shrugging out of her jacket or putting down her travel mug of tea before joining the fray. "What God among mortals stopped for these?"

"I did." Shae pulled the lids off the boxes—which now sat smack in the middle of Hollister's desk—and sent a glance over the group, starting and ending with Capelli. "I just wanted to say thanks for everything you guys did last night."

Capelli shook his head, utterly baffled at how any one person could be so brassy and so genuine all at once. "Doughnuts for a bunch of cops? Don't you think that's a little ironic?"

Shae's cat-in-cream smile told him the choice had been one hundred percent intentional, and Hollister tagged him with a look that suggested he was certain Capelli had taken leave of all five of his senses.

"Dude, shut up. There are apple fritters in here," he said, holding up a gigantic, golden brown pastry as proof. "Plus, even though we were just doing our jobs, I think it's pretty cool of Shae to enable our sugar high."

Capelli realized—a second too late, of course—how much edge his words had carried. But Shae just laughed that sexy, maddening laugh that managed to stir him up and smooth him out all at the same time.

"Thanks, Hollister, but believe me, we're square." Reaching down low, she plucked a glazed cake doughnut from the box on Hollister's desk. "Come on, Capelli," she said, her expression as sweet and as downright sinful as the pastry she offered up. "It's a doughnut, not the precursor to Armageddon. Live a little."

For a second, he was tempted, but not because of the doughnuts laid out in front of him in all their sugary, carb-laden, frosting-covered glory. It was the look on Shae's face that nailed him, and Christ, he had no defense against anything she did, however small.

And he really had to resist. Otherwise he *wouldn't*.

"No. Thank you," Capelli added, making sure his expression conveyed that he meant it. "But I'm all good."

Hollister shook his head, although his tone was all

laughter when he said, "Whatever, man. You don't know what you're missing."

"Well." Sinclair's gravelly voice scraped through the intelligence office from the spot where he stood by the crime scene board, grabbing everyone's attention and sobering the mood in the room in less than a heartbeat. "Looks like a party in here."

"Just breakfast, Sarge," Isabella said, moving purposefully to her desk while everyone else did the same.

Shae—having nowhere else to go—stood between Capelli's desk and Maxwell's unoccupied work space, holding up her hands in a nonverbal *mea culpa*. "That's kind of my fault. I stopped by to grab an update on the break-in and bring in some doughnuts, but—"

Sinclair cut her off with a small but definite shake of his crew cut. "Actually, I'm glad you're here, McCullough. It saves me a call. I trust you can all eat and listen at the same time," he added, sending a stare around the office, and damn, Capelli would recognize that all-business, no-bullshit expression even in the dark.

As would everyone else in the room, apparently. "If you've got news on the case, we're all ears," Hale said.

"Good. First things first. I just got off the phone with Captain Bridges and Frank Wisniewski over at arson, and we're all in agreement that in light of last night's threats and the strong possibility that they're related to our joint investigation, Shae should complete the rest of her work on the arson case here at the Thirty-Third under my supervision."

"Oh." Shae blinked in obvious surprise, and hell if that didn't make them a pair of fucking bookends. "If you think that's best and my captain agrees, then I'm okay with working here in intelligence."

"You'll be partnered up with someone at all times, and we'll take a few extra security measures for the next couple of days at least," Sinclair said. "They're mostly precautionary, but on the off chance this guy decides to get squirrely again, I don't want you working your end of the investigation solo. I trust that won't be a problem."

Shae must have heard the lack of wiggle room in his voice —God knew Capelli did—because rather than push back like she was normally inclined to, she gave up a slow nod. "I just want to help catch this guy."

"Which brings me to my next order of business," Sinclair continued. "Our crime scene unit is done in your apartment and the building manager installed a new deadbolt on your front door." He held up a pair of shiny silver keys. "So you're free to go home later today."

Capelli's pulse tripped. "Did CSU find anything workable that we can follow up on?" Damn, he was itching for something, *anything*, to key into the system and analyze.

But Sinclair killed the spark of hope with a single shake of his head. "Unfortunately, no. No prints on the note or the front door. The canvas came up empty, and even though it took a hell of a lot of time and manpower to go over the place, the rest of the apartment is clean. Whoever did this went to a lot of trouble to stay in the wind."

Hale lowered her doughnut to her desk and frowned, but only for a second before her glass-half-full mentality kicked into high gear. "We do have the rest of the surveillance video to go through. It's still possible we could get a hit off that, maybe grab an image to run through the DB for facial recognition."

"Good." Sinclair gestured to the laptop propped open amid the sea of papers on her desk. "You and Hollister keep going over the footage to see if anything pops. Moreno, I want you and Capelli and Shae on the ME's report and the fires. See if we can find a connection that links all these pieces together."

KIMBERLY KINCAID

"Copy that," Moreno said, and Capelli and Shae nodded their agreement.

"Maxwell's grabbing all the files from arson that haven't been put into the system yet on his way in, and he's reaching out to his contacts in the gang unit on anything we might have missed on the Scarlet Reapers. Let's get to work, people. And by the way...McCullough?"

Sinclair's stare arrowed in her direction as he walked across the office. Picking up a double-glazed cruller from the box on Hollister's desk, he tipped the pastry at her with a rare showing of his smile. "Looks like you'll fit right in."

"Thank you, Sergeant."

Dodging the pretty flush commandeering her cheeks, Capelli pushed his brain into go-mode. He turned toward his desk, firing up his computer and hitting the remote switch to illuminate the crime scene board.

"Okay, you two," Moreno said, pulling her chair over to Capelli's desk on the right-hand side of the now-bustling office. "We've got a pretty big mountain in front of us. Let's start at the bottom and work our way up."

Shae nodded, her green eyes chock-full of determination as she hooked a hand beneath Maxwell's spare chair and settled in next to Moreno. "I already sent you everything I had on both fires, and Maxwell's grabbing the rest, so..."

"The first thing we should do is get you up to speed on our end," Capelli said.

Isabella offered up a rundown of the facts, which he backed up with details from the case files, and both combined to sharpen the already elaborate images in his head. Shae tucked her brows as she listened, asking a handful of questions in between bites of her breakfast. While her brain didn't seem to operate by any organized rhyme or reason, her questions were straightforward and smart, and the facts that she threaded in from both fire scenes slid into Capelli's mental batch files, looking for a home.

"Let's look at the facts chronologically," he said to Shae. "What do we know about this restaurant fire, other than the fact that it looks like the same sort of arson as the meth lab fire?"

"Not much," she admitted. "The fire marshal went back out to the site yesterday for more detailed photos and another walk-through now that the fire is officially under investigation. He reached out to the owner—a guy named Nicholas something. Bonetti? Biello?"

"Bianchi," came Maxwell's voice from the doorway as he entered the intelligence office in all his gruff, tough, leather-jacket-and-knit-skull-cap glory.

Capelli's heart thumped out a warning rhythm as the name Nicholas Bianchi registered in his brain, and damn it, just when he thought this case couldn't get any more twisted.

"Yeah! Nicholas Bianchi. That's the guy." Shae pressed back in her chair, splitting a glance between him and Maxwell and Moreno, whose expression had just ventured into more serious territory. "He came up clean on all the public records for the building. Taxes filed on time, no health and safety violations for the restaurant. Although from the look of what was left of the grease trap in his kitchen, I'm not quite sure how. Do you guys know him?"

"In a manner of speaking," Maxwell said, lowering the box of file folders in his grasp to one corner of his nearby desk before turning to meet Shae's brows-up stare. "Nicky Bianchi's part of the local mafia, which is largely run by his uncle, Luca. They tend to stick to the racketeering basics—money laundering, loan sharking, with a little bit of gun-running here and there for grins."

Isabella nodded, picking up Maxwell's lead. "The Bianchis are well-connected, which explains the restaurant's inspections being aboveboard, and their security and counter-surveillance are ironclad enough that the Feds haven't been able to make anything stick to either Nicky or Luca."

"Local mafia. Ooookay," Shae whispered. But Capelli had to give her credit. A heartbeat later, she was right back to that chin lift/eyes glinting thing she did whenever she was about to dig her heels in, and fuck if it didn't make her twice as hot and about nine times more dangerous. "Well, Bianchi might be shady, but he barely had any insurance on the restaurant. He lost his shirt when Fiorelli's burned down."

Huh. The information made Capelli's forehead crease behind his glasses. A few keystrokes had the case file Shae had sent him yesterday up on Capelli's laptop, and with a handful more, he'd gotten the information to the center monitor on the array over his desk.

"So this definitely wasn't arson for profit, then," he mused out loud. Not that he was ultimately shocked—Nicky Bianchi might be thirty-one flavors of criminal, but he liked to stay under the radar. The payday from a scam like that wouldn't be worth the spotlight of the investigation.

"No. I don't think so," Shae said, then backtracked with, "unless whoever set the fire is really freaking bad at insurance fraud."

Moreno shook her head. "Bianchi runs scams for a living. No way is he screwing up insurance fraud. There has to be another motive for the fire."

"Yeah," Capelli agreed. "The question is, what?"

"How about revenge?"

Shae's query sent a pang through his rib cage, his spine unfolding against the back of his desk chair. "Revenge," he repeated. "You'd have to be a pretty heavy hitter to try and take a shot at a guy like Nicky Bianchi. Plus, he wasn't anywhere near the place when it burned."

"According to the transcripts from dispatch, the first nine-one-one call came in just after five in the morning. I think it's safe to say *nobody* was near Fiorelli's when it burned. Well, except for the arsonist, anyway," Shae tacked on.

Okay, so she probably wasn't wrong about that. The pier wasn't exactly home to a whole lot of early risers. Still… "The Bianchis own more than half a dozen businesses, and the rest of them have gone untouched. Why would our arsonist target just this one, especially when it was empty, if he wasn't trying to get at Nicky?"

"I don't know." Shae tucked her bottom lip between her teeth in a move that was far sexier than it had a right to be. "But somebody torched Fiorelli's badly enough for the fire marshal and the city building inspector to condemn the place all the way down to the bricks. That seems kind of personal, and if you ask me, there aren't a whole lot of things more personal than revenge."

"It isn't *too* far outside the realm of plausibility," Isabella said slowly. Although the logic pumping through Capelli's veins tempted him to disagree, he also knew Shae was likely to go all pit-bull-with-a-porterhouse until he gave her a damn good reason not to. Even then, it was a coin flip as to whether or not she'd actually let the idea go.

His mind whirled and spun, methodically processing facts and probabilities just as it always did, whether he liked it or not. This time, though, his brain snagged on a thought that took his heartbeat along for the ride.

Wait. What if—

"Hang on." Pushing his glasses higher over the bridge of his nose, Capelli slid closer to his keyboard. He routed all of Fiorelli's public records from the city's database to one of the screens on the array, then all the business records attached to anyone with the last name "Bianchi" to the monitor right next to the first, scanning the documents as quickly as his eyes would allow.

Which of course wasn't fast enough for his impatient and four-steps-ahead-of-everything-else brain, and come on—come on, come *on*—ah! There. That was precisely what he'd been looking for.

And nothing he'd expected.

Capelli's chin whipped upward at the sharp burst of realization that fell into place all at once. But despite his rising adrenaline, he was one hundred percent sure of where the facts had just led him, so he turned to look at Shae and said the only thing he could.

"You know what, McCullough? You're absolutely right."

CHAPTER 14

O f all the things James Capelli could have possibly said to her, this one stunned Shae the most. But truly, their attempt to work together last night was case in point that he lived to argue with her *and* her theories. No way was he really sitting here, wearing that fiercely serious expression that somehow managed to torque her up and turn her on all at the same time, telling her she was *right* about this case.

Was he?

"I'm right," Shae ventured, painting the words with a heavy layer of what's-the-catch.

But Capelli's nod was all certainty. "You are. Look."

Fingers flying over his keyboard, he scrolled through a handful of very official-looking documents on two of the screens on the lower section of the crazy six-way monitor-type thing mounted to the wall over his desk. "Nicky Bianchi is the sole owner of Fiorelli's. He bought the place from his uncle two years ago, and even though the restaurant seems to do very little business, from the look of things, their books have been oddly flush the whole time."

"You're not actually surprised the place is a front, are

you?" Maxwell asked, and okay yeah, even Shae—who didn't know extortion from embezzlement, thank you very much—had figured out that the restaurant couldn't possibly be a legitimate business.

"Hell no," Capelli said. "But it *is* the only front in Nicky's name. The rest of the Bianchi family's businesses either belong to Luca or they're registered to various shell corporations."

Isabella blew out a breath of understanding. "So Fiorelli's was Nicky's baby."

"Could be Luca needed someone to run the place. Or maybe it was a test to see if Nicky's ready to move up the ranks." Capelli gestured to the on-screen document, which looked like a deed to Shae, although her head was spinning hard enough for it to be a guess. Meth lab murders? Local mafia? This was getting outer limits.

Maxwell nodded, his dark eyes sharpening with the same sort of realization Capelli had reached a minute before. "Either way, if someone wanted to hit Nicky in a sore spot, burning the place down would be a pretty good way to do that."

"So we're looking at someone who had a beef not just with Bianchi, but the Scarlet Reapers too," Isabella said.

Annnnd cue up a whole lot of goose bumps. "You think the guy who was in my apartment has it in for gangsters *and* gang bangers?" Shae asked.

"I think the guy who was in your apartment doesn't want to get caught," came Capelli's quick answer, but it didn't escape her notice that his shoulders had just gone all lock and load around his neck. "Whoever did this is really meticulous. Enough that the fire was nearly ruled accidental."

"The local mob usually steers pretty clear of gangs, and vice versa," Maxwell said. "It's a turf thing. The good news is, the list of people associated with both is bound to be short."

But something in the detective's tone made her gut sink toward her boots, and before she could stop herself, Shae asked, "And the bad news?"

Maxwell crossed his arms over the broad expanse of his chest, his expression growing as budge-free as his body language. "Capelli is right. Whoever's committing these crimes is smart. We're going to have to dig pretty deep to catch him."

Shae's heart raced, her chest filling with too many emotions to name, let alone single out. Common sense dictated she should be scared out of her gourd at the thought of this maniac watching her yesterday, and yep, there was the familiar bloom of adrenaline she always felt when a call came in at Seventeen. But she wasn't a pushover, and scared or not, they were finally making headway on this case.

So she took a deep breath and said, "Then let's dig deep and catch him."

"Damn, girl." Isabella sent an appreciative grin across the office space between them. "Sinclair wasn't kidding about you fitting right in."

The words bolstered Shae's confidence another notch. Yeah, she was a little freaked out. Any normal person would be. But she could do this. She *had* to. "Thanks, but I just want to help."

Maxwell pushed up from his desk, reaching for the jacket he'd barely shrugged out of and shouldering his way into the dark brown leather. "I was going to head down to the Fifth to talk to Matteo Garza over in the gang unit this morning anyway, so this is good. He might have some intel on who'd have it out for both the Scarlet Reapers and the Bianchis. You feel like taking a ride, partner?"

He looked over at Hale, who had to have been able to hear every bit of their conversation despite having been lasered in on her laptop. "Sure," she said, proving the point. "I hate to say it, but this video looks like a bust. Plus, someone's gotta have your back."

"I'll take the rest of the video, just in case. Text me if Garza comes up with a name," Capelli said as Hale followed Maxwell toward the door.

"Copy that."

Sliding a glance at Hollister, Isabella said, "You know, we could go have a chat with Carmen."

At the *whaaaa?* that had to have made the move from Shae's brain to her face, Isabella added, "Carmen's one of my CIs. She works at Three Brothers Pizza, down on the pier. It's not far from where Fiorelli's was. She doesn't have any connections with the Bianchis that I know of, but still. She might've heard something."

"Great," Hollister replied with all the enthusiasm of someone about to be tossed into a Turkish prison. "Because Carmen's so much fun. Especially in the morning."

Isabella made a sound that was half-laughter, half-snort. "You really need to stop flirting with my CI."

A startled glint darted through Hollister's eyes, gone before Shae could be truly certain she'd seen it. "Are you kidding?" the detective asked, managing to look both bored and cocky at the same time. "What Carmen and I do isn't flirting. It's an MMA event."

"Okay, pretty boy." Isabella checked her badge and the gun in the holster at her hip, shaking her head with a wry smile. "Let's go get your ass kicked in the name of intel, then. Come on."

Shae watched the two of them head toward the front of the intelligence office, their banter fading into the hallway beyond, and a weird, unexpected pang spread out beneath the center of her dark red sweater. She pressed a hand over her breastbone as if she could literally snuff out the ache, realizing just a beat too late that Capelli's eyes weren't on the monitor in front of him, but firmly fixed on her instead.

"You miss Seventeen, don't you."

For a breath, she said nothing, just sat there in her chair with that squeeze still lingering in her rib cage. But bullshitting her way out of the conversation seemed stupid—not to mention useless, since Capelli's words hadn't held so much as a hint of a question.

So she didn't even bother trying. "I guess the biggest hazard of loving your job is that there's no place you'd rather be than up to your eyeballs in work. I'm happy to help you guys find whoever set these fires and killed those two men, but…yeah. I miss Seventeen."

Upon hearing her thoughts out loud, Shae punctuated them with a self-deprecating laugh that seemed to take Capelli by surprise. "Which, come to think of it, probably makes me sound a little weird."

"Actually, that doesn't sound weird at all."

His answer had been simple—seven words, less than a dozen syllables, all of which Shae had heard conservatively a billion times in her twenty-seven years on earth. And yet the way he was looking at her with nothing but pared-down honesty in those melty brown eyes made her feel like he got it.

Like just for a second, he really *saw* her.

But then Capelli was clearing his throat and enough heat had crept over her cheeks to let her know in no uncertain terms that she had to be visibly blushing, and God, this whole crime and punishment thing was seriously throwing her off her game.

"Right. So did you want to split the rest of this surveillance video?" he asked, and Shae nodded, all too ready to dive in.

"You got it, Starsky. Let's catch ourselves a bad guy."

~

CAPELLI LOOKED at the time stamp in the bottom corner of his laptop and cursed. Not because it was particularly late—although Hale, Hollister, Moreno, and Maxwell had all trickled out of the intelligence office one by one over the course of the last hour—and not because he'd had a terribly frustrating or unproductive day, either. No, Capelli's muttered F-bomb came courtesy of the fact that he actually *had* gained some ground on this case today.

Just in time for Sinclair to kick him out of the office for the entire freaking weekend.

"Everything okay?" Shae asked, her voice pulling Capelli back to the right-now reality of the softly shadowed intelligence office. She'd been reading so quietly in the work space she'd created for herself at the end of Moreno's desk that he'd temporarily forgotten he wasn't alone.

And wasn't that just one more reason to stay focused on this case, because damn it, he'd never forgotten anything—temporarily or otherwise—in his life.

"Everything's fine," he said, swallowing back the bitter aftertaste of the lie. But he couldn't exactly pop off with "I just don't want to go home and try to find something to keep my freakishly overactive brain busy so I don't end up defaulting to very bad things". Even if it *was* painfully accurate.

"Sorry we didn't get anything off the video," Shae said. "I looked really carefully, but the only person who wasn't a resident was that flower delivery guy who totally checked out as legit with the company."

Capelli shrugged. "Don't feel bad. My pizza guy did too. That footage was kind of a long shot, anyway. The movement we made on the arson side was good, though, so that's something." He let go of a slow exhale, reviewing the information they'd added to the crime scene board today one more time before shutting the thing down and packing up his laptop. "We should probably call it a night."

He knew from experience that if Sinclair booted him enough times in a row, it would lead to the sort of conversation that involved phrases like *you've racked up a lot of vacation time* and *maybe you should take a few days off*. Leaving pre-emptively would go a long way toward keeping him under the radar, and anyway, he could work almost as easily from home as he did from here. Thank God.

"It is getting kind of late, huh?" Shae said, but funny, she didn't pair the observation with any sort of movement.

"Almost seven," Capelli answered carefully. "We've been here for nearly twelve hours, and it's Friday night. Don't you want to go home?"

Her shoulders stiffened by a fraction beneath her dark red sweater, but still, she nodded. "Oh, yep. Mmm hmm. Absolutely." Closing her laptop, she pushed to her feet, hugging the thing to her chest as she glanced at the door. "So, um, all I have to do is ask the desk sergeant to have an officer walk me to my car, then text Hollister and Moreno when I get home and lock the door, right? That's it for the safety protocol?"

A hard pang spread out in the center of Capelli's gut. "There haven't been any more notes today, and all the patrols of your building have come up clean." They still hadn't found any hint of whoever had been in her apartment, but... "It looks like this guy was just trying to scare you, so yes. All you need for the protocol is an escort to your car and to check in once you're safely inside. But I can walk you out if you want. I'm headed home anyway."

"Right. Okay," Shae said. Lifting her chin, she turned to slide her bag from beneath Moreno's desk. To anyone else, she probably looked completely status quo, just a woman packing up to head home after a long week. But her movements were just a little too forced, her lips pressed together the tiniest bit more tightly than usual, and after a few seconds of analysis, the truth slammed into Capelli with all the grace of a brick.

"Shae, are you scared to go home?"

"No." Her answer arrived without hesitation, her tone surprisingly marking it as the truth. "I know you guys wouldn't let me go back to my apartment if it wasn't safe. So I'm not scared that this guy is waiting to pop out of my closet like some B-movie villain."

"That *is* highly unlikely," Capelli agreed. He'd gone over the reports from CSU himself. Sinclair had had her apartment triple-checked all the way down to the baseboards and hinges. No surveillance equipment, no signs the guy was really watching her or would be back. The place was completely clean.

And yet… "You still seem like you don't want to go home."

"That's probably because I don't."

For the billionth time, her honesty floored him, and for the billionth time, she didn't seem shy about coming out with the truth.

"I guess I'm just not too excited about the idea of being alone right now."

"Oh. Well, you could go to the Crooked Angel," Capelli ventured. "I'm sure everyone's there. Having a beer or two might take your mind off things."

"Maybe." Shae lifted one shoulder in a half-hearted shrug before slipping the strap of her laptop bag into place. "But it would just delay the inevitable. At some point, I'm going to have to go home and scrub the fingerprint stuff off the doorframes and the coffee table, you know?"

Capelli's pulse knocked a steady rhythm against his

throat. He didn't want to go home. Shae didn't want to be alone in her apartment.

Really, there was only one logical solution.

"As luck would have it, I'm pretty handy with a spray bottle and a sponge." He waited for her breath to catch—*there*—and God, the turnabout of being the one to surprise her felt more darkly satisfying than it should.

"You want to come help me clean my apartment?" Shae asked, her brows lifted in that bold, borderline sassy expression she wore so often, it was a wonder the thing wasn't permanently etched on her pretty face. But Capelli didn't just notice her moxie. He noticed everything, right down to the relief buried beneath her words and her bulletproof smile, and hell if that didn't make him feel a little bold, too.

"Sure." He grabbed his jacket and laptop bag, tipping his head toward the front of the intelligence office in a wordless *after you* before following Shae to the door. "You're going to have to feed me though. I have standards."

Shae laughed. "I hope your standards accommodate either Pop-Tarts or frozen dinners."

Capelli sent up a silent prayer that she was kidding. "Why don't we cross that bridge when we get to it?"

They made their way downstairs and past the desk sergeant in comfortable quiet. Capelli's senses sharpened once they crossed the precinct's main threshold, his careful stare measuring all the places someone could hide, either in the shadows or in plain sight. Thankfully, the path to Shae's Jeep and the vehicle itself were clear of anything out of the ordinary, and she popped the locks before turning to look at him in the ambient light shining down from the streetlamps illuminating the parking lot.

"You don't have to do this, you know."

It was, Capelli supposed, her way of giving him an out. But the thought of his quiet, empty apartment, of how much work he'd need to scrape up just to keep his brain on the straight and narrow, of the tough but grateful look on Shae's face right in this moment, and the truth flew out of his mouth unchecked.

"Yeah, I really do."

A few quick minutes had him in his car, following her through downtown Remington. One uneventful ride and one equally uneventful trip through the lobby of her building later, he and Shae were in the elevator, headed up to her apartment. She held the keys Sinclair had given her this morning in one hand, her shoulders level and her gaze alert as they stepped into the third-floor hallway, and Capelli followed as she led the way to her apartment door.

"Ugh," she murmured, the corners of her mouth turning down at the sight of the black fingerprint powder generously smudged over both the doorframe and the surface of the door itself.

But Capelli had promised to help, and *fuck*, as crazy and irrational and unexplainable as it was, he wanted nothing more in this moment than to erase that frown from her face.

So he looked Shae in the eye and said, "We should probably make a quick check of the place first, just as an extra precaution. Then we can gather up the right supplies and come up with a plan to start cleaning. Sound good?"

The straightforward response seemed to ground her, the gamble he'd taken to tempt her go-go-go side into action thankfully paying off.

"Okay, sure." Sliding the key into the shiny new lock, Shae turned the deadbolt with a heavy click. A flick of the light switch next to the door revealed a whole lot of quiet (albeit messy) apartment, and after a quick look in her pantry, hall closet, and powder room, they moved down the corridor toward what had to be her bedroom.

Whoa. Capelli surveyed the clothing-strewn yet definitely

intruder-free space, poking his head into her closet and adjacent bathroom for the sake of being thorough. A small but unambiguous frown formed at the corners of Shae's mouth, so at odds with her usual happiness that *his* mouth was open before his neurons had even stopped firing to make it happen.

"You didn't say this guy trashed your bedroom." Capelli pointed at the piles of T-shirts and jeans and hoodies flung to the four corners of the room. It took some extra effort not to linger on the four—no, five—lacy, satiny bras that accompanied each pile, and he forced himself to meet her confused stare.

"Nobody trashed my bedroom. It always looks like..."

Wait for it...wait for it...

Bingo.

Shae's eyes lit with realization, her frown falling away. "Oh my God. Are you...did you just make a joke?"

He grinned, unable to contain it. "Too soon?"

"No." She began to laugh, not hard, but enough to loosen her shoulders from their rigid line around her neck. "Actually, your timing is perfect. Although I'd like to point out for the record that contrary to what it looks like, I do have a very detailed filing system in here. Smartass."

Capelli lifted a brow even though his grin refused to lose steam. "I'll take your word for it. You want to get started on cleaning this place up?"

"Yeah, come on."

Turning on her boot heels, Shae led the way back down the hall, pausing to put her laptop bag by the front door before heading into the nearby kitchen and gesturing to a low cabinet.

"I've got a bunch of cleaning stuff under the sink in here. Do we need anything special?"

He switched gears, rolling through the facts in front of

him to come up with the most effective process in his mind. "Well, fingerprint powder is dark and tends to make a bit of a mess because it's graphite-based, but lucky for us, it's fairly easy to remove from most surfaces."

With a quick glance, he took in the open floor plan of her living area, setting his laptop bag beside hers and taking off his jacket before kneeling down beside her to look at the collection of soaps and spray bottles.

"It looks like CSU only dusted a handful of places for prints," he continued. Given the content of both notes, the crime scene unit had likely spent the bulk of their time checking her apartment for hidden cameras. Not that Capelli wanted to come out with that. Shae was tough, but she clearly had limits.

Hooking a finger beneath a red and white spray bottle, he liberated it from the bunch beneath her sink, and yeah, it would almost certainly do the trick. "This all-purpose cleaner contains ammonia, so it should work really well on pretty much everything. We can test it out on the door and go from there."

One honey-colored brow raised. "Do I even want to know how *you* know what cleaning products will work best on fingerprint powder?"

Capelli would put the odds of a *yes* at conservatively six billion to one, but instead he went with the safer and simpler, "Probably not."

Grabbing the cleaner and the roll of paper towels sitting on the countertop, he moved back toward the front door. He marshaled the tasks in front of them—*brush off any loose fingerprint powder with a dry paper towel, soak the affected area with cleaner before scrubbing*—then handed over a few squares from the paper towel roll.

"So just remove whatever dry powder you can to make less mess, then spray, and wipe away the rest." Capelli demonstrated on the inside of the front doorframe, which came back blessedly clean with just one pass.

"Gotcha." Her forehead creased, and of course, she jumped right in on the other side, as determined as ever. "Sorry you're blowing your Friday night on Mr. Clean detail."

"I'm not."

The admission was more than he'd meant to loosen—which naturally meant that Shae caught every inch of it.

"Seriously? What is it that you do to unwind at the end of the day?"

Capelli sprayed. Scrubbed. "I work."

"That's some pretty serious dedication." Shae took the bottle from his hands, working on the other side of the doorframe. "How come you're not a cop if you love working for intelligence so much?"

"I..." His heart catapulted into his sternum at the unexpected question, but he covered up both the sensation and the topic with a slow inhale. "I guess I don't have the same sense of adventure as you. Plus, I prefer tech and surveillance."

"The job does seem to suit you," Shae agreed, her lips twitching into a small smile. "Anyway, you probably have like nine Ivy League degrees in IT, just begging to be put to good use."

Again, warning bells clanged in Capelli's head. Divulging personal information was something he avoided at all costs —the less he came out with, the less vulnerable he was to a person having any sort of leverage against him. But Shae hadn't hesitated to put her feelings smack in the middle of the spotlight by admitting she didn't want to be alone tonight, and anyway, she wasn't the volatile woman he'd originally taken her for. She was surprisingly, *painfully* decent. The odds were fairly low that telling her a few cherry-picked details about his personal life would end up coming back to bite him.

"Actually, I never went to college." The words slid out far more easily than Capelli had expected, even when Shae's lips parted in obvious surprise.

"*You* didn't go to college?"

"That shocks you," he said, reaching for the spray bottle.

She handed it over with a nod, turning to clean the section of the doorframe she'd sprayed down a few seconds before. "You're just ridiculously smart."

"Intelligence and higher education aren't mutually exclusive," Capelli pointed out. "You're smart too, and you never went to college."

"I tend to be the exception to most rules," she said, her self-deprecating smile sending a spark of heat through his belly and making him crack one of his own.

"Well, I guess we can be the exception to this one together."

They worked quietly for a few minutes, finishing with the front door and moving farther into her apartment before he continued. "My family didn't have a lot of money when I was growing up, and I was raised in a pretty rough part of the city. College was never really an option for me."

"Oh." The slight hitch of Shae's shoulders was the only sign that he'd gone for a double in the surprising-her department. "That must have been hard."

"Yeah," Capelli said, because Christ, it was accurate. Well, all except for the 'family' part. Of course the money was only a fraction of why a normal life had never been on the table for him, especially once his mother had figured out exactly where his talents lay. But since that was a set of sinkholes he needed to steer far, far clear of, he stuck to a different group of facts.

"I've always been good with numbers and technology. Most of the time, I knew more than my teachers. They had no idea what to do with me," he said. He still remembered the keen disappointment he'd felt when his eighth grade math teacher, Mr. Ackerman, had finally admitted that the advanced calculus course Capelli had aced as a thirteen year old was all the school system could offer. "But I still liked to learn, so I'd hit the public library a lot, and I got a secondhand computer from a consignment shop near there. I taught myself as much as I could."

Shae lowered the spray bottle to her coffee table with a *thunk*. "So everything you know about computers and surveillance systems and all that crazy high-tech stuff you do for intelligence is self-taught?"

"Pretty much." He hadn't really had a choice. Even then, his brain had buzzed with the need to be busy. "Whatever I couldn't find in books I grabbed off the library's free Internet. I didn't learn it all overnight, but…"

Capelli shrugged to cap off the sentence as well as to counteract the weirdness of his admission, but one look at Shae's fascinated expression told him he'd failed spectacularly.

"Come on, Capelli. I can't even program my DVR when the customer service guy walks me through the whole process step-by-step, and you just"—she waved a hand through the air—"taught yourself how to run all the information technology for the most elite police unit in the city. Including their security and surveillance."

"I guess, yeah. That's just how my brain works. And all you have to do to program your DVR is follow the directions in the manual." Capelli took the spray bottle, cleaning the last of the fingerprint powder off of her coffee table.

She snorted. "Have *you* ever tried reading the manual for a DVR? You know what, on second thought, forget I asked.

You probably wrote the manual in your spare time, didn't you?"

"Funny," he said, gathering the dirty paper towels to trade them in for clean ones. But Shae's exaggerated smirk actually did make it funny, and he let go of a laugh that felt so good, he wouldn't have pulled it back even if he'd been able to.

"Seriously. I bet you'd be great at that." She straightened the cushions and throw pillows on her couch, draping the blanket she'd been wrapped up in last night over the back of a nearby arm chair. "In fact, I think you might've missed your calling."

"Right." Capelli crossed the living room to toss the paper towels in the kitchen trash, giving his hands a fast rinse before rejoining Shae where she'd plopped down on the couch. "Because *'Press the MENU button on your remote, then select the DVR icon'* is so riveting."

Shae's continued sweet and sexy laughter prompted him through the next half-dozen directives that had been jammed in his elephant-sized memory ever since he'd first read them in his own DVR manual ages ago. But by the time he was done, she'd traded her laughter for that wide, bright green stare that always managed to level him.

"Okay, seriously. How the hell did you know all that, word for word?"

"I remembered it," he said, all honesty.

She blinked. "Did you just reprogram your DVR yesterday or something?"

"More like two years ago, when I replaced the old one." It had actually been two years, one month, and seventeen days. But saying *that* would definitely be weird.

Of course, Shae's curiosity wasn't about to let the topic slide. Her brows creased in thought, but only for a second before winging upward. "Wait...do you have a photographic memory?" she asked, and although his defenses flickered, the truth was hardly classified information.

"Eidetic. But most people use them interchangeably."

"What's the difference?"

"Not much," he said. It was accurate—people confused the two for good reason.

Not that the response took so much as a chip out of Shae's obvious interest. "Come on, Capelli." She shifted over the couch cushions to nudge his knee with her own, the contact sending a pull of attraction deep through his chest. "Don't make me Google it."

He huffed out a laugh, holding up his hands in mock surrender. "Okay, okay. Having an eidetic memory essentially means that I only need to see something once, maybe twice if it's particularly heady or high-volume, and I'll remember it in vivid detail."

Shae blinked, and Capelli had to admit, shocking her instead of the other way around *was* kind of a turn-on. "So you can pull up even the teensiest little specifics about every single thing you've ever seen?" she asked.

"Not quite. Occasionally something will get lost after a while." Granted, it was pretty freaking rare, but... "I mean, I can't remember everything I've ever had for lunch. I do remember things most people don't, though—especially particulars. But the memories come back more like a movie replay than actual photographs, and I can usually call them up pretty quickly if it's something I'm trying to remember."

"Oh my God, that must be so cool," she murmured.

Although his pulse tapped out a steady rhythm of *careful what you wish for*, he oddly didn't shy away from the truth. "Not as cool as it seems, I'm afraid. Some things stick out more vividly than others, and I don't always get to pick what my brain will cough up and when."

"Oh. *Oh*," Shae added, her ponytail snapping over one

shoulder as her chin lifted in understanding. "I'm sure you see a lot of stuff in intelligence that makes an eidetic memory kind of a curse. But you must have a bunch of good memories too, right?"

The stuff from intelligence—as grim as some of it had been—wasn't nearly what haunted him most, but since he wasn't about to voice that little nugget, Capelli said, "Of course."

She didn't even skip a beat as she leaned toward him and brazenly said, "Name some."

"Huh?"

His graceless answer paved the way for Shae's laugh, and Jesus, her expression was so simple and wide open and beautiful that he felt it in a whole lot of places he shouldn't.

"Name some," she repeated, gently this time. "Tell me some of the good things you remember."

A feeling he couldn't easily define thumped through his chest, warning him and daring him closer to her at the same time. "We still have a bunch of cleaning up to do," he said, but shit, the attempt to stall so he could gather his wits was weak at best.

As evidenced by the fact that Shae only budged from the navy blue couch cushions to move closer to *him*. "The rest of the cleaning can wait. Seriously, Capelli. Is it really going to offend your sensibilities that much to tell me a couple of happy things you remember?"

Well, hell. She kind of had a point. "Okay." He sorted through the compartments in his mind until a memory unfurled like an instant replay. "I remember that freak blizzard we had five winters ago. You know, the one where we got nearly a foot of snow in less than a day?"

"I remember that too," she said with a grin. "I was a rookie, and we got stuck on shift. It was before Dempsey moved from engine to squad, and he and Faurier and I had an epic snowball fight in front of the fire house. For the record, Faurier fights dirty."

Capelli nodded. The guy was cocky enough for that to make perfect sense. "We were all stranded at the precinct too. Moreno was still on patrol then, and Sinclair had just taken over the intelligence unit. We all took turns crashing on the couch in his office. Which is how we found out Maxwell talks in his sleep."

Shae choked out a sound he was pretty sure she'd intended to be a laugh. "He does not!"

"Hand to God," Capelli said, his own laughter leading him closer to her as naturally as two magnets gravitating toward one another out of sheer instinct. "I remember the day Moreno was promoted, too. At the time, intelligence was just me, Maxwell, and another detective, Mike La Rocca, who retired seventy-nine days after that."

Her brows traveled up at the precise mention, and he lifted his back in an unspoken *I told you so*. "See? I meant it when I said the details are exact. I even remember what you were wearing the first time I ever saw you."

"You...what?"

Capelli froze to the couch cushions. Damn it, he hadn't meant to pop off with anything about her, specifically. But Shae had asked for good memories, and somehow, unexplainably, this was one of his best.

"It was April nineteenth, three years ago. Almost four, now. You were at the foosball table in the Crooked Angel. Playing blue. Kicking Gamble's ass." That part of the re-telling earned him a small smile, and the rest of the memory broke free to spill right out of his mouth.

"You were wearing jeans with a hole in the left knee and a green V-neck T-shirt and a silver necklace. It had an anchor charm on it that sat right in the hollow between your collarbones." He remembered—with fierce, preposterous clarity—

the play of her muscles where her neck met her shoulder, the glint of that necklace against her impossibly creamy skin.

"Your hair was longer," he said, his heart kicking harder beneath his dark blue button down shirt. "Still in a ponytail. And when Isabella introduced us, you said—"

"James Capelli. Don't you look like trouble," Shae finished on a whisper.

Her eyes glittered in the lamplight around them, her gaze unyielding and yet somehow still soft. She'd angled her body toward his as he'd spoken, and fucking hell, Capelli wanted her. But not in the same hot, urgent way of last night. No, this new want seemed even more dangerous, because unlike last night, this time Capelli *knew* he wanted her. Knew what she'd taste like when he put his mouth on hers. Knew exactly how the pitch of her voice would tighten and rise into a lust-filled cry when he made her come.

Yet *just* like last night, he didn't hesitate to close the space between them.

CHAPTER 15

Although Shae never would have been able to dial up all the details of the night she'd first said it to Capelli, her instincts had been spot-freaking-on when she'd told him he looked like trouble. Of course, at the time, the accusation had been a flirty little joke about how seriously he'd extended his hand and given up a solemn "pleasure to meet you". But with the way he was kissing her right now, so hot and so deep and with just the right amount of wrong, Shae couldn't deny the truth.

James Capelli *was* trouble. The best, baddest kind.

And *God*, the unexpected discovery only made her want him all the more.

Sliding her hands into his hair, Shae tightened her fingers to hold him close. He met her move for move, cupping first her face, then the back of her neck in a borderline possessive grip. A shiver worked a path up her spine as Capelli swept his tongue over the seam of her mouth. But it was a demand for entry Shae wanted to give, and she parted her lips without thought. Her tongue darted out, tasting the firm curve of his bottom lip before gliding up to deepen the kiss.

He only let her take for a minute, though, and then he was pushing back, pressing inside her mouth with greedy strokes, turning the spot between her legs molten.

Shae broke from his lips, although truly, she had no idea how. "You sure about this?" she asked. She wanted him— badly enough that she felt the force of it in her blood, thumping against her eardrums with every rapid-fire heart-beat. But as much as she wanted to strip off every stitch of their clothing and do unspeakably wicked things with him right there on her couch, what she *didn't* want were regrets.

Capelli's gaze winged up. Widened over hers. Darkened with intensity that transformed her breath into a dim afterthought.

"I'm sure," he said.

"Thank you, baby Jesus," Shae murmured, her hands flying out to start unbuttoning his shirt.

But he captured her fingers in one nimble grab. "Not so fast."

Her heart jackhammered against her rib cage as she tried —and failed—to balance his answer with his actions. She must've broadcast her confusion though, because before she could say anything, Capelli used his hold on her hand to pull her close.

"Do you remember last night, when I said I wanted to find every single place that makes you scream?"

"Yes," she said against his mouth, more sigh than actual word.

"I hope your walls aren't thin, because I'm starting here"—he reached into the sliver of space between them to drag his thumb over her kiss-swollen bottom lip, applying just enough pressure to the sensitive skin at the heart of her mouth for her to open up and taste him, and oh God, oh *God*, she was going to fly apart before they even started—"and I'm taking my sweet fucking time with the rest of you."

For a second, Shae just sat there on the couch cushions, lost in the sheer, hypnotically dirty promise. Then her impulses fired back, and she drew his thumb past her lips in one swift, sinful move.

"Fine by me, Starsky, because when you're done, I'm taking you my way. Fast"—she pressed her chest against his in a rush—"Hard"—added a kiss to back up her claim—"And so goddamn hot I won't be the only one screaming."

They crashed together in a burst of punishing kisses and bad intentions. Digging her fingers into Capelli's shoulders, Shae blew past every pleasantry she could think of to seat herself directly in his lap. Every part of his body went rigid beneath hers save his hips, which lifted off the couch in one rough thrust. But then his arms were around her rib cage, her center of gravity changing faster than she could fight it, and within seconds, Capelli had pushed to standing with her wrapped firmly in his grasp.

"Bedroom," he said, the word coasting down her neck as he strung a trail of open-mouthed-kisses there.

"Yes. Go." She took full advantage of the opportunity to knot her legs around his waist a little tighter when he started to walk, the friction of her thong against her already aching clit tempting her to bite out a moan. "Oh God, that's good."

"That's nothing." Capelli's smile was dark and wildly sexy as he moved over the threshold of her room, setting her down carefully at the foot of her bed. "You really want to know what good feels like? Take off your clothes so I can show you."

Shae's breath caught in her throat. Her fingers itched to yank off her sweater and jeans and throw them to the floor—shit, she'd throw them into the next county just to be one step closer to naked with Capelli right now. But something about the glint in his stare made her pause instead.

"You want my clothes off? Start stripping too. I'm an equal opportunity girl, and I'm not in the mood to wait."

For a second, she thought he'd balk. God knew his expression implied as much. Then suddenly, surprisingly, Capelli reached down to undo all the buttons on his shirt and cast the thing aside.

"Whoa." Want spread out, low and hot between her hips at the sight of his broad, bare shoulders. The flat plane of his chest gave way to chiseled abs and a leanly muscled waist, a dusting of sandy blond hair leading from his navel to the top button of his jeans, and seriously, who knew he'd been hiding all that under the cover of plain old clothes?

"You're staring," he said, and in that moment, Shae was powerless to come out with anything other than the raw truth.

"Because you're fucking beautiful."

Capelli surprised her again with a laugh. "I'm pretty sure it's the other way around, but I'm damn sure I'd like to find out." He stepped toward her, close enough to touch even though he didn't, and her heart hammered even faster in her chest. "Prove me right, Shae. Take off your clothes and show me how beautiful *you* are."

She didn't hesitate. Curling her fingers around the hem of her sweater, she lifted the cotton over her head, barely letting the garment fall to the carpet before she kicked out of her boots and jeans.

"Holy…" His eyes raked over her peach-colored lace bra and thong. "Don't your co-workers find that distracting in the locker room?"

"Are you kidding?" She laughed. "I don't wear this stuff when I work. Even if I did, I doubt Gamble and Walker and Slater would notice."

"Good," Capelli bit out, reaching out to pull her close. "Let me notice."

Hooking both thumbs beneath the ribbons that served as her bra straps, he slid the satin and lace from her shoulders. A quick turn of one wrist freed her breasts completely, but Shae didn't shy away from letting him look at her in the soft, golden light spilling in from the hallway. Capelli didn't speak, simply took her in with a long, loaded stare that moved over her like a touch, and wetness bloomed in hot demand between her thighs. Framing her face with his hands, he captured her mouth in a kiss, pulling her tight against his hard, bare chest.

"*Ah.*" Shae exhaled, half sigh, half something else she couldn't begin to name. The kiss blew past sweetness and went straight for pure pleasure, with Capelli taking and teasing and tasting, until finally, he broke from her mouth. But he didn't move on to touch her in any of the places she expected him to. He bypassed her tightly beaded nipples and the hot, aching spot between her thighs, tracing a path down the shell of her ear with his tongue instead. The feather-light contact sent flutters of want through Shae's belly, her pussy clenching as he slid lower to kiss the hinge of her jaw, and she arched up to get more of his touch.

"Now we're getting somewhere," Capelli said, smiling that dark, wicked smile she'd had no idea he was capable of, but *God*, it turned her on. "Let me find you. Let me figure you out."

Returning his attention to her body, he did exactly as he'd promised to the night before. He explored her with his fingers and lips, learning all the unexpected places that made her want to beg him to fuck her. The hammering pulse point at the base of her neck. The outer curve of her breasts. The shockingly sensitive spot inside her elbow. Each touch heightened her arousal, turning her sex slick and her breath into moans, until finally, Shae was certain she'd splinter apart.

"Capelli, please." She pushed up to kiss him, not gently. Whether it was the plea or the need-soaked tone with which she'd uttered it, she couldn't be sure, but something made him pause.

"You want more," he said, wrapping his arms around her waist and thrusting his hips against hers. The press of his cock, hot and hard and so damned close to where she wanted it, made Shae reckless, and she thrust right back.

"I want *you*," she said. But before she could reach out and back up her words with any sort of action, Capelli dropped to his knees in front of her.

"You want me? You can have me. Right after I have you first."

He tugged her panties down in one fast yank. Sliding off his glasses, he looked up at her, and sweet Jesus, Shae had never wanted anyone so badly in her life.

Capelli didn't wait. Shifting forward, he ran his tongue over the seam of her sex, and Shae had no choice but to cry out.

But the sound only made him bolder. Parting his mouth wider over her folds, he kissed her more deeply, stroking his way inside. Pleasure shot through her, powerful enough to make her bend at the waist, yet still, he didn't relent. Capelli licked and sucked, finding every last sweet spot hidden between her legs. Shae tilted her hips, greedy for more—for everything—and with punishing thrusts of his tongue, he gave it over and over.

"Oh my...*God*."

Shae's head dropped back as her hands lowered to make fists in Capelli's hair. His tongue slid up, turning firm circles over her clit and sending sparks across her field of vision. She gave in on a moan, gripping him close as he worked her core harder and faster with his mouth. Each movement coiled the tension in her belly tighter, bringing her closer and closer to release. Somewhere in the fog of her conscious-ness, Shae recognized the tiny desire to hold back, to wait until he was inside her before crashing over the edge. But the edge was right there, and Capelli seemed intent on pushing her over, and suddenly, the tension in her body was too big and too bright to ignore.

"I...I want..."

He read her without question, even though she knew she made no sense. With one final sweep of his tongue, he destroyed the last of Shae's resolve, and she started to tremble and shudder in waves.

"That's it. Right there," he grated, the vibration of his whisper against her hypersensitive clit twisting her need to come even tighter. "Let go, sweetheart. Scream for me."

God help her, Shae did. Her orgasm smashed over her in waves, and Capelli rode out every one with his mouth, his fingers, his words. Just when she was certain her legs would give out, there were his arms, folding tightly around her to guide her to the rumpled bedsheets behind them.

"Jesus, Shae. You really are beautiful."

The words made something snap deep inside of her, and she turned to kiss him, hard and fast.

"And you're overdressed. Now are you going to sit there, or are you going to let me do something about that?"

As if a pendulum swung to swap out their positions, Capelli gave up the lead. Shae made fast work of the rest of his clothes, until nothing stood between them but his boxer shorts and a whole lot of unfettered want. Reaching between their bodies, she palmed his cock over the cotton, and he bit out a curse as he rocked into her touch.

"There," she said, wicked satisfaction curling low in her belly, reigniting the desire he'd just fulfilled. Shae slid his boxers from his hips, his cock springing free from the last barrier between them, and her heart pounded faster at the sight of him. A muscle pulled tight over the line of Capelli's jaw, and in that second, Shae realized how hard he'd been fighting for his composure.

And just how badly she wanted to wreck it.

"You had me first." She moved over the bed, turning to the side as she trailed a line of kisses down his chest, the sculpted plane of his abs. His cock jerked when she reached the scattering of hair leading down from his navel, and she reached down to stroke him in one long, slow glide. "Now I'm having you."

"Shae—"

She slipped her mouth over his cock, and whatever else Capelli meant to say was replaced by a harsh exhale. A heady thrill raced through Shae's veins at the sound, daring her to dare *him*. She ran her tongue over his length from root to tip, pausing for only a breath before she took him into her mouth as far as she could. He arched off the bed, chasing her touch as she retreated, and she repeated the movement just to see him do it again. Splaying one palm over the sheets next to Capelli's hip, Shae pressed up to her hands and knees beside him, finding a steady rhythm of lift and lower with her mouth. Then suddenly, without warning, his fingers were between her legs, pushing inside of her with ease.

"*Oh*," Shae cried out, her inner muscles squeezing at the unexpected pressure. She wanted to stay where she was, to not be distracted from giving him the exact same pleasure he'd given her. But Capelli touched her with sure, perfect strokes, and when his thumb moved up to graze her clit, her impulses gave in to the now-right-now demand flying down from her brain. Sparing only a second to grab a condom from the drawer of her bedside table, Shae straddled his hips, rolling the protection into place before angling his cock over her slippery entrance and lowering herself over him in one hard push.

A sound flew past her lips, somewhere between a sigh and a swear word. For a second, she couldn't breathe, couldn't think, could only feel the undiluted pleasure flooding her senses at the feel of his cock filling her so completely. Then she shifted, and even though the move was only a slight lift and lower, Capelli went bowstring tight beneath her.

"Shae," he grated, a moan leaving his chest. "Jesus, you're so tight."

"You're not going to break me," she said, proving it by rocking her hips against his until there was no space at all between them.

His eyes met hers, locking into place. "I know. But if you keep that up, you just might break me."

Just like that, Shae was done hesitating. She hinged forward and began to move faster, and Capelli reached down low to wrap his hands around the flare of her hips. He guided her motions, his fingers grasping with firm intention to lift her up and down on his cock. The feel of him, buried inside her so hot and so hard, sent bursts of pleasure deep into her center.

Led by nothing but reckless desire, she began to thrust with more speed. But the faster she moved, the more Capelli stayed right there with her, holding her close as Shae took everything she wanted. Release built in her belly, fast and dark like storm clouds, until her body thrummed with the undeniable need to come. Capelli thrust upward, finding some undiscovered spot deep in her pussy that stole the breath right out of her lungs, and she unraveled with a keening cry. The more her body loosened, the tighter his grew, and Shae fluttered her eyes open to pin him with a stare.

"You don't have to hold back, Capelli. If you want it"—she

rolled her hips even though they were already fully joined —"lose control and take it."

He'd gripped her waist and swung her beneath him before she could fully register the movement. Hooking his hands under her knees, Capelli spread her thighs wide, filling her over and over in relentless thrusts. Shae moaned her approval, wanting each stroke more than the last, opening up to let each one bring him closer to losing control. But despite the intensity etched on his face and the power of his movements, he still somehow held back, and she looked up at him through the shadows.

"Let go, Capelli. Take what *you* need."

The tension in his touch shifted, his stare turning dark and fierce. He filled her faster, harder, until finally, on a long, pulsing thrust—*yes, God, yes, yes*—he came with a guttural shout.

With her heart still slamming in her chest, Shae slid back to her awareness slowly, like emerging from a fog. Capelli pressed against her, their bodies loose and warm and thoroughly tangled, their chests rising and falling in rapid rhythm. After some amount of time she couldn't begin to measure, he pushed up from the bed, moving down the hallway for a brief minute before returning to lie down beside her.

Shae knew the moment had the potential to get awkward —yes, they'd just had scorching hot sex, but not even that could change the fact that they were sitting here together in the near-dark of her bedroom, wearing nothing but a cotton bedsheet. But just because she and Capelli had lost their clothes together didn't mean their minds had to follow, so she propped herself up on one elbow and looked at him.

"I didn't feed you," she said, and after a beat, Capelli's laughter rumbled through her shadowy bedroom.

"A little random, but no. I don't suppose you did."

"I *did* promise." Shae bit her lip, trying on her very best remorseful expression. "I wouldn't feel right if I didn't deliver."

Capelli turned to his side, bringing them face-to-face. He didn't say anything, simply studying her for a second, then another, until finally, he broke into a smile.

"Given your culinary habits, I'm assuming you mean deliver literally," he said, and Shae's laugh flew out, unchecked.

"Hell yes, Starsky. I hope you're hungry, because I can order Chinese food like nobody's business."

CHAPTER 16

"Well, smack my ass and call me Sally."

Vaughn stood in his just-hidden-enough-to-go-unnoticed spot across the street from the firefighter chick's apartment building, watching her bedroom light go out with a disbelieving grin. It was well after midnight, and James's car still sat right in the side lot where the asshole had parked it five hours ago. Which could only mean one thing.

Someone had a liability, and it sure as shit wasn't Vaughn.

Truly, he hadn't thought his old buddy had it in him. Not that James had been a saint in the screwing-people department back in the day—or in any other department for that matter, because hey, a leopard couldn't change its spots no matter how badly it wanted to be a plain old house cat. But James knew better than anyone else how dangerous it could be to invest emotions in another person. His strung out, jacked up Mommy Dearest was case in point. Honestly, after the train wreck that had gone down eight years ago, the guy had to be an idiot to even consider emotions of any fucking variety, even the kind motivated by his dick.

Ah well. If James was going to be dumb enough to put a

queen on the board, no way was Vaughn not going to take it, if for no other reason than because he could.

"First things first," he murmured. He'd deal with James and his little screw toy and the rest of the intelligence unit when the time came. For now, he needed to get the rest of the pieces where he wanted them.

Slipping a burner cell from the front pocket of his hoodie, Vaughn dialed a number without looking. The phone on the other end rang once, twice, and Christ, what a fucking cliché. The third time was the charm.

"Kinsey," came the clipped voice over the line, but Vaughn wasn't fooled. The mayor's senior aide couldn't hide the traces of sleep in his tone from him the way he could from all the other yes-men and knuckle draggers.

"It's been a while, Kinsey. How are things on the primrose path?"

"Who is this?"

It was the split-second pause just before Jack Kinsey delivered the question that gave him away. He was buying time. Trying to figure out what Vaughn might want. How he'd deal with him. But not even an ice age would get the guy out of what Vaughn was about to throw in the mayor's lap.

"Clearly, it's been too long if you think I'm going to fall for that," Vaughn said, his voice as quiet and as dark as the chilly night around him. "You know exactly who this is. Or have you forgotten all of the services I've provided for you and ol' Brad in the past?"

This time, the silence on the line was all frost, and yeah, now they were getting somewhere.

"I'll assume this line is secure," Kinsey finally said, prompting Vaughn to laugh.

"Please. I've laundered millions of dollars in stolen campaign funds and bribe money for the mayor of our fine city over the last six years. You don't honestly think I can't safeguard one little phone line."

Kinsey exhaled his disgruntlement, presumably at the sound of the words having been spoken so clearly over the line. God, government officials were *so* uptight. Of course, Vaughn had known the out-loud mention would ruffle the mayor's senior aide. What was the point of having leverage if you didn't fucking use it?

Something Kinsey clearly recognized, because he said, "What is it I can do for you, Shadow, since I'm certain this isn't a social call."

Time for more expertly applied pressure. "What, you don't think I could be the mayor's fourth when he plays the back nine with Alderman Thompson and the CEO of Bushman and Park on Wednesday?" Vaughn asked.

Of course, he'd rather be dragged over a field of razor wire and broken glass than endure so much as a second's worth of that rich-person bullshit, but hey. Kinsey's grunt of surprise that Vaughn had clearly hacked into the mayor's private online planner was worth the asking. "Relax, Kinsey. Unlike your boss, I'm not interested in rubbing elbows with local figureheads or slick-ass real estate developers. You and I have bigger things to discuss."

Kinsey waited a beat before answering, probably in an effort to try and make Vaughn think he was bored. Reading people in order to get what he wanted on the mayor's behalf had always been Kinsey's primary job, no matter what his business cards claimed. Under other circumstances, Vaughn would consider being offended that Kinsey thought those preschool mind games would work on him. But since he had the upper hand—and was about to wield it like a fucking broadsword—he'd play along for another minute or two.

"You're paid in full at the end of every month for services rendered," Kinsey reminded him. "There's been no change to the mayor's needs for those services. What could we possibly have to discuss?"

"The mayor's needs may not have changed, but mine have."

Vaughn eyed the empty, well-shadowed street around him before slipping farther into the alcove of the corner market across from Shae McCullough's apartment building. The market had long since been deserted for the night, along with every other business on the block and the street around him besides, but still. There was no such thing as too careful.

"I'm listening," Kinsey said, and Vaughn smiled into the darkness.

"Good, because I'm not going to repeat myself. I want a million dollars transferred to an offshore account in the Seychelles by five PM on Friday."

"You must be joking."

Vaughn's smile morphed into a laugh that was all menace. "I never joke about money."

"And what is it exactly that you'll be providing for this million dollars?" he asked.

Jesus, for the right-hand man of the city's most powerful official, Kinsey could be *so* goddamn thick. But Vaughn was already getting tired of this conversation, so he cut to the chase.

"Security, of course. Here's the bottom line. I know all sorts of things about Bradley Aldrich III that I'm sure would be of extreme interest to his adoring constituents, not to mention the RPD. If he wants that information to remain secure, he'll pay me the million to keep it that way. You and I both know I've got enough dirt for the D.A. to indict him— and, oh by the way, you, too—on over three dozen counts of felony corruption."

Vaughn's heart pumped faster as he let the not-so-veiled threat sink in for a minute. Metering his voice to its softest, most insidious setting, he let his words slip into the phone, but no farther. "Fraud, money laundering, bribery, conspiracy. The mayor's been a very greedy man. Now it's time for him to share the wealth."

"So this is nothing more than common extortion? Hell, Shadow. All things considered, I'd have thought you'd be more creative than that."

Kinsey's tone was loaded with enough disdain to be thoroughly condescending, and Vaughn pushed off the bricks in the alcove in a move both swift and lethal.

"There's nothing *common* about it," he bit out, anger slithering up his spine. "I provide the mayor with services that no one else is smart enough to even dream of, and his top-one-percent, seven-million-dollar-estate-building ass is going to give me what I'm due. Need I remind you that you came to *me*, Kinsey? You sought *me* out to manage the mayor's private financial projects. And you still need me. I've been laundering Aldrich's dirty money for six fucking years. I can make prison orange his new color before the sun comes up if the spirit moves me."

"You get a cut of those proceeds," Kinsey reminded him, but Vaughn wasn't about to have his focus diverted. He'd already set too many fires. He wasn't going to be able to stay under the radar much longer, and he needed this money. Fuck, he *deserved* it. Without him, Aldrich would have been indicted years ago.

"Now I want more. Greed isn't so pretty when you're not the one wearing it, now is it, Jack?"

"A million is too much to move by Friday." Kinsey's voice had gone quiet, but the words were still an argument.

Frustration snapped, low and hot in Vaughn's belly. This shit was getting downright insulting. For Chrissake, how dumb did the man think he was? "Not if you do it right. Which I'm certain you can, because I showed you how."

"And if the mayor decides he's not willing to cooperate?"

"Then I'll burn old Brad all the way to the ground. Oh, and proof of every single bribe I've ever covered up for him will end up on the desk of the chief of police."

Kinsey made a sound that probably meant to be a laugh, but it was just a shade too nervous to pass. "You have no proof of anything. All the mayor's financial records are clean."

"Not the ones I have copies of," Vaughn said. Smartly, Kinsey didn't point out that their verbal contract for services rendered (seriously, for a herd of dolts, rich people were so fucking fancy) had been expressly dependent on no records being kept. Like there had been a snowball's chance Vaughn had ever planned to honor *that* bullshit.

"Anything you'd disclose to the police would implicate you, too," Kinsey pushed. "I know you. You're not about to risk going to jail. You'd rather take a bullet than be put in a cage."

Vaughn's pulse tripped in surprise. O-kay, time to kill this conversation, along with any hope Kinsey had of getting out of this situation without giving him what he needed.

"I can feel you thinking, Kinsey. Do yourself a favor and don't. Otherwise I'll be tempted to throw in all the video of Brad with those women who are so not the missus. The one with the redhead in the hot tub might be my favorite. Then again, I have a lot of honeys to choose from."

"There...there's no way you could access those," Kinsey sputtered, and Jesus, finally the jackass had tipped his hand. "They're completely private. You're bluffing."

Vaughn spent every ounce of the air in his lungs laughing into the empty darkness around him before he answered. "It is so *cute* that you think privacy is a thing. Friday. 5 P.M. I'll text you the account number at 4:55. And, Kinsey?"

He waited for just a breath, his pulse pounding faster and

his dick getting hard from the sheer arousal of twisting the knife the rest of the way into place.

"Don't bother trying to find me, catch me, or stop me. No one ever has, and no one ever will."

～

CAPELLI RUBBED the last of the sleep from his eyes, taking a long, hard look in Shae's pantry before shaking his head in defeat. "Seriously. I can't believe you live like this," he said, unable to keep a smile from creeping over his face as she came up beside him with a giant mug of coffee in one hand and both brows raised.

"Live like what?" she asked, and Christ, that sassy little grin of hers ought to be classified as a weapon for how quickly it rendered him fucking useless.

"Like you're running a fraternity house. Is any of this stuff even edible?"

Shae laughed, the loose neckline of her dark green sleep shirt falling away from one shoulder as she pressed to her toes to give the contents of her pantry a closer perusal. The sight of her bare skin made his dick twitch behind the fly of his jeans. Capelli pondered, not briefly, skipping breakfast and taking her back to her bedroom. Pulling the cotton from her body to map out the constellations of freckles on her smooth, creamy skin. Tasting each one slowly, learning and re-learning the most sensitive parts of her body until she shook with desire. Need. Release.

Right. Because what Capelli needed was to be *more* distracted.

"Don't be such a food snob," Shae said, delivering him back to the real-time of her sun-filled kitchen. "There's plenty to eat in here. Box-o'-noodles, canned chili, and— oooh! My favorite!" She whipped a yellow and blue can from the shelf in front of her with an exaggerated waggle of her brows. "Squeezy cheese!"

He bit back his laughter, but the move took all of his restraint. "I draw the line at cooking you breakfast with any ingredients that can be described using the word 'squeezy'. I told you, I have standards." He sent up a prayer that her refrigerator would give him more to work with than her pantry, and ah! Bulls-eye.

"Now we're talking," he said, pulling a carton of eggs from the top shelf of the fridge and holding them up in victory.

"Fine. Go the boring route," she teased.

"This isn't boring. It's classic." Capelli moved around her to put the eggs on the counter, mentally shuffling through a couple of potential recipes. "How do you like your eggs?"

"In a cake." Shae's laughter nixed any chance she had of nailing the joke, though, and she held up her free hand in concession. "Okay, okay. You don't have to make the serious face. I'm not a total breakfast heathen. How about scrambled?"

"Scrambled works."

A minute of comfortable quiet passed, during which Shae unearthed a bowl and a frying pan from one of the cupboards by the stove and Capelli took the milk out of the fridge. He lined up the necessary steps in his mind—*crack six eggs into the bowl, add one tablespoon of milk per egg to keep them tender when cooking, whisk thoroughly and then add*—

"So. You stayed last night."

Shae leaned against the counter, taking a draw from the mug in her hand like nothing doing. Meanwhile, Capelli's chin whipped up in total, heart-rattling shock.

"I, uh. Did," he finished lamely.

After their insanely hot, somewhat impulsive trip to her bedroom, he'd expected things to get a little awkward—when he'd come here last night, he hadn't even planned on kissing her, much less having mind-blowing sex with her. So coming up with something smooth when he'd gone back into her room after they'd done just that? Yeah, not exactly in his wheelhouse. Plus, even though it had been pretty far from his mind when he'd stripped off all her clothes, they *were* still working together on a case. The odds that they'd escape without any sort of weirdness had been astronomically high.

Except…that's exactly what had happened. Shae had simply thrown on that grin he was fast becoming addicted to, and the next thing he'd known, they were finishing their cleanup job and eating Chinese food and tumbling back into her bed for round two of crazy-good sex. Falling asleep next to her had felt like the most normal thing in the universe, even though nothing about him had ever been normal, predictable, or good in his entire twenty-eight years.

A thought trickled into Capelli's brain, pushing his heart into a hard thump against his sternum. "Did you not want me to stay?"

"Of course I wanted you to stay," Shae said, her smile wide-open and strangely sweet, and hell if his heart didn't thump even harder at the sight of it. "If I hadn't, I'd have kicked you out. Look"—she slid her coffee mug to the counter, stepping in front of him on the floorboards without invading his space—"I'm not really a hold-back kind of girl, so I'm just going to be blunt. I had a great time with you. I'm not saying I want to run out and get matching tattoos or anything, but it seems kind of stupid for us not to keep having a great time together just because we're working on this case."

"It's not technically a conflict of interest," he said slowly. There weren't any rules against them spending time together outside of work. Hell, after this week, they wouldn't be working together at all.

"It's not," she agreed. "And more importantly, I think

we're both far too determined to let anything, even sex, stand in the way of us finding this killer."

Ah, she definitely had a point there. "That's also true."

Shae tipped her chin at the eggs on the counter, giving up a little bit of a shrug and a whole lot of a sexy smile. "So what do you say we start with breakfast and see how things shake out from there?"

Capelli paused. He didn't do relationships, even casual ones like this, and for damn good reasons. Logically, he knew he should be cautious, on guard, defenses up.

The trouble was, he didn't *want* to be any of those things. As crazy and impulsive as it felt, what he wanted was Shae.

So he closed the space between them to kiss her.

"I say starting with breakfast sounds great."

Ten minutes, four pieces of toast, and a batch of scrambled eggs later, they were sitting at her kitchen table, forks in hand. "This smells fantastic," she said, gesturing to the pile of fluffy yellow eggs on her plate. "Even better than Pop-Tarts."

He laughed, startled at not only how easily the sound came, but how unassumingly good it felt falling from his lips. "Thank you, I think."

Shae took a bite, her little sigh of approval making eggs Capelli's new favorite food. "So does everyone call you Capelli?" she asked, and even though the question took him by surprise, he shook his head and answered as he always did: with the facts.

"Yeah. I mean, I've never really gone by anything else at the precinct. But to be fair, Sinclair introduced me that way on Day One, all the way back when he was still a detective and I'd been assigned to the equipment room to fix busted surveillance equipment and rebuild ancient desktop computers for the clerks and desk sergeants."

He counted his heartbeats in an effort to keep his pulse slow and steady, the way he'd trained himself to do any time the memory of that day became a slideshow in his mind. *Facts. Stick to the facts.* "Anyway, Capelli *is* my name."

"It's your last name," Shae clarified. "But your first name is James."

His spine stiffened against the ladder back of his chair, even though—like all the others—this was a fact, too. "Mmm hmm."

Most people took the expertly placed hint and changed the subject when he clammed up about his personal life. But there was nothing "most people" about Shae, so of course she just tilted her head and leveled her bold green stare right at him.

"Not to put too fine a point on it, but we did just kind of have wild monkey sex for half the night. I'm thinking a first name basis isn't entirely out of line here."

Capelli laughed, breaking the tension that had filled the space between them. "Fair enough," he said, because, really, she wasn't wrong. "It's just that my mother used to call me James, so no. I don't really go by that anymore."

"Ah." Now *that*, she seemed to know better than to push. Thank fuck. "Well, then. Capelli it is."

He nodded in a weird sort of gratitude. He'd never known the man whose surname he shared. Probably, his mother hadn't either. But it was better than hearing his first name over and over again in his memory in his mother's raspy, two-packs-a-day voice.

James, honey, go over to Coleman Avenue and run the stranded-kid con so we can pay rent and get the damn super off our backs. James! I need you to figure out a way to get past the password protection on these accounts. Me and Bruno wanna go to the casino this weekend. We're going to make a fortune! James, I know this thing at the bank is kind of a big job, but just think of the payday. Plus, we're not going to get caught. I'm your mother. Would I ever let anything happen to you?

"So." Capelli took a breath, and by the time he'd finished his exhale, his composure was locked back into place. "Is Shae short for anything?"

"Yep." She took a bite of eggs without elaborating, and after a handful of seconds, his curiosity burned a path right out of his mouth.

"If you don't tell me what it's short for, I'll be forced to start guessing," he said, straightening his glasses in an effort to look as scholarly as possible. "And with my memory, we could be here for a really long time."

Rather than concede, though, Shae gave up a shockingly angelic smile, and who the hell knew she had *that* in her arsenal? "Oh, you won't get it in a million years. Unless you're hiding a very weird, highly Irish side somewhere in there."

"Shae, I'm not even wearing a shirt," he pointed out. "But if you want me to start pulling ethnically specific names out of thin air, I guess I can take it from the top of the alphabet and—"

"Oh my God, fine!" Her laugh echoed through the sun-brightened space between them, and Christ, even in that wrinkled sleep shirt with her tangled hair in a sloppy knot on top of her head, she was beautiful. "But you have to swear you won't tell anyone at Seventeen."

"Damn. Is it that bad?" he asked.

"Not terribly." She lifted a shoulder in a haphazard shrug. "I mean, I'm not named after a vegetable or one of the Seven Wonders of the World or anything. But you don't get to pick your nickname in a fire house, and the last thing I need is to end up with one I've got to live down."

"Tell me about it." At her *oh really* expression, Capelli added, "Maxwell calls me Encyclopedia Brown."

Shae took a long sip of coffee, but he suspected it was more to hide her smile than for the purposes of properly caffeinating. "So you understand where I'm coming from.

Anyway"—she sat back in her chair, popping a bite of toast into her mouth before continuing—"in a very adamant nod to our ancestry, my parents decided to go all-in when it came to naming all three of their children. We each got 'S' names. My sisters are Siobhan and Sinead, which honestly, is bad enough. But being the baby, I got the prizewinner. Most people don't know how to pronounce it, let alone spell it."

Saoirse, Sheenagh, Sibeal, Sile…dammit, his curiosity was going to give him a brain cramp. "Try me," he finally said.

"Okay, smartass." She folded her arms over her chest. "My full first name is Seighin."

After a lightning-fast burst of *whoa*, Capelli's brain pounced on the lilt of the Irish accent she'd put to the syllables, the way she'd pronounced them "shay-eeeen", and a few seconds later, he pointed his fork at her with a smile.

"First of all, you didn't tell me it's normally a boy's name."

Shae's lips fell open on a gasp, but oh no. He wasn't losing steam now. "I'll let you slide on that one, though, since I'm going to spell it correctly. Speaking of which, I've got two options there, although I'm sure you know that, too."

Now her jaw dropped in full, which only pushed his satisfaction into deeper, darker territory. "It could be either S-e-i-g-h-i-n or S-e-i-g-i-n-e, but since your family seems pretty diehard Irish, I'm going to guess the former."

"Impressive," she said after a few beats of silence, her smile marking the compliment as genuine. "My parents are first generation Americans, so their values are still pretty old world. They believe names have power, that a person lives up to his or her moniker, blah blah. Mine means—"

"Little hawk," Capelli murmured, his eyes not budging from her stare across the table. "It suits you." An odd pang shot through his gut, and he shook his head to try and bring himself back to normal. "And for the record, I'm with your parents."

"They gave me a very weird, very Irish boy's name." She frowned, although the expression carried more humor than actual heat. "You're not seriously siding with them, are you?"

"I'm afraid I am. Names do have power. And by the way, yours might be unusual and untraditional, but it really is perfect for you."

Shae let go of a small laugh. "If you say so."

She turned back to her breakfast, beginning to eat in earnest. Capelli took a few bites of his eggs even though his appetite had taken an abrupt hike. He knew all too well how names could define people. Not just because he secretly hated his given name and the fact that it tied him to his mother in a way he'd never, ever lose.

But because he'd always be trying to escape from another name that haunted him at night, on the weekends, any time he was idle. A name that was part of him. A name that defined him no matter how hard he worked at the RPD and no matter how busy he kept his mind.

The Wraith.

The thought had come out of nowhere. But now that it had appeared, the memory that accompanied it unfurled in his mind's eye as if it had happened yesterday rather than nearly a decade ago. The shitty apartment with the rotting floorboards under the kitchen sink. The half-empty bags of stale, roach-infested chips that were meant to serve as his dinner. The stink of vomit and other, worse things he hadn't wanted to contemplate coming from the bedroom down the hall.

Damn, James! Don't be so uptight. We might not be living in a palace, but don't you see how much better we are than all those dumbasses putting in fifty hours a week at their stupid, mindless jobs? We'll never have to work for a fucking thing because we're smart enough to take anything we want, any way we want and never get caught. The world is different for people like us. We're cold and ruthless, like shadows and wraiths...

The voice—not his mother's, but one just as gut twisting —flew through Capelli's brain, leaving a chill on his skin in its wake. Memories of Conrad Vaughn, a.k.a. the Shadow, coughed themselves up from time to time, even though Capelli avoided them like the most viral strain of the plague.

And for good goddamn reason, because the guy was just as dangerous and every bit as lethal.

Vaughn had—unsurprisingly—kept a low profile after Capelli had begun working for the RPD. Still, Capelli would hear rumblings about the Shadow on occasion, jobs the guy had allegedly done and people he'd allegedly scammed. Most of those rumors had been credit where it was due—Capelli would know the Shadow's online quirks and signatures anywhere, and anyway, Vaughn had never been shy about his arrogant pride in his work. He'd also never been caught, although intelligence had gotten damn close three months ago when the Shadow had surfaced in the DuPree investigation.

The DuPree investigation. Forced prostitution. Sex parties. Two victims left to die in a flophouse fire in North Point. The strategically planned attack on Kellan, the raid that had brought the lunatic down...

The only person who had escaped that night.

Capelli's breath jammed in his lungs. The images in his head crashed into a different scalpel-sharp memory, this one of the scene of the meth lab fire he and Shae were currently investigating. The differences between both cases fell away, leaving the similarities to line up with astonishing clarity, one by one. Using arson to cover up murder. The sufentanil in both Kellan and the Scarlet Reapers' systems. The meticulous planning in both sets of crimes, the signature scrawled deeply but definitely beneath the surface of their current arsons, and all at once, the pieces clicked firmly and irrefutably into place.

"Holy shit." Capelli's fork clattered to the floor, his heart ricocheting through his rib cage like a freight train, and Christ, how had he not *seen* this before?

"Capelli? What is it? What's the matter?" Shae asked, her eyes wide and brimming with concern.

But his brain was spinning too fast, calculating too hard to form words. Pushing up from the table, he lasered a path to the front door, roughly grabbing his laptop bag with one hand while yanking the machine free with the other. Not even bothering with pleasantries like breathing or a chair, he sat in his spot, his lungs feeling like boulders and his fingers flying over the keys fast enough to ache.

"Come on. Come on." He whipped through the case file, his synapses firing like a Fourth of July finale. "I know you're in here somewhere, you cagey bastard. You never could resist. Just give me the proof."

"Okay, seriously. What is going *on?*" Shae's voice registered dimly from beside him. In a faraway part of his mind, Capelli realized she must have moved to sit next to him on the floor, but the rest of his thoughts—his pulse, his adrenal gland—were all pumping far too quickly for him to focus on anything other than his search.

Don't you see how much better we are...we're smart enough to take everything we want, any way we want and never get caught...

Realization smashed into him like a four-ton boulder. "The surveillance video."

Of course. Christ, it was just Vaughn's style. Smug son of a bitch.

Pulling up the security footage from the night of the break-in, Capelli clicked to the section of video Shae had reviewed. She'd never seen Vaughn in her life, so of course she wouldn't have recognized him. The guy made such a habit out of hiding in plain sight and blending into the shadows that most people never even *saw* him.

Not even when it was too late.

"The surveillance video? What about it?" Shae asked, and finally—*finally*—his mouth and his brain decided to take the teamwork path.

"When you reviewed the surveillance footage of your building's front door, you said it was all residents with key cards. Except for the floral delivery guy."

"Right. He was from one of those huge online florists who freelance their delivery people," Shae said. "But the manager confirmed the order as legit. I spoke with him right before lunch today, remember?"

Under different circumstances, Capelli would've laughed at the irony of her question. "I do. But the order wasn't legit."

"You think the manager lied to us?" she gasped.

"No. But I do think he was conned."

"By who?"

Anticipation made Capelli's heart kick faster in his chest as he fast-forwarded through the video feed. The proof had to be here. There were too many other similarities for this to be mere coincidence, and Vaughn would never pass up a chance to show the world just how smart he was—

There.

All the breath funneled out of Capelli's lungs in a sharp, hot burst at the image of Conrad Vaughn, carrying a giant vase of roses and all but smiling for the damned surveillance camera. Conrad Vaughn, who had broken into Shae's apartment while she showered.

Conrad Vaughn, who had killed two people, set two fires, and was almost certainly just warming up.

"I need to call Sinclair," he said, turning to look at Shae with one hundred percent certainty and just as much dread as he added, "I know who our killer is."

CHAPTER 17

Capelli sat at his desk in the intelligence office, his thoughts reeling and his heart still stuck in his windpipe. But now that the team was here, having been called into place as soon as he and Sinclair had come out of the sergeant's office less than an hour ago, Capelli had to gather his wits.

Conrad Vaughn was their killer. The evidence was there, albeit insanely well-hidden. The logic followed.

And Capelli had to focus on the facts of this case, to buckle down and sew up his emotions and catch Vaughn before the guy killed anyone else. Before anyone other than Sinclair found out exactly how connected he and Vaughn had once been. Before the team in intelligence discovered he was actually a fraud.

Before Shae, with her shrewd, sexy stare and her all-in attitude, found out that his work ethic was really just a survival skill, and that he couldn't even be a decent human being even on a dare.

"Okay, everybody. Listen up, because we've got a lot of

ground to cover. There's been a break in the Lawrence/Denton case."

Sinclair's voice cut through the office even though the room had been mostly quiet to begin with. Surprising, considering Shae and all four detectives on the team were gathered together in the work space. Then again, they had to know they weren't here for social hour. Sinclair never rallied everyone on a Saturday for anything less than a balls-out emergency.

Which was probably why he ditched the pleasantries in favor of the jugular. "Our primary suspect is Conrad Vaughn, a.k.a. the Shadow."

"The hacker from the DuPree case?" Isabella asked, clearly in shock, but Sinclair didn't hesitate.

"Affirmative. Capelli's the one who came up with the intel, so I'll let him get you all up to speed. Then we'll go from there."

The sergeant sent an ice-blue glance in his direction, lifting his chin in the briefest go-ahead. Scraping for a deep breath, Capelli took the first fact off the top of his mental pile and dove right in.

"On the surface, the DuPree case and our murders seem to have very little in common. Plus, DuPree is obviously dead, so even when the sufentanil turned up in our vics' systems, logic didn't dictate that the two cases were related."

Adrenaline combined with an odd twinge of emotion in his veins at the memory that had triggered his realization to the contrary. Both threatened to make his hands shake, so he busied them by firing up the crime scene board from the keyboard on his desk. *Facts. Evidence. Focus.*

"But now you obviously think they are," Moreno said, her surprise giving way to the slightest hint of unease. Damn it, as tough as she was, the DuPree case had still been hard as hell on her, for no less than a dozen reasons both physical and emotional. But she was one of the best cops Capelli had ever seen, so he answered her with the straight-up truth.

"Yes. I think Conrad Vaughn is using arson to cover up deeper crimes like murder, the same exact way Julian DuPree did when he killed Angel Velasquez and Danny Marcus. I also think he left those threatening notes for Shae."

Maxwell's dark eyes went hard and narrow from the spot where he sat behind his desk. "And you think that why, exactly?"

"Because Vaughn is the only person with detailed knowledge of DuPree's crimes who isn't dead or in jail, the M.O.s for the murders are a match, and we have him on the surveillance video from Shae's apartment less than ten minutes before the break-in."

In the two-ton silence that followed, Capelli paused to look at each member of the team. Sinclair standing at attention, observing from the back of the office. Maxwell, Hale, Hollister, and Moreno poised behind their respective desks in various states of shock and awe. But it was the faith and conviction in Shae's stare that bolstered him, and he sent her a tiny nod before turning toward the rest of the team to continue.

"I know it's surprising. I didn't expect the cases to be connected like this either. But the facts don't lie."

Capelli sent the image of Vaughn's face from his laptop to the crime scene board, setting his molars together for just an instant before saying, "Vaughn posed as a floral delivery man to get into Shae's building. The actual order was legit, but it was placed online using a stolen credit card."

"So he placed the order, then hijacked the delivery to get a free pass into the building," Hollister said, and enough of a question hung in his voice that Capelli nodded in reply.

"Yes. The floral company outsources its delivery services and they send all assignments to their drivers electronically.

KIMBERLY KINCAID

Intercepting a job itinerary and posing as the delivery guy would have been all too easy for Vaughn to do." Not to mention ballsy as hell, but since Vaughn had stones the size of a baseball stadium, they'd be getting to that soon enough.

Hale frowned in thought. "Okay, but this guy is obviously smart. Why not just slip in through a side door with a bogus key card like you said and keep himself off the surveillance feed entirely?"

"Because while he *is* smart, he's also self-righteous, remember?" Capelli asked. Vaughn had definitely proven both a thousand times over during the DuPree investigation. Even the RPD profiler had been impressed in the bad way by the asshole's lack of a soul. "Chances are, he did it because he could. Vaughn knows we have no physical evidence to tie him to the notes or the break-in. Sure, he was in Shae's building, but so were a hundred other people. Even if we could find him"—Capelli paused to let his expression deliver the likelihood that *that* would happen without a metric ton of work and luck combined —"we couldn't hold him for so much as a parking ticket."

Vaughn had been equally stealthy three months ago, triggering viruses on all of DuPree's hard drives that had rendered them useless just before ghosting to save his own skin. The move was textbook Cover Your Ass, and fuck if it hadn't done its job in spades.

"Ugh. This guy sounds like a real prince," Shae muttered, and Capelli hated that his only choice was to nod in agreement.

"Unfortunately, Vaughn is smart *and* dangerous, which is a bad combination by itself. Add in his narcissistic tendencies, the fact that he has a black hole for a conscience, and his job history running counter-surveillance for monsters like Julian DuPree..."

Moreno filled in the blank, her voice loaded with determination. "And we need to figure out what he's up to and nail him before he hurts anybody else."

Dread crawled an ice-cold path down Capelli's spine, but he wrenched himself back to the facts. "Given our past experience with him, odds are high Vaughn's got a very calculated plan. We just don't know what his endgame is, or who he'll try to kill next."

"Let's start from square one," Sinclair said, shooting a glance at the crime scene board where Capelli had posted the image of Vaughn at Shae's apartment building. "What do we know about his motive for these murders?"

"It could be money," Hollister said slowly. "I mean, this is a guy who freelances security and counter-surveillance to some of Remington's nastiest scumbags. Maybe he's expanding his résumé to include murder for hire."

Capelli shook his head. He wouldn't put murder for hire past Vaughn—Christ knew the bastard lacked even the barest shred of a moral compass. Still...

"There weren't any bodies at Fiorelli's." He turned to look at Shae, certainty and something else he couldn't name pumping through his veins. "Honestly, I think the most logical motive is revenge, just like Shae said."

Her shoulders hitched in the barest betrayal of her surprise, but she smoothed over the movement in less than a breath. "Both fires were designed to do a huge amount of damage. It definitely feels personal enough for revenge."

Maxwell lifted his chin in agreement. "If Vaughn did freelance security for both the Scarlet Reapers and Nicky Bianchi, and somehow things went sour, he *would* know how to hit them both where it hurt the most."

"Exactly," Capelli said. "But even though these crimes were personal in that regard, Vaughn is still methodical as hell. He might've used the same M.O. as DuPree for the murders at the meth lab fire, but he was a hell of a lot smarter about covering his tracks."

Pulling up the ME's report on Denton, he sent the information to the case board, highlighting the toxicology report. "Denton had the same amount of sufentanil in his system as Lawrence did, but he also outweighed the L-Man by a good fifty pounds."

"Which means the same amount of drugs would take longer to knock him out," Moreno murmured. "You thinking that's why his throat was cut instead? To be sure he went down? I mean, a guy like Vaughn doesn't take half-measures. He'd probably have a backup plan in place in case the drugs didn't subdue either victim fast enough."

Capelli nodded, having already run the odds in his head twice to be sure. "I think it's the most likely scenario, yes, but there's a catch with the wound, too. All this tissue damage was done post-mortem. Denton actually bled out from a very precise cut that severed his carotid artery."

"If the wound that killed him was inflicted first, why go back and do more damage after the fact? It's not like Denton could get any deader," Hollister said, and Capelli's brain shifted over the probabilities until he arrived at the most likely one.

"My guess is to throw us off. That cut was placed in exactly the right spot to do the most lethal damage possible in the shortest amount of time, which means Denton's murderer was not only calculating, but incredibly smart."

Realization flickered over Hale's face. "And almost certainly *not* a rival gang banger looking for a down and dirty revenge kill, like we originally thought."

"Jesus," Maxwell said. "This guy really *is* methodical."

A few seconds passed, and Capelli could tell from everyone's expressions that they were processing the intel. It was a lot, he knew—even Sinclair had given up a few signs of rare surprise when Capelli had first unloaded the whole story in the sergeant's office. Finally, Hollister broke the silence, his eyes not on Capelli or the crime scene board, but oddly on Shae.

"Vaughn clearly knows Shae is investigating the arsons, which is attention he might not have been banking on when he came up with his strategy." The detective paused as if he was selecting his words with extreme care, his voice softening as he asked, "Is it possible she's his next target?"

The thought sliced through Capelli as precise and sharp as razor wire, closing over the "*no*" lodged firmly in his throat. The sting grew teeth as he registered the shock-laced fear on Shae's face, and no amount of logic could explain the way his heart was currently trying to pry its way out of his rib cage.

"No." He swallowed—twice, because he didn't trust his throat to perform even its basic function past the single syllable. Facts. *Facts*. He needed the facts. They never lied.

The first one that appeared in his brain was that if Vaughn went near Shae again, Capelli would murder the man, bare-handed and smiling.

"I don't think so," he said, turning toward her and tamping down his emotions once and for all. "If you were a target, Vaughn would've hurt you when he had the chance. There's no way he doesn't know we have extra eyes on you now because of the notes, and he won't do anything that'll get him caught. No matter how arrogant he is, he's smart enough to know that going after you now would be strategic suicide."

The rationale took most of the terror out of her eyes and his chest—thank fuck—and a second later, Shae's chin lifted in that way that was as unique to her as her signature. "If this brainiac whack job thinks he can scare me off the case, he has another thing coming."

"We'll keep our current security measures in place anyway, just as a precaution," Sinclair said, one hundred percent unyielding. "McCullough, you'll still need to check with the team every twelve hours and be escorted to your car at night. No sense in giving this asshole any bright ideas."

She nodded, and Hollister took the opportunity to add, "We're not going to let anything happen to you, Shae."

"So where do we go from here?" Maxwell asked, and the straight to the point question tethered Capelli right back to his focus.

"Forward. If we want to take Vaughn down, we'll have to catch him in the act."

"Easier said than done," Hale mused, her eyes on the photographs of the two crime scenes on the board at the back of the office, and as much as Capelli hated it, she wasn't wrong.

"Vaughn knows how to stay four steps ahead of the system. We have to assume he's hacked the arson database and the RPD alert system at the very least. He's got tech just like ours—"

Hollister interrupted with a humorless pop of laughter. "Uh, we have you, dude. Nobody's got tech like ours."

"Unfortunately, Conrad Vaughn does." Unease coursed back into Capelli's veins at how thoroughly he knew the truth of it, but he pulled in a slow breath to cover the thought. "He's got a brain the size of a building and the power of the Dark Net at his back, which means for him, there are no rules. I put extra security measures into place on the intelligence database that should block him moving forward, and I have a call in to the RFD to do the same for the case files over at arson."

"*Should* block him," Moreno repeated, her brows lifting toward her hairline, and yeah, here's where things got thorny.

"The only way to absolutely guarantee that our network won't be breached is to unplug it, which we obviously can't do. We can keep certain things offline by going old school—burner phones and face-to-face coms." It would be a righteous pain in the ass to tap dance all over the grid, no doubt. But Capelli had worked with far less access to break a case. Plus… "Even if by some small chance Vaughn does get access to our database, that's not necessarily all bad news."

Both Hale and Shae chirped in surprise, but the detective found her footing first. "Um, correct me if I'm wrong, but won't we totally be tipping our hand if he can put eyes on our DB? Then he'll know everything *we* know."

"It's not an ideal situation," Capelli said in the interest of full disclosure. "But not everything we do and know will be online. And more importantly, if Vaughn can see us—"

"We can see him, too," Shae finished.

"Exactly." His heart thudded faster, his fingers twitching over the keyboard beneath them at the mere possibility. Christ, it would only take him two minutes—maybe three—to get a bead on the guy if he caught him lurking online. Yeah, Vaughn was smart, but Capelli knew him. Knew all his tendencies and quirks and maneuvers.

Which was why the dark, greedy hope in his chest fizzled with his next breath.

"Tactically speaking, that heightens the odds he'll stay away from the DB altogether. He knows we're on alert, and he thinks he can outsmart us without the intel anyway," Capelli said.

Sinclair took a step toward the group, his jaw set and his expression as serious as a sledgehammer in full swing. "Well, that's where he's wrong, because we're going to nail his ass to the wall like a Monet. I want to know everything there is to know about Conrad Vaughn. All known associates, last known address, anybody he might have done counter-surveillance for, anyone whose feathers he might have ruffled. If this guy has left so much as a breadcrumb of intel, I want every single one of you to know it inside and out, right down to what color socks he's wearing."

Sinclair slid a stare in his direction, but only for a second before his gaze moved over the rest of the team. "I want to know what this guy is going to do before he even knows he's going to do it. Let's get to work, people. Capelli?"

The sound of his name sent a prickle of warning over his skin, but ah hell, he couldn't let so much as an ounce of it show. "Yes, Sarge?"

"A word in my office before you get started."

Fuck. The non-request never, ever meant anything good. When Sinclair told you to close the door, the way he did when Capelli stepped over the threshold a few seconds later? You might as well put your head between your legs and kiss your ass goodbye.

Still, Capelli had no choice but to nut up and act normal for appearance's sake. "What's up?"

Sinclair ran a hand over his gray-blond crew cut, letting it rest on the back of his neck for a second before answering. "I know I don't need to tell you how badly we need to catch this guy. Just like you don't need to tell me how big a task that's going to be." His next pause had Capelli's heart stuttering behind the gray cotton of his Henley, because with it came that expression Sinclair almost never trotted out.

Regret.

"You and Vaughn have a history. One your team doesn't know anything about."

Every part of Capelli froze except for his eyes, which shot directly to Sinclair's. "I haven't had any direct personal contact with the guy in eight years. I gave you everything I know about the guy when we tracked him three months ago, and you and I have already agreed that my former working relationship with Vaughn doesn't have any bearing on the case in front of us."

Yeah, Capelli hated the truth, and no, he definitely didn't want to go broadcasting his past like a breaking news alert. But if disclosing his past with Vaughn would help the team catch him, Capelli would've done it the second the guy had surfaced.

"We did," Sinclair said past his frown. Although he didn't elaborate, he didn't have to in order for Capelli to hear everything he hadn't spoken but had somehow still managed to say.

"None of what happened in the past will keep me from being able to track him so we can take him down," Capelli said, and Sinclair's expression in return brooked no argument.

"If I thought it would, you wouldn't be here. But even if we catch Vaughn today and your teammates are none the wiser about your knowing him, that still doesn't mean your past isn't going to come back to haunt you."

My past haunts me every single day. It'll haunt me until I die.

Capelli bit his tongue just in time to trap the words burning there. Damn it, he needed to get it together. To clamp down on his emotions, to find his composure now more than ever.

He looked out the window facing the main intelligence office, eyes searching wildly until they landed on Shae, sitting at the end of his desk. She was focused on her laptop screen, her honey-colored ponytail brushing over one shoulder and her eyes determined. Bright.

Pure.

Unexplainably, Capelli's breath moved in. Out. In again before he said, "I'm good. Really."

"If the case depends on it—"

"If the case depended on it, I wouldn't think twice about

telling them everything." The same went for if any member of the team's safety was on the line, although he sure as shit hoped he didn't need to say that out loud. "But it doesn't. Either way, this thing with Vaughn isn't going to get personal. It isn't going to get in the way of us catching him."

"That may be." The lack of edge in Sinclair's voice backed up the words one hundred percent. "But I still think you should talk to them, Capelli. They know you. You need to trust that."

Slipping on as much of a smile as he could muster, he gave up a nod.

"Thanks. I'll think about it."

It was the first time in eight years that Capelli had ever lied to the man.

CHAPTER 18

"Well, well! Look what the breeze blew in."

"Ah, hell. There goes the neighborhood."

"Damn, they'll let every last troublemaker into this place!"

Holy *shit*, it was good to finally be back at work.

Swinging her duffle bag from her shoulder to the locker room bench in front of her, Shae didn't even bother trying to check her grin.

"Yeah, yeah. I missed you too." She spun a look from Kellan to Faurier to Hawkins before adding, "You jackasses."

"Glad to see you're back where you belong, McCullough," Dempsey said, pulling a battle-tested navy blue RFD baseball hat over his dark brown hair with a smile. "We were beginning to worry you might've gone over to the dark side and decided to become a cop."

"Not a chance," she said, although there was no disguising the pride in her chest or the weariness in her mind at having already put in over fifty hours this week, and it was only Friday morning. "Don't get me wrong. Working in intelligence was exciting and everything, but I'll take bunker gear over bullets any day. Plus"—her belly squeezed as she thought of the last six days she'd spent working tirelessly at the Thirty-Third, then did an outright flip at the thought of the corresponding nights she'd spent in bed with Capelli —"the team has a really good handle on the case I was assisting them with now. My hours at arson are complete, A-shift is up here at the fire house today, and...what can I say? I missed you Neanderthals."

Shae turned toward her locker, going through her pre-roll call routine as everyone around her joked and laughed and did the same. Okay, so the story she'd just given up had been technically accurate, but it had also definitely been the Cliff's Notes version of the truth. While the intelligence unit had amassed enough background information on Conrad Vaughn this week to have a pretty decent picture of his handiwork from the last five years, the only traces they'd been able to find of his actual location or his next possible target had been just that. Scraps. Details outdated enough to be useless. Information that was either scrambled or incomplete. She'd researched and investigated as much as she could on the arson end, but without evidence linking Vaughn to the scenes, she'd hit a standstill. The guy had lived up to his nickname, giving them only brief, shadowy glimpses before leading them to dead-end after dead-end.

Shae closed her locker, smoothing a hand over her RFD T-shirt and navy blue uniform pants. Yes, they'd been investigating two serious crimes, and *hell* yes, Vaughn was definitely the living embodiment of All Things Purely Evil. But he'd been church-mouse quiet all week, and while that sucked in terms of trying to pin him down, Shae couldn't deny her relief at the underlying facts.

They might not know where Vaughn was, but he hadn't threatened her again, and he hadn't burned anything to the ground this week, either.

And if he tried, this time they'd be ready for him.

"McCullough! You're back." Slater's blue-gray eyes went wide, his boots shuffling to a stop on the locker room linoleum just an instant before he broke into a smile.

"That's the rumor," she said, but not even her wry comeback could keep her genuine grin at bay.

Slater's expression slipped into more serious territory, and he lowered his voice even though everyone else had cleared out of the room. "I heard you were working on a pretty nasty case over at arson. Is everything okay?"

A pang centered itself behind Shae's sternum, fading to a dull thud as it spread out over her rib cage. Protocol dictated that she not discuss the particulars of the case with anyone other than members of the intelligence unit or fire department brass. Of course brass included Captain Bridges, and also Gamble, who had checked in with her in that quiet yet utterly badass way of his all week long. The truth was, there wasn't much—if anything—to check on now. All that was left was to wait for Vaughn to turn up so intelligence could tie him to the Denton/Lawrence murders and put him away forever, then arson could close the two cases they had against him, to boot.

And that would happen. Shae was one hundred percent certain of it. Because she and Capelli and everyone else in the intelligence unit had worked far too hard for it not to.

Covering any seriousness her pause might have given up, Shae looked at Slater and nodded. "Working in arson is definitely an eye-opener, but somebody's got to keep you guys on your toes around here. So tell me. What'd I miss?"

"Let's see," Slater said, leaning a shoulder against the bank of lockers beside him. "A half dozen fire calls that were more smoke than substance, a hit and run that turned out to be a mannequin that fell off the back of a truck, and a healthy baby girl delivered in the back seat of a Chevy Malibu."

"Ohhh, please tell me Gamble had to take point on the

baby." While she could count on one hand the number of things that freaked the big bad lieutenant out, squirming, squalling infants were *so* at the top of the list.

Slater's soft laugh said he knew it, too. "Nah. Parker and Quinn made it with plenty of time. Speaking of which"—he shifted, just a small straightening of his spine and shoulders, but it was enough to snare every last bit of Shae's attention —"I thought about what you said. You know, about managing the stuff that scares you. And I guess it turns out I'm not too crazy about blood."

"You wouldn't be the only firefighter with that phobia," she said. God, she'd heard dozens of stories of first responders who were terrified of blood, just like she'd been front and center at enough trauma scenes to know that in most cases, the fear was legit.

Funny, the glint in Slater's eyes looked far from scared, though. "Well, I decided to do something about it. I'm going to train as a paramedic. You'll still be stuck with me on Engine during A-shift," he added, likely in response to the fact that Shae's jaw had just dropped down for a meet and greet with the floor tiles. "But the best way for me to conquer my fear is to face it head-on. Plus, if I'm trained in both fire and EMS, I can pick up more extra shifts, and Quinn has already been really cool about giving me some pointers."

An expression moved over the rookie's face, something odd that Shae couldn't readily name. But before she could be sure she'd seen it, let alone identify what it was or what had triggered it, Gamble cleared his throat from a few feet away.

"McCullough. Slater. Roll call is in five. Thought you might not be interested in Bridges's bad graces until at least lunch time."

She'd give him this—he'd delivered the words with edge to spare. But then his mouth curved just the slightest degree, and she couldn't help it. Her grin came charging back at full steam.

"Aw, you missed me," Shae said, but of course, the big guy didn't budge.

"You're pushing your luck."

She turned what wanted to be a snort into a cough, just in the nick of time. "You're not really surprised, are you?"

One nearly black brow arched up over an equally dark stare. "Roll call's in four now. And McCullough?"

"Yes, sir?"

Gamble turned on his boot heels to face the doorway leading into the fire house, looking back over one gigantic shoulder just briefly as he said, "Good to have you back."

"No place I'd rather be, Lieutenant."

Shae's cheeks warmed with happiness, but it was a sentiment that wouldn't last if she didn't make it to roll call on time. After a quick "let me know if I can help" to Slater on the paramedic training, she aimed herself down the hallway leading to the main hub of the fire house, including the meeting room where they held their shift-change meeting every morning at oh-seven-hundred, sharp.

But she got no more than six strides from the locker room when her phone buzzed in her back pocket, and her cheeks warmed with something a whole lot naughtier than happiness at the sight of the text message on her screen.

You make it to Seventeen okay?

The words were ordinary. Ones any member of intelligence might use—God knew she'd gone the check-in route more in the last week than she had in all her years as a teenager combined. But the name next to the message sent a flutter through her like she was chock-full of butterflies, and okay, yeah. Fine. It was a little crazy, and a *lot* impulsive, but Shae didn't care.

She had it pretty bad for James Capelli. And his sort of bad was so. Very. Good.

Sliding her cell phone more firmly against her palm, she texted back, Come on, Starsky. It's a ten-minute drive. Even I have a tough time getting into trouble in a timeframe like that.

I doubt it, came the quick reply, and oh, she liked him more than a little. But I'll take that as a yes.

It's a yes, Shae thumb-typed back. But you don't have to check up on me. I already texted Hale when I walked in the door.

I know, and I know. Have a good day.

Despite their simplicity, Shae knew the cadence with which he'd speak the words, could hear in her mind the serious care that would go into them, and suddenly, they weren't simple at all.

Shit, she was going to be late.

Hustling down the hallway, Shae made it into the meeting room T-minus three seconds before Captain Bridges shut the door. Roll call became morning duties (okay, so she hadn't missed mopping the floors) which then became three fairly minor back-to-back calls and some ladder drills (ah, but she *had* missed looking down at the city from a hundred feet up on the aerial.) Shae moved from one thing to the next, falling back into her routine with ease until the afternoon coasted into dusk, then dusk into full-on darkness…

The all-call blasted her awake just shy of eleven P.M.

Engine Seventeen, Squad Six, Ambulance Twenty-Two, Battalion Seventeen, primary units, Engine Nine, Ladder Forty-Two, Ambulance Nineteen, secondary units, structure fire, nineteen hundred block of Winding Ridge Terrace, requesting immediate response.

Shae shook the sleep from her brain and stumbled in the direction of the bunkroom door, but after two weeks of uninterrupted sleep at night, she had to admit, clarity was a tough nut to crack.

"You good, McCullough? Because this one sounds like it ain't a Tupperware party," Hawkins said, and she nodded, chucking her hair into a close approximation of a ponytail as she beat feet toward the engine.

"Yes, sir," she said, her heart kicking into fifth gear. There was decidedly less banter during calls that hauled them out of bed, for sure. But for two houses to be called to a scene, right off the bat like that?

Shae would bet her paycheck this wasn't some yahoo burning leaves in his yard.

Stepping into her turnout gear, she yanked the heavy weight of her bunker pants over the sweats she slept in when she was on shift. The process jump-started her focus, the order of the steps oddly honing her adrenaline into sharp, streamlined calm.

Coat, helmet, breathe in. Hood and gloves at the ready, breathe out...

Her SCBA and mask were already in the rig, and anyway, they needed to get gone. Her muscles squeezed with familiar tension as she pulled herself into the operator's seat, sending the engine into a diesel-fueled growl with one hand while hooking the other under her seatbelt and snapping the thing into place.

"Address is in the GPS, McCullough. We're a go," Gamble clipped out, jerking his headset into place while she did the same.

Shae's inhale was surprisingly smooth considering how hard her adrenal gland was trying to commandeer her lungs. "Copy that. Engine Seventeen is a go."

She pulled out of the bay, her eyes on the road and her mind mapping out the path in front of them, and Gamble's hands moved briskly over the dashboard unit that displayed real-time updates from the city's dispatch center.

"Okay, boys and girls. Let's see what we're dealing with here. Dispatch has multiple nine-one-one callers reporting heavy smoke and flames showing at a large residence in South Hill. Looks like it's under construction."

"At least there won't be any entrapment," came Kellan's voice over the headset, but Gamble eighty-sixed the guy's silver lining with a grunt.

"Not so fast, Walker. Looks like one of the call-ins was from a construction foreman who had a crew at the site. He told dispatch two of his guys are unaccounted for."

"Are you kidding me?" Kellan asked at the same time Shae's pulse snapped in surprise. "It's twenty-three hundred, for Chrissake. Who works construction in the middle of the night?"

"That's not even the worst part. Looks like this place is huge, and it's already showing flames on the Delta, Charlie—shit. Everywhere. This fire sounds like a serious cluster fuck."

"Wait." Finally, the fog lifted all the way off Shae's brain and she lined up the location on the GPS with the map of the city in her head. "This is in the most upscale section of South Hill. Over where the mayor is…"

Oh shit. *Shit.*

"This is the exact location of that monstrosity the mayor is building," she breathed, her voice tight with shock as it echoed through the headset.

"The mansion that takes up the entire freaking block?" Slater asked.

Shae made a hard left onto Madison Boulevard, her foot pressing harder over the accelerator as she passed the Plaza hotel and the swanky shopping district that accompanied it.

"Affirmative." It was also the mansion currently burning down at a very hot, very unnatural rate of speed with two people trapped inside, and something hard and cold turned over in Shae's gut.

"Gamble," she said, channeling all her effort into keeping her lungs steady. *Breathe in. Breathe out. Breathe in...* "I need you to tell dispatch to call the intelligence unit at the Thirty-Third. Tell them we're all fine," she added before she even inhaled again, because God, the last thing she needed was for Capelli or Moreno or anybody else on the team to lose their minds when they'd need them most. "But they need to get out to this scene ASAP."

Gamble's brows shot toward his hairline. "I get that this isn't exactly a grease fire, McCullough, but the cops? There's no evidence this is a crime scene."

Shae knew it was a flyer. A gut feeling. A guess.

But she also knew she wasn't wrong. A fire this big, burning this fast, with two men trapped inside?

It had Conrad Vaughn's fingerprints all over it.

"I need you to call Capelli. *Please.*"

Whether it was the polite word or the decidedly impolite way she'd just bit it out, Shae had no idea. But something grabbed Gamble's attention enough to make him lift the handset on the dashboard radio.

"We'll need to radio Bridges too," she said, certainty and dread combining into a ball in the pit of her stomach. "I'm telling you, there's something very wrong about this fire."

Any doubt to her claim was obliterated when they pulled up to the scene a few minutes later, and sweet Jesus, this fire was *huge.*

"Gamble. McCullough." Bridges was on the asphalt beside the engine the instant Shae had it in *park.* "Intelligence is on the way. But we need to find those two men trapped inside this house and start knocking down these flames, and we need to do it now."

"Copy that," Shae and Gamble replied in unison. Her

heart pushed her blood on a circuit so fast, each beat pressed against her eardrums in a thump of white noise. The "house" in front of them was more Taj Mahal than actual residence, with its white stone façade and endless windows, porticoes, and columns. The power had clearly shorted out, although searing orange flames were already showing in more than half the smoke-clogged windows, and seriously, how were they supposed to find anyone in these conditions?

Analyze, then hypothesize.

The words anchored her calm into place. Buckling her helmet with suddenly steady fingers, Shae shouldered her SCBA unit, waiting for orders from Bridges as he moved back to his command post in front of the scene.

"Engine Seventeen and Squad Six, this is Command. We have reports of two men still inside the structure, last known location Bravo side. Hawkins, this place may be under construction, but it's also fully under roof, so we'll need a vent. Take Dempsey."

Shae craned her neck to look up at the roofline, her shoulders tightening at the sight of the slate tiles, the multiple gables and turrets, and the dramatic pitch.

But all Hawkins said was, "Yes, sir," turning to grab the circular saw from its compartment in the squad vehicle before he and Dempsey fell out in a clatter of boots on pavement.

"Engine Nine just arrived, and they are on lines," Bridges continued, his eyes never leaving the house, carefully scanning and assessing the scene. "The rest of you are on search and rescue. Gamble, take point. Time is an issue. Go."

The lieutenant didn't pause. Just moved, and Shae forced her legs to copy his strides as best she could with their nine-inch height differential. She had to analyze. Focus. Help find the men trapped inside before the roof collapsed or the fire flashed over.

They had minutes. *If* they were lucky.

"Alright," Gamble said, eyeing up the gigantic expanse of stone and glowing flames in front of him as they cut a path over the ridiculously long, ridiculously ostentatious stone-paved walkway. "We've got a ton of ground to cover, and visibility is going to be for shit. I'll radio Cap and see if he can get some spotlights going from the engine."

"Fuck. This place has to be twenty thousand square feet," Faurier murmured, his eyes sweeping over the house in front of them. Shae nodded in agreement—between the thick cover of smoke, the eerie shadows being thrown off by the emergency vehicles, and the sheer size of the house itself, she was struggling to keep up with her own scene assessment.

Doubt panged at her breastbone in a demand for re-entry, but oh no. No way was she scaling back on this call. "We can tether ourselves to anchor points to keep from getting turned around," she said.

Gamble nodded, just once in agreement as they reached the bottom of a set of stone steps leading up to two mahogany and stained-glass doors that looked like they belonged on a cathedral. "Good call," he answered, shifting forward to advance.

But Slater's arm shot upward, fist closed in the universal sign for *hold*. "Wait! Do you smell that?"

The unmistakable chemical scent pinched at Shae's senses, her gut dumping toward her knees. "That's gasoline," she said, and oh God. Oh God oh God oh God. "This is arson, Gamble. This fire was set deliberately."

Gamble swore in acknowledgment, radioing Bridges with the find. "We still have two men to find, so mask up and watch your backs. McCullough, you're with me on floor one, Bravo side. Walker, you're with Gates on second floor Bravo. Faurier, take Slater and sweep first floor Charlie side in case these guys tried to escape out the back and got jammed up. Copy?"

Without so much as a nanosecond's worth of a pause after their affirmative replies, Gamble smashed through the stained glass with his Halligan bar, reaching in to release the deadbolt he'd rightly assumed would've been a pain in the ass to breach any other way. The door—which had to be four inches thick—thumped inward on a heavy swing, and Shae followed Gamble into the near black depths of the foyer while everyone else fell out on their S&R assignments.

"We'll have to split up," Gamble shouted past his mask. "I'll take the rear section down this hallway, you take this part of the house right here. And Shae?" He spared her only a lightning-fast glance before continuing, because truly, it was all they had. "Do *not* do anything stupid."

"Copy that, Lieutenant."

Turning on her helmet-mounted spotlight along with the one clipped to the front left side of her coat, Shae stepped farther into the part of the house she'd been assigned to search. Sweat popped over her forehead in a near-immediate physical reaction to the blast of heat coming from the interior of the house, and her heart went from a steady rhythm to an out-and-out brawl beneath her gear.

Breathe in. Breathe out. Analyze. Make a plan.

Her voice flew out, clear and strong. "Fire department! Call out!"

She surveyed the room as quickly as possible for any potential hazards, cursing inwardly as she realized the whole fucking place was a potential hazard. Stacks of building materials, the unfinished sheet rock panels of all four walls, the rafters and sub flooring above her, all of them were covered in the deep glow flames.

Still, she wouldn't be deterred. Attaching the nylon tether she carried specifically for calls like these to the anchor on her coat, Shae wrapped the opposite end around the only support beam she could find that wasn't actively burning. Her muscles screamed beneath the weight of her gear and the heat swamping her from all sides, but still, she hollered, "Fire department! Is anyone here?"

Shae made her way into the space one step at a time. Although she hadn't thought it possible, the fire grew even stronger, the smoke and lack of daylight making it impossible to see more than a few feet in front of her even with her helmet lamp going full blast. A section of the rafters broke off and fell to the floor with a spark-filled crash, and okay, yeah. Shit had just gone from zero to pear-shaped.

Just as she reached for the two-way on her shoulder, though, Kellan's voice broke through the whoosh of the flames. "Command, this is Walker! We have two men down, Bravo side, floor two."

"Walker this is Command," came Bridges's voice. "Are you clear for the primary exit?"

The pause was excruciating even though it lasted only seconds. "Affirmative. Gates and I are a go for the primary exit."

"Copy that. Command to all units, fall out immediately. Gamble, McCullough, Slater, Faurier, I want you out of there right now."

God, Shae didn't need to hear the command twice. Pivoting on her boot heels, she reclaimed her tether, tracing her strides—*ten, eleven, twelve*—back to the spot where she'd started. She sent a quick glance around the foyer to make sure there weren't any new hazards in her path before she reached for her tether to release it, goose bumps chasing the sweat on her skin and freezing her movements at the sound of Gamble's voice crackling over the two-way.

"Command, this is Gamble. I'm on floor one, Bravo side…

I think. There's zero visibility in here, and I lost my anchor…"

He trailed off. Ice slid over Shae's spine despite the hell-hot conditions around her as she registered his tone, strung tightly with something she'd never, ever heard in his voice in the entire five years she'd known him.

Fear.

"Command, this is McCullough. I'm still in position, first floor, Bravo side, and I'm already tethered to an anchor point. Requesting permission for search and rescue."

"McCullough—" Gamble cautioned, and frustration welled in her throat.

"I'm the closest person to you, Gamble, and you're wasting time by arguing! Give me sixty seconds, Cap. I can do this. I *can*."

Bridges paused, but only for a breath. "Copy that. Gamble, hold your position and set off your PASS device. McCullough, you have sixty seconds. Go."

Shae was in motion before he'd even started sentence number two. With swift, methodical movements, she double-checked her equipment, forging a path down the hallway toward the screeching signal coming from Gamble's personal alert safety system. The hall branched off in what looked like two identical passageways, both equally twisty and clogged with smoke and flames. God, no wonder the lieutenant had gotten turned around back here—

Shae could barely see a foot in front of her. But that alarm on Gamble's PASS device was cranking out ninety-five deci-bels of Olly Olly Oxen Free, and she swung toward the noise blaring from the left-hand passage.

Damn it, she'd have to do this the hard way.

Hitting her knees, Shae crawled her way deeper into the house. Sweat stung her eyes, her breath impossibly loud in her ears over the hiss of her respirator, but still, she pressed forward carefully, hand over knee, until—*fifteen, sixteen*—yes! Her heart surged up toward her throat at the sight of the high-powered strobe light on Gamble's alarm flashing through the ashy haze. Like her, he had crouched down low for better visibility, and two more crawl-paces had her within arm's length of him.

"Hey, big guy. Fancy meeting you here," she said, her pulse spiking even faster as he jerked to attention as if he'd been trapped in a trance, eyes wide behind his mask.

"I told you not to do anything stupid, you know." The words were oddly quiet. In that scissor-sharp instant, Shae recognized the depth of the fear embedded in his stare, and she forced herself to speak even though she wasn't certain her throat would obey.

"I'm happy to see you, too, Lieutenant." Flames danced up both sides of the hallway over Gamble's shoulder, reaching toward the ceiling Shae could no longer see, and yeah, they could hug it out later. "Now what do you say we get the hell out of here?"

He focused his stare on the light attached to the front of her coat, his nod coming back stronger than his voice had been only seconds before. "Copy that."

She reached down to lock the snap hook on Gamble's coat to her secondary line, then reached for the radio at her shoulder. "Command, this is McCullough. Gamble and I are tethered and clear for the primary exit. Repeat, we are clear for the primary exit."

"McCullough, this is Command. The primary exit is unimpeded. Fall out."

Pushing her boots to the subfloor, she crouched down low while Gamble did the same. They needed the speed of their feet to cut a fast path to the exit, and anyway, now they had a lifeline. Getting out would be a hell of a lot easier than getting in. Shae turned, wrapping her gloved fingers firmly around the tether while Gamble fell in at her six.

They made it exactly four steps down the hallway before everything above them erupted in an over-bright flash, then faded instantly to black.

CHAPTER 19

Capelli stared at the massive fire in front of him, absolutely unable to breathe. His brain, which had refused to lose its hard-wiring even in the face of his body's adrenaline overload, catalogued everything in excruciating detail. The call he'd gotten from Sinclair that had roused him from his bed, where he'd slept alone for the first time in a week. The faster-than-was-safe drive to get to the scene. The fear and dread and high-octane tension that had ricocheted through his chest as he'd stood between Sinclair and Captain Bridges with the rest of the team, listening to events unfold on the Captain's radio.

"Walker and Gates are clear with the victims," Bridges said, and Capelli's brain registered the sight of Isabella's body loosening with relief from beside him. "Both men are unconscious, but breathing. They're being prepped for immediate transport to Remington Memorial."

His unfailing brain formed words, kicked them out of his mouth, and somehow, despite the riot in his chest, they were smooth, steady. "Have the trauma docs run a tox screen.

Chances are extremely high you'll find sufentanil in both of their systems."

Bridges's nod was interrupted by the crackle of static on the two-way radio at his shoulder.

"Command, this is Faurier. Slater and I are clear at the primary exit."

"Copy that," Bridges said. Tension that Capelli could neither rationalize nor ease cranked harder between his ribs. The countdown that had been steadily ticking down in his head ever since he'd last heard Shae's voice on the two-way was dwindling fast—*nineteen, eighteen, seventeen*—and he stared at the front door as if he could ridiculously, impractically will her over the threshold.

Damn it, it was just like her to want to go back for Gamble. Brash. Impulsive. Reckless—

At the fourteen-second mark, the house exploded in a rush of fire, shattered glass, and ungodly noise.

"*Shae!*" Her name tore from his throat, covered in raw terror. Capelli's brain—Christ, his stupid fucking brain that never *fucking* stopped moving—sent fragments of information past the slamming of his heart and into his awareness. The flurry of movement toward the fireball that had just blown through every window on the left-hand side of the first floor. The rough timbre of Bridges's voice as he yelled into his radio. The pressure of multiple hands and arms on his body, holding him back as he involuntarily launched himself toward the brightly burning flames.

Shae had been in the house. The fire had flashed over. Vaughn had set the fire.

Capelli was going to find that son of a bitch and murder him, slowly and without a scrap of remorse.

"*McCullough. Gamble. Report!*"

Bridges's repeat command echoed in Capelli's head, and the burst of static that arrived a beat later took a direct shot at his knees and the center of his chest simultaneously.

"Command, this is McCullough. Gamble and I are clear. Repeat, we're clear. We're okay, Cap."

Relief didn't even belong in the same stratosphere as the feeling that left Capelli's body on a sharp exhale.

Shae was alive. Talking. Unhurt.

He was still going to kill Vaughn.

"McCullough. Gamble. What's your location?" Bridges asked, and finally, the hands on Capelli's shoulders and waist —who he belatedly realized belonged to Sinclair and Hale— eased their vise grip.

"The ceiling collapsed in the hallway and blocked our primary escape route," Shae reported through the two-way. She was alive. Alive. "We had to cut our tether and fall out through the Charlie side, first floor, but we got out before the fire flashed over. Returning to the rendezvous point."

Less than a minute later, she appeared on the far side of the house beside Gamble, covered in soot and sweat and looking so beautiful it hurt, and of all the slideshows gathered in his brain, Capelli knew in that instant he'd remember this one the most.

His emotions surged in a rush so fierce and intense, it took him completely by surprise, paralyzing him to his spot on the pavement. He wanted to grab Shae and check every inch of her to be certain she was unhurt, to yell at her for her sheer stupidity, to kiss her until his lungs gave out. He wanted everything, he *felt* everything, with so much intensity that he had to fight it. He had to find his composure, his control.

Because if he so much as touched Shae right now, his emotions would flash over just like that fire, and he wouldn't be able to stop them from burning him to the ground.

"Jesus, you two. Not so close next time," Bridges said, his

own relief palpable even as he sent a string of commands to the secondary firefighting units with the rest of his breath.

Shae nodded while Capelli forced himself to go numb. It was that or go crazy, and he could not—*could not*—let his emotions ruin him.

"It was a little hairy for a second or two, but we're fine." She slid a barely there glance at Gamble before trying on a lopsided smile. "I mean, my ears are ringing from that flash over, and I'm pretty sure I'm going to smell like a charcoal briquette for a couple of days, but other than that..."

Shae's voice faded for only a second, then came back with the sort of determination that could only belong to her. "This fire was set intentionally. It's definitely arson." She looked around, her startled expression a clear indicator that she'd just registered the intelligence unit standing a handful of feet away. "The place was doused in gasoline, Capelli," she said, and God, he felt the way she said his name in the deepest part of his bones. "There's no way this wasn't Vaughn."

Capelli swallowed hard and focused on the curve of her earlobe, half-covered by a wisp of errant honey-brown hair. "We know."

"The fire marshal has been called in," Sinclair added. "Patrol officers are already canvassing the area for anyone who might have seen him."

"There might be evidence inside the house. We can run secondary lines from Seventeen to help knock this fire down faster," Gamble said, but Bridges stopped the guy's forward movement with a hard shake of his head.

"Dispatch has three more engines en route, and their ETA is less than two minutes. You and McCullough have had enough for one call. You're off-shift for the rest of the night. Not as a punishment," he added, because of course, Shae had just opened her mouth to protest—"but because I like my firefighters in one piece, and that includes their minds."

Gamble and Shae looked equally pissed off and put out, although neither one argued. Sinclair sent a glance over all the members of the team, starting and ending with Capelli, and fuck. *Fuck*, he needed to work, to push his mind to exhaustion in order to buy himself some order, some sanity.

And yet the only thing he wanted was Shae.

"CSU is on the way," Sinclair said, his voice low enough to keep the conversation between the team, yet firm enough to allow no argument. "Once the fire is out, we'll have them work with arson investigation to comb whatever's left of this scene for any traces of Vaughn. Moreno, you and Hollister check in with the patrol officers running the canvas and pull all security cam footage within a mile of here. See if anything pops. Maxwell, you and Hale head over to Remington Memorial to sit on those victims. I want full statements as soon as they're able to make them. In the meantime, I'll go deal with the mayor myself so we can figure out how he's connected to Vaughn. Capelli…"

Sinclair paused, and to anyone else, even the detectives in the unit, he probably looked like his regular old hard-assed self, giving out orders and running a case. But Capelli had no choice but to notice everything, right down to the muscle in the man's jaw that tightened ever so slightly when he was about to say something he wasn't about to budge on, and he braced for impact.

"Take Shae home," Sinclair said. "I'll call you if we find anything." This part, he aimed at Shae herself, who had stepped into the circle of the conversation as soon as she'd been excused by her captain and looked primed to object to being sent home twice in one night. "But Bridges is right. You've had a hell of a night, and I'm going to need you both clear-headed in the morning once we get these reports lined up. So go. Get some rest."

Capelli nearly argued despite the double dose of *don't you dare* flashing in Sinclair's steel-edged stare. But logic warned that the words would be a waste, so instead, he took a deep breath and locked his armor over himself as tightly as possible as he tested his voice with, "Copy that."

He fell in next to Shae, mirroring her precise footfalls toward Engine Seventeen. They made it six steps—five of which had probably driven her crazy—before she looked at him and asked, "Are you okay?"

Capelli swallowed the "no" on his tongue in one gulp. He needed his default. He needed the facts. He needed them *now*.

"You had a really close call," he said. "Are you sure you don't want one of the paramedics to check you out?"

"Yes. I'm sure."

Oddly, miraculously, she didn't push further. His next series of movements were a blur—arriving at the engine, waiting for Shae to carefully store her gear in one of the vehicle's side compartments, leading her to his car on the other side of the police barricade. The acrid smell of smoke permeated the air around them, leaving a bitter aftertaste on his tongue with every exhale. Capelli tried to smooth his tangled nerves by cataloguing everything around him, by keeping his brain busy with facts and tangible truths that might prove useful later. But his heart kicked in protest, as if Shae had suddenly switched places with true north and his default had been recalibrated to focus on her and only her, and oh hell. He needed to stamp out his emotions now more than ever.

"Let's get you home."

The trip to her apartment passed quickly enough. Blessedly, Shae had grabbed her keys and her cell phone and stowed them in the engine before Seventeen had left on the call, and Capelli walked her from the elevator to her door—twenty-two, twenty-three, twenty-four steps—and waited for her to free the deadbolt with a turn of her wrist.

"I need to take a shower," she said, looking down at her sweat damp RFD T-shirt and sweatpants without chagrin. "Can you…" Her green eyes closed, just briefly. "Can you wait for me?"

It occurred to him in that second that for all her fierceness, Shae was still afraid. Exposed. Able to be shaken, and his answer was all instinct, out before his brain and lips knew it would form.

"Of course."

Her thank you came by way of a smile that should have been simple, but instead, it was everything. She disappeared down the hallway, followed by the quiet yet definite rush of running water and the passing of time, and Christ, he shouldn't be here. Shae was naked, vulnerable, less than twenty-five feet away in her shower, the same way she had been when Vaughn had broken in. The thought made something dark and sharp snap free in Capelli's gut, and his hands cranked to fists so tight, his knuckles throbbed.

He wanted to kill Vaughn for what he'd done. He didn't want to think twice. Didn't want to ask smart, logical questions. Just wanted to put his fingers around the motherfucker's neck and squeeze the life right out of him, to crush tissue and steal air and snap bones even though he knew it was deeply wrong.

And didn't *that* just make him the man he'd been trying to hide for the last eight years.

Shae appeared in the entryway to the living room a few minutes later, her hair loose and damp over the shoulders of her bathrobe, and Capelli's composure slipped by yet another degree.

"Do you want to talk about this?" she asked. His defenses lined up a logical answer, one that involved phrases like *I should let you rest* and *I'll just be on my way*. But his legs—Christ, his stupid, mutinous legs—moved toward her like a magnet, his pulse joining the conspiracy by knocking faster at his throat.

"No."

"Do you want to go home?"

"No." Capelli took another step toward her, close enough to smell the citrusy scent of her shampoo and see the flash of gold at the ends of her sand-colored lashes. He wanted her so much he was dizzy with it, wild with it, absolutely fucking consumed by it, and his calm fractured like a hairline split along fragile glass. "I don't want to talk, and I don't want to go home."

Shae's eyes widened, but she remained unmoving, her voice perfectly level as she asked, "Do you want to tell me what you do want?"

"You, Shae. I want *you.*"

And just like that, his composure shattered.

Capelli rushed forward, slanting his mouth over hers as their bodies crashed together. He devoured her mouth in greedy kisses, hooking his fingers in her hair and tightening them—ah, God, *yes*—to hold her close. The deep strokes of his tongue were far from gentle, the dark, primal need fueling them even less so, but he couldn't stop. Hell, he wanted Shae so thoroughly, he couldn't even *think*, couldn't hold back or hide.

But then there she was, kissing him back just as desperately and digging her hands into his hair just as hard, matching his movements as if she needed him with the same brand of intensity, and Capelli's instinct flared. The urge to strip her naked and see every inch of her, to be certain she was unharmed, roared up from behind his sternum, and he slid his fingers to the edges of the thick cotton crisscrossed over her heart.

"Take this off." He shoved the material aside without waiting for a response. His cock stiffened as he realized the reason her robe had fallen to the floor with so little effort was because Shae had reached down to loosen the belt before he'd even been done telling her to undress.

She stepped out of the light blue cotton pooled at her feet, completely and beautifully

bare in the light spilling through the living room. The firm, lean muscles of her shoulders gave way to the plane of her chest, the swell of her breasts forming a generous curve on either side of her body. The soft, blush-pink of her nipples juxtaposed the firmness of the tightly beaded points, but then again, it was just like Shae to be sweet and full of sin, all at once. A bruise was starting to form on her rib cage, still just a shadow hiding beneath her skin, and Capelli's breath slid between his teeth in a hiss.

Her chin snapped up. Realization burned in her eyes, sudden and hot. "It happens from time to time at fire scenes. I'm fine, Capelli."

He looked at the bruise, the shape and size of it instantly stamped in his memory. He'd thought she was dead. He'd thought—

"I'm not fine," he said.

But instead of filling with concern, her eyes flashed with pure, uncut certainty. "You need to see it, right?"

"What?"

The question shocked him into stillness on the floorboards in front of her, but God, she didn't hesitate.

"That's the way your mind works, isn't it?" Reaching up, Shae brushed her fingers over his temple, the move oddly reverent given the flush of desire that colored her naked body, and Capelli wouldn't have been able to rip his gaze from her if his ability to breathe depended on it.

She closed the space between their bodies just shy of actual touch. "If you see something happen, you'll remember it in detail. You'll know it's true, and you'll never forget it."

255

"Yes," he said, his voice caught in the no-man's-land between a whisper and a growl.

"Well, if that's what you need to know that I'm here and I'm okay"—her fingers skimmed a path from his face to the tip of his chin, coming to a rest directly over his slamming heart—"if it's what you need to *be* okay, then take it. Fuck me any way you want. Just make sure you watch."

The last scraps of Capelli's composure disappeared as if they'd never existed. He yanked at his clothing, his shirt flying over his head and to the floor beside them in one swift movement, his boots and jeans and boxers following suit. Pausing for only the briefest of seconds to grab a condom from his wallet, he placed it on the coffee table before turning back toward Shae, walking her to the end of the couch and angling her ass against the well-cushioned armrest.

"Look at you," he said. He'd never had to try to memorize anything in his life. But right now, with this woman standing in front of him, bold and unabashedly naked and brimming with trust, he made sure to catalogue everything. Like it was a movie rolling out in his mind's eye, Capelli saw her peach-colored mouth part, her breasts flushing with desire as his eyes raked over them and lingered. His cock—already hard as a rail against the lower part of his belly—jerked in encouragement, and there was no holding back his moan as he pressed forward to taste one nipple with a hard swirl of his tongue.

"*Ah*." Shae's cry melted into his sharp exhale. With his eyes wide open, he wrapped one arm around her rib cage below her shoulder blades, cupping her breast with his opposite hand while keeping his attention on her nipple. Focusing on the rapid-fire flutter of the pulse point at the base of her neck, Capelli learned the topography of her body with his lips and teeth and tongue. He watched her pulse leap when he licked softly, and he saw the hitch of her chest when he abandoned lighter touches in favor of ones filled with dirty purpose. He watched Shae's nipple darken and grow slick from his ministrations, his brain greedily taking in her lust-blown pupils and the arch of her back as she wordlessly begged for more. And even though he knew, in the very far-off place that housed what had once been his decency, that he should slow down to regain the control he'd clung to for the last eight years of his life, he didn't.

Instead, Capelli did what Shae had told him to do.

"You want me to see everything, right?" he asked, and there was no hesitation in her nod.

"Yes."

"Good, because I want to watch you come before I fuck you. I want to see exactly what you look like when I make you scream."

Grabbing the condom from the coffee table, he tore open the package and rolled it into place even though each touch made his cock ache with equal parts pleasure and pain. He shifted back to the spot where Shae stood, coaxing her up to the arm of the couch with little more than a press of his palms. Her spine bowed as she arched up to kiss him, and he instinctively stepped toward the cradle of her hips at the same time her thighs parted to allow him access.

"You're a work of goddamn art, you know that?" Capelli asked, and oh, how he meant it. Christ, she was perfect, so passionate and fierce. "You're so fucking beautiful."

"You're beautiful too," Shae said, the words vibrating against the sensitive skin of his lips.

Unable to cage it, he laughed, even though the sound held little joy.

She heard plenty, though. "You still don't believe me?" she asked, widening her thighs in invitation. "Let me show you.

Watch while you make me come. Watch how beautiful you are."

He didn't need to be told twice. Reaching down, he gripped his cock and slid it over the seam of her sex. But rather than burying himself in the sweet heat of her pussy the way his instinct screamed at him to, he stayed where he was, with his length notched where she seemed to need it the most.

"Oh, God. Capelli, please don't stop."

Shae thrust against him, testing every bit of his fortitude. But he let her, dropping his stare to the spot where the length of his cock slid up and down over her clit, and good Christ, he'd never seen anything so perfect in his life than this woman working him with her body.

"I won't stop, baby." His words were all promise. Affirmation. Oath. "Let me see. Let me see what you need."

She did. Bracing one hand on the arm of the couch beside her and the other on his shoulder, Shae anchored him in place. Canting her hips against his, she rocked again and again, the hard knot of her clit rising and falling against his dick until the tension in her body began to break.

"Oh God. Oh *God*," she swore.

To Capelli's ears, it was all benediction. "There. There you are. Show me."

She thrust again, one last time before she started to shake. Blood rushed in Capelli's ears, and the sight of Shae's face, so completely caught up in the pleasure of her orgasm, branded itself into his memory for just a split second before his instincts took over. Shifting back, he grabbed her hips, turning her roughly and burying himself between her legs before she'd even stopped trembling.

"*Oh...*" The noise that crossed his lips was more moan than word. Sensations crashed through him like a tidal wave —her soft skin beneath the bite of his fingers, the sweet yet insanely erotic pressure of her slick inner muscles, gripping him hard with the force of her continued release. Capelli dropped his chin, focusing on the spot where his cock disappeared inside Shae's body, and something primal unraveled in his chest, commanding him to move. He edged her feet a little farther apart on the floorboards, testing her body with a shallow slide of his cock, out an inch, then right back home.

"Fuck." The word came from her mouth, not his. But he loved the pared-down sound of it, the way she wielded it with the power of what she was feeling and what she so clearly wanted.

So Capelli gave it to her. "You like this," he said, pulling out of her pussy a little farther this time before removing all the space between his hips and the provocative swell of her ass.

Although her moan was answer enough, Shae whispered a "yes" anyway. His position behind her gave him the perfect vantage point to watch, and as he started to move, he captured everything. The fall of her hair over her back. The flare of her hips. The flex and pull of the muscles where her leg tapered up to the sugar-sweet curve of her ass. With each thrust, he took everything Shae had wanted him to see, every last part of her wide-open and willing and unequivocally his for the taking.

"Capelli." Her voice was thick and loaded with need. Arching her back, she slid her feet wider, exposing the cleft of her ass. His heart beat so fast that he was nearly dizzy, but he didn't care. His physiology was nothing compared to how badly he wanted her.

He moved one hand from her hip to the base of her spine, watching his fingers trail over her skin as he continued to fuck her from behind. Fanning his fingers over that deep, wicked curve of her lower back that he'd loved since he'd first glimpsed it in the grocery store, he skimmed his thumb lower over her ass until he found the tight ring of muscle hidden there. Capelli pressed, not hard enough to gain entry, but with just enough pressure to heighten the pleasure of it.

Shae gasped, not in surprise, but something darker. "Please," she whispered. "You want to see what I need? I need *you*."

She looked at him over one shoulder, and Christ, she was perfect.

"I need you, Capelli. Let go and come for me."

The words made his balls tighten in dark, dirty pleasure. But they also made something break free deep in his chest, something warm and good that said *I have you*, and the feel of it shoved him right over the edge. He thrust into the heat of her, over and over, filling her fully each time. Release built, fast and hot between his hips, but there was no drawing it out or holding back. He fucked Shae in deep, hard strokes, his thumb pressing again until she cried out in bliss. Her orgasm squeezed his cock, and the sensation, the sight of her body that went with it, was too much. Capelli's climax rushed at him from every direction, wringing a shout from his chest as he went bowstring tight on one final thrust. Pleasure flew apart beneath his skin and stole his breath, but still, he never took his eyes off Shae.

And in that moment, with her name on his lips and the image of her fierce, flawless face tattooed in his memory, Capelli knew he was in trouble.

Because not only was he falling for Shae, but he didn't want to do a damned thing to stop it.

CHAPTER 20

Capelli stared at the ceiling in Shae's bedroom, his body perfectly still even though his brain was less than a step away from self-destructing. They'd gone through the motions of getting ready for bed, with her trading her bathrobe for a tank top and a pair of sweatpants and him throwing on a pair of nylon basketball shorts he'd left at her place earlier this week. Teeth brushed, lights out, blankets up —all the methodical steps followed, just like always. Yet all the step-by-step processes in the universe wouldn't change the fact that Vaughn had nearly killed four people tonight, one of whom was Shae.

And they *definitely* wouldn't change the fact that no matter how hard Capelli had worked to fight it, he didn't just know Vaughn from their shared past. He knew him because his brain worked in the exact same calculating, always-moving way, and it would never, ever change.

The world is different for people like us, James. We're cold and ruthless, like shadows and wraiths...

Shae turned to her side, close enough to touch him even though she didn't. "Do you want to talk about this yet?"

Capelli's heart slapped against his sternum before lodging firmly in his throat. The answer, he knew, should not just be no, but hell no. He needed his composure now more than ever. Needed to steel himself against his past, against the emotions that would ruin him if he let them see the light of day.

But all Shae had to do was look at him with those wide green eyes, and his brain stopped functioning altogether. He'd spent the last eight years not letting anyone see who he truly was. He dodged and strategized. Worked to stay busy. Hid while he tried to atone. Then Shae came along, wearing every last one of her feelings like a fucking billboard, loud and bold and proud as hell, and damn it, even though it defied every ounce of logic he'd ever known, Capelli wanted to show her everything right back.

Consequences be damned.

"Haven't you ever wondered how I know so much about Vaughn?" he asked, and her body stilled at the same time her brows tucked in the scant moonlight filtering in past her bedroom blinds.

"He was the prime suspect for all the counter-surveillance in the DuPree case," she said slowly. "Plus, he's clearly not an altar boy. Intelligence must've suspected him in other cases, too. I'm sure his list of alleged crimes is three inches thick."

A beat of silence opened up between them, but somehow, the shadows made it easier to admit the truth, like some sort of conduit for all things dark and ugly.

"It is," Capelli agreed. "But that's not how I know."

"Okay." Shae drew the word out into a question, and for once, he didn't calculate the bare minimum of information required for a sufficient answer.

"I know what Vaughn's like from firsthand experience. I've known him for more than a decade."

The unease in Capelli's chest twisted sharply between his

ribs, reminding him he'd just scratched the surface of the truth, that the layers beneath were darker and more treacherous, unforgivable at best. But Shae was right there next to him, her breath steady and her body warm and her stare bold on his in the near darkness, and his words flew out despite the danger of what they'd expose.

"Vaughn and I used to work together."

"Oh my God," she gasped. "Vaughn was a cop?"

Capelli took a breath. Sealed his fate. And said,

"No, Shae. I'm a criminal."

~

SOMETHING WAS wrong with Shae's brain. Or maybe it was her ears, or possibly both, because there was no universe in which the words Capelli had just said could be right.

I'm a criminal.

"I don't understand," she finally managed, although it was the most gargantuan understatement she had ever uttered. Nothing about this made any sense. "How…what are you talking about?"

Capelli exhaled, the sound soft compared to the sudden soundtrack of her racing heart. "I'm talking about who I am. Do you remember how I told you I had a rough upbringing?"

"Yes," Shae said, trying to make her brain fall in line enough to follow the facts. "You said you didn't have much growing up. I remember."

"We weren't just poor. My mother wasn't exactly what you'd call…stable."

The words sounded strange, as if they were somehow rusty, and it occurred to her in that moment that this was the first time he'd spoken them in a long time. Maybe ever.

So she fought the deep-seated urge to start impulsively asking questions and she listened.

"I never knew my father," Capelli said, his shoulders rustling against the pillow behind them as he capped the statement with a shrug. "To be honest, I'm not sure my mother did, either. It was always just me and her, although most of the time, I was the adult. She had a substance abuse problem," he added, sending Shae's heart into a full twist. "Meth mostly, but she wasn't picky. If you could snort it, swallow it, or shoot it, she was usually game."

Shae released a sharp exhale, unable to cage her emotions entirely. "Shit. Capelli, I'm so sorry."

He laughed, a soft, joyless sound. "I remember thinking I was lucky, if you can believe that. Don't get me wrong—she was hardly Mother of the Year material. But she never hit me or lost her temper, or…worse."

His voice tripped over the last word, just enough to let Shae know how much worse he'd seen growing up, and oh God, how had he kept this inside for so long?

"Still, I took it on the chin in other ways, more times than I can count," Capelli continued. "Sleeping in cars. Cleaning up after her all-night benders. Begging for food and eating whatever I could salvage from trash cans or restaurant dumpsters. It was all just part of my normal."

"Oh my God," Shae whispered, realization becoming reality in one swift, heart-rattling stroke. "Is that why you're so careful about what you eat now?"

One corner of his mouth lifted slightly, like an attempt at a smile that didn't quite stick. "It's part of it," he said. "When I was younger, I didn't realize that wasn't how things were supposed to be, though. I mean, we lived in the deepest part of North Point. The people around us had difficult lives too, and while my mother was a pretty bad parent, she wasn't really a bad person. Not in the beginning, anyway."

Anger sizzled in Shae's veins, sudden and hell-hot. "You were her kid, and she let you sleep in cars and eat from garbage cans," she snapped, but Capelli simply shook his head.

"I'm not denying that she was a terrible parent. But I couldn't rely on her to always be *un*reliable. Every once in a while, she'd throw me for a loop and straighten up. We'd move into a less shitty apartment or she'd get a steady job, and for a while, things would be okay."

He paused, seeming to get lost in thought. "On those nights when she was sober and didn't have to work, my mother would break out the microwave popcorn and DVDs she'd borrowed from God only knew where. We'd camp out on a blanket and watch movies and laugh, and she'd promise me she'd stay clean, that things would only get better."

In less than a breath, Shae's anger melted into gut-punching heartache. "But they didn't, did they?"

"No." He shook his head. "A couple of weeks would go by, maybe a month, and I'd find my mother passed out on the bathroom floor or shacked up with some new guy who had a fresh stash and a bad look in his eyes," he said quietly. "The craziest part was that even then, I knew how to read people. How to tell if they were hiding something or lying. And every time she said she'd get clean, she really meant it, so every single time, I believed her."

"And then the cycle just started again," Shae said softly.

"For a while, anyway." Something hardened in Capelli's voice, and it sent a spray of goose bumps over her bare arms. "I've always known my mind works differently than most people's. But it wasn't until my mother caught on that it really hit me how different I am."

"I'm sorry." Shae blinked, trying and failing to read him in the moonlight. "I don't follow."

He lay perfectly still beside her even though the sudden tension in his body radiated out to fill the room. "When my mother figured out that I could calculate odds and read people and memorize things after only seeing them once, she used the skills to her advantage. At first, it was low-level stuff here and there, like counting cards at local poker games or running small cons when we were desperate for extra cash. But then she caught me with that secondhand computer and she realized what I could do with it."

Shae's anger whipped back through her like a boomerang, stretching her voice thin and tight. "How old were you at the time?"

"I did my first black hat hack six days after my fourteenth birthday," Capelli said, and oh yeah, it was official. She wanted to throttle this woman for no less than a dozen *super* legitimate reasons.

"Online security was a lot different back then," he continued, quietly enough to capture her full attention. "It pretty much barely existed in places other than the FBI and NSA. Hacking into retail sites to access credit card information or local businesses' payroll accounts to siphon some change off a handful of 401Ks was far too easy. I knew it was wrong," he said in a rush of breath, and of all the truths he was letting her see, this one felt like the biggest. "But my mother kept telling me how much we needed the money, and that the companies had insurance and loss protection plans, so it didn't actually hurt anyone. And just like all those times she told me she was clean and sober, like a fool, I went with my emotions instead of my head, and I believed her."

Shae's throat threatened to close. "Of course you believed her." Tears pricked at her eyes, born of equal parts anger and emotion, but she held fast to her determination in spite of them. "You were barely in high school, you had no one else to turn to, and you needed a place to sleep at night. Your mother manipulated the hell out of you. None of that was your fault."

"Of course it was my fault," he said, adamant. "I knew

stealing money from those people was wrong, Shae—I certainly knew it was illegal. And I did it anyway. Not once or twice, but *hundreds* of times, over the course of years, until I was so good at lying, stealing, and hacking that it wasn't just all I did. It was all I knew."

Realization flashed in her mind, pinning her into place on the bedsheets as she came full circle with the start of their conversation. "Is that how you know Vaughn?"

Shoulders locked around his neck, Capelli nodded. "Vaughn came up on the streets, just like I did. His mother was in and out of jail—prostitution, possession, all the usual songs on the playlist. His old man's doing back-to-back life sentences for a double homicide he pulled when Vaughn was seventeen. We ran in the same circles, and we had the same set of skills. It didn't take long for us to connect."

"So you worked together on cons and scams."

"For a while." At Shae's silently raised brows, he added, "Enough times to know he's as smart as he claims and that he's got no soul."

She did her best not to wince. It worked for the most part. "Okay, but then how did you get out of that life and start working for the RPD?"

Here, he paused, and her gut tapped out a warning she didn't understand. Turning his life around should be the best part of this story, not something that should put a look of sheer dread on his face.

"After a while, my mother got greedy, and that made her brash. She pushed me to do bigger jobs," Capelli said quietly. "She'd find potential places to scam or rob, and I'd do the counter-surveillance to show her the weak spots and the best way not to get caught. If she needed muscle for on-site robberies, she'd convince the boyfriend-of-the-month to help out for a cut. But then, eight years ago, she fell in with some guy who worked as a night-shift security guard for Holden Federal Savings."

Whoa. "Hardly a small company." They were the second biggest bank in Remington, with branches all over Charlotte, besides.

"Nope," Capelli agreed. "And their security systems are top of the line. The only way to kill the live feed on the surveillance video was to patch it on-site during the actual job. I told my mother the whole thing was too risky—the odds of something happening that we couldn't predict were a lot higher than usual. But she and her boyfriend went full court press because the payday was bigger, and I was the only one who could put the patch in place to make the whole thing work."

"Oh my God." Shae's heart pounded and broke all at once. "What happened?"

Capelli said exactly what she knew he would. "The whole thing went completely south. I got the patch in place, but my mother's boyfriend tripped the motion sensors, and we both got arrested. Of course he lied to cover his ass. Said the entire job had been my idea and that I'd coerced him into it. The cops had me on the surveillance footage doing all the recon in the days leading up to the job, so the story stuck. And the next thing I knew, I was taking the weight for the whole robbery."

Shae gasped. "Okay, but your mother must have—"

"She didn't."

"—said something," Shae finished softly, and oh God. Oh *God.* "She let you take the fall?"

Capelli nodded. "She knew that if her boyfriend couldn't hang what had happened at the bank on me, he'd try to hang it on her instead. Me, my mother—that guy would've implicated fucking Santa Claus if it would have lessened the charges against him."

Shae's lips pressed into a tight line, trapping her deeply rooted temptation to curse, but only by a thread. She sensed a tiny shift in Capelli's voice, some measure of sadness that hadn't been there a second ago, and as she kept listening, her temptation to curse became something else entirely.

"My mother knew it wouldn't take much digging for the RPD to figure out she had been partying beyond her means for years. If I didn't go down for the one crime, neat and tidy, she knew she might go down for everything. So she did what she was best at."

"She lied," Shae whispered.

"She lied," Capelli said, his resignation on full display even in the dusky shadows of her bedroom. "I didn't have any recourse. Telling the detectives that my mother was the guiltiest party of all would've only gotten me in deeper in the hole for all the other jobs I'd helped her pull, and more importantly, they weren't wrong. I'd committed the damned crime."

Shae's breath slapped to a stop in her lungs. Okay, so technically, that was true, but still... "You shouldn't have been the only one to pay for it. God, Capelli, you shouldn't have even been the *first* person to pay for it."

"Funny you should say that," he answered, all irony. "Turns out, someone else felt the same way."

Shae's confusion must have been slathered all over her face, because he went on with, "One of the detectives who arrested me came into the interview room just as I was about to be booked. He told me he thought my mother's boyfriend was lying, and that he knew I'd gotten caught up in something I hadn't wanted to be a part of. He also said he knew there was a third party involved."

Understanding lit like a tissue paper touching open flames. "The boyfriend ratted your mother out as a safeguard, didn't he?"

"Yeah." Capelli's chin dipped in the smallest of nods. "Although at the time, I didn't know that. The detective said the plan was too detailed to have been a first crime, and he made me an offer, right then and there. A full statement and testimony against my mother for the bank job along with all of the other crimes she and I had committed in exchange for no jail time."

"It sounds like that detective knew who should take the brunt of the blame," Shae said, slowing her breath to accommodate the rush of relief filling her lungs.

But Capelli surprised her with a firm shake of his head. "It was a massive risk on his part. I was just as guilty of those crimes as my mother. But he said he didn't quite see it that way, and in the end, once the DA heard everything the detective had to say, he agreed, too." Capelli paused to laugh, a joyless sound that cracked Shae's heart. "Even though I knew it would keep me out of jail, I didn't want to take the deal. But I also knew that if I didn't, I'd end up back at that precinct—or worse—eventually anyway. So I agreed. I told the detective everything, and he had my record cleared in exchange for my testimony."

Shae looked at him, at the wistful sadness dominating his features in the silvery, barely there light slanting in past her window shades, and in that moment, everything clicked. "The detective was Sinclair, wasn't it?"

The realization earned her the tiniest of smiles. "Yeah. It was pretty obvious from the investigation that I had a skill set the police department would find useful, so he offered me a job, helped me find a place to live, and I've been with him at the Thirty-Third ever since."

"What happened to your mother?" she asked.

"She and her boyfriend were both convicted, him for the robbery at the bank, her for a lot more than that. She was..." Capelli stopped to clear his throat. "She was two years into her thirty-six year sentence when she was stabbed to death in prison. Some drug smuggling thing gone bad, I guess."

Ice coated Shae's gut, her chin whipping up with the force of her sadness and shock. "Oh, Capelli."

"The thing is, what I did to her isn't even the worst part."

"What you did to her?" Shae repeated, but he kept talking as if what he'd said was some universal truth, some unarguable constant like the color of the sky.

"I'm always trying to figure things out," he said, his voice rising in frustration. "Strategies and systems and schemes—Christ, all of it! My brain doesn't rest, Shae. *Ever.*"

He pushed up to a seated position, turning swiftly to pin her with the full force of his stare. "I was twenty when Sinclair arrested me. An adult. I could've walked away from those crimes I committed a thousand times, but I didn't. Because I'm not like normal people, like *decent* people," he bit out, gesturing roughly to his temple. "Figuring out those cons and crimes is my default! It's how I'm wired. It's what my *brain does*, and it's never going to stop."

The words stunned her into place so completely that for a second, Shae couldn't even breathe. "You think you're a bad person because of how your mind works?"

"I think I'm the *worst* sort of person because of how my mind works," he shot back. "Jesus, Shae, don't you get it? I might work for the RPD now, but I'm not different. If my brain didn't do this, my mother wouldn't have been able to talk me into all these crimes in the first place. But it does. It always *will*. I'm ruthless and cold, just like Vaughn."

The mere suggestion sliced through her, foregoing muscle and hitting bone. With nothing but impulse in her veins, she swung toward the bedside table, fumbling with the lamp—come on, come *on*—until her fingers clumsily found the switch. The sudden brightness burned her eyes and tempted her to squint. But she couldn't hold back on this, not even a little bit.

She needed to make Capelli see that she meant every goddamn syllable of what she was about to say.

"No, you're not." Jamming her knees into the mattress, Shae stabbed a finger through the air, making contact with his bare shoulder to be sure she had the full measure of his attention. Her affirmation shook under the weight of the pure emotion sailing through her veins, but she didn't care. "You are nothing like him, do you hear me? Your mother exploited you! You did what she told you to because you needed a place to sleep at night, then you kept doing it because it was all you knew."

He opened his mouth—presumably to argue—but oh no. Not fucking happening.

"Yes, you did bad things, and yes, they were wrong," Shae said, and the words seemed to shock him into silence. "But you did the right thing when you needed to. What happened to your mother in prison isn't your fault." Her vocal cords wanted to falter at the sudden flash of grief in his eyes, but she dug deep for what she knew. "You're not a bad person, and you're *nothing* like Vaughn. You work your ass off to catch guys just like him, and you care about everyone in that intelligence unit like they're your family."

"I'm not..." His voice caught, all gravel and rough edges. "I'm still not a good man, Shae."

"Yes, you are," she whispered, flattening her hand over his chest, her own heart tripping as his pounded against her palm. "Your brain might never rest, Capelli, but your heart doesn't either. You're just too smart to see it. That's okay, though. I see it. I see *you*, and I know you're a good man."

Shifting her hands to cup his face, she leaned forward until she was close enough to feel his shaky exhale on her cheek. Yet she'd never been more steady or sure of anything in her life.

"Look at me, James Capelli. Know what I'm telling you. You're a good man."

And as he pressed his forehead to hers and let her fold her arms around him to hold him close, Shae knew he believed her.

Just like she knew she was in love with him.

CHAPTER 21

C apelli stood on the sidewalk in front of the Thirty-Third and waited to be overcome by the urge to vomit. A minute passed, then another, with nothing but the muted rush of nearby traffic and a whole lot of business as usual, and he released a slow exhale into the mid-morning sunshine.

"You good, Starsky?"

He returned Shae's brows-up, sassy smile with one of marginal doubt. "I'm still not a cop, you know."

"I'm not either. But if the badge fits…" She stepped in front of him, her hands in the pockets of her dark brown leather jacket, her eyes so bright and beautiful, it almost hurt. "We're going to catch Vaughn. He's going to go down for everything he's done. And you're still nothing like him. You know that, right?"

Capelli paused. It defied all logic, but the fact that Shae saw goodness in him made him want to *be* good. He didn't even know if he'd ever truly been good before; at least, not in the way of anyone truly decent. His brain always unraveled things, pared them down, stripped them all the way to their lowest common denominators and basest, barest parts. But when Shae looked at him, all of that shifted, and suddenly there was a chance—however slight—that he might have a shot at redemption.

"Yeah," Capelli said slowly, testing the idea out in a brain that had known a different reality for so long. "I know."

Just like he knew what he had to do right now.

Pressing forward to place an essentially chaste kiss over her mouth first, Capelli turned toward the building. He and Shae hadn't spoken much since he'd unloaded the story of his past on her last night. Then again, they hadn't needed to. He'd pretty much splattered his feelings all over the place, leaving no messy, horrible details left unsaid.

And rather than running like she should have, Shae had not only listened, but held him tighter for it.

They walked up the steps in front of the precinct, side by side. The lobby was fairly empty—not a huge shock considering their nine o'clock-on-a-Saturday-morning timing. But as they went through security and made their way up to the second floor, the dread Capelli had been expecting to fill his belly and send ice through his veins was strangely absent.

They *were* going to catch Vaughn. He'd do whatever it took to make it happen.

"Oh, hey!" Hale was the first person to see him and Shae cross the threshold into the intelligence office, where the rest of the team was already unsurprisingly hard at work. "You two okay? You feeling alright, Shae?"

"I'm totally fine," Shae said, pairing her answer with a smile that backed it up. "Thanks for asking."

Hollister looked up from his laptop screen, leaning back slightly in his desk chair. "Close call, McCullough. You had us worried for a second, there."

Although the detective's expression was pretty much unreadable—even Capelli had to admit Hollister had a killer poker face when he chose to trot it out—enough concern carried through his tone to give him away.

Concern Shae must have heard loud and crystal clear, because she made sure to give up a full twirl before saying, "I'm in perfect working order, which I'm sorry to say means you're all stuck with me helping on this case until my next shift at Seventeen. How are the two contractors who were pulled from the fire?"

"Serious but stable," Maxwell said. "They both inhaled a lot of smoke, but with some breathing treatments, they should pull through. And you were right." He looked at Capelli. "Substantial amounts of sufentanil turned up on both of their tox screens."

"If you want to fire up the crime scene board, we can get you caught up on the case," Isabella offered, just as Sinclair appeared at the back of the room by the now-open door to his office. While Shae nodded and went to sit in her usual spot at the far end of his desk, though, Capelli's feet remained rooted to the spot where he stood on the linoleum. His heart conspired against him, tripping faster in his chest. The part of him that had buried the past warned that this would make him vulnerable, that it was too dangerous, too personal to share.

But the other part of him belonged here, in this intelligence unit. And for the first time ever, that part knew it was way past time to tell his teammates the truth.

"Before we do that, there's something you all need to know." Capelli pulled in a large breath. Held it for just a second. Then went with the facts. "I know Conrad Vaughn."

Isabella was the first to break the stunned silence. "You *know* him," she said slowly, her shock clearly mirrored by Hale, Hollister, Maxwell, and even Sinclair. While a not-small amount of surprise had also flown through Shae's gaze when he'd first spoken the words, her lips curved into a smile that led the truth right on out from the space where he'd kept it hidden for eight long years.

"I do."

Capelli opened his mouth and didn't stop talking until the whole story was out, from his upbringing to his history with Vaughn to his arrest. Sinclair stood at the back of the office, his face revealing nothing as Capelli spoke, but the rest of his teammates' expressions made up for it tenfold.

"Jesus, man. That's a lot to keep bottled up," Hollister finally said after Capelli had finished. "Not that we don't all have skeletons we don't want to dig out of the closet," he added, his normally laid-back persona slipping into surprisingly serious territory for only a second before he tacked his easy-does-it poker face firmly back in place. "But how come you never said anything until now?"

"Lots of reasons," Capelli replied slowly. In truth, there were hundreds of them, but finally, he stuck with, "I guess it was just hard to get my head around being the only criminal among a bunch of cops. I was worried…" He broke off for a breath. "I committed a lot of crimes. My brain is kind of hard-wired for it."

"Bullshit." Moreno's answer was unequivocal enough to stun Capelli into place on the floor tiles. "Your brain is hard-wired to figure things out. That might've made you a good criminal once," she admitted. "But it makes you an irreplaceable part of this team now."

His deep-seated instinct kicked, clearly not wanting to ease its grip on him so easily. "I stole from people. Cheated. Lied."

"And the DA wiped your slate clean," Maxwell said, crossing his arms over the well-muscled expanse of his chest. "If there's one thing I can promise you, it's that none of us in this unit are angels."

If anyone was qualified to make the statement, it was

definitely the rough, gruff detective with more tenure as a cop than anyone save Sinclair. "It took balls to come clean about this. I respect that. If Sarge stands by you, I stand by you," he said, and Hale nodded her agreement.

"Me too. I know I'm the baby of the unit, but I'm proud to work with you, Capelli."

Capelli released the breath he'd only just realized he'd been holding. "Thanks."

"I am too." Isabella's nod sent another flare of relief through Capelli's gut. "If there's one thing this job has taught me, it's that we're a team, all of us, together. Nothing that's happened in your past changes that."

Speaking of which… "I want you to know that I'd never jeopardize an investigation," Capelli said, and God, despite all his instincts to keep the side of himself that belonged to the past well-hidden, he meant it. "I never withheld anything that would've helped us catch Vaughn, not in the DuPree case or this one. I do know him, and he knows me, but I haven't had any contact with the guy in eight years."

Hale's shoulders hit the back of her desk chair, her dark blond brows knitting together beneath the heavy fringe of her bangs as she gestured to the laptop on her desk. "Consider yourself lucky in that regard. It looks like he's culling his list of friends. Including, apparently, Mayor Aldrich—who not only had his house burn down last night, but seems to have a penchant for bikini models who aren't his wife. At least, according to the less than virtuous video that was leaked to all the major news outlets about an hour ago."

"Whoa. Talk about a plot twist," Shae murmured, and damn, Capelli had to agree. "No way that timing is a coincidence, right?"

He shook his head. "If Vaughn was also trying to shake the guy down? It's extremely unlikely."

Shrugging out of his jacket, Capelli moved over to his

desk and booted up both the array and the crime scene board. He might not be great (or, okay, even passably decent) at emotional disclosure. But processing the facts and probabilities, even when they related to a subject as potentially pothole-laden as Vaughn? Now *that*, he could do.

"At first glance, the mayor doesn't seem like he'd be on the list of Vaughn's usual suspects, and we're not quite sure how the video fits in with things yet," Hollister said. "But the M.O. for the blaze fits the other two crimes. No way are they not related."

"Extortion *and* blackmail. Vaughn's stepping up his game," Capelli realized out loud, the variables falling into place in his mind. "Which means he's either pissed or getting desperate for a payday. Maybe both."

"What have we got to work with from last night's fire?" Shae asked, the question as natural as if any other member of the team had voiced it, and Sinclair stepped over toward the crime scene board at the same time Capelli pulled up the case files for display.

"Arson and CSU are still working the scene, but preliminary reports corroborate Shae and Slater's statements that large amounts of gasoline were present and likely used as an accelerant."

Shae shook her head in thought. "Dousing the mansion in gasoline is pretty brash. Vaughn really is ramping things up if he's not even bothering to hide the fact that this is arson anymore."

"Yeah, well, he's still slippery as hell," Moreno said, frowning as she gestured to the photos Capelli had just posted of last night's crime scene. "The canvas didn't turn up a single witness who could put Vaughn anywhere within a mile of the scene. Hollister and I are still going through the footage from the city cams though."

"The two contractors aren't much help either." Maxwell's

add did nothing for the knot in Capelli's gut. Well, except make it bigger, anyway. *Damn* it.

"They don't remember anything at all?" Shae asked, eyes wide in surprise, and Maxwell shook his head.

"They were working in different rooms, doing overtime at the mayor's request." The tone the detective slung around the last word made it clear the mayor's "request" hadn't involved the option of saying no. "Both men said their assailant snuck up on them from behind, they felt the needle stick, and the next thing they remember is waking up at Remington Memorial."

Confession, physical evidence, witness... Capelli flipped to the next logical variable most likely to yield a lead. "What's Aldrich saying?"

"Nothing yet. We haven't been able to reach him," Hale said.

Sinclair planted his hands over his hips, and—oh shit, the glint in his steel-gray stare was a serious harbinger of Very Bad Things. "That's about to change. Maxwell, you and I are going to go have a chat with the mayor and find out what he's been up to when he thinks nobody's looking. In the meantime, I'll have the DA subpoena his financials for the department's forensic accountant to start going over. Let's see if Aldrich is as slick on paper as he is with his constituents."

Unyielding, Sinclair turned toward the crime scene board, where Capelli had just posted the mayor's headshot. "He's the key to nailing Vaughn, and it's past time for the Shadow to go down for his crimes. I don't care if we have to go all the way back to Aldrich's third grade report card. Kick over every rock you can to prove these two are connected. Phone records. Bank statements. Campaign donations. I want everything under the microscope."

"Actually, Sergeant, there's no need for all that digging."

Capelli's heart pumped out a steady stream of *what the hell* at the sound of the unfamiliar feminine voice coming from the doorframe of the intelligence office.

Sinclair—along with everyone else in the room—swung his full attention toward the woman, who was accompanied by a uniformed officer on one side and a man Capelli had never seen before on the other.

"I'm sorry, you are?"

Capelli placed her before Sinclair had finished asking, and holy shit. What was a defense attorney from one of the best law firms in Remington doing in their office?

"Tara Kingston," she said, her glossy black corkscrew curls bouncing over the shoulders of her suit jacket as she crossed the linoleum to offer Sinclair a handshake that looked firm as hell upon delivery. "Glad to finally have the pleasure. I've cross-examined a few of your team members at various criminal trials. You run quite the sharp unit."

"Thank you, but something tells me you didn't come all the way out here to blow sunshine up my skirt." Sinclair kept his expression as neutral as possible while still retaining all of his hard edges. Not that it seemed to faze Kingston much.

She lifted a brow. "Right to business. I like that. I represent Jack Kinsey, the mayor's senior aide."

Kingston gestured to the man still standing in the entryway who, despite his impeccable charcoal gray suit, looked like the poster boy for Insomniacs Anonymous.

A fact that surely hadn't been lost on Sinclair, or anyone else on the team, all of whom were watching the exchange intently. "And how is it that I can help you and Mr. Kinsey, counselor?"

Kingston offered up a smile that was all teeth. "You can start by calling the DA. My client has a boatload of information that's going to interest you, and he's willing to make a deal."

~

"THAT SHIT-SUCKING SON OF A BITCH!"

Vaughn glared at the breaking news update flashing over his laptop for a heartbeat, then another before slamming the thing shut. Given the level of the threat, he'd been a little surprised—not to mention a *whole* lot pissed off—that old Brad hadn't paid up last night like he should have. But come the fuck on. Now his senior aide was singing to the police like a goddamn canary, and Vaughn was wanted as a "person of interest" in the investigation?

He'd been sold out by Kinsey? The mayor's *handler*?

"Oh, screw this."

Vaughn shoved to his feet, prowling a path over the crumb-laden carpet in his stolen, fancy-ass apartment. So maybe he hadn't predicted Kinsey's balls would shrivel up and he'd go to the cops like a little bitch. According to the news, Aldrich wasn't corroborating whatever intel Kinsey had given up, and anyway, Vaughn was still smart enough to strategize a way around this little moronathon.

After all, he did still have a hell of an ace up his sleeve when it came to the RPD.

An idea formed in his brain, taking shape with speed and enough malice to make his dick hard, and yes—fucking A, *yes*, this was perfect. Reaching for the latest burner phone in the sloppy pile of them on his kitchen counter, Vaughn moved back to his laptop and pulled up a cell phone number he'd squirreled away for a situation just like this one.

Blast, meet past.

The phone at the other end rang twice, three times, and Jesus, how typical that James would try to figure out "Unknown Caller" even though Vaughn knew there was a zero percent chance the guy could track so much as what country the call originated from.

"Hello?"

"James! Long time no see. Tell me, how's life with the lemmings?"

Ah, the pause. Christ, it was so full of emotion and tension, it was practically goddamn delicious.

"Vaughn. I've been wondering when you'd call."

"Wondering, or worried? You've got a lot of secrets locked away in that vault of yours," Vaughn said, wanting to draw blood quickly.

Surprisingly, James had grown thicker skin since they'd last spoken. "This isn't really about me," he answered, not even skipping a beat. Oh, fine. So the guy was prepared. Vaughn was still smarter.

"Actually, it's totally about you, you lucky bastard. But you can do yourself a favor and stop trying to trace this call." He didn't even need to check his signal-blocking software to know every move James was making right now. The guy was more reliable than Old Freaking Faithful. "I'm pinging my signal off every cell tower between here and Singapore. I figure that'll give us a minute or two to catch up."

"Great," James said. The telltale click that said he'd put the call on speakerphone followed, and ha! Just like clockwork.

"Aw, speakerphone. Now it's a party. Let me guess…" Vaughn paused for the sake of drama. "Your sergeant—who has a lot of skeletons in his own closet, just FYI—I'm sure he's listening. Say hi, Sergeant."

"Vaughn." Sinclair's voice cut through the silence, and Vaughn grabbed the upper hand with a laugh that held no joy.

"Ah ah ah, that's the Shadow to you. And your girlfriend, Firefighter McCullough. It wouldn't be a soiree without her." Time to test the water a little. "She's a little brash for my taste, but hey, I'm sure you've figured out a way to put that mouth of hers to good use."

"Screw you, asshole," McCullough said, proving his point with startling predictability.

Vaughn laughed. God, this was going to be all too easy. "So now that we're all here, let's get down to business. I'm sure you think you can catch me now that you've listened to Kinsey's song and dance, but I'm here to tell you, that's not going to happen."

"You killed two people. You left innocent men to die in that fire, and you nearly killed two firefighters on top of it," James said, and there. *There* was the sore spot. The bruise to dig at in order to gain leverage.

The microscopic hitch in the word "firefighters" was everything.

But first things first. "Like anyone's going to miss a couple of gang bangers." Vaughn scoffed with the full power of his scorn. "I did you a favor."

"What about the other people you put at risk? All the people you've hurt by working for dirt bags like Julian DuPree?" James shot back. God, he was making this so fucking easy.

"Collateral damage," Vaughn said, utterly bored. "Come on, James. You know how risk/reward works. Shit, you made a killing off of it for years."

More bruises. After a pause that was more telling than any words could possibly be, James said, "I never killed anybody."

"You always did think you were so much better than everyone else." The truth of it slipped under Vaughn's skin, making his heart beat faster and his anger surge. "Tell you what. Let's cut through all the bullshit, shall we? I have a deal for you."

"You have a deal for me?"

There was no masking the surprise on the line, so Vaughn went straight for the jugular.

"By now you know the game I have in play, so I'll make this easy for you. I want two hundred and fifty thousand dollars."

"You're not seriously trying to extort a quarter of a million dollars from *me*," James said dubiously. "I don't have any assets like Nicky Bianchi or the Scarlet Reapers do. For Chrissake, I work for the RPD."

Vaughn stopped mid-pace on the stupid, snobby-as-hell eco-friendly bamboo floorboards in his kitchen and fought the urge to gag.

"Please. Let's not sprinkle sugar on this bullshit just so we can call it candy. We both know you could pull any one of a dozen scams that would earn you that money in less than a day. Hell, if you really want to be upstanding about it, I'm sure your precious police department has reserves for this sort of thing. I don't care where you get the cabbage, or how. But you're going to wire it to me by eight o'clock tomorrow night."

"It's the weekend, Vaughn," James started, and the anger that had been simmering in his chest broke free and bubbled upward at the obvious diversionary tactic.

"I don't give a shit if it's Christmas fucking morning, *Wraith*," he hissed, hammering his point home with the name. "Be grateful I didn't ask you for the million Aldrich should've given me."

Vaughn knew his limits, even if he hated them with the intensity of a thousand white-hot suns. But he was getting far too much pushback on these threats to be able to stay under the radar when he turned them into reality. Leave it to the vilest of Remington's underbelly to be as dumb as they looked. Still, he needed one last payday so he could go underground and regroup, and thanks to that spineless wonder, Kinsey, Vaughn was now exposed in a way he hadn't accounted for. No way could he risk stealing the money himself now that the spotlight was flying around. He might be good (okay, yeah, he was *that* good), but even a blind squirrel stumbled across a nut every now and then.

That the final payout would come from James and the RPD was honestly just poetic.

"Two hundred and fifty thousand is still a lot of scratch, even for a hacker," James said. "What if I can't come up with it by tomorrow night?"

Vaughn's smile tasted like decadence and pure, dark evil. "You can. I don't care who signs your sad-sack, hard-earned paychecks now, or how much you think you've repented. Underneath all that righteousness, you're still just a common criminal. I'll send you the account information tomorrow, and you'll transfer the two hundred fifty K. If you *decide* not to, I'll burn you to the goddamn ground. And not even an army of cops will catch me."

CHAPTER 22

S hae stared at the cell phone sitting in the middle of the desk in Sinclair's office, wanting nothing more than to hurl the damned thing across the room. Logically, she'd known there was a chance this case would end up in a show-down—Kinsey's statement had been pretty damning for both the mayor, who was now in custody, and Vaughn, who was still in the wind. Using the news of Kinsey's deal with the DA to draw Vaughn out of the woodwork had been a calculated risk. They'd known that once it went public, Vaughn could just as easily run as swing for the fences.

What they hadn't known—what Shae had *never* expected —was that the move would put Capelli directly in that little bastard's crosshairs.

"We're going to need to craft one hell of a plan here." Sinclair's voice was surprisingly calm as he sent an unreadable stare across his desk at Capelli.

Oh, that she should be so lucky in the cool-and-collected department. "Can our strategy involve me having five minutes alone with this guy?" Shae muttered, her temper flaring enough to snap her arms into a knot over the front of her cream-colored sweater. "Sorry," she amended. "I know we need to stay on the level. This guy just burns my freaking toast."

"I don't think you're the only one who feels that way," Sinclair allowed, putting just enough edge on the words to let Shae know a potshot at Vaughn was sky-high on his wish list, too. "But Vaughn is dangerous, and our move with Kinsey obviously pissed him off enough to take a serious dig. We're going to need to play this exactly right in order to nail him without anyone getting hurt."

Shae chanced a look at Capelli from the spot where she stood next to him on the business side of Sinclair's desk. He'd been enviably stoic during the entire conversation with Vaughn, most of which they'd thankfully been able to record. Not so thankfully, Vaughn hadn't been exaggerating about scrambling the cell signal like a dozen eggs at breakfast, and no way, no fucking *way* could they let him get away with any of this.

"Vaughn's pissed, but he's also strategizing. He's looking for a payout to get him back underground," Capelli said. His chocolate-brown stare was more serious than she'd ever seen it, and wait…

"You're not honestly thinking of *giving* him the money." Something twisted deep in Shae's chest, the sensation doubling as he looked at her and nodded.

"Making the payout is the safest play. He knows he can't stay in Remington. Between the heat and the bridges he's burned, it's too dangerous not to run, but he can't get far without the means."

"Agreed," Sinclair said. "He's got to be prepping to clear out. What are you thinking for bringing him down?"

Capelli tugged a hand through his hair, rocking back on the heels of his thickly soled boots. "We give him the money. There's no way I can fake it," he added quickly, before

Sinclair could ask or Shae could get a renewed protest past her lips. "Vaughn's far too smart not to have safeguards in place to make sure the transfer is legit. But once he gives me the account number, I can hack into the bank's security system to track his activity. When he draws off the funds, we should be able to locate him and take him down."

"Should be," Shae echoed. "But it's not a guarantee, right? And if he's in some other country, or something, there's nothing you can do."

Sinclair's ice-blue stare shifted from Capelli's to hers. "No. It's not a guarantee, but a clear and present threat has been made against a member of my team, and we know Vaughn will follow through if we don't pay him off. If I'm going to make a riskier move, it had better be for a damned good reason."

"Look, I know paying Vaughn off for now isn't ideal," Capelli said, almost certainly for her benefit. "But it's strategically sound. We'll recover the money when we take him down, and this is the most logical call if we want a solid chance at catching him."

"And he's counting on you to make it," Shae shot back, her pulse clattering in her veins. "Like it or not, this is personal. He knows you. He knows exactly what you'll do. He's going to be ready for that."

The look on Capelli's face said he knew she was right. "That may be, but there isn't a better option here. Look"—he let out a slow breath—"Vaughn is a narcissist. He thinks he's too good to get caught, but the reality is, he's terrified of it. His biggest fear is being exposed as a fraud. As smug as he is, he'll do anything to stay out of our crosshairs, which means we're only going to get one chance to nail him."

"So let's *take* it." Shae looked at Sinclair, and God, here went nothing. "I have an idea."

One gray-blond brow rose. "Am I going to hate it?"

"No." Her palms went slick, her gut pitching with unease. Still, she didn't hesitate. "You're not going to hate it. But Capelli is."

"Shae," Capelli started, but Sinclair—*yes*, thank you, sweet Jesus—leaned back in his desk chair and lifted one hand.

"Hang on a second. I've heard your pitch. Now let me hear McCullough's."

Shae inhaled, standing as tall as her frame would allow before saying, "Vaughn is armed with an awful lot of knowledge right now. He knows RPD protocol, and he knows how Capelli runs counter-surveillance. We can't just outsmart him. We have to outmaneuver him, too. Which means that if we want to take him down, we have to do something he's not expecting."

Sinclair tilted his head. "So we don't take the safe move and pay him. And then?"

Annnd here was the part Capelli was going to hate even more than bucking logic. "Vaughn's M.O. is to destroy the thing that means the most to his target when he doesn't get paid out. For Nicky Bianchi, it was the restaurant he used as a front. For the Scarlet Reapers, it was their meth lab and the men who ran it. For the mayor, it was status and political position. And for Capelli…"

Capelli's chin snapped up with the full power of his obvious surprise. "It's you."

"So use me as bait."

"*No.*"

The word fired from Capelli's mouth before Shae had even finished her suggestion, and for once, he wasn't hiding a single emotion. "Are you crazy? Using you to draw Vaughn out is way too risky."

"It is risky, but that's exactly why it'll work." Heart racing, Shae turned toward Sinclair. She had to keep her cool if she was going to get him on board with this. As much as it would drive her bat-shit crazy, she had to take impulse out of the equation and make a calm, logical argument.

"Yes, not giving Vaughn the money will piss him off and make him dangerous, but it'll also make him sloppy. He threatened Capelli, and he thinks we'll put all of our energy and resources into protecting him if we don't pay up. Vaughn is arrogant enough to think he can get to me. If we give him the right set of circumstances, he won't be able to resist making a move to try and hurt me."

"And this is a smart move how, exactly?" Capelli asked from between his teeth.

Steady. Breathe in. Breathe out. "Because he won't know we're watching him. We'll be in control of the whole situation. You'll have me on coms, the team can run full surveillance. Then when he closes in, you can take him down before he gets a hand on me. We'll have to sell it," she emphasized, because even sloppy, Vaughn would still be cagey as hell. "But we can outplay him. *You* can outplay him, Capelli, but only if you take him by surprise."

His shoulders snapped upward, forming a hard angle on either side of his neck. "We're not doing this. We're not even *talking* about doing this." He must have calculated his odds of convincing Sinclair versus getting her to change her mind, because he turned to his boss and said, "Sarge, this is crazy. She's a civilian. No matter how much backup she has, we can't guarantee her safety. And if Vaughn gets his hands on her—"

"I understand the risks," Shae said before he could finish the grim thought out loud, and God, she really did. But they weren't going to catch Vaughn any other way. "I'm volunteering anyway. Run the odds, Capelli. You know using me as bait is our best shot at catching him."

Before Capelli could launch the counter-argument he was clearly formulating in his mind, Sinclair gave up a slow nod.

"I'm inclined to agree with McCullough on this one." He flicked a glance at the window overlooking the intelligence office, where all four detectives sat at their desks, hard at work, and Shae stood firm even though her knees threatened to wobble in relief. "Drawing Vaughn out will be easier than tracking him down, and no one does better counter-surveillance than you, Capelli. The team will take every possible precaution to keep Shae safe"—he shifted his stare to hers, and whoa, he meant business—"and I expect her to follow *all* plans and protocols to the letter. But coming up with a strategy to nail Vaughn before he ghosts is our best shot at taking him down. If we can catch him red-handed trying to hurt Shae? Even better."

Capelli went bowstring tight beside her, like a coil being pushed hard and primed for release, and for a second, Shae was certain he'd fight back. A beat passed, then another, his expression growing more and more impenetrable, until finally, he let go of an audible exhale.

"I'll start canvassing locations. We've got a lot of work in front of us if we have a prayer of outmaneuvering Vaughn, and not a lot of time to get it done."

Eleven hours, three pizzas, and a metric ton of team strategizing later, Shae had to admit that neither her brain nor her body could keep up with her Kevlar-reinforced determination any longer.

"Hey," she said, swiping a hand over her burning eyes before chancing a glance at the spot where Capelli sat at the far end of his desk, methodically reviewing the plan they'd all kicked into motion over the course of the day and evening. "Everyone else has gone home. Well, except for Sinclair." Not that *that* really counted. In the handful of weeks she'd been working with the intelligence unit, she'd grown fairly certain the sergeant was just a permanent fixture at the Thirty-Third. "I don't know how much more we can do tonight. Did you want to head out, too?"

Capelli adjusted his glasses, his plaid-shirted shoulders hitting the back of his desk chair with a soft thump. His expression was just as inscrutable as it had been ever since Sinclair had okayed the plan to use her to bring Vaughn out of hiding, but Shae knew far better. She knew *him*.

He'd probably rather die than admit it, but beneath that serious façade and even more serious work ethic, Capelli was scared.

"Sure. I guess." Shutting down his laptop and the crime scene board, he skinned into his black canvas jacket and slung his bag over one shoulder. Shae followed him to the door of the intelligence office, going through the motions of saying goodnight to the desk sergeant and completing a covert yet complete check of their surroundings, just as she had for the last few weeks. Something unspoken pulled between her and Capelli, as constant and tangible as gravity, but oddly, it wasn't uncomfortable. It was more of a tying together than a pressing apart, the way two magnets just seemed to know where they belonged and traveled toward one another by sheer instinct, and by the time they'd gotten to his apartment, she couldn't hold back anymore.

"You're mad at me for suggesting we go after Vaughn like this," she said, crossing the floorboards until less than a foot of space remained between them.

"No." At her arched brow, he amended, "Okay, I *was* mad. And I still hate the plan. But strategically, it's sound. I know because I made it that way. And I'd trust the team with my life, so..."

"I trust you with mine." Shae captured his face between her palms, looking him in the eyes so he would know how much she meant it. "This plan is going to work, Capelli. I know it."

A smile, slight and wistful, pulled at one corner of his mouth. "Gut feelings are still largely unsubstantiated and mostly illogical, you know."

Despite the gravity of the topic, she had to smile. "Not this one. This one says you'll keep me safe and that we'll catch Vaughn." Her heart began to beat faster, but she followed it without a second thought regardless. "This one says the risk is worth taking."

Capelli pressed his forehead to hers, his voice going ragged. "It's still a risk. If anything happens to you—"

"Nothing's going to happen to me. I'm right here," Shae said. She shifted back, but only far enough to slide one hand between their bodies, letting her fingers splay over the center of his chest. "I'm yours."

"I know," Capelli whispered. "That's what scares me."

Her heart pressed against her breastbone, filling her rib cage with a strange brand of emotion she couldn't quite identify. "It scares me, too. But I'm still here, and I'm not going anywhere."

Sliding her hands to his shoulders, she slanted her mouth over his. He cupped her neck, his hands wide and strong on her skin, fingers moving up to hook in her hair. Capelli held her fast while he explored every part of her, swiping his tongue over her bottom lip, finding the sensitive spot at the corner of her mouth, deepening their contact with his lips and teeth and tongue. Unlike all their other kisses, this one wasn't frenzied or rushed. Slow and far from sweet, this kiss was deeply erotic, urgent in a way that could only belong to the two of them together, and understanding sparked, low and hot in Shae's belly.

The seriousness, the intensity, the keen intelligence that

noted everything down to the last detail and always held it close. *This* was Capelli.

He was letting her see him. In his own way, with this kiss that Shae felt in every last part of her breath and bones and blood, he was letting her in.

Without speaking, she broke the kiss, sliding her fingers through his to lead him to his bedroom. The space was cloaked in shadows, nothing but the light from the hallway spilling in to cast a muted glow over the room, but that was okay.

Even in the pitch dark, she'd still be able to see what he was showing her. She'd know him, and he'd know her right back.

By heart.

Shae's breath caught, but she stood firm beside Capelli's bed. Her fingers curled tight against her palms—sweet Jesus, she wanted to touch him so badly. As if he'd zeroed in on her thoughts, he reached up, freeing the buttons on his shirt until the cotton fell away, then repeating the process with his jeans and boxers until he stood in front of her, completely and utterly bare.

Desire pooled between her hips, dark and needy. "Capelli. You are…"

"Yours." He slid off his glasses, eyes glinting with need in the scant, gold light. "Nothing else matters. I'm just yours."

In that moment, Shae didn't think. She moved out of raw instinct, pulling her sweater over her head, letting her jeans find the floorboards next to his.

And then she dropped to her knees.

"Shae." A note of warning touched Capelli's tone, but she met it with a smile.

"If you're mine, I'm taking you. Just the way I want." She let her fingertips drift up the rock-hard length of his cock, her sex going instantly wet as he shuddered at the touch. "Is that what *you* want?" she asked, looking up at him through the fan of her lashes.

"Ah, God." A moan grated up from his chest, his hips canting forward, chasing her touch. "Please, baby." Another thrust, and Shae's heartbeat grew wild in her chest.

"Please, what?"

"Take me." He looked at her, spearing her with his lust-blown stare. "Put your mouth on me and suck my cock."

Pressing forward until there was no space between their bodies, Shae parted her lips to take him deep. But much like the kiss they'd shared in the living room, she didn't rush. She kept her movements slow and full of purpose, touching and tasting and licking, and Capelli responded to every move. His hands shaped her shoulders, his exhales growing thicker, but still, she didn't hold back. She wanted this, *craved* the provocative sounds he made, the taste of him, heady and hot on her tongue. Wrapping her fingers around the base of his cock, she let her hand follow the motions of her mouth, up, then down, then up again, until finally, his breath became erratic and his body coiled tight.

"Shae."

This was a different sort of warning, one she recognized but didn't even think to heed.

"It's okay," she murmured, not breaking with the rhythm of her fingers as she looked up at him, their gazes locking. "I have you. Come for me, Capelli."

Shae angled forward, sucking his cock as far past her lips as she could. She took him in deep, sure strokes, and a quake worked a path over his muscles, sending a pulse of unfettered desire right to Shae's core. She didn't scale back or slow down, staying right there with him as her name tumbled from his lips and his body went loose in release, taking all he had to give before slowly shifting back on the floorboards.

In an instant, she was in the middle of his bed, her shoulders flat against the soft cotton comforter and her heart knocking hard at her throat.

"I have you, too," Capelli said, coaxing a trail of goose bumps over her skin as his tongue skated a path over her collarbone, his mouth curving in a wicked, wanton smile. "And we're not nearly done."

He moved lower, pulling a sigh past her lips. Shae opened her thighs wider to accommodate his body, and ohhhh *God*, he didn't disappoint. Stringing a trail of hot, open-mouthed kisses down the plane of her belly, he let his mouth hover over the low rise of her white lace panties before slipping them aside to bare her sex.

"Christ, you're so fucking perfect. So wet and ready." Capelli dragged the blunt edge of one finger over the seam of her pussy, the slow, slight contact sending sparks behind her eyelids.

"Yours," she whispered.

And the one word was enough. He lowered his mouth, pressing a provocative kiss between her thighs. Shae's back arched with the force of her pleasure, and he met it without pause. Hooking her legs over his shoulders for better contact, Capelli parted his lips over her clit, working the hard, sensitive knot with deep pulls. The pleasure was so much dirtier, so much more intense, so much *more*, period, than anything she'd ever felt. Desperate, she ground her hips against him, thrusting in search of every lick and suck.

"Mine," he said, the single syllable vibrating over her hyper-sensitive skin. There was nothing rough or proprietary in his tone. But his reverence just made the claim sexier, and with one last swirl of his tongue, Shae flew apart.

"*Yes*." Her moan tore out of her as her body trembled from the force of her orgasm. Capelli worked her through every shudder, softening his touch and lessening the contact between them in slow degrees before returning to her side. A quick glance through the shadows showed clear evidence of his arousal, his cock hard and flush against the lean muscles of his lower belly, and desire stirred again, low between Shae's hips.

Quickly, she took a condom from the spot where she knew he kept them in his bedside table drawer. A few seconds later, Capelli was exactly where she wanted him, his body pressed over hers from shoulders to chest to hips and his cock buried deep inside of her.

"Shae." He began to move, filling her pussy with every stroke.

God, she loved him, with his intense stare and his sinful touch and his hidden heart that only she could see.

"I'm right here, baby." Shae wrapped her arms around his shoulders as proof. "Right here with you."

And as they found a perfect rhythm and rode it all the way over the edge together, she knew that right there with Capelli was exactly where she belonged.

CHAPTER 23

Capelli flipped through the channels on the TV in his apartment for the fiftieth time in the last two minutes. Vaughn's text with the offshore account number had arrived like clockwork at 7:55, and it had taken all of Capelli's willpower to ignore the message, especially when Vaughn had followed it up ten minutes past the deadline with a gif image of a mushroom cloud and a single, chilling word.

BOOM!

Scooping in a breath, Capelli let the oxygen soothe his accelerated heartbeat, lifting a hand to the state-of-the-art microphone transmitter resting just out of sight in his right ear canal. Although he was closely monitoring everything from the precinct, Sinclair had given him point on the case for tactics and coms, and so far, Vaughn had been every bit the shadow his nickname implied.

"It's almost twenty-two hundred hours," Capelli said. "Can we get a check-in?"

"Another one?" Hollister asked, punctuated by an "oof" as Isabella landed an expertly placed elbow to her partner's rib cage from the spot where she sat next to him on Capelli's couch.

"Don't be a dick, H. He's just being careful. Moreno and Hollister, in position," she said for the benefit of everyone else on their ears-only coms, sending a lightning-fast wink in Capelli's direction. They had to assume that Vaughn had been monitoring their locations, and Shae hadn't been wrong when she'd said they had to sell this thing hook, line, and hacker. Vaughn would never buy the intelligence unit not putting Capelli into some sort of protective custody after a viable threat had been made against him. So for appearance's sake, here they were, even though they all knew Vaughn had likely stopped watching *him* as soon as Capelli didn't make the payment. But they needed Vaughn to think Capelli was well-guarded and Shae wasn't so he'd make a move to try and get at her.

Yeah, it was official. The plan might be tactically solid, the team even more so, but he still fucking hated being seven point six miles away from Shae right now.

"Maxwell and Hale, in position. Eyes on McCullough's location. All clear," came Maxwell's gruff voice. Capelli pictured the surveillance spot they'd chosen for the two detectives yesterday, the vacant apartment that just so happened to be one floor up from Shae's unit and had a great line of sight on the surrounding street as well as the market across the way where Shae was currently out in the open and grocery shopping like nothing-doing, and his exhale came just a fraction easier that—for now—all was quiet.

"McCullough, in position. Aisle nine at the Food Market. And just so you know, this earpiece is really freaking cool."

The sound of her voice, so confident and bold and so uniquely Shae, sent a bolt of something to Capelli's gut that couldn't be defined with words.

If anything happened to her, if she sustained so much as a

fucking scratch on her honey-brown head, Capelli would search the ends of the earth and most of hell besides to find Vaughn and make him pay.

"Garza, in position, aisle six at the Food Market," said Maxwell's buddy from the gang unit who—thankfully, since they'd needed someone whose face Vaughn didn't know— had been willing to jump in for an assist. "And for the record, McCullough? You're buying the weirdest assortment of groceries I've ever seen."

"Hey, it's not my fault this place has Atomic Cheez Puffs *and* dill pickles on sale at the same time, okay?" she murmured quietly, since she was the only one of them other than Garza who was in public with her coms on. "At least the pickles are a vegetable. Sort of."

Capelli snorted, unable to help it, and Shae conceded, "Okay, fine. They're green. It's close enough."

He sobered less than a second later, remembering why she was at the grocery store in the first place. Who she was luring out of hiding. "Any sign of Vaughn yet?"

"Negative," Shae said, both Garza and Hale's voices layering in over hers in the same breath.

It was Hale who continued. "The market's pretty empty since it's closing in a few minutes. Vaughn might not want to risk making a move until Shae gets back to her apartment. But all the precautions for that are in place and good to go."

Another thing Capelli knew for a fact, since he'd been the one to wire the hell out of the place. Still, Vaughn was arrogant enough to try and make good on his threat in public, so... "Shae, are you sure you don't want to go over your exit strategy for the market one more time, just to be on the safe side?"

"*I* am, but something tells me you're not, so..." The smile in her half-whisper edged out the underlying tinge of seriousness that Capelli was certain no one could hear but him.

She might be calm on the surface and brash to her bones, but she was scared, too, and damn it, they needed to end this thing with Vaughn tonight. Once and for all.

Quietly, Shae said, "As soon as I'm done shopping, I'll check out and leave through the primary exit, then load my bags into the Jeep and head directly home. I'll keep my cell phone in my back pocket at all times so you can track my exact location via GPS. And before you ask, yes. I made triple sure to activate the backup device before I left, just in case."

"Okay," Capelli said. The plan of action—along with how thoroughly Shae knew it—kicked his unease down a notch. "Hale and Maxwell have eyes on the street, and Garza's got your back in case Vaughn tries anything before you get home. But whatever happens, be sure to play it safe. Fall out if anything goes sideways, and keep your phone on you and your coms on until you're back at your apartment."

"I've got it, Starsky. Coms on. Phone in pocket. No exceptions. I'm headed to the checkout right now."

Capelli blew out a wobbly breath. He listened to Shae chat up the clerk, cataloguing her progress through the line by the number of electronic beeps—*twenty-one, twenty-two, twenty-three*. He pictured the scene in his mind's eye: the checkout line, the brightly lit alcove by which she'd exit the market, the equally well-lit path to the spot where she'd parked her Jeep at the end of the street. He'd worked through the plan no less than a thousand times. If Vaughn surfaced, Maxwell and Hale would see him far before he could get his hands on Shae. Even if by some utterly unexpected turn of events, Vaughn closed in on her, Garza was right there in the market, close enough to keep her safe. Logic dictated that she'd be fine. Even their backup plan had a backup plan with the GPS locator Capelli had embedded in the heel of her right boot.

Christ, maybe Shae had been right after all. Maybe this whole thing would go off without so much as a—

"I've got a visual on Vaughn," Maxwell said, and the words slammed into Capelli with the force of a freight train. "Jesus, this guy really is a shadow. He's on foot, just past the corner of Hanover and Grammercy. Came out of fucking nowhere."

"Shae, what's your position?" he asked, his heart thundering against his sternum. *Cold and ruthless...like shadows and wraiths...*damn it, they needed to get her out of there. Fast. *Now.*

"I'm at the Jeep, loading my groceries." She slid the words under her breath, just loud enough for the coms to pick them up. "I have eyes on Vaughn. He's at my ten. Passing the market right now."

"Garza, get on this guy so we can take him down," Capelli bit out. The scenario unfolded in his head, his brain mapping out moves and counter-moves fast enough to make him dizzy. Vaughn was on foot. He'd never make it far, with or without Shae, no matter how well he hid.

"Copy that. I'm heading out of the market—"

Garza's words crashed to a halt.

"Garza?" Moreno asked, and only then did Capelli realize that she and Hollister had thrown on their Kevlar and geared up to fall out.

"Vaughn stopped," Hale said. "Shit. He's got eyes on Garza. Caught sight of him when he passed the market. I think he smells a setup."

"I'm holding in the alcove pretending to be on my cell, but I don't have a whole lot of options here if you want to keep our cover intact," Garza near-whispered. "Vaughn is definitely suspicious. If I don't fall out, he's going to ghost."

"Can you take him down from your current position?" Capelli asked, silently begging God and every other deity he could drum up that Garza would give up an affirmative.

But the detective's pause was answer enough. "I don't mind giving it a go, but he's got a decent lead on me, and I'm willing to bet he's got an exit strategy ready to roll. Your call."

Capelli opened his mouth, ready to give the go-ahead anyway, when Shae's voice filtered over the line.

"Hang on. I think I can get him to make a move."

"No." Adrenaline replaced the air in his lungs. "Shae, you need to get out of there. Right. Now."

"I'm good without Garza. I know how to get Vaughn to close in rather than run."

"*Shae*—"

"I said I'm *good*," she insisted on a low hiss. "He doesn't know I see him. He's trying to decide whether or not to make a move. If Garza falls out, I think I can get him to bite."

Fear combined with anger, both funneling into Capelli's gut. "Shae. Listen to me. Don't do anything stupid. Just get in your Jeep and lock—"

"Ah, damn it," Maxwell bit out, and no, no. This couldn't be happening. "Shae just took her cell phone from her pocket and put it in the front seat of her Jeep."

Her cell phone. The same cell phone Capelli had told her a million times she needed to keep on her, no matter fucking what. But not having the phone would tell Vaughn she couldn't be located, and in a soul-shaking instant, Capelli realized exactly what Vaughn was going to do. How he'd probably planned it from the beginning, right down to baiting Shae when she was supposed to be baiting him instead.

He was going to kidnap her, and they weren't going to be able to stop him.

"Vaughn's on the move," Hale confirmed, her voice not entirely steady. "Coming in at your nine, Shae. *Fast*."

Capelli's heart locked in his throat. "Garza, go! Shae, you need to—"

"Bad move with the cell phone, sweetheart," came Vaughn's voice over the coms.

"*Shae!*" Capelli screamed.

But the only response was silence.

~

HOLY HELL, Shae felt strange. She tested her eyes in a series of slow-motion blinks, trying to get her bearings, all to no avail. She was moving—maybe?—possibly in a car, although she couldn't remember how she got here or who she was with. Her mouth felt packed with cotton, her brain even worse, and wait…wait…she needed to figure this out.

Yeah. Not happening.

"Good morning, sunshine," came a voice from beside her, insidious enough to chill her into awareness. The market… packing her bags in the back of the Jeep…the strange, highly chemical smell on the cloth that had been pressed over her face after Vaughn had appeared in her line of sight, and oh God. Oh God oh God oh God.

He had kidnapped her.

Shae bolted upright, although her brain worked on a full five-second delay. Her first instinct was to lunge for the passenger door, which of course was locked. God *damn* it!

Vaughn laughed, his cold, evil features flashing on-off, on-off in the passing street lights. "Gotta give you points for moxie. But since we're moving at like"—he paused to flick a glance at the speedometer in a car that—shit!—wasn't hers —"fifty miles an hour and I did recently dose you with chloroform, it's probably better for you that I locked that door. Unless you've got a particular fondness for becoming road pizza, that is."

"It's better than being anywhere with you," she shot back, but that only earned her another round of laughter.

"Feisty. I like it. Too bad it won't get you very far."

When she sent a gaze around the car to grasp for particulars, landmarks out the window, street signs—God, *anything* would be helpful at this point—Vaughn only smirked.

"You didn't really think I was dumb enough to take you very far in *your* car, did you? What with its GPS and everything? Tsk tsk. We switched vehicles a while ago."

Her stomach bottomed out with dread as Vaughn continued. "Oh, and I tossed your cell phone on the street before we left. You're not going to find your earpiece still in place, either. I'd say I'm sorry, but, you know. It'd be a rookie move if I didn't check you for coms, and I'm far from a rookie. Took off that pretty necklace of yours, too. I know how much James loves to hide GPS trackers in those. He's nothing if not completely predictable."

Oh God, her GPS tracker. Shae's heart stuttered with hope. She surreptitiously wiggled her toes, relief spilling through her belly that her boots were still in place and seemed intact. Intelligence could still track her. Her failsafe was still in place, and Vaughn didn't know it.

Now she just had to be smart and stall for time. "Where are you taking me?"

"Ugh, I liked you so much more when you weren't conscious," Vaughn said, giving up an exaggerated eye-roll. "Buuuuuut since no one can save you even if you know, I'm taking you somewhere where we can finish this. You and I are going to an abandoned freight tunnel system, where I'm going to bring you far enough underground that no one will be able to hear you scream. I'm going to tie you up—while James and that whole useless intelligence unit of his watches via secure video feed, by the way—and then I'm going to douse the place in gasoline and set it on fire. You're going to burn alive. And you of all people should know you won't be dying quickly."

Shae's throat clogged with fear, her breath hitching at an unnatural pace. "Don't," she said, immediately regretting the impulsive slip.

Vaughn's brows took the slingshot route up toward his hairline. "Oh, come on, now, Firefighter McCullough. You don't strike me as the type to beg for your life."

If only it were that easy. But she was already in for the penny. At this point, she needed to go down fighting for the whole damned pound. "You got what you wanted. You've got me. Kill me, if that's what will get your tiny little rocks off. But don't make him watch."

A heartbeat passed, then recognition stole over Vaughn's face, his features eerie and twisted in the near-dark of the car. "Holy shit, that's just priceless. You know he'll remember every detail until the day he fucking kicks it, and you want to spare him the agony of watching me cook you alive while he can't do a thing to save you."

Breathe. Breathe. Breathe. There had to be a way out of this. *Analyze, then hypothesize.* All she had to do was buy time and think.

"That's not going to happen." How Shae managed to make the words so steady when her heart was rioting so hard in her chest, she had no freaking clue. "You're not going to kill me."

She still had her boots on. The intelligence unit was tracking her with the GPS. Capelli had followed protocol to give her a failsafe, and he *would* come for her.

Vaughn's expression was covered in scorn. "Your blind faith is so sweet. Too bad it's also naïve and completely brainless. You're going to die screaming, sweet cheeks, and James is going to watch every single second."

Without warning, he jerked the car over to the side of the narrow road they'd been traveling, their surroundings dark and deserted enough to make Shae's spine crawl with cold, clammy dread. The only thing she could see was an ancient metal sign in the over-bright glare of the headlights.

HAZARDOUS CONDITIONS. FREIGHT TUNNELS CLOSED. NO TRESPASSING UNDER PENALTY OF LAW.

Oh...God.

Vaughn unhooked his seatbelt, his stare as cruel as it was utterly uncaring. "See, I started planning this whole thing the second I threatened your boyfriend, and the two of you made it far too easy for me to get my hands on you. You're going to pay for your stupidity, and I *will* get the satisfaction of showing James how much smarter than him I've always been."

And then there was a blinding pain in her temple, and the whole world went black.

CHAPTER 24

Capelli sat in the passenger seat of the unmarked police car Moreno was driving, his belly full of pure, uncut rage. Seventeen—no, eighteen minutes had passed since Vaughn had drugged Shae and pushed her into her Jeep, tossing her cell phone to the sidewalk and nearly running over Garza as he'd sped away from the scene.

A lot could happen to a person in eighteen minutes.

"A patrol unit just found Shae's Jeep six blocks from the Food Market," Hale said over coms from her own unmarked vehicle, and the words filtered past Capelli's anger just enough to ground him. Facts. Facts. His brain needed facts to keep the rest of him from going ground zero. "There's no sign of her or Vaughn anywhere nearby."

"Let's get a canvas going anyway, just in case somebody saw something," came Sinclair's gravelly voice over the line. He'd joined in on coms as soon as he'd heard that Vaughn had Shae, managing the kidnapping scene and making sure an ambo had arrived to tend to Garza's minor injuries. "Maxwell, get someone at the precinct on the footage from security cameras in the surrounding blocks, too."

"Copy that, Sarge," Maxwell answered from his and Hale's unmarked car, which was presumably not far behind Moreno and Hollister's.

After less than a second, Sinclair came back with, "Capelli, where are we on the backup locator in McCullough's boot?"

"It stopped moving three minutes ago, at a location in North Point just past the docks. We're about seven minutes out." He swallowed past his slamming heartbeat, forcing his focus over the in-dash computer in front of him. "But there's no street address for it on the GPS grid. In fact, there aren't any discernable roads within a five-block radius of the location. It looks like it's just empty space."

Which made no logical sense. Vaughn might want revenge, but even desperate, he wouldn't risk getting caught. He wouldn't take Shae somewhere out in the open, not even in the cover of night.

Capelli's thoughts coiled and spun as he pictured the map, the images of the city burned into his mind's eye that accompanied it, and wait... "This is down by the entrance to the freight tunnel system the city shut down ten years ago."

"Those tunnels are sealed off and almost impossible to navigate unless you've been down there before or you have blueprints," Hollister said from the back seat. "There are like a hundred passageways in the old system. Seems like a place Vaughn might find handy."

"For a lot of reasons," Capelli said, dread punching through him as the chessboard changed yet again. "The GPS in Shae's boot won't transmit from underground. I doubt Vaughn knows it's there." In fact, he'd stake his life on it. Vaughn would never lead the cops to him that closely, no matter how arrogant he was. "But it's still good strategy. Taking her underground is a failsafe against our failsafe. No matter what, we won't be able to see her, *or* to track her."

As if on cue, the blinking red icon on the computer screen in front of him went dark. Capelli's lungs squeezed under the force of the adrenaline that wanted to fill them, but no—*no*—he could see the chess board now. He had to focus on finding Shae.

Otherwise his brain would start churning up things like exactly what Vaughn might do to her once he got her all the way underground, and how many times the soulless son of a bitch might do them.

Capelli shook his head and marshaled his thoughts. "The GPS is dark," he said. With a voice that only shook a little, he relayed the coordinates over the line. "He's definitely got her underground, Sarge. We need to get to those tunnels."

"Copy that. Moreno, drop some lead on it and get to the scene. Take point until I get there. Hale, you and Maxwell follow. I'll call in a backup unit and meet you on-site. I'm out on coms until I'm en route."

Capelli sent the coordinates from their dashboard unit to both Maxwell and Sinclair's GPS systems, trying like hell to keep his hands on the level despite the fear in his veins and the distinct increase in pressure Moreno had just applied to the accelerator.

But his composure refused to stay locked in place. "Moreno. I…"

Shit, there were so many ways to end that sentence, and each one scared him senseless. *I can't let anything happen to Shae. I know it's illogical and probably even downright insane, but I can't picture anything without her.*

I love her. God, I'm so in love with her.

Ironically—and somewhat thankfully—Capelli didn't need to say anything else.

"I know." Although Moreno's eyes never left the windshield, he recognized beyond the shadow of a doubt that she meant every ounce of her words. "We're going to find her,

Capelli," she said. "We're going to find her, and she's going to be okay. We'll be there in less than five minutes."

Before Capelli could respond, his cell phone buzzed from his back pocket, and what the hell? Sinclair had the radio, and the rest of the unit was on coms. Anyway, ever since Vaughn had called his cell yesterday morning, the entire RPD had known the number was compromised. Why would anyone—

Sweet Jesus.

Unknown Caller.

Capelli hit the FaceTime icon on his iPhone and braced for impact. Sure enough, Vaughn's face appeared on the screen, backlit by the unearthly glow of overhead emergency lighting and deep, creepy shadows that made Capelli want to scream.

But he couldn't tip his hand. He couldn't. Vaughn already had too much leverage.

Capelli needed to take it back so he could dismantle the motherfucker.

"Vaughn."

The laughter he got in reply was all malice. "For fuck's sake, Wraith. For someone so touchy about names, you'd do well to remember mine. Especially since I just kidnapped your girlfriend right out from under you. Say hi, Firefighter McCullough."

"Screw you." Shae followed the words with a lungful of invective from just off-screen, and Capelli released a silent exhale, full of relief that she was alive and alert.

The emotion, however, died a quick death, replaced by scalpel-sharp anger as Vaughn turned the camera to Shae. A fresh, blood-crusted bruise bloomed at her temple, unmistakable fear mixing in with the strength in her stare, and Capelli's heart folded in half at the sight of the restraints tied thickly around her wrists and ankles.

Focus. Analyze. Assess.

Capelli's brain overrode the screaming command from his adrenal gland to stand down. "You're not going to get away with this," he said, scanning every millimeter of the image on the screen for something, however small, that he could use to pinpoint their location within the tunnel system.

But Vaughn swung the camera back to his own face before Capelli could capture so much as a scrap of detail. "Good Christ, all that emotion is making you the king of the 40-watt club," he said, rolling his eyes and making a gagging noise. "I have to say, of all people to lead with their dipstick, I didn't peg you for the type. As for me not getting away with this"—Vaughn paused to hook air quotes around the words, and truly, Capelli had never wanted to destroy anyone more in his life—"Puh-leaze. I've *already* gotten away with this. You want to know why? Because I'm fucking smarter than you, that's why. And now you're both going to pay for even thinking for a second that you could outsmart me."

"Vaughn—"

"*Shadow,*" he spat. "I know we've all been to this party before, but let's review. I'm going to drench this room and everything leading up to it in gasoline. Then I'm going to lock Shae, here, inside—sorry, not sorry—and I'm going to burn the place down. And here's the most fun part!"

Vaughn's features twisted into a grin that turned Capelli's blood to ice. "Since I'm certain you're scrambling like an idiot to try and track the signal from my phone, you, my friend, are going to need to stay on the line. Which means you are going to watch every. Fucking. Minute. Of her dying."

Capelli froze to the passenger seat, his traitorous, bullet-proof memory coughing up every gruesome crime scene image from every fire intelligence had ever worked. His throat went tight as he fought the urge to scream, and come on, come *on*. He needed to think—God damn it, he needed facts, data, something he could use, even if it wasn't true.

True...true...

His strategy hit him all at once.

This whole time, Vaughn had used fear to gain leverage. It was time to turn those tables. As counter-intuitive as it was, Capelli needed to stop covering things up and tell the truth.

He needed to take the risk.

"No."

"*No?*" Vaughn's voice faltered under the weight of his surprise, and Capelli didn't think. Just spoke.

"I didn't stutter. I'm not watching you do anything, you little shit. I don't need your location, because I already know it," he said. "In less than five minutes, your not-so-secret hideout in the tunnels is going to be swarming with every cop in the city. You don't even have time to strike a match, let alone douse anything with gasoline and watch it burn. Not if you want a goddamn prayer of getting out of there without handcuffs on."

"You're not smart enough to know where I am. You couldn't possibly have tracked me," Vaughn snapped, but oh, his eyes put his doubt and fear on full display. "You're bluffing."

"You think so? Try me and find out," Capelli said.

And then he ended the call.

"Jesus Christ, that took balls," Hollister said, checking his Glock as he rapidly geared up in the back seat. "But Vaughn's underground, right? How the hell did he even get a signal to call you?"

Capelli's brain threw the facts past his surging adrenaline and out of his mouth by pure default. "GPS signals operate on different wavelengths than cellular connections. Location devices cut off as soon as there's no direct line to their satellites, but cell phones can still work just as long as the caller isn't too far below ground."

"Which means Vaughn can't have gone too far into the tunnels, and we have a good chance of cornering him when he tries to bolt," Moreno said. "Damn, Capelli, that's brilliant."

Capelli nodded, although his movements were shaky at best. "Odds are extremely high he took the bait and decided to run, but we're still going to have to track him down." If Vaughn got away, he and Shae wouldn't be safe again, ever.

Assuming the narcissistic bastard didn't decide to screw the odds and set fire to the place instead, and fuck. *Fuck*, they needed to hurry.

"Call the fire department, just in case," Capelli said, and Maxwell's voice filtered in over their coms.

"Forget the fire department. I just called the cavalry. Backup units, air support, patrol officers. Vaughn's not coming out of those tunnels unless he's in bracelets or a body bag."

For the first time since he'd impulsively hung up on Vaughn, Capelli's heart overrode his brain, pumping with pure rage as Moreno screeched to a stop at the path leading to the freight tunnels.

"Now we just have to find him. And Shae."

Moreno slid out of the driver's seat and turned toward the entrance to the tunnels, Hollister falling in behind her. "Okay, Capelli. You set up a command center here, and Hollister and I will fall in with Hale and Maxwell in two teams."

Oh *hell* no. "I'm going in with you."

"No, you're not," she shot back. "This is an active manhunt for a highly dangerous killer. You might be brilliant at strategy and tech. But you're not trained for this."

Yeah. Still no. "I do my weapons and tactical safety certifications every year, just like everyone else on the RPD's payroll."

"Capelli—"

"Let me put it another way," Capelli said, not giving one shit that he was breaking about ten different safety protocols in a single breath. "You can either let me go in there with you, or you can shoot me. Because that's the only goddamn thing that will keep me from going into those tunnels to find Shae, and we are wasting time."

Moreno exhaled in defeat. "Fine. But you're with me and Hollister. And for Chrissake, give me two seconds to get you in some Kevlar so Sinclair doesn't shoot *me* if something happens to your crazy ass."

True to her promise to act quickly, she had her extra vest and her backup Glock 19 out and at the ready less than a minute later, just as Maxwell and Hale pulled up beside them on the narrow access road.

"Backup units are seven minutes out," Hale said, her Kevlar in place and her badge on display. "They'll start an immediate search of the area aboveground, just in case Vaughn's already out of the tunnels."

Capelli flipped through the knowledge stuffed away in his brain, rummaging through everything he knew about the freight tunnels before shaking his head. "Unless he can run thirty miles an hour, the odds are pretty much against that."

"Well, good," Moreno said, slamming a fresh clip into her Glock with a smile. "Then let's go drag his ass out."

The five of them headed down the weed-choked gravel path leading to the tunnels, and Capelli's pulse went full throttle at the sight of the rusted chains laying in a useless heap beside the heavy double doors, along with the narrow stone staircase leading down and out of sight.

"Our coms operate a lot like cell phones. Once we get far

enough underground, they're likely to get pretty sketchy," he said.

Maxwell frowned but didn't hesitate. "We'll have to go a little old school and use hand signals as a backup."

"Okay. Let's see what else we're dealing with," Moreno whispered. She slid through the entryway with as little sound as possible, coming to a halt after they'd all made it safely down to the bottom of the stairs. "We've got the emergency lighting, so at least that's something."

"Vaughn must've tapped into the electric company's servers before he grabbed Shae," Capelli said quietly, the words making him want to spit out the nasty aftertaste they'd left behind in his mouth. But as badly as he wanted to go ripping through the tunnels, screaming his lungs out until they found her, they had to be covert if they wanted to find Vaughn, too.

Moreno exhaled, swiveling a sharp gaze over the shadow-cloaked freight tunnel, complete with all of its smaller passageways snaking off from the main track line. "Yeah, well, emergency lights or no, this place still looks like a freaking funhouse, so we're going to have to split up. Maxwell, you and Hale take that branch on the Bravo side. Hollister, Capelli, and I will take Delta. Watch each other's backs, and call out if you get eyes on Vaughn. Go."

"Copy," came the collective whisper of all three detectives. With his heart wedged in his windpipe, Capelli followed Moreno down the branch of the tunnel leading to the right, Hollister falling in at his back. The air pressed against his lungs, growing mustier with every step, and he funneled all of his mental energy into collecting the details. The ancient rail tracks laid in the rocky ground beneath his boots. The dank smell of air that had gone largely undisturbed for over a decade. The scuffle and scurry of rats scattering as they moved farther underground, and Jesus, Shae could be anywhere in this mess.

So could Vaughn.

"Hold." Moreno's hand lifted, her fist closed tight, and Capelli's breath snagged at the sight of the three low-ceilinged corridors snaking off from the main tunnel.

"These look like service passageways," he said. "Some of them might lead aboveground. If Vaughn wanted a quick getaway once he set the fire, chances are decent Shae might be in one of them."

"Okay. We'll each take one for a thorough sweep. Call out if you need backup."

Moreno started down the first corridor and Hollister took the last, leaving Capelli to the one in the center. He listened carefully, although it was an absolute chore to process anything over the squall of his heartbeat.

The sensation didn't get any more manageable when he reached a small door about halfway down the cave-like passageway. But Shae could be on the other side of the rust-covered metal, and he gripped the door handle, pushing over the threshold in one quick burst.

And saw her huddled on the ground next to a bright red can of gasoline.

"Shae," Capelli breathed, his relief so strong, it smashed his equilibrium to pieces. Her green stare went wide and she choked out a sound—Christ, Vaughn had *gagged* her, too—and Capelli lowered the Glock he'd held in his clammy grip as he hit his knees beside her.

"Okay. Okay, I've got you, baby," he said, curling his arms around her instinctively before realizing she'd been bleeding in the FaceTime video.

He rocked back on his heels, his brain in go-mode. "Where are you hurt?" he asked, forcing his eyes to do a visual assessment for any injuries as his hands loosened the rag tied over her mouth.

"I'm okay," she said hoarsely, her face smudged with a layer of dirt and dust.

And blood. "You don't look okay," Capelli said, his molars coming together in a hard clack at the closer examination of the cut-and-bruise combo spanning from her temple up into her hairline.

"Look at you, with all the sweet talk." The tiny smile she'd managed to work up disappeared half a breath later. "Vaughn knocked me out before he dragged me down here, probably so I wouldn't kick his scrawny ass and run. But really, other than feeling like a bunch of squirrels are having an all-night rave in my cranial cavity, I'm fine."

A tendril of dread and something much, much deeper uncurled in Capelli's gut, and he sent a glance over his shoulder, toward the door. "Do you know where he went?"

"No." Shae shook her head, then winced and added, "But you completely spooked him, and you were right. He didn't have any time to start a fire, or to try and hurt me. He just gagged me to keep me quiet and took off as soon as you hung up on him."

"Good. I'm glad the plan worked." Capelli knew the words were lame, but his emotions were churning all over the place, threatening to swamp him, and he had to keep them in check. He had to get Shae out of here.

Not wanting to call out on the off-chance that Vaughn was still nearby, Capelli dug deep for an inhale and formulated an exit strategy. "First things first. Let's get these bindings off you."

He pulled a pen knife from the pocket of his jeans, flipping it open with a snick. Although the vicious rope burns and raw skin at Shae's wrists tempted his fury to make another appearance, the methodical act of cutting through

319

the rope went a long way toward getting his brain back in the vicinity of calmness.

Finally, the last strand of rope popped free and fell away to the dirty concrete floor, and he took another breath. On to step two. "We're not too far from the exit. Follow me."

Picturing the path he'd taken into the tunnels, Capelli easily reversed it in his mind. He grabbed the Glock with one hand and Shae's fingers with the other, ducking past the doorframe, out into the twisty passageway that would lead them back to the main corridor.

And found himself face-to-face with Conrad Vaughn for the first time in eight long years.

CHAPTER 25

"Ah!" Capelli's gun hand whipped upward out of sheer instinct, the distance between him and Vaughn so close that the guy smartly chose to freeze in place. "Don't fucking *move*."

"Hello, James." Vaughn actually had the nerve to crack a grin, albeit a small one, and a strange chill started moving through Capelli's mind. "Fancy meeting you here."

"If you were looking to double back and slip out of the tunnels through the service exit at the end of this hallway, I'd say that was a tactical error," Capelli said, dropping Shae's hand and angling his body in front of hers to advance a step closer to Vaughn in the narrow space of the hallway.

"I don't make tactical errors," Vaughn said, the words dipped in steel despite the fact that Capelli had a gun pointed at him. "But it does seem that on occasion, *you* get very, very lucky."

Capelli's brows winged upward, his shock escaping in a huff. "I see. So knowing you'd run rather than carry out your plan to burn this place down was just luck?"

"It was strategy." Vaughn shrugged. "Covering my ass now gives me the opportunity to come back and fight another day. But you know all about that from squealing on your mother, now don't you?"

He hadn't been expecting the blow, and it landed right in his solar plexus. "That has nothing to do with this."

"Oh, it has everything to do with this."

Capelli was aware on some logical level that Shae was behind him, that the hallway had two viable exit paths, that they were still pretty far from backup being more than halfway down the passage. But in that moment, the only thing that mattered was the cold, visceral sensation spreading out over him, and Capelli took another step toward Vaughn, this one fueled by menace.

"And the fact that I pinpointed your location here in the tunnels even though you thought you trashed all of Shae's coms? Is that luck too?"

Well, *that* shut Vaughn's cake trap. "Good guess," he finally said, and Capelli allowed himself the pleasure of a laugh.

"It's not really a guess when it's that close to the mark, now is it? There's a GPS tracker in her boot heel. One you missed," he added, a swirl of dark pleasure rippling through him at the muscle tightening in Vaughn's jaw.

"So how are we going to do this, Wraith? You gonna rat me out, too? I heard your mother died in the clink. Stabbed with a screwdriver." He clucked his tongue. "Such a shame. Could've been avoided if she hadn't been there in the first place, don't you think?"

"Shut the fuck up."

Capelli wasn't shocked by the words until he realized he hadn't been the one to say them. But it was Shae's voice that hung in his ears, and all at once, he realized how close he'd come to losing her.

How Vaughn had had every intention of killing her. Slowly. Painfully.

His free hand was around Vaughn's throat in a blinding, white-hot instant.

"There we go," Capelli hissed, backing Vaughn against the wall for leverage and pressing the Glock to his rib cage for insurance. His anger pulsed through him, sliding under his skin like a living, breathing, mind-altering thing. He could call out, he knew. He could hold Vaughn at gunpoint until the rest of the team arrived to back him up. He could have him in full custody in less than two minutes.

But he wasn't going to.

Surprisingly, Vaughn wheezed out a strained laugh. "Yeah," he grated, and Capelli kept his grip firm enough to be painful, yet loose enough to let Vaughn speak. "There we go, indeed. There's the ice-cold son of a bitch I always knew."

Capelli's grip tightened of its own volition, but still, Vaughn sputtered on. "You haven't cleaned up, James. You've just gotten a whole lot better at being dirty. So go on. Do it. Shoot me and get it over with."

"I'm not going to shoot you."

Even in his utterly outmatched position, Vaughn had the balls to laugh again. "I always knew you were a pussy."

"Oh, I didn't say I wasn't going to kill you," Capelli said, and there. There it was.

Fear.

But the flash in Vaughn's eyes only lasted for a second before turning flat, cold and lifeless. "You were raised by wolves, brother. So go on. Show me your fangs."

The dare collided with the adrenaline in Capelli's veins, forming a four-hundred proof cocktail of dark and nasty. He wrapped his fingers more tightly around Vaughn's throat and started to squeeze. He knew the anatomy, trachea, hyoid bone, external carotid artery—which was hammering away beneath the pad of his index finger. Funny, how delicate it all was. How all it took was one move, one snap decision to change everything.

"Capelli."

The voice sounded far away. He was aware—quite vaguely—of movement beside him, of Vaughn's eyes bulging wider, of a more earnest struggle, but he didn't care.

"Capelli!" came the voice again, yet still, he pressed harder, his fingers digging deep.

"*James.*"

The single syllable pierced his awareness at the same time his conscience came roaring back to life, carrying out the plan he'd had all along.

"I didn't say I *was* killing you, either," Capelli said. "But you deserve to know what it's like to be scared for your life. Just like you deserve the one thing you're afraid of more than dying."

"You wouldn't," Vaughn coughed, staring up at him in true fear. "You *can't.*"

"Oh yeah, I really would. You belong in jail, asshole. And I'm going to make it my personal mission to be sure you rot in there for the rest of your nice, long life."

Keeping the Glock trained on Vaughn just in case, Capelli took a step back and aimed a shout down toward the main corridor.

"Suspect in custody! Repeat, suspect in custody in passageway two, requesting backup!"

The heavy riot of footfall echoed off the damp tunnel walls, and seconds later, Moreno and Hollister arrived on each other's heels, Glocks drawn.

"Jesus. Nice work, Capelli," Hollister said, turning Vaughn around roughly while Moreno slapped handcuffs over his wrists. "McCullough," he added, relief flooding his voice. "Are you okay?"

"I am now," she said, launching herself into Capelli's arms, and Capelli didn't even care that the hallway was starting to swarm with all manner of RPD personnel, all of whom could see every last one of his emotions.

He held her back even tighter.

CHAPTER 26

Shae sat back on the pancake-flat gurney, arming herself with a full-on scowl as she looked at the paramedic-in-training in front of her.

"Seriously, Slater. Do we really need to go through the *entire* concussion protocol?" All she wanted was a hot meal, a hotter shower, and about a week in bed. Preferably not alone. But since protocol was protocol, here she sat, in the back of Ambulance Ninety-Three, where Slater just happened to be riding along tonight.

Hell if the rookie didn't look far more pleased than he should. "Considering you have a head injury, and I'm your paramedic?" he asked, barely containing his smile as he recorded Shae's vitals. "Yes, ma'am."

"You know what, Slater? You go ahead and take your time," Capelli said from his spot beside her in the ambulance, and Shae threw her hands up in defeat.

"It isn't fair when you two gang up on me," she groused. "But fine. Whatever rocks your cradle, boys."

Under the watchful eye of the senior paramedic on duty, Slater completed a thorough exam and pronounced her—

shocker—just as fine as she'd claimed to be, thank you very much.

"That cut is pretty nasty, but I don't think it needs stitches, and your concussion protocol is all clear."

"So am I good to go?" Shae asked, and Slater nodded his nearly shaved head.

"I can clear you for release in about fifteen minutes. You'll need to sign the waiver just like regular people, but…yeah. I can't find anything wrong with you," he said.

She laughed, and okay, yeah. She might not have a concussion, but her head still smarted like crazy. "I know you're in training and everything, but don't sound so disappointed."

"I'm not." The rookie surprised her with an expression of sudden, sincere gratitude. "I'm really glad you're okay, McCullough."

Her heart squeezed unexpectedly. "Thanks. And hey, Slater?" When he looked back at her from the back door of the ambulance, Shae said, "You're a great firefighter, but you've got a real knack for this paramedic thing, too."

"Thanks." He smiled, a blush creeping over his light brown cheeks. "I'll give you a few minutes to rest before I write up those release waivers."

"Thanks, Slater," Capelli said, staying quiet until the guy was out of earshot. But then he turned back toward her, and God, she loved his sweet, serious face.

"You scared the hell out of me, Shae. Putting your cell phone down to keep Vaughn from bolting was risky as hell."

"I know," she said, because she really, really did. "But I didn't just do it impulsively, without thinking. I knew we had a backup plan, and that you'd follow it to the letter to find me and bring Vaughn down."

"Let me guess." Capelli lifted a brow. "Another gut feeling?"

Shae shook her head. "No. Fact. You're smarter than he is. I knew you'd form a strategy that would work."

Capelli braced his forearms over his thighs, his gaze dropping just slightly as he nodded. "Yeah. Moreno and Sinclair brought Vaughn down to the precinct. He'll be charged with your kidnapping and attempted murder, but we also found a key to an apartment in South Hill on him. Hollister said techs just recovered several laptops, along with a ton of other evidence that can link him to both of our other crime scenes and a ton of other crimes, too, so…"

"He really is going to rot in jail for the rest of his life."

"Looks that way," Capelli said.

Shae looked at him, weighing her words in her mind for only a second before giving them voice. "You let go."

Capelli frowned. "What do you mean? I'm right here."

"Not of me. Of Vaughn, in the tunnel. You had him by the throat. You could have easily killed him. But even before I said your name, you let him go."

"Not really. I mean, physically, yes. I let go of his neck. But Vaughn took away the thing all of his victims held the most valuable. It only seemed fitting to take the thing he needed most in return."

"His freedom," Shae whispered, reaching out for his hand and squeezing tight. "It was a hell of a risk."

He squeezed back with equal measure. "Yeah, well, a very beautiful, very brash person taught me that sometimes, risks are worth taking."

"Beautiful, huh? Should I be jealous?"

"Nope. Because I am completely, insanely, irreversibly in love with you."

Shae's heart swelled in her chest, but wait. Wait. Capelli couldn't have possibly said… "You what?"

"I love you, Shae." Shifting forward, he cupped her face gently in his hands. "You saw parts of me that I didn't even see, and you showed me who I am. You make me laugh, you frustrate the hell out of me. You drive me the very best kind of crazy, and I don't ever want to be without you."

"Oh." The word collapsed past her lips, happy tears wobbling on her lashes, and she pressed forward to hold him close. "Well, when you put it that way...I love you too. God, I love you so much."

He brushed the softest of kisses over her mouth, then pulled back with a grin.

"Okay," he said. "I'll be Starsky. But only if you'll be Hutch."

ALSO BY KIMBERLY KINCAID

Want hot heroes, exclusive freebies, and all the latest updates on new releases? Sign up for Kimberly Kincaid's newsletter, and check out these other sexy titles, available at your favorite retailers!

The Station Seventeen series:
Deep Trouble (prequel)
Skin Deep
Deep Check

The Cross Creek series:
Crossing Hearts
Crossing the Line

The Line series:
Love On the Line
Drawing the Line
Outside the Lines
Pushing the Line

The Pine Mountain Series:
The Sugar Cookie Sweetheart Swap, with Donna Kauffman and Kate Angell

Turn Up the Heat

Gimme Some Sugar

Stirring Up Trouble

Fire Me Up

Just One Taste

All Wrapped Up

The Rescue Squad series:

Reckless

Fearless

Stand-alones:

Something Borrowed

Play Me

And don't forget to come find Kimberly on Facebook, join her street team The Taste Testers, and follow her on Twitter, Pinterest, and Instagram!

ABOUT THE AUTHOR

Kimberly Kincaid writes contemporary romance that splits the difference between sexy and sweet and hot and edgy romantic suspense. When she's not sitting cross-legged in an ancient desk chair known as "The Pleather Bomber", she can be found practicing obscene amounts of yoga, whipping up anything from enchiladas to éclairs in her kitchen, or curled up with her nose in a book. Kimberly is a *USA Today* best-selling author and a 2016 and 2015 RWA RITA® finalist and 2014 Bookseller's Best nominee who lives (and writes!) by the mantra that food is love. Kimberly resides in Virginia with her wildly patient husband and their three daughters. Visit her any time at www.kimberlykincaid.com